Also by Liana LeFey

To Love A Libertine

Once a Courtesan

Scandal of the Season

Liana LeFey

This book is a work of fiction. Names, characters, places, and incidents are the product of the author's imagination or are used fictitiously. Any resemblance to actual events, locales, or persons, living or dead, is coincidental.

Entangled Publishing, LLC
2614 South Timberline Road
Suite 109
Fort Collins, CO 80525

Entangled Select is an imprint of Entangled Publishing, LLC.

Visit our website at www.entangledpublishing.com.

Edited by Erin Molta
Cover design by Erin Dameron-Hill
Interior design by Toni Kerr

ISBN: 9781633757028
Ebook ISBN: 9781633757035

Manufactured in the United States of America

First Edition May 2017

10 9 8 7 6 5 4 3 2 1

For my daughter—you are a constant source of joy and light in my world, and I adore you. Thank you for being so patient and understanding. If you learn anything from your mother's example, I hope it's that working hard to make your dreams a reality is always a worthwhile pursuit. Don't ever be afraid to reach for those stars, baby.

Prologue

London, 1812

He's back!

Sorin Latham, her family's closest neighbor—and her dearest friend—had returned at last.

Eleanor raced down the stairs, keeping tight hold of her skirts and a sharp eye out for Rowena. The last thing she wanted was another scolding about running in the house. The carriage must have made it down the drive by now. He should be getting out by the time she reached the front hall.

A grin split her face as she contemplated sliding down the banister, but good sense overruled the rash impulse. She'd be sixteen in two days. Sliding down banisters was out of the question now—at least whenever there was a chance one might be seen.

Will he have exciting news to share? Will he be happy to see me? Did he bring me a present from Paris, like he promised?

He'd been gone three whole months this time. It had seemed an eternity. Not for the first time, she wished Cousin

Charles had a sister he could marry so they could truly become family. But, like her, Charles was an only child. At least Sorin's bride would one day come to live with him here in Somerset.

Now all she had to do was find a way to remain here, herself. Eleanor gritted her teeth. If only Charles would see reason! But both he and Rowena were bent on the idea of her marrying. It was to be her debut Season, and no expense had been spared to see that she made a good impression. Daughter of a duke, she was expected to make a fine marriage. Her cousin had even gone so far as to show her a list of possible matches he deemed "acceptable."

A grimace tugged at the corners of her mouth. *I'll never wed.* Her family would be annoyed at first, but they'd get over it. *They don't* really *want me to leave Holbrook.* Why, this very morning Charles had told her that, in his opinion, no man was good enough for her, but that he'd be pleased, as long as she was happy.

For some reason, he simply refused to accept that her idea of "happy" was for things to remain exactly as they were. *I don't need a husband. I already have a home.*

The front door opened as she reached the bottom step, and joy surged at the sound of Sorin's voice. Quick as a fox, she ducked beneath the stairs and waited. After the servant had welcomed him and taken his hat and coat, their guest was told Lord Cramley awaited him in the blue salon.

Eleanor emerged just as he rounded the corner. "Surprise!"

Stopping short, he greeted her with a broad smile that crinkled the corners of his hazel eyes. "Ellie!" His gaze travelled downward, doubtless noting the absence of her customary pinafore, and his brows rose. "Gracious, I think you've grown another inch."

Too happy to take affront at his reference to her height, which had indeed increased during his absence, she dashed forward to embrace her friend. "I've missed you so! It's been dreadfully lonely here without your visits."

Her joy turned to bewilderment as he stiffened in her arms and then, bracing his hands against her shoulders, thrust her away. The ungentle manner of his rejection caught her off guard and she stumbled backward, only just managing to catch herself on the newel post and avoid an ungraceful fall.

When she looked up, a thunderous, disapproving frown was fixed upon his face, which was turning scarlet. A dull, throbbing pain erupted in her chest, and a queer, numbing sensation settled over her. Sudden tears stung her eyes as he backed away another step. She wanted to ask why he looked at her as one might a leper, but words would not form on her lips.

It was he who broke the silence. "Ellie, I'm—" He stopped and took a deep, unsteady breath. "Forgive me." Without another word, he turned and strode away.

Shaking as if a palsy had taken her, Eleanor sank to the floor in a state of utter shock and confusion.

What did I do wrong?

Chapter One

1817—Five Years Later

"Go and find out whether Sor—I mean Lord Wincanton—has arrived," Eleanor ordered her maid Fran for the third time in the space of an hour. She turned to her friend Caroline. "I keep forgetting he is the earl now."

Caroline frowned and patted a fiery red curl back into place. "Earl or not, why you should bother waiting for him is beyond comprehension."

"He's my cousin's closest friend and our neighbor, and he has just returned home after a long absence." Going to the mirror, Eleanor gave her tiny, puffed sleeves a final tweak. She had to admit the new gown was very becoming. The deep, square neckline was most flattering, and the long swath of celadon-striped muslin that fell from just beneath her breasts to the tips of her matching beaded slippers was simply divine. "It would be the height of ill manners to begin the festivities without one of our honored guests."

Her words had no effect other than to elicit another

exasperated sigh. "Some friend," complained Caroline. "He's been away for five years." In the reflection, Eleanor watched as her friend pinched her cheeks to make them pink. "It seems to me his importance might have diminished after so long an interval. Besides, it's *your* birthday. Why should you have to share the celebration with anyone, much less a man who means nothing to you?"

Because the thought of sharing this evening with him made Eleanor want to burst with both joy and trepidation, but she chose not to correct Caroline's assumption. She glanced at the locked box by the window seat, which contained his letters to her. They had exchanged correspondence throughout his absence, and she'd never shared them with anyone but Charles and Rowena. Caroline was a good friend but she could be insensitive at times, and those letters were personal and precious.

"He's the one being discourteous," said her obstinate companion. "Holly Hall is but a short distance from here. I cannot think what has delayed him." She began to pace the room.

Eleanor smiled. "What's really bothering you is that Lord Penwaithe's son is downstairs."

As usual, Caroline didn't bother prevaricating. "He is indeed. At this very moment. And Elizabeth Ann, if I know her, has probably already sunk her claws into him!"

"Well, you needn't wait for me," Eleanor said, chuckling. "Why don't you go on down? I'll be along soon enough."

An indelicate snort answered the suggestion. "And have you run off? I should think not."

"I would never do such a thing to my cousin." *Especially not tonight.*

Another snort. "You would. You hate these things."

"I do hate being paraded about like a slightly overripe

fruit in danger of spoiling," Eleanor confessed. "But tonight is not about my cousin trying to marry me off. This is simply the celebration of another year—and the return of a friend."

"I still don't know why they bother to celebrate his return," grumbled the other girl. "As I recall, he was never much fun. Always so proper. Never a smile or laugh. A sober sack if ever I've seen one."

"You disparage him, yet you knew him less than a month."

A raised auburn brow queried her accusation.

"It is only because you never understood him," Eleanor insisted. "He's reserved, as a gentleman ought to be—a quality one might consider a benefit, as opposed to a fault." She hadn't meant that last bit to come out with such sarcasm, but Caroline's taste in men ran rather unfortunately to the rakish. "I just feel you ought to look to men like him as a proper example."

"Proper indeed," said Caroline with open disdain as she touched perfume to her wrist. Her bright blue eyes narrowed. "Manners are all good and well, but I like a man who laughs every once in a while. Not to mention one who understands this modern age. Remember when Lorraine Montagu was ill and missed a Season? One Season, and she was completely hopeless the following year! Wincanton has been away for five *years*. It might as well have been fifty."

Eleanor bit her tongue. Sorin probably knew more about this "modern age" than many a London dandy. And while it was true he rarely laughed, it didn't mean he *never* did. The first time she'd had the occasion to witness it would live in her memory forever. Out of rebellion over being scolded by Rowena for ruining yet another dress, she'd defiantly climbed a tree down by the pond—and had gotten stuck. Naturally, Sorin had been the one to find her. He'd climbed up as far as possible and then had carefully talked her down to meet him.

Just before they'd reached the lowest limb, however, she'd lost her grip and had fallen on him, knocking them both into the murky water below. The very *cold* murky water.

Instead of being wroth, however, he'd taken one look at her and had started laughing. She'd been covered from head to toe in muck, and he'd laughed until he was nearly blue. After getting over her own wounded pride, she'd laughed, too—for the first time since her parents' death. It would have been completely wonderful—had she not accidentally broken his nose a moment later while he was helping her up the slippery bank. But, even then, he hadn't yelled at her.

Caroline wasn't quite finished with her rant. "Waiting for his high-and-mightiness to arrive is a complete waste of time. We should already be down there."

"Caroline, I will n—"

The door opened, cutting her off. "His lordship has arrived, my lady," said Fran.

"At last," muttered Caroline, sweeping away.

After stepping aside to let her pass, the servant leaned back in. "Shall I tell them you're coming down, my lady?"

"No, but thank you," Eleanor said quickly. Nothing, *nothing* was going to mar her entrance. Tonight was her twenty-first birthday, and by George, she would be a perfect lady for once. Or at least appear to be one.

"Come on!" said Caroline from the hallway.

Eleanor followed meekly, but stopped when they neared the stairs. "Will you just check first to make sure the way is clear?"

Caroline rolled her eyes, but did as asked. "It's safe enough—no one is looking. I'm going down." She did so without a backward glance.

Eleanor listened as the crowd below hushed. *Damn. I ought to have gone first.* She waited until the murmur of the guests returned. Stomach aflutter, she began her descent.

Hand grazes the rail rather than gripping it tightly. Head high. Shoulders back. Spine straight. Don't look at your feet. Six steps down, silence again fell. She forced herself the rest of the way down and paused on the last step to seek out the faces of her guardians.

"Dearest Eleanor, happy birthday," said Rowena, coming forward to kiss her cheek.

"How very generous of you to host this party in my honor," Eleanor said to her. "I cannot thank you enough for your many kindnesses over the years." To her surprise, her eyes began to sting. Rowena had indeed been kind. More than kind. Though they were near enough in age to be sisters, she'd been a mother in so many ways.

Charles beamed as he joined them. "The pleasure is all ours, Cousin Eleanor. Come, let us toast this special day with a glass of champagne."

As he turned to seek out a glass for her, another figure came forward, his face as familiar and dear to Eleanor as any on earth, though it had been more than five years since she'd last looked upon it. Sorin. Unlike the other men in this room, his skin was golden—from days spent on the deck of a ship. Faint lines fanned out from the corners of his hazel eyes, and hair that had once been darkest walnut was now tinged with lights from exposure to the sun and the faintest sprinkling of gray at the temples.

Eleanor sank into a deep curtsy. A perfect curtsy. "Lord Wincanton. How delighted I am to share in celebrating your return home." Flawless. Just the right tone. Cultured. Polite. No unseemly squeals or unladylike displays.

Not like last time.

What an awful day that had been. Though he'd later sought her out to make amends for his ungentle treatment of her, his words had cut her to the quick.

...I shall always count myself your friend, Ellie—Lady Eleanor, I should say from now on—and much as it pains me, I would be a poor friend indeed did I not speak plainly with you. You are a young lady now and must behave like one. You simply cannot go about hugging men, not even me, lest you risk your good name and that of your guardians. Certainly, I expected you to know better by now. As such, I shall at the first opportunity speak with Ashford regarding your edification on matters of propriety, for you certainly cannot enter London society otherwise...

To have earned such censure from him, of all people, had been devastating, and the effects had lasted much longer than a mere day.

Before he could make good on his promise to speak with her cousin, however, Rowena had discovered herself again with child. Unable to make the journey to London, Rowena had arranged for her to stay with her elderly aunt. She'd then prevailed upon Sorin and his mother to help bring her out, as Charles had refused to leave her side. Thus, it had been Sorin rather than Charles who'd presented her at court, Sorin who'd squired her about to various events, and Sorin who'd kept strict watch over her every word and action, correcting her at every turn.

Much as she adored her friend, Eleanor had found the whole experience most awkward. He—apparently—had found it mortifying. Less than a month into the Season, he'd returned to Somerset without explanation, leaving her with two elderly matrons for company. Upon arriving home, she'd found him cool and distant. Then he'd left again "to see to his family's foreign investments." Following that absence, he'd received orders to command a vessel in His Majesty's Royal Navy. She'd expected his return after Napoleon's defeat, but it was another two years before he came home.

It had taken all her courage to write that first letter and send it enclosed with Charles's correspondence. Thankfully, he'd written back, and their friendship had resumed. Numerous letters had been exchanged between them since, with "the incident" never mentioned, but she knew he'd not forgotten—any more than she had. And now here he was, and still, it felt awkward.

Gracefully, she extended her hand—and the bottom dropped out of her stomach. She'd forgotten her blasted gloves. *Damn that Caroline for being in such a rush!* Behaving as though nothing was amiss, she waited, her innards all hollow and wobbly as he bowed, as his hot, dry fingers slid beneath her own. He released her almost immediately and folded his hands behind his back.

Heat flared in her face, but she held her head high. So not everything was perfect, but no one could possibly remember to follow every one of a thousand rules all of the time! "Tell me, Lord Wincanton, are you planning to remain in England or do you intend to return to the East?"

Sorin tried hard to ignore the ominous tingling as it spread from his fingers throughout the rest of his body. *God have mercy…* Could this poised, elegant female possibly be Ellie?

The silence was becoming conspicuous. He cleared his throat to ease its tightness and spoke through suddenly parched lips. "It would of course please me greatly to never again leave England's shores, but none of us knows what the future holds. Fate has a way of interfering in the best laid plans." His plan to stay away until she was safely married had failed miserably.

"Indeed it does," she agreed. "But if it is truly your desire to remain, then I should hope Fate will allow it."

Though her cheeks were as red as pomegranates, her tone was light and airy. Anyone else might have thought they were two strangers meeting for the first time. In a way, they were. But for all that she had matured, she was still Ellie, and her flush told him she was remembering *that* conversation. A conversation he desperately wished he could erase.

"Lord Wincanton?"

Sorin realized he'd been staring. "My apologies. It is only that I cannot believe how much you've changed. It is as though a different person stands before me." He forced a smile. "Where is the mischief-making pixie who climbed trees and ran about with no bonnet until her nose freckled?"

The corners of her mouth curled slightly and her nose, utterly devoid of freckles, lifted a fraction. "Those were the antics of an impulsive youth. I am a lady now. In every respect."

Clearly she had *not* forgotten. "That pixie was my friend. I would not have changed her for the world, and I shall miss her if she is indeed truly gone."

His carefully cloaked apology had the desired effect, for her lips now formed a sweet, rueful smile reminiscent of days past. "She is still here. And she will always be your friend."

The pressure in Sorin's chest eased. "It gladdens me to hear it."

"Come now and share a toast with us," she said, blinking eyes that were suspiciously bright. "A toast to celebrate your return."

"Indeed," said Rowena, coming forth. "It has been far too long since you graced us with your company. You used to spend weeks at a time here with us. We have all missed you."

"Indeed we have," agreed Charles, handing him a flute of

champagne. "Waterloo was necessary, I suppose, but for the life of me I'll never understand why you personally had to take care of all that bother in the East."

Against his will, Sorin's gaze fixed on Eleanor. "Neither assignment could be delegated to another and both were equally necessary," he said, distracted as he watched her accept a glass.

"Well, at least it's all over and done now," said Charles. "The hunting has been dismal without you along, you know. I hardly bothered with it last year. As such, the deer have just about overrun the place. My gardener has been having fits over the beasts. The pheasant have been unchecked as well. Droves of them at every turn. But we'll soon sort it out now that you're back."

"I shall be glad to help, of course," Sorin replied absently. Eleanor was wearing an interesting shade of green that complemented her eyes, and her deep-caramel hair was piled high in the Greek fashion currently so popular. It made her look cool and regal—like the woman she was, rather than the child he now struggled to remember.

Pushing aside such thoughts, he tried to concentrate as everyone raised glasses to first toast Eleanor's twenty-first birthday and then again to toast his return. Her cheeks remained pink with excitement as she sipped her champagne, and the smile she gave him over the rim of her glass made his heart constrict.

Of all the things Sorin had experienced, his visceral reaction to her innocent embrace five years ago had been one of the most alarming and unwelcome. He'd hoped the time away would cure him of the affliction, but it seemed to be stronger than ever. His hand still tingled where hers had touched it. It was obvious now that his perception of her had been irrevocably altered. Gone was the little girl he'd discovered crying in the garden after her parents' funeral the day he'd returned from his own tragedy in London. He'd never see her as that little girl again.

"Why not start tomorrow morning?" asked Charles, jolting him back to the present. "Since you'll be staying the night with us, we may as well make the most of it and bag a few birds, eh?"

Stay the night? Remaining under the same roof as Ellie overnight was the last thing he needed to do right now. "That is very kind, but I should never wish to impose upon your hospitality when I live so near and you have so many other guests."

"Nonsense." Charles waved away his excuse. "Rowena would have my head if I let you ride back now when your favorite room has been prepared for you."

There was no refusing him without raising questions, so Sorin nodded acceptance.

"Excellent!" said Charles. "We'll rise early and head south down by the lake where the little devils like to roost. In the meantime, I believe the music is about to begin. As we are celebrating both Ellie's birthday and your homecoming, why don't you two lead the first dance?"

"I would be honored." Heart racing, Sorin offered his arm to Eleanor and led her out onto the open floor, keenly aware of her feather-light touch on his sleeve.

"I remember my first dancing lessons were with you, here in this room," she said with a wistful smile as other couples began to form the line. "I was all but hopeless."

He remembered. She'd been eleven and determined to trample his toes to a pulp. He'd had the good sense to come prepared wearing his heavy boots. Those were such innocent, happy times. "Indeed you were," he agreed. "But you improved."

Her gentle laugh fell on his ears like rain on a thirsty field.

"I did, thanks to your patience. You were a very good teacher."

"I was mediocre, at best. Charles ought to have sent for a real instructor for you."

"He did. Andre LaValle. But he was only here for two days."

"Just two days? That's not nearly long enough."

"It was for Charles," she said, pulling a wry face. "He discovered the blackguard attempting to seduce one of the new maids and sent him packing at once, in the dead of night, no less. Rowena had taken great pains to secure his services and was absolutely livid."

Of that he had little doubt. To this day, LaValle was one of London's most sought-after instructors.

"But when Charles told her what had happened, she agreed with him," continued Eleanor. "She said she'd sooner bring a serpent into the house than expose me to such a man." Her expression softened as she looked up at him. "That's why she asked you to teach me. She wanted someone trustworthy."

Trustworthy. Wonderful. The knot in his gut drew a little tighter.

The music commenced, ending their conversation and intensifying the already pitched battle of will-versus-want taking place inside Sorin. In and out the dancers twined, the pattern first separating them and then bringing them back together again and again. With every touch of Eleanor's bare fingers against his, the inexorable pull of desire grew stronger.

As soon as the dance came to a close, Sorin bowed and gave her hand to another gentleman, excusing himself. Coming back was a mistake. Nothing had changed, save that his predicament was worse than ever.

Chapter Two

Eleanor lounged beside Caroline on the picnic blanket and watched her idly strip the petals from a wildflower. "You'll stain your fingers," she warned.

"Do you know, I think you may have been right about Lord Wincanton," said her friend.

Tilting back the broad brim of her straw hat, Eleanor peered at her. "Oh? How so?"

Caroline discarded the now-barren stem and sat up to face her. "Well, most men seem to share the opinion that we females have nothing between our ears but air. They often speak to me as though they believe me incapable of intelligent thought, but not him. Of all the gentlemen present last night, excepting your cousin, of course, Lord Wincanton was the only one to treat me with respect, as though I was his equal."

"That has always been his way," Eleanor replied, readjusting her hat so that it provided better shade. It was still quite chilly out this early in the spring and the sunlight felt heavenly, but she could ill afford to spot her face. "He would not dream of disrespecting anyone, least of all a lady."

A dimple appeared in her friend's cheek. "I asked him what it was like being at sea, whether or not he'd seen any whales and, if so, were they truly as large and terrifying as it is said. I once asked the same questions of a visiting navy captain, and the man laughed and told me only that I need never worry about such things. But Lord Wincanton described for me a whale in detail and then told me about a terrible storm his ship had survived. It was dreadful! The way he described it made me feel as if I were right there with him," she finished dreamily.

Eleanor refrained from scowling—just. He'd told her about the whale, too, but he hadn't mentioned any storm in any of his letters. A sense of unease settled in her stomach as she looked at Caroline, marking her misty eyes, her blushing cheeks. "I take it you've changed your opinion of Lord Wincanton since we last spoke of him."

Caroline's gaze slid away, her color deepening. "I really cannot say. We spoke only briefly after we danced. I should need more time to come to any final conclusions about him."

They danced? It must have been while she was occupied elsewhere. But why had he danced with Caroline? She was nowhere near his rank.

Cool reason applied itself almost at once. He'd danced with many women of all stations last night…but he hadn't spent an inordinate amount of time talking with anyone else afterward. Certainly not long enough to tell tales of storms and whales. *He practically ran the instant the music stopped after dancing with me.* She forced a pleasant smile to her lips. "Well, since it appears he is to remain in England—for the time being, at least—you may well have your chance."

She watched her friend's face carefully, but Caroline was now concentrating on weaving together long blades of grass to form a fairy basket. "That would be nice," she said, holding up the half-finished product and smiling. "Remember when we used to make these and leave them filled with dandelion fluff for the fairies' beds?" She bent once more, returning to her handiwork. "The real question is whether or not he plans to come to London. Though his mother is quite insistent on the matter, he's still undecided regarding whether or not to put himself up on the block this Season."

Eleanor sat bolt upright. "Surely you did not ask him such an impertinent question?"

"Of course not!" answered Caroline, clearly appalled that she would think such a thing.

Which meant he'd volunteered the information. *Why would he tell such a thing to Caroline and not me?* "And?" she prompted. "Did it seem like he was leaning in any particular direction?"

A sly smile crossed Caroline's face. "I cannot imagine him staying behind to molder away in the countryside while everyone else frolics in London. No, I'm certain he'll be going. Have you ever been to Holly Hall? He told me about it a little, but I cannot quite picture it in my mind."

"Yes. I've been there many times," Eleanor answered, trying to calm herself. He'd told someone—someone other than her—of his adventures abroad. He'd included details he had not shared with her, he'd talked about his estate, and worst of all, he'd mentioned the Marriage Mart. To Caroline. Surely he wasn't planning to woo her? She looked at her friend with new eyes, seeing her fine, freckle-less skin, dark auburn hair, and blue eyes in an entirely different light. Caroline had always been very pretty. But she was also impatient, short-tempered, pouty when she didn't get her way, and generally impulsive in her conduct—all qualities Sorin frowned upon. But still, she was quite pretty.

And she couldn't be more wrong for him.

"Are you unwell?" asked Caroline.

Following her friend's concerned gaze, Eleanor realized she was holding a hand to her stomach which, to be honest, was feeling a bit unsettled. She snatched it away. "I'm perfectly well. But I think perhaps I might like a cup of tea. I'm a bit chilled." She rose.

But before she could take even one step toward the house, Caroline pointed down the hill and let out a little squeal. "Oh, look! They've returned. See? Here they come!" Tossing aside her half-woven basket, she leaped to her feet.

At the edge of the wood, a group of men was emerging amid a boiling sea of rowdy hunting dogs.

"Halloo there, ladies!" called Charles, grinning and waving. "Just look at this lot we've brought back—enough to feed the whole county for a week!" He pointed proudly at the string of dead birds dangling from a pole slung across the shoulders of two sturdy men.

Eleanor laughed and waved back, but her eyes were not on the birds. Sorin, his face lit with one of his rare smiles, strode alongside her cousin. It filled her with pleasure to see him here, back where he belonged.

"You were right—he does smile," whispered Caroline, ruining the moment. "Quite nicely, in fact. He really is a handsome gentleman, is he not? I don't know why I failed to see it before." She giggled softly.

An odd impulse swept through Eleanor, an unpleasant one that made her long to shove her friend down the hillside. Head first. "Well, of course he smiles. He's not made of stone."

Caroline turned to her, brow puckered. "You needn't bite my head off. I meant no insult. I was simply admitting I'd been mistaken about him."

Eleanor opened her mouth to say something, but then thought better of it. "I'm sorry. I'm a bit out of sorts from lack of sleep, I suppose. It was a long night." *Yes. That's it. I'm tired.* "Come, let us go down and meet them."

"With all of those dogs running about loose?" said her friend with a look of horror. "Are you not afraid for our gowns?"

"My cousin's hounds are very well trained, I assure you." If one knew the proper commands, which she did.

Caroline looked doubtful, but followed anyway.

Eleanor waded right into the churning mass of dogs without any hesitation, leaving Caroline to cautiously pick her way through with many a gasp and squeal of dismay.

"A successful hunt, I see," Eleanor said, grinning at the men. "I suppose I should run and tell Cook what we'll be having for dinner for the rest of the week."

Her cousin beamed at the compliment. "Blasted creatures were so complacent I could have simply plucked them from the ground like fallen fruit and shoved them into sacks." He turned to Sorin. "You will take some of them with you, won't you?"

"I've got plenty of my own, I'm sure," replied Sorin with a shake of his head. "Mine have had five years' respite, whereas yours have been undisturbed for only two. Perhaps you might render me the same assistance in thinning them out next week?"

"I should be delighted," said Charles with gusto. "But look at these lovely creatures that have come to witness our triumphal return!" he exclaimed, gesturing to the two women. "How brave of you ladies to risk your slippers and hems amongst this unruly lot. Down, Albert!" he commanded one particularly excited dog that had decided to personally greet Caroline—who was even now squeaking a horrified objection.

Eleanor repressed a laugh as the dog obediently put its

forepaws back on the ground. Caroline's previously pristine skirt now bore an enormous pair of muddy streaks down its front. "You cannot let them know you're afraid," she tutted without sympathy. "As long as you appear fearless and in command they won't bother you."

"Yes, well I rather wish you'd told me that *before* coming down here," said her friend crossly. "Just look at my gown—it's ruined!"

"Not to worry," Eleanor soothed, flicking a glance at Sorin. "Fran will have it out in a blink." Good, now he'd see what a petulant ninny Caroline could be. She turned to him. "You did enjoy yourself, I hope?"

He barely glanced at her, so intent was he on retying a knot that had worked loose on one of the birds during their walk back. "Very much indeed." He turned away from her to face Caroline. "And I'm glad to see we were not the only ones taking advantage of the spring sunshine. How sorry I am to see your lovely gown spoiled, Miss Caroline. I'm sure Eleanor meant it when she said it could be quickly put to rights."

Shock suffused Eleanor as he smiled down at Caroline—and as Caroline blushed to the roots of her hair in happy response. Her heart began to hammer in her chest in a peculiar, almost painful manner.

"Cousin Eleanor?"

She started and looked to see Charles staring at her expectantly. "Yes?"

"I asked if you would be so kind as to run to the house and tell Rowena we've returned. Oh, and do let her know the menu will need adjusting. We'll feast on pheasant tonight!"

"Yes, of course," she replied woodenly. Turning back, she again stared at Caroline, who was now batting her lashes in the most preposterous manner. Despite her foolish appearance—she looked as if she had something in her eye—Sorin was being quite cordial toward her. Attentive, even.

Her cousin cleared his throat, clearly impatient for her to get on with it. Feeling alone and put out, she began walking up the hill. It didn't make any sense at all. Sorin *loathed* women who behaved like Caroline. Or so she'd thought. Hadn't he always told her that a lady who flirted too brazenly was no lady at all? Hadn't he always adjured her to conduct herself with more dignity?

Confused and nettled, she trudged across the lawn and into the house. Pausing on the doorstep, she turned and listened. Faint sounds of laughter drifted back on the breeze—Sorin's and Caroline's. As there was no one about to care, she gave in to a sudden fit of ill temper and slammed the door behind her with a resounding bang, causing the glass panes to shudder in their frames.

The noise brought her up short. *Why am I so tetchy this morning?* Sorin was only being…Sorin. Obviously, he'd come to accept Caroline as part of the family, that's all. She stared at the floor in shame and noticed how damp and dingy the hem of her skirt had become from the walk through the grass.

By the time the other three had finished their leisurely stroll back to the house, she'd changed her gown and was waiting for them with Rowena in the salon, a pot of fresh tea at the ready. In they came, still red-cheeked from the chilly air and talking excitedly of the shoot.

Caroline, still bearing the muddy paw prints, hung at Sorin's elbow, her eyes shining with admiration. "Do tell me about the elephants, Lord Wincanton. I'd give anything to see one myself, but since that is, of course, impossible, I should love to hear about them in every detail."

If Eleanor was irritated before, she was now positively ready to take her friend by the ear and toss her out of the nearest window. "Tea, anyone?" she offered brightly. "You must surely be chilled to the bone. This just came from the kitchens so it'll be nice and hot."

"Ah, yes!" boomed Charles. "How very thoughtful of you, cousin. Wincanton, have some tea. And if that won't drive away the bite, there's always a nip of brandy, eh?"

Eleanor watched with bewilderment as Sorin seated himself by Caroline rather than taking the seat beside her as he'd always done in the past. *What in heaven's name is going on?* Carefully, she thought back over the evening prior, trying to remember if she'd done anything that might have offended him. But other than forgetting her gloves, nothing came to mind. While they talked, she poured. "Lord Wincanton?" she said, handing him a cup. "Dash of cream and half a spoonful of sugar, is that not how you take yours?"

"Yes, thank you," came his absent reply as he reached out and took it from her. She shivered as his fingers briefly brushed against hers. Strange, she'd thought it quite cozy in here a moment ago. Her temper warmed her quickly, however, as he immediately turned his attention back to Caroline, who was talking about the nature sketches she'd been working on over the winter.

Frustrated by his short answer and lack of attention, Eleanor poured for her cousin and Caroline. The temptation to put lemon in her friend's cup instead of sugar was strong, but she decided against the juvenile prank. Caroline was not to blame for his odd behavior, after all, even if she was making a complete cake of herself. For the life of her, Eleanor couldn't understand why Sorin was paying her any mind at all. He intensely disliked women like Caroline—or at least that was what he'd always claimed.

But if that was so, then why was he acting like this?

It took every ounce of self-discipline not to look at her. Sorin could feel the strain as every one of his nerves tugged in her direction. Doggedly, he instead kept his eyes fixed on her vapid little friend, refusing to give in.

He still couldn't get over how much Eleanor had grown and matured. She'd taken the trouble to change her gown and looked radiant in pale yellow muslin. Like sunlight and daisies. How very like her to remember just how he liked his tea, too.

"We'll be staying the whole Season this time," Charles was saying.

"And we'll have young Miss Caroline with us," added Rowena. "When her parents informed us they would not be making the journey this year, Eleanor insisted we have her come and stay with us."

Eleanor smiled sweetly. "London is always so much more fun when shared with a friend."

He watched as she reached out to refill her cup from the pot. Though her neckline was perfectly modest and her bosom entirely covered with a fichu, the material pulled tightly across the swells beneath it. The temperature in the room went up a bit. He had to get out of here, and soon. Before Charles invited him to stay another bloody night. Before his traitorous desires and emotions could give themselves away through some stray word or misdeed.

Eleanor was speaking again to her friend, "I dread to think of some handsome swain wooing you away and depriving me of your company. But though I lose you to your groom, I wish you good fortune in the hunt."

"As do I," said Rowena.

"Indeed, I wish you the best of luck," added Charles with a chuckle. "After all, the whole purpose of the thing is for the unwed to find a ring." Though the rhyme was spoken with humor, the look he directed at Eleanor was pointed.

"Not *all* unwed ladies go to London with that singular purpose, Charles," she replied calmly, taking a sip of her tea. "I certainly shan't."

"Why not?" Sorin blurted before thinking it through.

"Why should I?" Her tone was light. "Thanks to Papa, I have wealth enough of my own to live comfortably for the rest of my life, provided I manage it well."

In for a penny… "You mean *not* to marry?"

Her shoulders lifted in an elegant shrug. "Well, I suppose if I should happen to meet someone who makes me completely happy, I might feel inclined toward matrimony." She sighed. "But I think it highly unlikely that I shall ever find such a person. I may be young, but I'm woefully set in my ways, as my dear cousin will be quick to tell you. Besides which, the company I most enjoy is already right here."

"But what of children?" asked Caroline, seemingly as shocked as he was to hear her announcement.

"Oh, well. I suppose I should like to have children someday," she replied. "But not at the expense of being bound to someone with whom I cannot truly be happy. No. I would rather remain unencumbered than compromise my joy." A beatific smile curved her lips. "Besides, what need have I that cannot be fulfilled through such friendships as I already possess?"

An awkward silence fell, and Sorin barely refrained from snorting aloud into it. *What need, indeed?* Wicked thoughts on that subject ran amok, and it was all he could do to keep the chief—and highly inappropriate—answer behind his teeth.

"Surely your heart longs for something deeper and more meaningful?" asked Caroline, oblivious to the barely audible sigh of relief from the men in the room.

The girl had taken the words right out of his mouth, for

which he was grateful—until he noticed she was looking at *him* rather than at Eleanor, and with far too keen an interest.

"Not at all," said Eleanor, smiling. "I'm quite content with my life just as it is, I assure you. All the longings of my heart are met."

Such blithe words from one so clearly inexperienced! A hair's breadth away from bursting into laughter, he sought to cover his amusement by taking a sip of tea. Above the rim of the cup, he watched Rowena level a quelling stare at Charles, who looked near to asphyxiation.

"And what of you, Lord Wincanton?" asked Caroline, drawing his gaze. "What are your views on the institution of marriage?"

A mouthful of tea went down the wrong pipe. Fighting the urge to cough, he took another sip and carefully cleared his throat. "Me? Ah, well. I suppose I shall be obliged to marry, naturally. Eventually," he amended as the girl's eyes took on a distressingly hungry gleam. He looked at Eleanor and saw her lips quirk just as she ducked her head over her teacup. The little imp was laughing! Well, it took two to waltz. "Unlike some, I have not the option of remaining unencumbered. I have a duty to my family—one with demands that, unfortunately, cannot be fulfilled by mere friendship."

Charles's brows collided, and Sorin realized he'd alluded to a bit more than was appropriate for present company. The conversation needed to move forward and quickly. He glanced at Eleanor, but then immediately swung his gaze toward Caroline, feeling as though he were navigating a battlefield. "I was engaged once. But she was taken from me only weeks before we were to marry."

Jane. She'd been killed in a riding accident during a hunt almost ten years ago. The horse, a borrowed mount, had thrown her and then stepped on her, crushing her. As long as he lived, he would never be able to expunge the sight of the life ebbing from her blue eyes. It was his fault she'd died. He'd put her on the accursed beast, dismissing her reluctance and encouraging her to put aside her timidity and be more adventurous, to live more fully.

Never again.

"I've yet to find her equal," he continued, shoving his guilt into a dark corner. It amazed him how such an old wound could still feel so raw. "And now, like Ellie, I'm woefully set in my ways. Yes. I'm afraid the lady I marry will have to be eligible for sainthood."

Caroline's hand flew to her bosom, and she leaned a little closer. "How can you say such a thing about yourself when you are the very soul of accommodation and kindness? Any lady would be honored to call you her own."

Sorin felt the carved arm of the couch, an immovable barrier, dig into his ribs on the opposite side. She would be in his bloody lap in a moment. "So says a kind-hearted young lady of little experience with ill-tempered old men like myself."

"Old?" The redhead's smile turned coy. "You are not yet forty years of age, sir. My own dear papa was forty and five when he married, and Mama but seventeen."

He opened his mouth, but then shut it again. There was no possible response that wouldn't cause him endless trouble. Opposite, he saw that Eleanor's shoulders were shaking so now that she was barely able to keep her tea from spilling.

Charles came to his rescue. "If I remember correctly, Miss Caroline, your parents met for the first time on their wedding day. An arranged marriage, was it not?"

Caroline looked at him with barely concealed irritation. "Indeed."

"Well, there you are then," said Charles, slapping his knee as he turned to regard him with a smirk. "Perhaps there is the solution to your problem, eh? I'm certain your lady mother would be delighted to handpick her own daughter-in-law, would she not?"

Sorin breathed a quiet sigh of relief as the fickle tide again turned in his favor. "Indeed she would," he agreed with a chuckle. His traitorous eyes again found Eleanor and lingered on her for a moment. "However, I prefer to choose my bride-to-be myself."

"And who can blame you?" said Charles, his face breaking into a smile as he looked to Rowena. "After all, I chose my own lovely bride and look how happy it has made me."

"Oh, was it *you* who made the choice, then?" Rowena's smile was soft in spite of her teasing tone.

Sorin looked on with a touch of envy. Indeed, his friend's joy was complete. He was the lord of a fine estate—several, in fact—while still young enough to enjoy it, his wife was both beautiful and affectionate, and his line assured.

It was the sort of life he'd have had with Jane, had she lived. But Fate, in her caprice, had dealt him a different set of cards. He looked at Eleanor, sitting there serving them tea, so composed and elegant, completely unaware of the ardent feelings she evoked in him. Truly, she had grown up to be every inch the lady he'd always told her she must be. He refused to believe she wouldn't marry. The call to matrimony was not something many young women denied for very long.

All it would take was a little pressure. Her friends, like the eager Miss Caroline, would marry and their lives would become vastly different. Then those friends would begin having children and motherhood would add yet another layer of separation. Left behind, she'd begin to feel lonely and want to rejoin their ranks. Then a handsome young man would come along with all the right words to unlock her heart, and she'd traipse down the aisle with a smile on her lips to slide that man's ring on her finger.

And then she'd be gone.

The thought lashed at him like a whip. He pushed it aside. She *would* marry. It was only right that she should have a life filled with all of the happiness she deserved. And he'd ensure that it happened, even if it meant tearing out his own heart. "Rowena, I meant to ask how the children were this morning." A safe enough subject. Better than talk of marriage, certainly.

"As good as may be," she said with a wry laugh. "Michael is giving Nanny fits, insisting on keeping a pet toad in the nursery. Emily is still coughing, which has us a bit worried, but she seems to be steadily improving."

"And young George?"

"Is doing very well with his lessons," she said, her expression one of immense pride. "His tutor has told us that he's quite a promising little scholar. Naturally, he'll go to Oxford—"

"Ahem. Rowena my gem," interrupted Charles gently. "I thought we agreed he would attend King's College in Cambridge."

Her smile broadened just a little and she patted his arm. "Did we? I can never remember, darling. But there are many years yet to come before we must make a final decision. None of us knows what things will be like by the time George is of an age to attend." She rubbed his arm soothingly. "I'm sure there will be many fine institutions from which to choose by then, and we don't yet know his natural bent."

This seemed to mollify Charles, somewhat. "Well, being a King's man, I *am* naturally biased toward Cambridge. But...I suppose we should wait and see the direction he takes before carving anything in stone."

"You are ever reasonable and fair-minded, my love," said his wife, giving him a final pat.

Sorin hid a smile. He had no doubt whatsoever that little

George would be an Oxford man, if she wanted it that way. She had the benefit of time to exert her gentle influence. Again, he looked at Eleanor. Her sharp eyes and ears never missed much, and he wondered if she was taking notes on how to properly handle a husband of her own.

All at once he pictured himself with that coveted title, a blissful image of them discussing plans for their own children. He allowed this fantasy to live for no more than an instant before snuffing it out. It was an impossible dream.

How could he violate Charles's and Rowena's trust by admitting amorous feelings for their cousin, whom he'd practically helped them raise? Especially when she looked on him without the slightest romantic interest whatsoever. If that wasn't enough, then there was the fact that they were all wrong for each other.

Unlike his shy, quiet Jane, Ellie was a force of nature. Despite what she'd said, he knew from her many letters that she craved adventure and excitement. And though she'd apparently taken his admonishments to govern her impulsive nature to heart, he could still see its mutinous spark in her eyes. He wouldn't be the one to put it out.

He'd tried to shape Jane into something she wasn't and the outcome had been disastrous. His brushstrokes could be plainly seen in Ellie's demeanor now, and he longed to undo them, to take back his censure. He'd wanted to protect her, to teach her caution, to make her more like Jane—for her own good.

It had been a mistake.

Even if by some miracle he could convince her to accept his suit, the act would only result in her misery and eventual resentment of him. She could never be content as his wife. Ellie needed a husband who was like-minded, a kindred spirit. Someone young and idealistic, someone ready for an adventure. He was not that man. Not anymore.

No. The only way out of this was to see Ellie married—to someone else. Someone better suited to her. Someone worthy of her.

"I believe I shall go to London this Season," he announced, watching as eyes widened around the room. One pair in particular—the wrong pair—shone with undisguised delight. Miss Caroline looked like a child who'd just been promised a pony of her very own. Eleanor's gaze, however, was fixed on the teapot. "I've been away for far too long and must get reacquainted with everyone," he continued, hiding his disappointment. After all, why should she care whether or not he went to London?

"How wonderful!" said Rowena. "You'll come with us to all of the balls and parties, of course?"

"Naturally," he answered. It would be torture, but he'd do it if only to see Eleanor safely married by the end of it. At least then he would have a measure of peace. Above all, her marriage would force him to get on with his own life. "It'll be like old times," he said, trying not to sound pained.

"By George, I think it a marvelous plan!" said Charles. "You'll come with us, have a jolly time of it, and we'll find *you* the perfect wife!"

Sorin repressed a groan. That Charles had the same strategy for him as he did for Eleanor was irony at its finest. "Why not?" he said, forcing a laugh. "It's better than allowing my mother to choose my bride, certainly." He fought the impulse for a moment, and lost. "What think you, Eleanor?"

She looked at him and smiled serenely. "I think it a fine plan. I should like nothing better than to see you as happy as my cousin."

Again disappointment stung hard, and with it the certainty that seeing her happily married was the right thing to do—for her sake, as well as his own.

Chapter Three

Eleanor fought for inner calm as she watched Caroline shamelessly flirt with Sorin. Such behavior was to be expected whenever Caroline encountered any reasonably decent-looking male of the species—but his favorable reaction to it was most certainly not.

"Eleanor?"

She jumped and saw that Charles was staring at her expectantly. "I'm so sorry. What were you saying?" If the heat in her cheeks was any indication, she was turning as red as a beet.

"I said that with any luck some young buck will persuade you to marry, as well," he reiterated. "Oh, I know you mean to stay 'unencumbered' and all that rot, but you never know." He turned to Sorin. "This may be the year our Jericho finally falls."

"Charles," admonished Rowena, giving him a sharp look.

"Jericho?" said Sorin at the same time.

Her heart sank.

"Yes, well, Lady Jericho, to be precise," corrected Charles, ignoring the elbow his wife nudged against his side. "One of the fellows dogging Eleanor's heels last Season, a young reverend, in fact,"—he broke off and chuckled for a moment—"declared he would bring down her walls even if it meant marching 'round her house seven times while blowing the matrimonial trumpet." He dissolved into laughter.

Eleanor cringed. It wasn't all that funny, really.

"A most persistent young man, as I recall," added Rowena, shooting Eleanor an apologetic glance. "He proposed to her three times."

Caroline turned to face her with a wounded expression. "Did he? You never told me."

"Well, to be honest, I did not think it noteworthy."

"Not noteworthy?" said Charles with another incredulous laugh. "The man proclaimed before the entire assembly at the Darlington ball that God Himself had promised him in a dream that our Eleanor would be his wife. Not noteworthy!" he scoffed. "You should have seen the bloody book at White's. Entire pages were devoted to wagers on whether or not she would succumb to his siege. Every man in London with a shilling to spare likely bet on the outcome."

Sorin's face was deadpan. "How disappointed they must have been when she made good her escape."

"Ah, indeed." Charles wagged a playful finger. "But he did not make it easy, oho no. Our Eleanor ran, and wherever she went, the good reverend followed."

Indeed he had. Like a biblical plague.

"He tried everything to catch her," continued Charles. "I understand he even shammed an injury at one point."

"An injury?" exclaimed Caroline, her hand rising to her bosom.

If Sorin's gaze hadn't been fixed on the region over which that hand rested, Eleanor would have found her dramatic display hilarious. As it was, she was not at all amused. "Yes," she bit out. "He 'hit' his head on a low branch during a garden party—quite intentionally, I assure you—and then in front of everyone requested that I accompany him back to the house so that he might recover. I could not decline without seeming rude, so I agreed. As soon as we were out of sight, however, the horrid little toad miraculously recovered his ailing faculties and then proceeded to behave in a manner most untoward." He was still staring at Caroline. Her temper flared. "He kissed me."

That got his attention—along with everyone else's. Her palms grew moist as Sorin's hazel eyes pierced her.

"And?"

The single, gruffly uttered word affected her like a finger plucking a harp string. From the top of her head all the way down to her toes, which began to curl in her slippers, everything inside her began to resonate in the strangest manner. "He—I—"

"Ellie," gasped Rowena. "You never told us he assaulted your person. You said he accidentally stepped on your hem and caused you to fall."

"He did," she finally replied. He had, only it had been quite deliberate. He'd stamped down on it with his heel, tearing the bottom and bringing her crashing to the ground like a felled tree. "And I did fall. He reached down to help me up, and before I knew what he was about or could stop him, he kissed me. I can only surmise that he must have been overcome by ardent emotion." The lie tasted bitter on her tongue. He'd been overcome with lust and had fallen on her like a ravening beast. She'd barely been able to fend him off and get away.

"Merciful God, Ellie," whispered Rowena, her face white. "Why did you not tell us?"

"Because there was no need," she answered, trying to ignore a pang of guilt. She hadn't meant to tell *any*one, ever, for fear of being labeled "compromised" and ending up forever bound to the miserable barbarian. Reverend indeed! Lecherous brute was more like it. At least she was safe now, for he'd since gotten married. "I can assure you he regained his senses very quickly and that the matter was resolved."

"Is *that* what happened to his eye?" asked Charles, his own narrowing. "I knew something was wrong when you came back so quickly. When we all returned to the house, the good reverend's eye was blacked," he explained to his wife. "He claimed it was the fault of the tree, but I now suspect otherwise."

All eyes turned to Eleanor. "I'm sure I don't remember all of the details. It was almost a year ago, after all." A weak excuse, but better than none.

"Yes, practically an eternity," her cousin drawled.

"Eleanor, tell me you did not actually *strike* him?" asked Caroline, her mouth forming a perfect little "o" of shock when she failed to reply.

"I suspect she did, and quite roundly," Charles answered for her, his eyes twinkling. "His eye was swollen completely shut. Never have I seen a man's face look so battered, save after a jolly good brawl. She had to have hit him square on and hard."

"Indeed?" murmured Sorin, still staring at her.

"Most ladies would have simply called out for help," said Rowena sternly. "I consider it very fortunate that he did not return the blow, as some men might."

Charles's face darkened. "There would have been a calling out and sure, had he laid a violent hand on her."

"I, for one, am glad she was able to defend herself," said Sorin, shooting her a quick conspirator's smile.

Eleanor returned it. After all, hadn't he been the one to teach her how to curl her fingers into a proper fist? It was one of the few times he'd ever condoned unladylike behavior.

"Still," continued Charles, a frown marring his normally good-natured face, "Rowena is right. You should have told us of his presumption at once so that I might have addressed the matter properly on your behalf, as is my duty. I am most distressed that you did not come to me."

She bowed her head meekly. "I did not wish to burden you with so trivial a matter when you were already so worried. Rowena was indisposed, if you remember, which—"

"I'd just learned that I was *enceinte*," interrupted Rowena softly, smiling at her husband. "Remember?"

The look he shot her was one of pure adoration. "I do indeed."

"Which was why you escorted me to that particular party," finished Eleanor. "Regarding the reverend, the matter is now moot. The gentleman has married."

Charles settled back in his chair. "Married or not, if the blackguard should attempt to make a nuisance of himself again, you must promise to tell me at once."

"Yes, of course." The promise was completely unnecessary. The reverend had not so much as looked at her since the incident.

"Goodness me, Eleanor," said Caroline with a weak laugh. "I've known you for many years, yet I should never have imagined you so bold as to strike a man with a closed hand."

"Yes, well, I suspect the injury to the good reverend's pride was far worse than the one to his eye," Eleanor mumbled, hoping she would drop it and move to a different topic. No such luck.

"Had I been in your place, I would not have known what to do," breathed Caroline, her eyes wide. "I should have likely fainted, or at best screamed in the hope that some brave soul might come to my rescue." She cast a smoldering look at Sorin.

But to Eleanor's delight, Sorin wasn't looking at Caroline. "For my part, I'm very glad your courage did not fail you," he said, the warmth in his eyes reaching down into her. "I am appalled that a man charged with acting as a shepherd would be so sorely lacking in self-control. I believe you did his flock a great service by teaching him the error of his ways. One can but hope the lesson was henceforth reflected in his conduct and not merely in his sermons."

Though his tone was dour, the twinkle in his eye instantly restored her spirits. She had no doubt whatsoever that he, too, was remembering his clandestine instruction on proper punching technique. She smiled at him fondly. "One can but hope."

Damn me for a thrice-blind fool. Sorin tried—and failed—to look away, to ignore the pull of that smile. He reminded himself that the tenderness in her eyes was at best nothing more than sisterly affection. Charles cleared his throat, and he realized he'd been staring and that an awkward silence had fallen. Glancing at the clock on the mantel, he stood. "By George, it's very nearly noon. I'm afraid I've lingered here far too long."

"You're leaving?" blurted Eleanor, half rising from her seat. Almost at once, she sank back down, a faint blush beginning to stain her cheeks. "My apologies, I meant no imposition. It's just that we've been so long deprived of your company," she amended lamely.

His heart leaped at the knowledge that she had missed him, but it was too late to change his mind now. "I regret having to depart as well, but I must return. I promised Mother that I would go over the accounts with her today."

"Of course," agreed Charles, standing. He, too, appeared crestfallen. With visible effort, however, he brightened. "And there'll be plenty of opportunities to visit now that you're back to stay. You are of course welcome here at Holbrook any time—no invitation necessary, just as before."

"Indeed," said Rowena. "You must visit us again soon."

It would never be the way it was before, but Sorin couldn't deny the fact that he'd missed this place even more than he had Holly Hall. And he couldn't deny the fact that it felt wonderful to be here even though it presented him with a dire problem in the form of Eleanor. "Thank you," he replied, bowing to them both. "I certainly will. Rowena, Charles, it has been a delight."

Rowena smiled fondly. "The pleasure is all ours." She turned to Eleanor. "Will you please accompany our guest to the stables? I have something to discuss with Charles and Caroline."

From the corner of his eye, Sorin saw that the redheaded girl wore a look of undisguised rancor at the announcement. Her misplaced ambition to bag him was clear. And it was his own bloody fault.

Rising, Eleanor smoothed her skirts. "I shall be delighted, of course."

He didn't quite know what to expect as they sauntered down the otherwise empty hall that led to the rear of the house, but it wasn't this silence. Eleanor had always been so talkative, ever excited to relay to him the latest bit of news from her world. The quiet, composed woman beside him seemed almost foreign. Though he knew it for foolishness, he much preferred her blushes and outbursts. "I suppose you'll be happy to return to London?" he finally asked.

"I shall be happy to see some of my friends, but in truth I

much prefer quiet living." She looked at him sidelong. "I'm not nearly as frivolous-minded as Charles believes."

"I've never thought you frivolous-minded."

It earned him a faint smile. "Charles thinks all women are bent on gaiety. He teases me over what he calls my 'false temperance' and vows that I secretly harbor the same giddiness and whimsy as other ladies my age. I vow to be bullheaded and disagree with him."

That's better. "One would think he might appreciate your taking the more sober attitude."

"Indeed, one would," she said with a small sigh. "But I'm afraid that as long as I fail to agree with him that marriage is the only sensible course, my cousin will continue to view me as a child incapable of any sort of wisdom."

His gaze was drawn to her mouth, which was curled in a wry smile. "I've met a great many matrons sorely lacking in wisdom. It's not some mysterious gift to be instantly imparted upon speaking one's wedding vows. It can be obtained only through experiencing the travails of life."

She laughed softly. "Perhaps my cousin is correct after all. I've certainly suffered very few such trials. My life here at Holbrook has been idyllic."

He stopped. "Eleanor, you have suffered such loss as can only impart wisdom far beyond your years." He referred to her parents' untimely demise when she was but nine. Did he dare bring up the more recent past? "I must confess I'm astonished to find you so reserved."

"If I appear so, it is because that is what is expected of me," she replied, her voice taking on a crisp edge. "I would not shame my guardians by conducting myself in a manner unbefitting my station. As you once said, 'a true lady always exhibits an attitude of polite reserve.'"

Damn, and damn again. "Yes, but there is a vast difference between reserve and gravity. Reserve is merely the veil that conceals one's true sentiments from being inappropriately displayed."

"And gravity?"

"Gravity is the hallmark of a soul that no longer experiences joy." Such would likely be his fate once this was finished. He pushed the black thought aside. "You had a foot on that path when I first met you, and I was quite relieved to see you abandon it. May God grant that you never again find it."

"You showed me a better path," she replied softly, her irritation fading. "And you've been my faithful guide ever since."

"Yes. But I have perhaps been wrong about a few things along the way." At her puzzled look, he hurried on. "I cannot help but feel there is something between us that remains unresolved. I know you've long since forgiven me for my harsh words the last—"

"Of course I have," she interrupted, looking away uncomfortably.

"Eleanor, please just hear me." He took a step closer, forcing her to again meet his gaze. "I wish there to be no bitter stones between us. In the past, I might have been a bit… over-zealous in my correction of you, but I never wished you anything but happiness."

"I've never thought otherwise," she said, straightening her shoulders to address him with dignity worthy of a queen. "And you needn't worry. I recognize that what you did was for my own good. I have since seen several of my peers fall prey to a lack of reserve. They displayed their sentiments openly, only to be rejected and humiliated—or worse, ruined by an unscrupulous man's whim. Because of your wise and timely instruction, I've avoided such pitfalls and the misery that accompanies them. For that, I cannot thank you enough."

Sorin bit back a groan. "Please, don't thank me," he managed at last. "It was not an entirely selfless act, you know. I was just as concerned for my own reputation as I was for yours."

"I know," she said, surprising him. "I admit that at first I failed to understand, but in time I grew to comprehend the untenable position in which I had put you. I was impetuous and indiscreet, and you were right to correct me before I could publicly shame us all." She bowed her head. "I doubt anyone else would have done so as gently."

Remorse piled onto his shoulders until the weight of it was almost unbearable. "Eleanor, Charles has told me of your many rejected suitors. You have, to his utter bewilderment and despair, refused to consider any and every gentleman that has expressed interest in you, and I cannot help but feel that the fault is in some way at least partly mine. While it is true that I'd hoped to impart to you a sense of decorum, I never intended that you should withhold yourself so entirely as to become isolated."

In the silence that followed, he braced himself.

But in spite of her reddening face, she spoke with chilling calm. "You confuse reserve with a lack of feeling. Reserve is the veil behind which we conceal those sentiments inappropriate to display, is that not what you said?"

"It was indeed," he replied, now regretting the fact that he'd ever broached the subject.

"Then consider it fortunate that I maintained my reserve, because to have displayed my true feelings for those so-called suitors would have been insulting to their dignity and very likely ruinous for me." Her eyes flashed, belying her cool tone. "I've given every gentleman before which Charles has paraded me an opportunity to prove himself worthy of my regard. It's not my fault that all have failed to meet my standards. If I've been reserved, it is because I have yet to find a gentleman possessing the qualities necessary to engender my trust and affection."

Prudence warred with curiosity—and promptly lost. "Might I inquire as to these...standards you've set forth? Because it seems to me you've set some lofty requirements, if indeed no less than four—six if you count the good reverend's repeated attempts—proposals of marriage have been turned down due to lack of their fulfillment. Are you certain the fault lies with the gentlemen?"

In an instant, he knew he'd gone too far. Her eyes widened, and the flags in her cheeks brightened to a cherry red that spread to the tips of her ears.

"Perhaps I *am* too harsh a critic," she said a bit unsteadily. "My only excuse is that my expectations have been set by the examples with which I was provided in my youth. My father, Charles, and..." A suspicious brightness rimmed her lower lashes for a bare instant before she averted her gaze.

Comprehension dawned. "If you mean to say that *I* am at fault for—"

"Who else was there?" she snapped, glaring at him through leaf-green eyes that glittered with unshed tears. "Had I been exposed to lesser men, I should perhaps be more willing to accept such a one. However, as I was not, I shall continue to hope for better. Had you been here to see what has presented itself thus far, I would like to think that you would agree with my decision."

The words had been spoken softly, and yet they cut like the sharpest steel. He took a step toward her, intending only to offer comfort and reassurance, but she quickly edged away.

"Regardless, my standards are my own and I will not compromise them," she said, her tone once again brisk. "Now if you will excuse me, I believe you know your way out."

Brushing past him she stalked away, leaving him to stare after her in shock—and to wrestle down the fierce joy that had begun to kindle in the ash pit of his heart. Just because she'd made him part of her standard for comparison did not mean she desired him. When evaluating suitors, young ladies often looked for the qualities exemplified by the older gentlemen in their acquaintance. That he should even dare to dream that she might have meant more was a measure of his idiocy.

Still...her blush had been quite spectacular. *Had* she fooled herself into thinking him her husbandly ideal? If so, he must disabuse her of the notion at once, no matter how much the selfish part of him would rather do otherwise.

He walked the rest of the way to the stables, torn between guilty elation and fear for both her and himself. He'd ruined one young woman's life by trying to change her—he wouldn't ruin Ellie's.

The truth must be learned, and the damage—if any—must be undone. The question was how to do it without her suspecting anything.

Chapter Four

It was all Eleanor could do not to bolt. Her back stung like a thousand angry bees had alighted on it, but she kept her spine straight and her pace steady and stately, refusing to give in to the childish urge to run. If she did, he'd only come after her, which would result in even more humiliation. No. This was the way a mature, dignified woman would handle the situation.

Inside, however, she longed to tear out of the house and hide in the wood until the heat left her face, until her blood settled down and her head cleared. She could retreat to her room, but there was always a chance that Fran might be there or that someone else might see her state and inquire. So instead of doing either, she ducked into the deep shadows beneath the grand staircase to compose herself.

Lightheaded and trembling all over, she leaned against the wall. The tears she'd tried so hard to hold back now streamed down her face unchecked. Digging into her pocket, she found a kerchief and carefully blotted them away, listening for any sound of approaching footsteps. If anyone saw her like this…

In his eyes she was still a child. The pathetic, tearful child he'd found hiding in the garden the day they'd met. The disobedient brat who'd fallen out of a bloody tree and broken his nose. The impetuous hoyden he'd had to chasten for being too demonstrative. Would he never see her as anything but that child? She wanted to think they'd become friends—*real* friends—now that she was grown. Friendship between adults should be comprised of mutual fondness and respect between equals. But while his respect for her was a given and his fondness assured, he most certainly did *not* consider her his equal.

Hot tears again pricked her eyelids. Furious, she swiped them away, taking care not to rub too hard lest she further redden her eyes. Down the hall a clock struck half past twelve. The others would be waiting for her, wondering. She couldn't stay here, and she couldn't appear to have been crying or there would be questions.

Breathing deeply, she counted to one hundred and then peeked to make sure no one was about before tiptoeing across the hall to have a look in a mirror. Her cheeks were still a bit pink and her lids a little swollen, but she looked well enough to escape undue notice provided she was careful. Squaring her shoulders, she made her slow way back to the salon, making sure to pause and listen at each corner for a moment before emerging—in case *he* was still lurking about. Fortunately, she encountered no one. By the time she neared the salon, she felt reasonably composed.

Caroline's voice issued out into the hall. "Might I inquire as to whether we can expect Lord Wincanton to share our coach for the journey to London?"

The inquisition had already begun.

"Of course not," answered Rowena at once. "He and his mother have their own conveyance."

"Oh. I did not think of that." Disappointment colored Caroline's voice.

"I dare say you did not," replied Rowena.

Eleanor smiled grimly. It was as much a relief to know she wouldn't have to sit across from him for the journey as it was to know he'd be beyond the reach of Caroline's claws. She was just about to make her entrance when Rowena again spoke, sending her back to her place of concealment.

"Though I hesitate to do so for fear of offending you, Caroline, I have been asked by your parents to chaperone you this Season and therefore feel I must speak."

Holding her breath, Eleanor strained to hear.

"Your demeanor toward Lord Wincanton this morning came very close to being unacceptable. Not only do I disapprove of such bold flirtation, but you ought to know that Lord Wincanton deplores forward behavior in females."

"I apologize for any perceived impropriety, Lady Ashford," she heard Caroline say after a moment. "I was merely attempting to put Lord Wincanton at his ease."

Eleanor almost laughed aloud at the bald-faced lie. She would have been in his lap had there been no one else present!

"Lord Wincanton has been our friend for many years and has always been perfectly at ease here at Holbrook," said Rowena. "In the future, I expect you to behave with proper decorum, especially when we have guests."

"Yes, Lady Ashford."

The meek answer seemed to close the conversation. Quietly backing up a few paces, Eleanor schooled her features, shook her skirts, and rounded the corner.

"Well, that was quick," said Rowena, her brows rising. "I would have thought you'd spend at least a few minutes talking, though I suppose all the letters between you made it unnecessary."

Eleanor suppressed a curse that would have in previous years earned her a mouthful of strong soap. "I would have enjoyed further conversation but he was in rather a rush to return home." Quite deliberately, she sat down beside Caroline so that she wouldn't have to face her. "But truth be told, you are right. Neither of us can have much to say that hasn't already been said." Let Caroline ponder *that* and wonder what she meant by it. It was a childish thing to do and she knew it, but that didn't make it any less gratifying.

Rowena's brow furrowed, causing the knot in Eleanor's stomach to tighten. "I suppose it is the mark of a good friendship that you understand each other so well," she said at last, dismissing the subject.

But I don't understand him at all! Slowly, Eleanor released the breath she'd been holding. Still refusing to look at Caroline, she reached out to pour herself another cup of tea. "Oh, pity. The pot has gone cold. Shall I ring for a fresh one?"

Rowena shook her head. "There is no time for it, I'm afraid. You must both go and change. Eleanor, see that Fran takes care of the stain on Caroline's skirt."

She made it to the top of the steps before Caroline stopped her.

"You never mentioned to me that you and Lord Wincanton corresponded during his absence."

Affecting the same too-sweet tone, Eleanor answered, "I did not think you would find our discussions of any particular interest. You've always—at least until today—made it quite plain that you thought him stuffy and boring. Had I known you were interested, I would have been glad to share them," she lied.

"Oh really, Eleanor!" said her friend, dropping all pretense. "You've been exchanging letters with a man traveling abroad and you thought I would fail to find them interesting?"

Shrugging, she resumed progress up the stairs. "Not unless you find observations regarding the price of goods and sketches of scenery fascinating," she said over her shoulder. Opening her door, she went in fully expecting to be followed. She was not disappointed.

"Still, you could have told me," grumped Caroline, making herself comfortable on the edge of the bed. She heaved a sigh. "Don't you think he looked handsome in his hunting coat this morning?"

"If you think a man in muddy boots tromping behind a gaggle of dead birds swinging from a pole is a handsome sight, then I suppose so," she said sullenly, determined to be disagreeable. Flinging her shawl aside, she gave the bell pull a yank.

Caroline sat up straight and stared hard at her. "My, but something has curdled *your* cream this morning."

Thankfully Fran chose that moment to enter, and for a few minutes the women busied themselves disrobing. The instant the maid stepped out to fetch a forgotten item, however, the inquisition continued.

"Well?"

"Well what?" Eleanor replied, dismayed that her friend was still interested enough to persist. "Which do you think I ought to wear, the blue or the green?"

"Don't try that trick on me, Ellie," said Caroline, her hands on her hips. "Tell me."

"Tell you what?" she asked blankly. *That I think you a ninnywit for even contemplating a man like Sorin for a husband?* She bit her tongue. "I'm just a bit out of sorts," she said at last, walking over to snatch the blue gown from the wardrobe and lay it across the bed. "I'm sure I'll be perfectly fine as soon as I have something to eat."

Caroline followed and forced her to face her. "You've been out of sorts ever since *he* arrived. Don't think I failed to notice it. And the way he acts around you…" Her blue eyes narrowed. "Is there something between the two of you?"

A strangled laugh burbled up from Eleanor's chest. "Good heavens, no! At least not in the way you mean. He's known me since I was a child. We are merely friends. Old friends."

"Well, I'm glad to hear it, because I've decided that I want him."

Though she knew it already, hearing it said aloud almost made Eleanor drop the ribbon she was holding. She tried to sound nonchalant. "You cannot be serious, Caroline. He is not your sort and you know it. Why waste your time?"

Her friend was having none of that, however. "Was it not you who said I should look to him as a shining example of what a gentleman ought to be? Well, why not take the original rather than settle for an imperfect copy?"

If she'd been irritated before, Eleanor was now quite thoroughly vexed. But she dare not show it. She had no desire to ruin their friendship or incite the redhead's wrath. Reason told her that once they were in London, Caroline would forget all about dull, older, sober Sorin. "I suppose I did tell you that," she said, turning with an apologetic smile. "I'm so sorry—I don't mean to be ill-tempered. I'm just hungry and rather tired, if you want to know. I hardly slept after the excitement of last night."

This excuse seemed to mollify Caroline, for the sparkle returned to her blue eyes. "And who can blame you? After all, you'll be your own woman this Season, won't you? How wonderful it must be to know such freedom!"

Eleanor knew she hadn't meant it as a dig, but it certainly felt like one. Yes, at twenty-one she was no giddy greenling ready to fall for the first handsome face or dulcet word. She was worldly-wise, unencumbered and independently wealthy—a prize not easily, if ever, to be won. Curiosity pricked her. “Caroline, if you had the means to avoid marriage, would you do so?”

Caroline’s brows rose. “Well, as I have not the luxury of any other alternative, I’ve not really thought about it. But I must suppose I would. Unless I found someone I could truly love, of course.”

“Do you hope to marry for love?”

A soft snort answered that question. “Every woman hopes for a love match, Ellie. But I’m too practical to allow fancy to get in the way of a successful match and security.”

“You would choose money rather than love, then?”

“Love won’t keep one from suffering privation, will it?” said Caroline, her manner cool. “Oh, don’t look so horrified. If possible, I should very much like to have both money *and* love. But not all of us have the means to pass up a good opportunity in order to wait for our ideal.” Coming over, she grasped Eleanor’s hands. “I promise I won’t marry a brute. Nor shall I wed a fool—unless he’s ridiculously rich and happy to allow me to guide him in matters concerning his purse.” She giggled. “No. I shall marry the first tolerably wealthy man to make an offer. Better to have done than have none, as my grandmother once said. As for Lord Wincanton, he seems a fine match indeed.” Another giggle. “And the best part is that I’ve the advantage of being in his acquaintance *before* the cats in London can get a claw in.”

A cold, hard lump settled in Eleanor’s stomach at the thought of Caroline marrying Sorin. She would make him utterly miserable! In that moment, she knew what had to be done. Sorin might think of her as a naive child who needed his benevolent guidance to avoid making a terrible mistake, but in truth *he* was the one in danger. Whatever happened, even if it ruined both friendships, she could not allow him to fall into Caroline’s nets.

Sorin managed to stay away from Holbrook—and Eleanor—for an entire week. The days were easy enough as long as he remained busy, which was not at all difficult considering how long he'd been away and how much work there was to be done. The nights, however, were a different story altogether.

No matter how exhausted he was, he lay awake in the dark for hours, his mind overrun with thoughts of Eleanor. Every word she'd spoken to him since his return. Every detail of her face. The scent she wore that drove him mad.

There was no peace to be found in slumber, either. Most times, the Eleanor of his dreams answered the longings of his heart and the cravings of his body with a passion that awakened him in a state of need bordering on torment. There were other dreams in which she featured as well, dreams that were far less pleasant. From these he awakened drenched in cold sweat, and nothing—not reading, not walking, nor even copious amounts of brandy—could dispel the sense of utter hopelessness they left behind.

By the time Sunday arrived, his nerves were taut and his temper short.

"Stop your grumbling," admonished his mother as he climbed into the carriage ahead of her. "You may have lived like a heathen while abroad, but you have no excuse for it now."

"I'm not grumbling—and I did *not* live like a heathen," he snapped, helping her up and then taking the seat opposite. He would have avoided attending church but for her insistence on having him along.

One steely gray brow lifted.

Damn. "My apologies, Mother. I did not intend to be harsh."

"Whatever is the matter with you of late?" she said a few minutes later as they trundled down the road toward the village. "You've been cross ever since your visit to Holbrook. Did you and Ashford have a disagreement?"

"No, Mother," he answered, wishing now that he'd insisted on staying at home.

"Well, something has certainly been weighing on your mind."

Indeed it had. "There is much to be done now that I'm home," he said with a weary sigh. "The finances are in decent shape but the estate itself is going to need a great deal of work. The east wing badly needs a new roof. The workers that repaired it after that storm did a shoddy job. It will have to be redone before the winter or we'll have snow in the staff quarters—and quite possibly fewer staff."

"I'm still wroth over having been so easily rooked." Her bony knuckles turned white as she gripped the handle of her cane.

"And then there is the matter of the ruined harvest and the nonexistent rents," he went on, glad to have found an adequate distraction for them both. "I doubt whether we'd have seen full payment from any of our tenants, given the impact that storm had on the crops, but there might have been partial payment at least. So there is that to consider as well. A minor loss in the grand scheme of things, but a setback, nonetheless."

She settled back, her face filled with contrition. "Perhaps I went a bit too far in forgiving the rents entirely for the year," she said with a sniff. "I managed things to the best of my ability in your absence. I knew there would be dire hardship if I held them to even half the expected amount, and hungry men with hungry families are apt to turn to criminal activities to meet their needs. In any case, I could not in good conscience hold them accountable for something over which they had no control and from which they had no recourse."

"Of course not," he agreed, now feeling churlish. "I did not mean to insinuate that you'd done poorly, Mother. Had I been informed of the situation, I might have made the same decision. I'm simply taken aback at learning of it almost a year after the fact."

"I did it on your behalf, you know," she said, examining her gloves. "You should have heard the blessings heaped on you the Sunday following. Two of the children recently born in the village were named for you—a boy called Latham and a girl named Sorel."

"How...lovely." Having the village children named after him out of gratitude over a charitable act he hadn't even committed felt wrong in so many ways. "Father must be railing at Saint Peter to let him come back and sort us out."

"Your father was a good man, but you are likely right," she admitted with a grimace. "He never would have been so generous. He would have taken what he could when it was due and expected the rest after the following harvest."

"That, I will never do," he vowed. "I've never thought that a fair practice. What God has ordained for a season is a burden of responsibility beyond any man's right to place upon another human being."

His mother's eyes warmed. "Your father was from another age, Sorin. A much harsher one. He would have wanted to be merciful, but he would have feared being taken advantage of and thought a fool more."

"More the fool for allowing those in his care to suffer needlessly," he muttered. "You acted rightly. I would much rather have the loyalty and gratitude of those living on our lands than their resentment. Thanks to my success abroad, we can absorb the financial loss."

She peered at him with open curiosity. "You were very enigmatic in your communications regarding said success."

"I did not want to risk such information falling into the wrong hands and you being subsequently targeted by dishonest men," he said grimly. "Not to overestimate the success of the plans I've laid, but if all goes as it should, our income will more than triple each year for at least the next decade."

Her eyes went wide. "Triple?"

"Yes. However," he held up a hand to forestall any further exclamation, "we should be careful until the company is well established."

"You said you were absolutely certain of this investment. Are you not?"

The worry in her face tugged at his heart. "I'm quite certain; however, it would be imprudent to count the pounds before they are in the bank. I prefer to remain cautiously optimistic until at least three years have passed with solid gains." He'd saved the best for last. "But lest you worry yourself, know that I've taken the liberty of diversifying our interests." He grinned. "America has such potential."

Again, her eyes widened. "Sorin, the risk! The hostilities have only recently ended and there is the—"

"Relax," he laughed. "It was only a small investment, but already it has resulted in some handsome profits. And it is growing exponentially. Whereas many of our countrymen shun the idea of doing business with them, the Americans are not so prideful as to turn down any relationship that promises them profit, and neither am I. Should our eastern investments take a bad turn, we'll have western ties to fall back on. In fact, they may even perform better."

She fixed him with a gimlet stare. "I know you would not do anything to displease the Crown, of course."

It was exactly the reaction he'd expected. "I had His Majesty's approval before ever putting pen to contract. My little side endeavor will feed the royal coffers as well as ours. After all, England somehow must replace what was lost during the war. His majesty is quite delighted at the prospect of having some of it back from the Americans."

She sagged back with a sigh. "Thank heaven!" Her eyes narrowed. "You ought to be ashamed of yourself, frightening an old woman like that. Have you no respect for my nerves?"

"Nerves? You?" he teased, ignoring her glare. "Truly, it was not my intention to frighten you, but rather to offer you comfort. I'm attempting to secure our family's future before things decline beyond the point of redemption."

"What do you mean, decline?" she said, suddenly sharp again.

"What I've seen abroad does not bode well for those choosing to remain stagnant," he explained. "Refusal to accept and embrace progress now will only result in impoverishment."

To his surprise, she nodded. "Well do I know it. Many of our friends have recently been forced to retrench. They've done it as quietly as possible, of course, and many of them under some plausible pretext, but it's not something easily kept hush. A few weeks ago, Lady Demby let slip that they almost had to forgo London this year. She and Lady Afton, who has also been showing the telltale signs of declining economy, managed to convince their husbands to 'make a party of it' and share a London residence between their families. They've told everyone that their girls, who are the very best of friends, begged them to do so that they might stay together for their first—and what their families hope to be their last—Season. All of their hopes are pinned on them making good matches and quickly, for it is likely that neither will be able to afford another Season. And they are not the only ones. It's happening all over."

He nodded. "Those against dirtying their hands with the business of making money are finding it increasingly difficult to keep up with industrious commoners eager to better their lot in life."

"You mean eager to emulate us, and poorly at that," she retorted, her tone sour. "The gentry have been thoroughly infiltrated, and now the peerage is being invaded. 'Merchant-barons' are springing up everywhere, marrying into quality families, quite literally buying their way in with the promise of solvency." She shook her head. "It's shameful. And yet that is exactly what the Dembys and the Aftons seek. Not only does Lady Afton look to marry her daughter off to such a one, but she admitted that she hopes to find an heiress for her son from among them. I can hardly imagine the lad being attracted to any woman of common origin, but I've no doubt Lord Afton will insist upon the most lucrative match."

"Don't be such a snob, Mother. After all, am I not equally guilty of lowering myself by engaging in business?"

"What you are doing is quite another thing altogether," she snipped. "You are of noble descent—and you are being far more discreet about your entrepreneurial activities than some I can name. I doubt anyone knows of your dabbling."

"I see. By allowing marriages below their rank, these families are essentially tainting themselves, is that it?"

She shifted in her seat, and he knew he'd gotten to her. "I did not say that. But at the same time I feel Society is losing its refinement, and I blame this new invasion. I just think it a shame to see our culture diluted by the coarseness of the newly affluent," she said, pursing her lips as though the words tasted bad.

"Not all of them are coarse," he rebutted. "Over the last few years I've met a number of the 'newly affluent' and have made several friends among them. If anything, most are keen to refine their manners and rise above their humble origins." Though he knew it would rile her, he said it anyway. "And who knows? Perhaps some new blood will serve to revitalize our lofty ranks."

"New blood? I do hope *you* are not considering such a union," she said with undisguised alarm. "In fact, I expressly forbid it. My delicate sensibilities would not tolerate such a daughter-in-law."

"How fortunate for you then that I have no need to marry money." He grinned as she glared. "As for the Aftons and the Dembys, I've found that fear of poverty always overcomes the delicate sensibilities of those in the midst of financial strain. The uncouth can always be trained or ignored, a far more palatable solution than being demoted to a lower social echelon over a lack of means. If our friends can find suitable matches for their children from among the nouveau riche, they will be saving themselves from the indignity of a slow decline."

"I cannot decide which fate is the worse," his mother muttered, shaking her head. "Speaking of making a suitable match, you ought to consider doing so yourself—to a woman of appropriate family, of course."

He hesitated for only a heartbeat. "I've been thinking about that, actually, and I've decided to go with you to London this year. It is high time I married."

"Oh, Sorin! I'm so very pleased to hear you say it," she exclaimed softly. However, her joyful smile transformed almost at once into a frown of worry. "Heavens! You've only just arrived, and the Season is right around the corner. There won't be enough time to have a new set of clothes made for you or to—"

"There is no need. I have several trunks filled with the very latest from Paris," he said, enjoying her surprise. "I took the liberty of having them made while I negotiated the final contracts for the King's fleet."

Her eyes narrowed. "This is no spontaneous decision, is it?"

"I confess it is not. Nor is it solely for the purpose you deem it. All of the clothes are made from *our* imported fabrics," he said, careful to conceal his enthusiasm. He couldn't let her know just how much he really liked "dirtying his hands" with entrepreneurial pursuits. "When everyone sees the beauty and quality of the materials, they'll wish to know where they can find them. Naturally, I'll direct them to those shops offering our goods."

A single silvery brow arched. "I assume the bolts and patterns you sent to me were to the same end?"

"Those I sent because they were beautiful and I thought it would cheer you."

"And it certainly won't hurt our pockets if my friends wish to imitate me, either," she added with a knowing smirk.

"My first desire was to lift your spirits."

"Of course it was," she said, eyes twinkling. "You're a good son *and* a shrewd businessman. I'll wear the gowns and gladly tell everyone where they can find the material as long as you can promise they'll never find out we're profiting from their covetousness."

"No one will ever know," he assured her. "The shops purchase the material from a distributor. He gets it from ships whose captains know only that they work for the Triple Crown fleet, which is managed by a man I pay handsomely to keep the identity of its true owner a secret." A man he trusted because he knew his life was forfeit if he ever revealed that information to anyone other than the king himself.

"You must pay him a pretty sum indeed," she said, eyeing him.

"He is well content with his lot. I've made him a rich man."

"I thought you said we needed to be cautious," she said, frowning. "How rich?"

"Rich enough to marry into quality," he said just to poke at her "delicate sensibilities."

"Heaven forefend," she said with open contempt.

He shot her a quelling look. "Earning an honest living should bring shame to no man. Many of our peers will fall because of their overweening pride."

"And yet pride has its place," she replied, her chin rising. "Your father would have sooner suffered gentle poverty than abandon his."

"A fool's pride!" he snapped, his patience drawing swiftly to an end. "Woe to the man who holds to his pride while doing naught to prevent his ship from sinking, for hunger and regret will be his chief companions in the days to follow—if he does not immediately drown. Anyone who romanticizes poverty shows a privileged ignorance of its brutality." Now that they were safe, it was time she knew. "Five years ago, poverty knocked at *our* gate, Mother. Father's stubborn refusal to modernize, or to at least employ better economy, very nearly ruined him, and us along with him."

Her expression grew stricken, and he softened a little. "I did not share that knowledge with you because I did not wish to tarnish your memory of him while your grief was yet fresh. Much as he had done, I continued to shield you from the dire reality of our circumstances."

"Dire?" The word was small and filled with disbelief.

"Our debt was monumental," he said quietly. "I sold off some of the smaller unentailed assets in order to fund my recent endeavors as well as pay at least some of the amount owed to the worst of the creditors lest our situation become public knowledge. And I have since worked tirelessly to drive poverty off our doorstep. If my efforts are discovered, then so be it. I will bow my head in shame to no man."

She had no chance to respond, for they had reached the church.

Sorin disembarked in haste, still fuming. Had Father lived, they would be in the same, if not worse, situation as the Aftons and Dembys. He ground his teeth. It had taken five years of careful planning, stealthy negotiations, and some bloody hard work, but he'd turned their fortunes around.

He hadn't told Mother, but the estate now had more income than ever before in its history, so much in fact, that it would have been an easy matter to pay off all their debts at once. He would have done so, save that such an act would be equivalent to announcing his activities in *The London Gazette*. Instead, for the past two years he'd been paying creditors off in small enough increments to keep them satisfied without tipping his hand. They now owed no more than anyone else and certainly far less than most, and no one knew it wasn't "old" money being used to pay it down—which was exactly how he wanted it.

Well, almost no one. There was one other person privy to his secret. Two, actually. Charles, who'd invested along with him in order to save his own family's fortunes, and Eleanor. Eleanor, who'd been quiet witness to their early discussions. Eleanor, who'd told them it made more sense to risk Society's censure than to accept hardship and pretend it was anything else. Eleanor, who was practical and wise beyond her years. If he could find a woman even half as sensible…

He let out a loud snort of self-derision, and a passerby shot him a startled glance. Such thinking was useless. Not only did he not want any other woman—much less one with only half her sense—but it was likely that any female from the loftier circles of Society would be mortified to learn that her noble husband's income was newly minted.

Any woman but Eleanor.

Even as he thought it, his eyes found her. Her cheek curved as she turned to say something to Rowena, and he knew she was smiling. He yearned to see it, to feel its warmth directed at him. But there was little hope of that, given their most recent interaction.

"Well? Are we to stand here all day or are we going in?" asked his mother, who'd come up beside him.

In answer to her testy inquiry, he offered his arm.

Chapter Five

He'd arrived. Even if Eleanor hadn't felt the prickle of awareness on the back of her neck, she'd have known it thanks to Caroline, who'd gone all stiff beside her before proceeding to primp and preen. Determined to ignore his presence for as long as possible, Eleanor kept her hands folded in her lap and her eyes fixed on the pulpit.

Dear Lord, please help me not to make a fool of myself today.

An hour of listening to the vicar deliver scathing indictments concerning the innately sinful nature of humanity was all the reprieve she could expect. As soon as it was over, Charles would spot Sorin and drag them all over to stand and politely listen to, if not actively participate in, their conversation. She closed her eyes. *How can I face him?*

There had to be a way to avoid him. Immediately, she crossed Caroline off the list of possible excuses—her friend would delight in any opportunity to hang at his elbow and upon his every word. Her desperate eye fell on Rowena, who was speaking to Mrs. Quimble about an upcoming charity fundraiser. In that instant, Eleanor determined that should Rowena go to speak with her after the service rather than stay at Charles's side, she would accompany her. No matter how tedious the conversation, no matter if it meant a month of embroidering napkins or stitching quilts, she'd do it and be glad.

The church bell rang, and as everyone moved to take their seats, Eleanor marked the presence of an unfamiliar gentleman sitting beside Lady Yarborough. A hiss of dismay escaped from between her lips as the man turned to speak to his companion.

"What is it?" whispered Caroline, following her gaze. "Oh, I see," she murmured, appraising the young man with an appreciative eye. "A handsome fellow, is he not? I assume from your reaction that you know the gentleman?"

"That's Donald Yarborough, and he is no gentleman," Eleanor replied, keeping her face averted so he wouldn't see her. "He was a terrible bully when we were children," she added in response to her friend's blank look. "I knocked him down once in this very churchyard."

"You appear to have a strange penchant for hitting handsome, eligible men." Caroline's eyes twinkled. "Well, I don't suppose he'll remember it now all these years later."

"Oh, I can only imagine he will, and all too vividly," Eleanor muttered, busying herself with her hymnal.

"You were only children. Surely he's forgiven you by now?"

"I very much doubt it. I humiliated him in front of half the village."

"Well, be that as it may, I don't think he holds it against you anymore," said her friend. "The man is staring at you as if he would eat you with a spoon."

What? Before thinking better of it, Eleanor looked. Yarborough *was* staring at her. Their eyes met, and after a momentary furrowing of his brow, his face broke into a wide grin of recognition.

Quickly, she turned away. He was supposed to be at university! Ignoring him, she looked to the other side of the aisle—a mistake, for Sorin and his mother had taken their seats there. His gaze met hers for an instant and then, without so much as a nod of acknowledgement, he turned to stare impassively at the front, as though he hadn't seen her.

Her stomach clenched. He'd given her the cut. Him. Sorin. Her oldest friend. She ought to have looked away, too, and pretended not to have noticed, but the little muscle jumping at his jaw fixed her attention. She knew that expression all too well. He was annoyed. With her, apparently. Pain lanced through her, and her eyes began to smart. Steeling herself, she poured all of her concentration into singing hymns. Then the sermon began—a treatise on, of all things, the many blessings bestowed by the institution of marriage.

Beside her, Caroline giggled softly. "It seems the good vicar has taken a liking to the eldest of the Braithwaite girls," she said, indicating a pretty, young blond woman sitting near the front.

Eleanor bit back a sigh of frustration. Was heaven against her, too? She'd rather suffer the usual blisteringly cautionary diatribe than this! She spent the entire service in a state of utter wretchedness.

...Trying not to look at Sorin.

...Resisting the urge to elbow Caroline, who kept wriggling about and making little noises to draw attention to herself.

...Attempting to ignore Yarborough, who was trying without much subtlety to attract her notice. She sucked her teeth in irritation. Really! Couldn't he at least wait until after church to make a laughingstock of her?

When the final blessing was issued and the congregation

dismissed, it was all she could do to keep from hiking her skirts, jumping the pew, and bolting for the door. *Dignity*, she reminded herself. Donald Yarborough must never have the satisfaction of knowing he'd troubled her. As for Sorin, he would have no excuse to reprove her this day either, and he would certainly never know how much he'd hurt her with his coldness.

Two could dance that waltz.

Holding her head high, she exited her row just as Sorin, who was following his mother, came to the end of his. The Dowager Countess she greeted with a sweet smile and a nod before allowing the lady to go before her. Sorin, on the other hand, she did not deign to acknowledge, though he waited politely for her to precede him. Without so much as a glance, she gave him her back.

Her teeth clenched with frustration as behind her she heard Caroline's enthusiastic greeting. Hoping for a quick exit, she made to follow Rowena who, much to her relief, was making a beeline for Mrs. Quimble. Before she'd gone ten steps, however, a male voice—not Sorin's—called out her name.

"Lady Eleanor! Wait—I say, do stop a moment and greet an old friend, won't you?"

Damn. And how dare he call himself my "old friend"? Groaning inwardly, Eleanor stopped and turned to Yarborough with as blank an expression as possible. "My humble apologies, but have we met?"

"Do you not recognize me?" His mouth stretched into a saucy grin. "I certainly remember *you*. How could I ever forget? Why, it was in this very churchyard that you taught me the meaning of humility."

At that moment, Sorin passed them by—again without seeming to see her. Blood boiling, she looked to her old nemesis, let out a little feminine squeal, and clapped a hand to her chest in a manner that would have made Caroline proud. "*Donald Yarborough?* Upon my word, you are so changed that I did not even know you! You've grown so very"—she ducked her head, feigning embarrassment, but then peeked up at him coyly—"so very tall."

Satisfaction filled her as Sorin halted in his tracks, stiff as a poker. *Ha!* "Goodness, but it seems to be the time for old friends to return," she said to Yarborough. "You cannot have been home for very long?"

"I arrived just yesterday. Felicitations on your birthday, by the bye. Mother informed me that I missed the festivities," he continued, his smile turning sheepish. "I'm afraid she was most displeased with the lateness of my coming, though it could hardly be helped. One of the horses drawing my coach stepped in a hole and lamed itself."

"Oh, well I'm truly sorry to have missed you," she replied with an exaggerated pout, watching with glee as Yarborough stood a bit taller and as, behind him, Sorin half turned around. "You *are* home to stay, I hope?" she added for good measure.

"Indeed. Well, after the Season, of course," amended Yarborough. "You will be going to Town as well, I suppose?"

"Oh, but of course. We'll no doubt run into each other quite often, won't we?" It was, perhaps, a bit heavy—but she was set upon making a point to yon eavesdropper. It was no lack of civility on *her* part that had determined her current marital status!

"I certainly hope so," said Yarborough, his gaze roaming for a moment before settling on her bosom. "I should like to see you as often as possible."

Ugh! But even as she forced a smile, she saw from the corner of her eye that Sorin was still listening. Perhaps it was time to give him a little taste of his own tonic. "But come, you must greet my cousin, Lord Ashford. I'm sure he will be as delighted as I am to welcome you home." Taking the arm he offered, she sailed right past Sorin, keeping her eyes fixed straight ahead. *And here's some sauce for the gander!*

Sorin bit the inside of his cheek as the pair sauntered away. He'd not wanted to ignore Eleanor—far from it—but there was no possible way for them to talk safely as long as his mother was present. She knew him too well and saw far too much with her keen eyes. Already he'd been admonished for his distracted state.

Wherever Eleanor was, there his focus seemed to be fixed and there wasn't anything he could do to stop it. Especially now, when he didn't like the look of the fellow upon whose arm she'd just draped herself. The man's walk was more of a swagger, and his demeanor conceited. He looked a right rogue.

"That's young Donald Yarborough, if you're wondering."

Jerking around, he found his mother had come up and was now staring in the same direction he'd been looking. *Damn.* "Ah, yes. I thought he looked familiar. He was a childhood friend of Eleanor's, I believe."

"I doubt he views her in such benign terms now," she replied drily. "I hear he is determined to find a bride this Season."

The acid-gnawing sensation redoubled in the pit of his stomach. "He's not the sort of man Ellie would consider."

Her lips pursed. "You would know better than most, I'm sure, but Lady Yarborough would never forgive him if he didn't at least try. The same will likely be true of every unattached, fortune-hungry male in London, until she marries."

She was right, he knew. Were Eleanor as homely as a

hound, her inheritance would still guarantee a certain level of desirability on the marriage market. Her fortune and beauty combined made her an irresistible target. "Which is why Charles has already enlisted my help to keep an eye on her," he said quietly. "I'll see that she does not fall prey to any trickery. If he is a roué, I shall soon learn of it."

"I see. And then what?"

"I'll inform Charles and he'll make an end of it."

Her soft chuckle startled him. "And when she finds out you've gone to her guardian behind her back and sabotaged her chances with him or any other lad for whom she sets her cap, she'll—"

"I have no need of subterfuge. I'll speak openly with them both."

"*Mmm*, and I'm *sure* she'll hear every word from the man to whom she gave the cut little more than an hour ago."

Taking a deep breath, he counted silently to ten before answering with equanimity, "She has always valued my counsel. She'll listen to me."

An indelicate snort erupted from his mother. "Eleanor is no longer a child to be so easily led, my son. But I think you've already discovered that."

Her penetrating look sent a guilty flush creeping up his neck.

"I knew it," she breathed, a triumphant gleam entering her eyes. "*She* is the reason you've been avoiding Holbrook, not Ashford. I gathered as much when you failed to greet each other this morning."

"Mother, I don't—"

"There is no point in denying the obvious," she interrupted, raising a wrinkled hand. "And you need not explain how it came about. Just tell me what happened to cause the rift. Perhaps I can help."

"I do not require assistance," he said, hot with embarrassment. "And there is no need for me to explain anything because there is nothing to explain. We had a difference of opinion. That is all."

"Well, it must have been rather a significant one," she said, arching a brow. "A woman does not cut a man, much less one she considers a friend, unless she has been mightily offended. Come. Tell me. What did you say to elicit such ire?"

"It was nothing, really," he said, shrugging. "I simply inquired of her as to why she'd turned down so many proposals. She told me her reasons, and I questioned her logic."

"In other words, you behaved like a condescending ass."

An exasperated breath exploded from him before he could contain it. "I was *not* an ass!" Several people turned and frowned. He lowered his voice. "I merely made the observation that her standards, such as they are, are unlikely to be met by any mortal man."

"And I suppose you expected her to be grateful to you for offering up your enlightened opinion?"

"No," he snapped. "But neither did I expect her to behave in this manner. After all, it was in her best interest that I point out the unrealistic nature of her expectations."

"Her best interests…or yours?" she asked lightly.

Again, the blood rushed to his face. "I wish only for her happiness."

"Of course you do."

For a moment he thought he'd succeeded in closing the conversation. No such luck.

"I must assume that you have not informed her concerning the true nature of your regard?" she persisted.

Oh, bloody hell. "There is nothing of which she need be informed. This is not the first time we have disagreed," he said, steering the subject back on course. "You know, as well as I, how intractable she can be at times. But I'm confident her irrational ire toward me will dissipate once she comes to acknowledge that I am correct."

When she finally spoke, his mother's voice trembled with barely repressed laughter. "I don't wonder that she is vexed with you if your attitude was such. My dear boy, you may have traveled the world but you have a great deal to learn about women. Men are not the only ones with pride, you know, and you have sorely wounded hers. You must make amends if you wish to enter back into her good graces."

"By make amends, you mean apologize."

"Precisely."

"I won't apologize for speaking the truth. She *will* eventually come to see reason."

"Not if that young man has anything to do with it," she said, nodding at a point beyond his right shoulder.

Unable to help himself, he looked, and across the green saw Yarborough bend to say something at Eleanor's ear. A throbbing began at his temples as Yarborough bent closer—without any resulting protest, he noted—and she laughed in response to whatever it was he'd said.

Pain shot through him. The same suffocating, gut-wrenching pain he'd felt all those years ago when he had watched her effortlessly win the adoration of every man she'd encountered. The same pain he'd hoped never to experience again. Her inheritance might be the lure that first drew them and her beauty the second, but it was her own unique charm, her warm spirit that thereafter held them helplessly prisoner.

Behind him, he heard a delicate cough. Turning, he found his mother staring at his hands—which were curled into fists at his sides. "You should tell her how you feel."

"I cannot," he blurted, knowing it was useless to try and hide from her anymore.

"Why ever not?" she asked, frowning. "Surely you don't believe Ashford would object?"

"Ashford views me as a brother and trusts me with his family—with Eleanor, whom he has worked tirelessly to shelter from the world's licentiousness. I've worked alongside him in this, such that he asked *me* to stand in his stead as guardian during her debut. How will he feel when I, whom he has so entrusted all these years, reveal unchaste sentiments toward her? I fear our friendship would not withstand such a betrayal."

"Nonsense," she scoffed. "Once you assure him of your honorable intent, I'm certain he'll be both understanding and amenable. Doubtless he'd prefer that she marry you over certain others I could name. Friendship is always a desirable state within one's family."

"Even if Ashford were to be agreeable, there is Eleanor herself to consider," he persisted. "I'm too old to be of interest to her."

"Rubbish. Young ladies marry gentlemen twice, sometimes even thrice their age every day and are quite happy. At a mere twelve years her senior—"

"Nearly thirteen," he corrected her.

"You are far short of either mark," she continued without acknowledging him. "You'll need a better excuse than that, I'm afraid. Why should she not welcome your suit? She's known you more than half her life and cares for you greatly."

"Yes, she cares—but not in the way a wife should for a husband. She grew up with me lecturing her on comportment, correcting her every lapse, always urging her to better herself. She once told me I was worse than any governess. I'm not exactly a romantic figure in her mind."

"Then you must change how she sees you. But first you must apologize—be sincere and contrite, and pray she accepts it," she said over his irritated rumble of objection. "And in the future, I would advise you *not* to criticize a woman's logic—no matter how flawed you think it is."

"Yes, I believe I've learned that lesson," he said with chagrin. "Very well, I'll apologize. The revelation of my changed sentiments, however, remains a dilemma. I cannot simply propose a different sort of relationship between us."

"No indeed. I do not myself entirely understand how you arrived at such feelings considering your long separation from each other, but if I'm surprised by it, it is likely everyone else will be doubly so. If at all possible, it would be better for you to ease slowly into an understanding with her. Achieving your purpose will require great care and discretion."

"I will, of course, employ the utmost discretion," he promised, shocked to hear himself say it. So much for his decision to selflessly refrain from pursuing his heart's desire. "As for my altered attitude, I believe it can be explained by the letters we've been exchanging." It wasn't wholly untrue, and he needed some legitimate excuse.

"Letters?" She frowned again. "What letters?"

"We exchanged letters while I was abroad—she enclosed her correspondence along with Charles's. I told her of my travels and she wrote back concerning the happenings here. When I returned, it was as though we'd never been apart."

"With the exception that she's grown now, and into a very beautiful young woman," she said with a thoughtful nod. "I certainly hope she comes to return your feelings, but you ought to prepare yourself in the event that she does not. The friendship was forged when she was young, and such perceptions as she has concerning you may be difficult or even impossible to overcome." Her grim expression softened into one of sympathy. "But I suppose you've already given that a great deal of thought."

"Indeed I have." Nothing more could be said on the matter without further embarrassment. He cleared his throat. "May I assume, based on this conversation, that she has your approval?"

"Naturally," she said in an equally dry manner. "She's a duke's daughter and a fine catch. But were she a pauper, I would still grant my blessing." His surprise must have been evident, for she began to chuckle. "Surely you did not think I would object? I've always been fond of the girl."

"I thought you had your eye on Lady Billingsley's daughter?"

"Given the circumstances, I no longer consider her an appropriate choice—unless of course matters don't turn out," she replied, her usual business-like demeanor returning. "Now, I shall leave you to plot your course without further maternal interference." She shot him a knowing glance as she straightened her hat and veil. "Despite your fears to the contrary, I shan't act on your behalf unless you specifically request it—and you needn't look so relieved. There *are* times when a mother's meddling can be both useful and effective."

"I shall bear it in mind," he muttered.

"See that you do," she replied with a hard glance. "Now, go and rescue her from Yarborough before everyone here thinks them forming an attachment."

Chapter Six

Despite his polished manners and gentlemanly appearance, Donald Yarborough was still an arrogant, puffed-up roisterer. Eleanor's teeth were already on edge and she hadn't been subjected to his company for even half an hour. To be fair, her encounter with Sorin—or rather the lack of one—had put her in a black mood, and she was finding it more and more difficult to quash her vexation.

"I hope you won't mind if I tell you how lovely you've grown since last I saw you," said Yarborough.

She didn't dare tell him how very much she *did* mind, not while he held her hand prisoner on his arm, at least. Instead, she ducked her head as though embarrassed.

"I would be dishonest did I not admit it," he went on. "I cannot tell you how pleased I am that you did not simply walk away earlier. I know I was a terrible trial to you when we were children. I do hope you've forgiven me my errors."

His smile was very pretty indeed, but one look in his eyes told her his words were nothing more than that—empty words. She remembered with perfect clarity the way he'd tormented her and how he had delighted in her tears. Still, better to have the appearance of friendly relations than open hostility—at this early juncture, at least. "Of course I have. The past is long gone and we are different people now."

"Indeed we are," he said, again letting his eyes wander.

She felt herself coloring and, looking away, marked the approach of the one person in all the world she wished most to avoid. But unlike earlier, Sorin was looking directly at her now and smiling as though he had not completely ignored her earlier.

"Hello, Lady Eleanor, and I believe it's Mister Yarborough, is it not?"

Beside her, she felt Yarborough stiffen. "Actually, it's *Sir* Yarborough now."

"I see. Please accept both my apology for the oversight and my condolences to you and your mother for your loss," said Sorin. "I've been away and was unaware you had inherited."

"Thank you, Wincanton," said Yarborough, seemingly mollified. "It is a little more than a year since I took on the burden. But let us not dwell on the melancholy. I'm most pleased to renew your acquaintance. It has been many years since we last greeted each other, has it not?"

Eleanor had not missed his familiar manner of address—and neither had Sorin. "At least five," he answered, his flat reply making clear that it had not been nearly long enough.

"Indeed," she interjected brightly, hoping to ease the tension. "I wondered whether you would remember each other."

Sorin looked to her, a hint of a smile curling one side of his mouth. "His face has not changed so much as to be unrecognizable, and neither am I so old as to have forgotten it."

The warmth and humor in his eyes elicited a queer

fluttering in her stomach.

"How happy I am to know that I'm so memorable," said Yarborough, drawing her a bit closer.

Instinct made her shrink from the contact before thinking better of it. She kicked herself mentally as Sorin's gaze sharpened.

He'd seen. "Lady Eleanor, might I borrow you for a moment to ask your opinion regarding a gift?"

Her irritation with him evaporated. She'd go anywhere as long as it gave her an excuse to get away from Yarborough. "Oh, a gift? I would be delighted." But her attempt to ease away from her captor was met with resistance. "What sort of gift?" she asked lightly, as though nothing was amiss.

"A gift for my mother," he said, his face hardening as he stared at Yarborough. "Her birthday is next month, and I wish to commission a piece of jewelry for the occasion. Perhaps you and Lady Ashford might be of help?" He offered his arm and waited.

With ill-concealed reluctance, Yarborough at last let her go.

Relieved, Eleanor quickly transferred her hand to Sorin's sleeve, where it received a quick, reassuring pat. Well, it would have been reassuring—had it not been for the blossoming warmth his touch left behind. So unsettling was the sensation that when they turned to depart, she missed her step and had to hop in a most undignified manner to right herself. Sorin, thank heaven, appeared not to notice. She glanced over her shoulder, hoping Yarborough had already turned away, only to have her hopes dashed.

"I shall see you again soon," he called, grinning. "If not here, then certainly in London."

Such presumption! "I shall be sure to tell my cousin to look for you," she called back, hoping she sounded cheery.

She would warn Charles about him at the first opportunity.

Sorin chose that moment to lengthen his stride, forcing her to almost run to keep up. A faint, smothered sound beside her made her look up at him. His lips were quivering. The devil was laughing! "And what has you so amused?" She winced. That had come out as sour as lemon juice.

"That young man looked quite put out at my intrusion. I do hope I was not interrupting anything of import?"

"Not at all," she said, discomfited to find her face growing hot beneath his gaze. "Sir Yarborough and I were merely becoming reacquainted."

He held her eyes a moment longer before looking away. "I admit I was surprised to see you behaving so amicably toward him. As I recall, you both spent much of your youth at odds. I suppose it is yet another mark of your maturity that you're able to set aside the past and conduct a civil conversation with an old enemy. I do hope such patience extends to those you consider your friends." Before she could compose a reply, he stopped and faced her, his voice lowering to a quiet rasp. "I could not fail to notice your cool demeanor toward me this morning, Ellie."

Despite having every intention of concealing her hurt, it poured out unchecked. "Mine? What of yours? I might as well have been made of glass the way you looked right through me. I've never felt so small and inconsequential, or so—"

"Such was not my intent, I assure you."

"Well, it certainly seemed so from my perspective." Her voice shook almost as much as her knees. He was near enough that she could see the flecks of gold in his hazel eyes. The silence stretched as, to her amazement, he appeared to struggle for words.

"I had no right to question your judgment," he finally said. "I can only ask your forgiveness and promise you it will never happen again. As for this morning, I was quite simply at a loss as to how to conduct myself in your presence after my egregious behavior. Please accept my most humble apology for both offenses."

After a moment, she realized her mouth was hanging open. "Of course," she answered weakly, flabbergasted by his awkward admission.

"Thank you," he said with evident relief. "You must understand, I spoke only out of concern for you. I had no way of knowing you'd looked to *me* as any sort of example."

She couldn't help smiling. "A young lady could do no better," she told him, her spirits rising as he smiled back. The shadow over her heart returned, however, when it faded after only a moment. "Come," she said quickly, taking his arm once more. "Let us put our silly little misunderstanding behind us. The sun is out, the sky is blue, and I'm quite over it."

"It gladdens me to hear you say it," he said, his smile returning as they proceeded onward.

"So, is it to be a necklace, a ring, or a brooch?" she asked, anxious to move to a safe topic.

His face went blank for an instant before he answered. "My mother's birthday. Yes. A brooch would do nicely I think."

Clearly, his "gift" had been nothing more than a contrivance to get her away from Yarborough. He'd always been protective, and Yarborough *had* overstepped a boundary when he'd refused to let her go. That Sorin had so readily leaped to her defense elicited a feeling of great warmth and happiness.

"Or perhaps a ring might be a better choice," he said, glancing at her sidelong. "I've marked how much women seem to like rings."

Despite the sunshine, a chill settled over her. *Perhaps he is considering a ring for Caroline…best to dissuade him of* that *idea!* "Then again, maybe she already has so many rings that another might not be considered special." She watched him carefully, looking for any clue as to what was going on inside his head.

But his face remained inscrutable. "As I have little expertise in the area of selecting gifts for ladies, I shall bow to your superior perspective."

"Rubbish," she chided, her disappointment turning to delight at having been provided a perfect opening to change the subject. "You underestimate yourself, as usual. The gifts you sent me from abroad never failed to bring me great pleasure. I especially liked the clever little puzzle box you sent me last Christmas." Inside, nestled on a bed of fragrant exotic herbs, had been a miniscule ivory elephant encrusted with tiny, sparkling gems. It was one of her most prized possessions not because of its value but because of the thoughtfulness it represented. She'd once mentioned how very much she wanted to see an elephant.

"I'm gratified to know you enjoyed it so much." He stopped. "I wonder if perhaps…"

She turned to face him. "Yes?"

"I don't wish to impose, but would you consider accompanying me to Rundell & Bridge's when we arrive in London? I cannot help thinking it would be better to have a woman's opinion while making my selection."

A telltale shifting from foot to foot belied a nervousness she'd never before observed in him. *Oh no! He* is *considering a ring for Caroline!* Why else would he ask her best friend to accompany him to a jeweler's? "I would be more than happy to accompany you. And I'm sure Rowena will be equally delighted at the prospect of such an outing, although I doubt my cousin will share her enthusiasm."

"I'm sure she'll be able to convince Ashford otherwise—

provided she is not already engaged elsewhere."

Heart in her throat, she forced out her next inquiry. "What of Caroline?"

He frowned. "What of her?"

"Well, should she not come along as well?"

"If you wish her company, then by all means invite her to join us," he said with ill-concealed impatience. "Invite anyone you like. We'll make a party of the event."

Eleanor felt like sinking into the ground. *I knew it!* Taking his arm again, she propelled them forward to disguise her upset. "Actually, now that I think of it, it might be better if we did not ask her. It might be an unkindness."

"Oh? How so?"

Sighing, she shot him a sorrowful look. "Not to be indelicate, but her prospects are not such that she's likely to ever be able to afford the kind of merchandise offered at Rundell & Bridge's. Her lack of a significant fortune destines her for a baronet, at best."

His brows crashed together. "Her lack of money is an unfortunate circumstance, certainly. But why should it limit her in so definite a manner? Not all men marry solely for money, Ellie."

"Perhaps," she said, keeping her tone light, in spite of her panic. "But I've learned that most give it a great deal of consideration when it comes to the selection of their bride. Marriage has ever been a mercenary practice for the aristocracy—for both genders. Of course I hope Caroline marries for love, but I'm forced to be as pragmatic about it as the lady herself."

"Pragmatic? A week ago the girl was prattling on about longings of the heart and meaningful relationships."

"That was strictly for the benefit of her audience," she said in her driest tone. "Later when we were alone, she confided in me that she plans to marry the fattest purse she can catch this Season." She felt no guilt for having said it, for it was the absolute truth.

"Is her situation so very desperate?"

Alarm traced a cold finger down her spine. The last thing she needed was for him to feel sympathy for Caroline! "You misunderstand," she said with a little chuckle. "While Caroline's family is limited in means, they are nowhere near destitute. Should she decide not to marry, she will certainly suffer no privation—but she would be ill content with such a life. More than anything, for her, marriage is a vehicle for improving her station. She, like so many, aims to marry up. I only hope that in her ambition she does not set her cap at too high a mark and miss an opportunity to make a perfectly agreeable match with someone nearer her rank. Ah! There is Rowena over by the gate."

Satisfaction filled her. *There. That ought to put an end to it.*

The motivation behind her rather unsubtle warning was something Sorin dearly wished to explore, but the fact that Eleanor had forgiven him for embarrassing her and was now conversing so affably was enough to make him let the matter drop.

Her demeanor toward him was vastly improved compared to this morning. Perhaps her friendliness was simply due to his having delivered her from Yarborough's clutches, but he hoped it was more. He'd wait and see whether she mentioned the lout's interest to her guardians. Given her apparent eagerness to escape, he didn't think she would speak of him in favorable terms. If she did, then there was a whole new set of unpleasant variables to consider.

For now, however, it appeared he had the advantage. Rundell & Bridge's had been a stroke of genius. The "birthday present" had been a complete fabrication, of course—he'd obtained a suitable gift ages ago—but such an outing would provide him another opportunity to gain useful insight, maybe even make her see him in a new light. After all, how could a woman look at rings with a man and *not* think of marriage?

A rush of anticipatory pleasure washed over him—as well as anxiety. As much as he wanted to tell Charles of his intentions prior to revealing them to Eleanor, his heart told him it would be a mistake. Despite their long friendship, he didn't doubt for a moment it would cause complete uproar, and he could ill afford to risk losing access to Eleanor even for a short time. Also, Charles was very bad at subterfuge. Like his cousin, he possessed an open temperament. One could often guess what he was thinking just by observing his face. Eleanor, for all her naïveté, was no fool and would see right through him.

What he needed now was time, time to let her get to know him as a man, time to forge a new relationship with her, one of equals. He marked the roses in her cheeks and the closeness of her hold on his arm as they crossed the churchyard. It was heavenly being near her like this.

"Remember the day you taught me how to make a proper fist?" she asked suddenly.

He smiled. "How can I forget?" He'd ridden into the stables to find her huddled in a corner, hay in her hair, mud on her dress, and her face streaked with wrathful tears. He'd been livid when she'd told him the reason behind her condition, though she'd never revealed the culprit's name.

"Well, the boy who pushed me down that day was Yarborough."

"I wondered about the identity of your bête noire," he said far more calmly than he felt. He liked Yarborough even less, now that he knew for certain.

"Yes, well the next time he tried to shove me down, I knocked him flat on his…" She glanced at him guiltily. "Derriere," she finished, a sheepish grin on her lips. "He never bothered me again."

Until today. "You could have told me, you know. I would have been pleased to correct his misconduct."

She gave a disdainful snort. "And what a coward he would have thought me, running to tell the tale. No, far better that he learned for himself I'm no weakling to be trifled with."

"Weakling is never a term I would associate with you," he said, earning a quick smile. "But even as courageous as you are, you might find that being sheltered and protected is not such a terrible thing. The world can be a very harsh place, especially for women."

This sage advice was met with a long sigh. "I shall have no need of protection because I have no intention of provoking anyone's enmity. Did you not just witness how I handled Yarborough? The wounds of the past are long healed over. I have no enemies to fear."

Indeed he had witnessed it. And he hadn't liked it one bit. "If only provocation was a requirement for conflict, but that's not how the world works."

"I'm not so naive as to think it does," she answered testily. "I well know the injustices this world is capable of visiting upon those undeserving of punishment. But it does so far less often to those who choose to live simply and quietly. I have the means to achieve that end."

Stopping again, he turned to face her. "Is that really all you desire, Ellie? A simple, quiet life on your own?" Her silence revitalized his hope. "Though you might not think it, independence—a highly relative term in my opinion—involves such complications as you have likely never considered."

"I am perfectly capable of caring for myself," she insisted, lifting her nose a fraction higher.

He couldn't help smiling. "Tell me, how much longer do you plan to remain at Holbrook?"

She blinked at the sudden change of topic. "I imagine I shall stay for as long as I like. It is my home, after all. Charles and Rowena are certainly happy enough with my company. Just yesterday, Rowena told me how appreciative she is of my help with the children."

He'd suspected she was unprepared for the reality of her situation. This was going to take a light touch. "For now," he said gently. "But is that what you really want? To act as a sort of governess to your cousin's children until they are all grown?"

"I'm no governess, even if I do help with the children from time to time," she retorted with pride. "Nor am I an impoverished relation to be taken advantage of so meanly, not that Charles and Rowena would ever do such a thing."

"Of course not, and I would never impugn them by implying they would," he said at once. "But at the same time, Holbrook is *their* home. As long as you remain under his roof, you are Charles's responsibility and live under his auspices. Do you really wish to linger, even as an honored member of the family, where you will never truly be in command of your own direction?" It was time to put it plainly. "Neither he nor Rowena expect you to remain at Holbrook forever. They *expect* you to establish a permanent home for yourself elsewhere."

The color slowly leached from her face. "They have told you this?"

"Not in those exact words, but it has been implied in

every conversation I've heard between them concerning you. Rowena has expressed high hopes for you this Season and has in fact begun quietly making preliminary plans for your wedding. Charles, too."

"But I've *told* them that I never want to—"

"It's not uncommon for young ladies to swear off marrying," he cut in gently. "But very few ever follow through on such a vow. Your guardians fully anticipate your marriage and departure within the year."

Her expression went from stricken to mutinous. "Then I shall have to make arrangements of my own, shan't I? I'll—I'll contact Charles's solicitor and have him procure a property for me, and I'll ask Rowena to help me hire the appropriate staff for it."

"A well-born young lady cannot live alone, no matter how wealthy she is," he reminded her.

"Though you may think otherwise, I have not forgotten the rules," she snipped. "Naturally, I shall require a suitable companion. Caroline would do nicely enough."

"I think we both know how unlikely that is," he said with a chuckle. "She's sworn to 'marry the fattest purse she can catch,' if I remember correctly."

But having her words tossed back at her only caused her to bristle. "Were I to make her an offer of independence, she would no doubt be most willing to alter her plans."

"Shall we go now and ask her?" he suggested, unable to resist goading her.

"I would rather ask her in private," she replied, flushing deeply. "Even if she does not agree, there are plenty of other like-minded ladies who would be delighted to be offered control of their own destiny. Why should I, or any other woman with the means to do otherwise, be forced to answer to a man for her every decision?"

I was right, he thought. He knew why she longed for autonomy. She'd felt powerless for nearly her whole life, beginning with her parents' deaths. And now she was being pressured to marry and effectively give up what little control she had over her own fate. "I did not mean to offend you," he said gently. "I merely wish to help."

"You may best help by persuading Charles and Rowena not to anticipate an event that is unlikely to happen," she snapped, not mollified in the least.

"Unlikely, perhaps, but not impossible—even for one so stubborn as you," he teased, in spite of the danger.

Her burnished gold brows collided. "I shall not marry, I tell you! There is nothing that could make me—" She faltered, and for an instant he saw something in her eyes that made his pulse jump. Then it was gone, replaced by a recalcitrant glare. "There is not a man on this earth to persuade me otherwise," she ended briskly.

"At the risk of again incurring your wrath, I will once more advise you against surrounding your heart with walls so high that none can scale them," he said. "I tried to hide from life once and found that doing so brought me only loneliness and misery. I watched my friends move on while I remained stagnant and was left behind. I wasted so much time and missed out on so many wonderful things, and all out of fear. That is time I will never recover." It was terribly risky telling her this, but she needed to know. Even if she never saw him as a potential mate, she needed to hear it for her own sake. "I would not wish you to endure that kind of regret. I live with it daily, and it is a most unpleasant burden."

Her mouth parted in surprise. "I—I did not know. I never thought you'd…not after…" Blushing, she ducked her head. "After you lost Jane, I simply never imagined that…I mean, you certainly never appeared to desire anything but to be left alone in that regard," she blurted, her color deepening. "What I mean to say is that it is entirely understandable that you would wish to be left in peace after suffering such a tragedy." Taking a deep breath, she squared her shoulders. "But that is all to change now that you've determined to marry, of course. I'm sure you'll be very happily wed in no time at all."

The prediction had been uttered with forced cheer, giving him hope. "Wed perhaps, but 'happily' is debatable. At my age, I don't hold much hope for a love match."

"Then you will compromise where I will not," she said, her discomfiture vanishing in the face of firm resolve. "But perhaps I'll be more fortunate than you in the area of regrets, for I make my choice without any reason save my own preference. I have neither the need nor the desire to marry. Therefore, I shan't. And nothing Charles says or does can change my mind." Again, she began to walk.

Bloody hell. "Eleanor, wait," he said, hastening to catch up. Without thinking, he reached out and grasped her elbow.

When she turned, he saw pain written on her features. Almost at once, however, her former mask of nonchalance returned. "Have you yet more sage advice to offer?"

He wanted to answer her, but nothing came out of his mouth. The sight of her beautiful face upturned and lit by the gentle morning sun drove all coherent thought from his mind. One of her dark-honey brows lifted. *Say something, you idiot!* "I never wanted to—"

"Eleanor!"

It was Rowena, and she was fast approaching. Smothering a curse, Sorin stepped away from Eleanor and bowed to greet Rowena as she dipped a hasty curtsy.

"I've some wonderful news to share," she said, a bit breathless. "But first, Charles bade me extend to you an invitation to dine with us tomorrow night."

"I should be much obliged, of course." Good. Another opportunity.

"Excellent."

"What news?" prompted Eleanor.

Rowena turned to her with a smug gleam in her eye. "Lady Yarborough has just announced that she and her son will be coming to London for the Season."

"Yes, I'm aware—he told me himself just a short while ago," Eleanor explained.

She looked none too pleased about it, Sorin noted with satisfaction.

"Yes, but my news is that we are to be a party for the journey," continued Rowena. "Their carriage suffered an incident while bringing her son up from London. As such, I've offered her a seat in ours. I did not think you'd mind."

"Not at all," Eleanor answered at once. "I have Caroline to keep me company. Why should you not also have a friend along?"

"I knew you would be agreeable," said Rowena, beaming. She turned again to Sorin. "Sir Yarborough will, of course, ride out front with you and Charles. If it looks to rain, they will both likely need to beg a seat in your carriage."

Sorin could feel his jaw tightening. He forced himself to relax. "It would be my pleasure, and I'm sure my mother won't mind the company."

Rowena's cheeks pinked. "Lady Wincanton is, of course, welcome to join us in the ladies' carriage any time she desires."

"I'm sure she will be delighted to join you at intervals," he said, hoping to ease her embarrassment over what he knew to be an unintentional omission. Despite his mother's interest in Eleanor, he very much doubted she would wish to join an already full carriage. The presence of both Lady Yarborough and Miss Caroline would be too a strong deterrent. His mother demanded a certain level of decorum—and while dignity could be found in nearly every societal rank, it was most definitely lacking in both of those ladies. Even so, if it did rain, she would likely still prefer their company to that of the menfolk.

In an unexpected show of support, Eleanor spoke up. "I think it a most sensible arrangement, considering the condition of the roads and the recent predations of highwaymen along the route. Sir Yarborough was fortunate to have survived his carriage's mishap and to have been close to a town when it happened. He was even more blessed not to have fallen prey to thieves while seeking assistance. The larger our party, the safer we shall all be."

Sorin found it difficult to hide his surprise and disgruntlement over her seeming concern for her supposed enemy. "Indeed. Most sensible. I shall relay the news to my mother so that preparations may be made." Preparations for battle. Across the yard, he saw Charles talking to none other than Lady Yarborough and her odious offspring. Eleanor had no doubt noticed as well, but he could read nothing in her face. *Damn and blast!* It was time to strike a blow.

Chapter Seven

Eleanor's face ached with the effort it took not to scowl. While she'd been strolling slowly to stretch the time with Sorin, Yarborough had gone straight to Charles! No doubt the blackguard was hoping his presence during the journey to London would endear him to her family and give him an edge over other suitors.

Mingled with vexation was a burning desire to know what Sorin had been about to say before they'd been interrupted. His strange hesitation and awkwardness had vanished the instant Rowena had appeared. It was all very curious.

"Might I prevail upon you for a moment, Rowena?" she heard Sorin ask, jerking her attention back to the present.

"Of course," answered Rowena.

"I will be going to Rundell & Bridge's in a fortnight or so to commission a special birthday gift for my mother. I would very much like to take Ellie—and you, if your schedules permit—along to assist with making a selection. I know you ladies have likely made your plans far in advance and I don't wish to interfere. It would require only an hour or two of your time."

"I'm sure we can find the time," said Rowena. "Come, Eleanor. We'll be late for luncheon if we don't leave now, and we needs must disentangle Charles." She dipped a curtsy, which he returned with a short bow. "Don't forget to come to Holbrook for dinner tomorrow. I'm having Cook prepare your favorite."

"I look forward to it," he replied, a smile in his hazel eyes. "Until then, I bid you both good day."

"That was a bit...irregular," murmured Rowena as he disappeared into the crowd.

"Oh? How so?"

There was a long pause, during which two pink spots appeared on Rowena's cheeks. "Eleanor, I don't know how to say this delicately."

Puzzled, she frowned. "You need never mince words with me."

"Very well, I shall speak plainly. We are going to London soon. While there, you must not allow yourself to be as familiar with Lord Wincanton as you've been here—at least not in public—lest others make certain...assumptions about your relationship that are untrue. *We* know him as a sort of extended family member, but others don't."

Eleanor's scalp prickled with shock. "If I've behaved inappropriately, then I can only apologize and ask you to tell me in what way I have erred."

"You have not," assured Rowena. "I just wish you to be mindful of appearances, that is all. I don't want the two of you becoming the subject of malicious gossip. He has suffered enough for one lifetime."

Her words felt like a slap. Had Sorin indeed told her cousin of her gross impropriety all those years ago? "I would never do anything to cause him discomfort. If you object to my accompanying him to see the jeweler, then—"

"I have no objection whatsoever," interrupted Rowena. "All I wish is that you keep in mind how things might appear to those outside our intimate little circle. London, as you know, is an entirely different world than the one to which we are accustomed out here in the countryside. I fear we'll have enough to worry about this Season without any disparaging whispers concerning you." Her gaze flew to Charles and company, which Eleanor noticed now included Caroline.

"That's another thing I've been meaning to discuss with you," said Rowena, her tone taking on an edge. "I know Caroline is your friend, but I hope we do not come to regret allowing her to accompany us."

"I hope not, too," Eleanor muttered without thinking. She shrank under Rowena's sudden, sharp gaze. "Do not mistake me—I adore her, but I'm well aware of her impulsive nature."

"Then I shall prevail upon you to at all times adjure her to curb her impetuosity. As she is to be under our sponsorship, her behavior will reflect directly upon us. I should greatly dislike having to inform her family of any unfortunate circumstances resulting from misconduct on her part while she is in our care."

"Of course," Eleanor replied soothingly. "But I beg you not to think too harshly of her. She is simply...gregarious. I'm certain she comprehends the level of decorum expected of her."

"I pray so, too, for all our sakes. But come, we must leave now or the meal will be overcooked."

Yarborough and his mother were still attempting to ingratiate themselves with Charles when they joined the party, and Eleanor couldn't help but notice the sly wink her old nemesis gave her as he bowed. She marked also that Lady Yarborough's curtsy to Rowena was little more than cursory, though Rowena was a duchess and she the mere widow of a baronet. Their familiarity was presumptuous and more than a little insulting. Then again, perhaps she was being overly sensitive in the aftermath of Rowena's little chat with her. Still, she liked it not. It smacked of arrogant assumptions concerning their relationship with her family.

"Husband, I do hate to intrude, but we must away home," said Rowena, taking Charles's arm.

"Yes, of course," he replied, absently patting her hand. "Sir Yarborough and I were just discussing the state of the towns between here and London. According to him, there has been a good deal of improvement in the town of Hindon since we last passed through it. There is a new inn there, now, the Ellington Arms. I was thinking we might stop there to overnight rather than going on to Chilmark. It would shorten that leg of the journey a bit and allow the horses a longer rest."

"Whatever you desire, my dear," said Rowena mildly. "But come, already the day grows long and there is much yet to accomplish before it is done." She cast him a beguiling smile, and his eyes brightened.

Eleanor hid a smile of her own as her cousin bid the Yarboroughs a hasty farewell. If ever she were to attempt to ensnare a man, Rowena's example was surely the one to follow. Her methods were subtle and elegant. Unlike Caroline, who was even now casting coy glances back over her shoulder at Yarborough as if she'd never talked of bagging Sorin an hour before.

To be fair, she'd known her friend would be far too shrewd to put all of her eggs in one basket. Thanks to a terribly botched courtship during her debut, Caroline had come up short of beaux these last two years. This being her third—and likely final—Season out, Eleanor had no doubt she'd get down to business and ensnare several serious suitors before all was said and done. Her chances were improved by the fact that only four "prize purses"—*three*, Eleanor corrected, removing herself from the equation—would be out this year. Those who hadn't been lucky enough to catch an heiress last Season would perhaps be more amenable to the idea of marrying a young lady of more modest means.

"I think Sir Yarborough is quite a nice gentleman," reflected Caroline, confirming Eleanor's suspicions as she settled into her seat. "I found his mother most agreeable. She extended an invitation for me to join her for tea while in London. Her son is of an enjoyable temperament as well. Nothing at all like the mean little boy you described to me this morning."

"I should hope not," Eleanor snapped, forgetting her intent to remain impassive. "I would rather hope the years have matured him beyond feeling a need to push people down in the mud."

Charles frowned. "I had no idea he'd done such a thing, Eleanor. Had I known, I can assure you I would have been less willing to have them join our party. No man should ever raise his hand to a lady."

"Indeed," agreed Rowena. "Such an act, though committed in his youth, shows a serious lack of breeding. You should both be very cautious in your dealings with him."

"We were only children," Eleanor sighed, though she was loath to take Yarborough's side.

"Did you perhaps…provoke him in any way?" asked Caroline, her tone hopeful.

"No," she answered flatly, her temper growing shorter by the second. "He was a bit of a bully to everyone, if you want to know. He enjoyed antagonizing people, in general. I was but one of many. Surely he is a different person now."

"Boys are betimes unruly and forgetful of their manners," said Charles with a noncommittal shrug. "Perhaps he has changed, at that."

Rowena's lips pursed. "I'm not so certain. The stripes don't wash off a tiger when it takes a bath, and neither do they fade with age. Regardless, it is too late now to alter our plans. The Yarboroughs will be joining us on the road to London, and we shall likely be obliged to entertain them once or twice while there, being that they are acquaintances from the same county."

Wonderful. Eleanor kept a neutral face, but inside she was already thinking of ways to get out of it. Being "indisposed" would work only once. As for the overly-eager Caroline, she would indeed do well to have a care with the Yarboroughs. Very likely, Lady Yarborough's invitation to tea was merely a means of gathering information on how best to cast the net for the bigger fish.

She shook herself. *Enough of this bitterness and old bile!* There were more important things to think about, like tomorrow and Sorin's visit.

Almost as if she'd read her mind, Rowena spoke his name. "Oh, Lord Wincanton will indeed be joining us for dinner tomorrow, Charles. He sends his regrets for not having been to see you again sooner. He has been much occupied with matters at home."

Charles's brooding expression lifted into a smile of delight. "Ah! Excellent, excellent! I cannot begin to tell you how glad I am that he's returned to us. Like a brother to me, really. Better than a brother, actually—a brother would be hankering after m'title," he added with a chuckle.

Beside her, Eleanor heard Caroline snicker softly. The gleeful, calculating look on her friend's face told her there would be trouble from that quarter tomorrow.

After a slightly overcooked luncheon, she went to her room to have a look through her wardrobe. The new gowns

Rowena had ordered for her were all being sent directly to their London residence, but there were a few from last year that Sorin hadn't yet seen. Her fingers lingered over the deep-aqua silk. It would do nicely—the cut emphasized her maturity. Holding it up against herself, she stood before the mirror.

I'll look anything but childish in this. And since silk is so difficult to get these days, I'll stand out. The thought brought her up short, and she frowned at her reflection. *Stand out for whom?*

The answer was plain, but the reason behind it was all muddled and confused. She wanted her old friend to acknowledge her as an adult, of course, to see her as an equal. But her mind would not let it rest there. *Is that the only reason? Why should his opinion matter to me so much?*

Eleanor's middle tightened for a moment before logic asserted itself. *Because if he sees me as an adult, so will my cousin. Maybe then Charles will stop all this nonsense about marrying me off.*

The tension in her midsection eased. Laughing at herself, she hung the gown back in the wardrobe and dismissed her foolish worries.

Dismounting almost before his horse had come to a full stop, Sorin handed the reins over to a lad and climbed the familiar steps of Holbrook. The anticipation of seeing Eleanor again had been almost more than he could stand. Upon entering, he handed his hat and coat to the waiting servant.

"You're early."

Looking up, he saw Caroline coming down the stairs. "My

apologies," he said with a short bow.

"Oh, there is no need to apologize," she said with a sultry smile. "You are practically one of the family here."

"I'm a very fortunate man when it comes to my friends."

Turning to the servant, the girl dismissed him. "I'll see to our guest. You can go."

"I presume everyone else is already in the drawing room?" Sorin asked as the man disappeared.

Caroline shook her head so that her curls bounced, and then proceeded to narrow the gap between them. "Eleanor is still upstairs making ready. I don't know the whereabouts of Lord and Lady Ashford." She drifted a bit closer, far more so than was proper. "But I would be happy to accompany you to the drawing room to await them."

The look in her eyes was positively predatory. He resisted an urge to back away. "Ah. Perhaps I'd better wait h—"

"Lord Wincanton," said a blessedly familiar voice from above. "How good of you to join us this evening."

For a moment Sorin nearly forgot how to breathe. A vision in swirls of starlight and sea foam, Eleanor glided down the stairs like a goddess descending from the clouds. Her caramel hair was swept up in a crown of curls with wisps about her temples and forehead, and her creamy skin glowed in the candlelight. The curve of her cheek lifted in a soft, welcoming smile as she gazed down at him.

The thought of coming home to such a sight every day was almost enough to make him drop knee on the spot. Instead he bowed deeply. "Lady Eleanor, a pleasure as always."

Her returning curtsy was elegant perfection. "The pleasure is ours." As she moved to take his arm, her friend had no choice but to defer and step aside, which she did with ill-concealed rancor.

The girl was instantly forgotten as Eleanor drew near. The

gown she wore—or rather what it revealed—turned his mouth into a veritable desert. Its wide neckline revealed an expanse of décolletage to tempt the most hardened misogynist, which he was most definitely not. The shallow bodice was gathered tightly beneath her breasts by a band of silver mesh from which fell layers of diaphanous aqua silk embroidered with silver flowers and tiny pearls. Each step she took revealed a tempting suggestion of shapely legs and hips.

God help me… Hers was the lush form of a woman built for carnal pleasures, a fact that had heretofore been for the most part concealed by lace fichus and high necklines. "I'm afraid I've arrived a bit early," he said, praying no one noticed the sudden, urgent stirring in his breeches. "Please accept my apologies for any inconvenience."

"I should never be so unwelcoming as to chastise you for gracing us with your presence a few minutes ahead of schedule. Come. Charles and Rowena will join us in a moment or two. Caroline?" she inquired over her shoulder as they turned away.

"I'm coming," muttered her sulky friend.

Sorin hid a smile. He really couldn't say he felt sorry for the girl. Eleanor's warning about her mercenary designs was certainly no lie, and he sincerely hoped her attentions would be directed elsewhere once they were in London. The fewer distractions he had to deal with, the better.

"I hope you brought your appetite with you," said Eleanor with a mischievous glance that made his mouth go dry again. "Cook has been busy since before dawn preparing a feast worthy of the king himself, and I've been told there is to be entertainment afterward."

"I'll be spoiled by such lavish treatment," he said, laughing. "But in truth, I need no entertainment save that of conversation with good friends." He silently cursed himself for using the "f" word. The last thing he wanted was her thinking of him as a friend, damn it all! But it was too late now.

"You are too kind," she replied. "Somerset must seem interminably dull compared to the sights you've seen in your travels."

"On the contrary. I take great interest in the goings-on here. I always have." He smiled at her dubious look. "I never wanted to leave, you know. By the time I returned to England's shores, my longing for home was a sickness. I was never so happy as when I rounded the turn to see Holly Hall awaiting me with her green lawns and solid walls. For me, the beauty of home far outstrips that of any other place on earth."

"Well, you are here now and you are most welcome indeed," said Eleanor, her voice suspiciously thick.

"I suppose absence does make the heart grow fond," said Caroline from behind, her voice tinged with sarcasm.

The tender moment was gone. "Indeed it does, Miss Caroline," he tossed back, trying not to sound irritated.

"Such sentiments will likely fade after you've been home awhile," the girl continued with an exaggerated sigh. "I've heard it said that anyone who has been away for more than a year can never get the wanderlust out of their blood."

"I'm afraid I must disagree," Sorin replied. "The call of home is stronger than any wanderlust. I've traveled the world, and never once did its pull on my heart diminish." That much was true, though it was more than Holly Hall he'd yearned to see.

As if answering his private thoughts, Eleanor murmured, "Travel abroad is all good and well, but I should never wish to be forever parted from all that is familiar. My heart of hearts longs to remain here, among those dearest to me."

His heart leaped as her wistful gaze settled on him.

But Caroline wasn't done yet. "I long to remain, too," she

added lightly. "However, with a male cousin who is to inherit everything and two younger sisters to help bring out before he does so, I've no choice but to leave."

Beside him, Eleanor stopped in her tracks and turned, aghast. "Oh, Caroline, I'm so sorry. I sometimes forget that—"

"Please don't," interrupted Caroline, her expression stoic. "It is simply the way of things for those of us without the means to do as we please." Her mournful eyes turned to Sorin. "But my humble upbringing has prepared me for the inevitable."

He would have laughed at her artifice if he'd known it wouldn't anger Eleanor, who in her undeserved chagrin no doubt felt a complete louse. The thought of her suffering any distress over such an obvious attempt to garner sympathy peeved him. "A humble upbringing is no cause for shame," he said, much to Caroline's delight. "Indeed, I believe it will be a great asset to you, Miss Caroline. Your future husband will no doubt appreciate your sense of economy when it comes to the judicious employment of his income."

His inference must have hit the mark dead on, for her mouth dropped open just as he turned back to Eleanor. He pretended he hadn't noticed. "I do hope your cook saw fit to make some of those strawberry tartlets I so love," he said quietly. "I confess that I missed them almost as much as I did home."

"Oh, I—I believe she did," said Eleanor, half turning to look behind her, obviously still concerned for her friend.

"One day, I shall find a way to woo that talented woman over to Holly Hall," he said, calling her attention back again.

"Ah, but then you would have one less reason to come and visit us," she said, the smile returning to her eyes.

"I need no such impetus. The pleasure of your company is quite enough to bring me here." It was bold and flirtatious, and he marked how her cheeks pinked at the compliment.

Before she could answer, they rounded the corner and entered the drawing room where Charles was waiting, a glass of brandy in hand. "Ah, here you are! I hope you're prepared for an evening of culinary delights. The table is fairly groaning from supporting such a feast, and I've broken out the best of my brandy to wash it down."

Rowena swept in. "Yes, and I see you've decided to precede the meal with it as well. Good evening, everyone. I do hope you will pardon the delay. Our other guest has not yet arrived."

"Late in the coming, as usual," chuckled Charles, avoiding his wife's gaze as he drained the last of the brandy from his glass. "Marston always did like to make an entrance."

"Is Marston to join us, then?" Sorin asked, grinning. A retired Master and Commander in the Royal Navy, James Marston was a good friend. The gentleman had been in command of the first ship to take him from England, and they'd become fast friends on the journey. Upon leaving the service after the war, he had come to live in Somerset because Sorin had described it as a paradise—and it was within a day's journey of the sea. "I did not see him here last week and assumed he'd gone off to London early."

Rowena shook her head. "He was unfortunate enough to be laid up with a cold and missed the festivities."

"But I'm here now and ready to make amends," said a man's voice from the doorway.

Sorin turned with gladness. "Well met again, Marston! It seems an age since we last saw each other."

"Well, I consider myself fortunate to be here. Damnable cold brought me low for a bit, but I'm back in Bristol fashion." The blond, mustached man was indeed gaunt, but seemed in good spirits. He bowed to the ladies. "Lady Ashford. Lady

Eleanor. Miss Caroline."

Observing Eleanor, Sorin was pleased to note nothing extraordinary in her greeting. Caroline's reaction, however, was most surprising—she behaved with indifference bordering on outright rudeness.

Rowena gestured for them to follow. "Now that our party is happily complete, let us dine."

Sorin started as Caroline all but leaped to his side, where she remained like a tenacious burr all the way to the dining room. Thus it was that when it came time to be seated, Sorin found himself across from Eleanor rather than by her side as he'd desired. Sandwiched between Rowena and Caroline for the duration of the meal, he was given little opportunity to do more than glance at her every now and then.

Half an hour later, his head began to ache. Frustration mounted by the minute as Caroline alternated between assaulting him with questions and regaling him with witticisms that were no doubt intended to make her appear sophisticated and clever. They did neither. He sneaked another peek at Eleanor, who'd turned to ask Ashford a question he couldn't hear—because the flirtatious chatterbox beside him seemed to require no breath.

Heat crept up his neck as Eleanor caught his eye and shot him a quick look of amused sympathy. *Bollocks*. He'd been staring at her like a damned lovesick schoolboy. Reluctantly, he returned his attention to the still-nattering Caroline. George's gout, the woman was a bloody magpie! Her voice grated. Her high, tittering laugh annoyed. Her subtle innuendoes alarmed.

By the time dessert—the much anticipated strawberry tartlet—had at last been eaten and their hostess invited her guests to join her in the music room, he was fit for Bedlam. Rising with haste that very nearly upset his chair, he fled to the other side of the table to offer Eleanor his arm, no longer caring how it might appear. His talkative table companion was left no choice but to pair off with Marston, and he marked that neither of them looked very pleased over the fact. Their strange aversion to each other was a mystery that would have to be solved—later. For the moment at least, he'd been granted a blessed reprieve and was going to take advantage of it.

When they reached the music room, he deliberately led Eleanor over to a settee that would accommodate only two occupants. "I've missed these little gatherings," he whispered to her as Rowena settled herself at the pianoforte and began to play. "I meant what I said earlier. I missed home…and this, more than anything."

"You were missed as well," she whispered back with a sweet smile. "Tonight was planned specifically for your enjoyment, you know."

"Oh? And what of Marston?" he replied in a teasing manner. "Is he not also a special guest? Or is he here so often as to be considered commonplace—as was I, once upon a time?"

A faint grimace crossed her lovely face. "Lord Marston is here because Rowena wanted a dinner partner for Caroline. Unfortunately, I think Caroline already had someone else in mind," she said, wincing. "I do hope she was not too much of an imposition."

"Not at all," he replied instantly.

The look she gave him told him she wasn't convinced.

Laughing softly, he gave in. "Though I should like to have made it through at least one mouthful without interruption," he admitted. "I feel as if I've been through an interrogation at the Tower."

"I'm so sorry. Caroline can be absolutely relentless, and I

fear she has developed a taste for your company that might not be easily dissuaded. If you wish me to speak to her, I shall."

"No," he answered at once. "Despite her foibles, I know her to be your friend and I would never wish to cause strife between you. I believe she will turn to other pursuits once amid London's distractions. If not, I shall handle the matter with as much delicacy and regard for her feelings as possible."

"Thank you," she said with obvious relief.

He looked to the other side of the room where Caroline sat pointedly ignoring the gentleman beside her. "I cannot help noticing her cool attitude toward Marston," he commented. "There is a history there, unless I am gravely mistaken."

"You are not," she murmured, dropping her voice so low that he had to lean closer to hear her. "He once attempted to court her."

The scent of lilies clung to the creamy flesh of her neck. "Attempted?"

"Yes," she answered with an infinitesimal nod. "He began his pursuit here in Somerset about a month before her debut. At first she received him with great enthusiasm, enough so that we all thought he would make an offer before the end of the Season and that she would surely accept. But he never came to scratch."

"I cannot believe a man as honorable as Marston would trifle with any young lady."

"I don't believe he did," she replied, leaning a little closer. "He was very kind and attentive toward her, and she appeared much taken with him—at first. But after she arrived in London she seemed to forget him. She set her cap for another, a titled fellow who charmed her with a handsome face and false promises. Lord Marston lingered for a while, but left off his pursuit when he did not receive any further encouragement from her. Then the devil she'd been mooning over married another by special license. It was an enormous scandal, one that left Caroline to return home having only barely escaped disgrace. When she again set her sights on Lord Marston last Season, he would have nothing to do with her."

"Small wonder after having been cast aside in so callous a manner," he said, immediately regretting his caustic tone.

"Yes, but there is more," she breathed. "Caroline went without a single suitor last year and she blames Lord Marston for it, though there has never been any evidence to support her assumption. I believe there were several contributing factors. Eligible gentlemen were thin on the ground last year while there were several wealthy heiresses on the market, and then there was the matter of her reckless behavior the year prior. She'd come within a hair's breadth of scandal, and people remembered it. But she chooses to fault Lord Marston rather than accept her own culpability."

"If there is rancor between them, then it again begs the question: why is he here now?"

"My cousin and Rowena know nothing of her animosity toward him," she answered, so close now that the wispy curls at her temple brushed against his ear. "Rowena thinks it failed to work out the first time because Caroline was too proud. Ever the optimist, she invited him here tonight in the hope that they might rekindle their initial liking for each other."

"Do you think it possible that she still loves him?" He stared at her as she contemplated the question, fixing in his mind the curve of her cheek and the graceful line of her neck.

"I'm not certain, but I think it might be."

"Her greeting tonight would say otherwise, as would her behavior at dinner."

A wry smile tilted her mouth. "I think tonight was about attempting to take two birds with one stone, if you want to know. Not only is she out to bag you, but I think she was determined not to have to speak to him."

"Perhaps she was trying to make him jealous."

"I doubt it. She's still furious with him. He came home without a bride last year even though Caroline made it clear she was available for the asking and more than willing to accept. Even if he was able to prove his innocence regarding the alleged gossip, she'll *never* forgive him for that humiliation."

The song ended and it was her turn to entertain. He sighed with relief when she called Caroline, who'd just risen and was now making her way toward him with frightening determination, to accompany her on the pianoforte. The twinkle in Eleanor's eye told him she'd done it purposely, to spare him further exposure to any marital machinations.

While the pair was deciding which song to play, Marston came over and sat beside him. "I've been waiting all evening to have a word with you, my friend. You've been so popular with the ladies tonight that I'd begun to despair."

"A fortunate happenstance that is unlikely to be repeated," Sorin murmured, sipping the sherry handed to him by a passing servant.

"Oh, I don't know," said Marston. "Seems to me you've captured more than one heart here tonight."

"Oh? What makes you say so?"

A broad grin creased the other man's sun-weathered face. "Oh, come now. I saw the way Miss Caroline looked at you during dinner—as if she would dine on you rather than the meal in front of her. And were you not just now sharing whispered confidences with Lady Eleanor? Your heads were bent close for quite nearly the whole of the song. Is she not the same Lady Eleanor for whom I carried many letters from you?"

"One and the same. But you already know that such correspondence was the result of a friendship forged between us in her childhood."

"*Mmm.* Well, not to be blunt, but she is no child now," murmured Marston as the subject of their discussion began to play. "And the way you've been staring at her all evening…" One shaggy, straw-colored brow lifted. "I won't be boorish enough to point out the obvious. I only hope you can reach an understanding with her before it is too late. I would caution you about the temptations of London subverting your cause, but I know Lady Eleanor is not one to have her head turned easily. All the same, I advise you to leave nothing to chance. You ought to let her know how you feel, and soon."

The blood began to pound in Sorin's temples. "Am I so easily spotted for a fool?"

"Never a fool," answered Marston kindly. "I think she would make you a fine wife, if you can convince her. She has sworn off marriage, you know."

He met Eleanor's smiling eyes over the top of the pianoforte, and his face prickled with heat. "I'm aware."

Beside him, Marston chuckled. "This would be most entertaining did I not know you so well and so deeply sympathize with your plight."

Turning, Sorin regarded his friend with all seriousness. "Sympathize?"

"Oh, come. Do you think I don't know what the pair of you were whispering about over here? And even were you not, you cannot have failed to mark the manner in which I am treated by Miss Caroline."

"I won't lie and tell you that it went unnoticed, or that I did not express to Lady Eleanor my curiosity regarding the matter."

"Then you must know that I've very likely made a lifelong enemy in Miss Caroline," said the other man. "She despises me utterly."

"An unhappy circumstance for you, unless I'm mistaken."

"Indeed," said Marston, his brisk manner at odds with the

sadness in his eyes. "And to make matters worse, I absolutely must marry this year. I forfeit my inheritance to the next in line if I do not, and such is not an option as I must support my mother and two younger sisters, one of whom is a widow and the other unwed and unlikely ever to marry. Mother begged me to ask for Miss Caroline's hand last Season. I very much wanted to comply, but I simply could not bring myself to do it."

"Why? I was given to understand she was quite willing to accept you."

Marston stared at his folded hands for a long moment. "I was too afraid," he said at last. "The first time I pursued her, she dropped me for a more tempting prospect and I was humiliated. I was reluctant to bind myself to a woman whose affections I could not be certain of, so I avoided her while we were in London. My plan was to wait and renew our acquaintance upon returning home, where I'd at least have some privacy in the event of another rejection. But she would not see me. I was offered no explanation. When I finally cornered her and demanded to know why I was being treated thusly, she informed me that I was the cause of all her woes and then accused me of spreading lies about her in London." His eyes were devoid of hope. "I swear to you on my honor that I never said anything about her that was unflattering. Though we are friends, I would not have even spoken to you of what lay between us had you not let on that you already knew part of the tale."

Sorin disliked meddling in other people's lives, but he disliked his friend's misery more. "I would like to help you if it is within my power."

"There is nothing to be done." Marston's pronouncement had a disturbing ring of finality to it. "She made her choice and has left me with none but to seek a wife elsewhere."

"Do you still care for her enough to want to marry her?"

The other man didn't speak for a long moment. "I loved her once. She was sweet and unspoiled when we first met." His voice hardened. "But London infected her with its caprice, and now it is too late."

"Perhaps not," Sorin suggested. "She might be more forgiving if she knew the truth. Young ladies are often tempted to foolishness in their first Season. Might you not try just once more?"

Marston shook his head. "I thank you for your kind offer, but I beg you to leave it be. She did not find me worthy then, and she likely never will." He fixed Sorin with a piercing stare. "As for you, my friend, don't let this opportunity pass you by. If you love Lady Eleanor, you must be swift to claim her heart. Do not allow her to— "

But he was interrupted by applause, which both gentlemen hastily joined as the two women rose and curtseyed before their audience. Eleanor sent him a quizzical look that he returned with a smile. Caroline, however, had the demeanor of a thundercloud.

Chapter Eight

"That *beastly* man!" hissed Caroline as they rose from their seat at the pianoforte. "How I wish your cousin had not invited him! I hope he dies this very night of...of—the pox!"

Eleanor looked to her in shock. Caroline had always been quick to vent her spleen, but rarely had she seen her friend in such a state of rage. Her face was nearly as red as her hair, and her eyes were bright with unshed tears. Linking arms with her, Eleanor quickly propelled Caroline straight out into the hall, ignoring Rowena's look of concerned inquiry as they passed her by.

"What are you doing?" squeaked an indignant Caroline, trying to pull away.

"Saving your neck!" Eleanor told her. "Now keep your voice down before the whole house hears you." Quickly, she dragged Caroline into the room across the hall. "If anyone asks, we'll tell them you felt faint," she said, shutting the door behind them.

"No!" said Caroline, wrenching her arm free. "We must

go back before he spreads lies about me to Lord Wincanton!"

"Lies? How can you possibly know for certain what they were discussing?" Eleanor prudently blocked the door. "Let us not be so hasty in condemning the man."

But her friend's red curls shook from side to side with a violence that made them look like dancing flames. "Any fool could see from the look on Wincanton's face that something untoward was said—and I am no fool!" Her eyes narrowed. "I shall have to mend the damage as quickly as possible. I cannot afford to lose even a moment! Now stand aside."

"You're making a terrible mistake!" Eleanor warned, flinging out her arms to prevent the angry girl from dodging past. "Caroline, you *cannot* pursue Lord Wincanton!"

Caroline stilled, and Eleanor cringed at the cold fury that stole into her eyes. "Oh? Pray tell me why not?"

"Because he is not within your reach," she said bluntly, wincing as Caroline's mouth opened on an offended gasp. "Please, just listen! Although you are of good family, you cannot expect him to make an offer to someone so beneath him in rank and thus so unqualified t—"

"How dare you!" raged Caroline, her cheeks becoming mottled.

"—unqualified to assume the duties of a countess," Eleanor pressed on. "There are certain expectations to be met when it comes to his marriage. Even if his mother does not demand that he meet them, his sense of duty will. His rank is an obstacle you simply cannot overcome."

"Why not? Others have done so. If he felt passionately enough about me he would not let something as meaningless as rank get in the way."

It was time for the hard truth. "Do you know anything at all about running an estate that size?" Eleanor asked, deliberately harsh. "I speak of much more than just Holly

Hall, Caroline. His estate encompasses several properties, some of them quite large. As his wife, you would be expected to help him manage their upkeep, including oversight of their servants. And then there are the associated villages, farms, and tenants that come with each. You would be duty bound to visit their sick, provide charity to their poor, and succor their elderly in his name. Have you never wondered what Rowena does when she goes out or why she's so tired when she returns? It's not all parties, expensive clothes, and having people fawn over you. You have *no* concept of the responsibilities that come with such rank!"

"I can learn," the redhead bit out.

Damn, but she was muleheaded! "Right. Then we'll leave that aside for the moment, along with the great multitude of societal rules to which women of such rank must adhere, and focus on the more vital issue. Has he given you any encouragement to engender such determined pursuit?"

Caroline's color deepened. "It is still very early. And I will *not* have that perjurer putting him off me before I have my chance!" she said, stamping her foot. "I'm going this instant to confront him and put things right."

Eleanor didn't budge from her position in front of the door, but squared her shoulders and stood firm. "If you go in there now with cannons ablaze, what do you think will happen?" Her calmly posed question had the desired effect, for Caroline stopped cold. "If you lose your temper now, it can only end in embarrassment and disaster. My cousin will send you home rather than allow you to accompany us to London, and then you'll have no chance at all of making a match—with *anyone*."

"What would you have me do?" replied Caroline angrily. "Let the blackguard spread rumors without contradicting them? Without fighting back?" A tear slid down her face.

"Am I to do nothing to cleanse myself of the blight on my character?"

Eleanor's own eyes smarted. How could she make her understand that the way the aristocracy handled such matters was very different from that of the bourgeoisie without deeply insulting her? She thought for a moment and then seized upon the one thing she knew would work. "You shared your desire to bag a titled husband. Well, there are strict social rules by which all ladies of quality must abide. To confront a gentleman publicly or to speak ill of him to others in secrecy would only serve to lower you—not him—in the sight of those whose ranks you aspire to join. There is only one way a lady can truly defy a smear against her character, and that is by exhibiting irreproachable behavior, behavior that puts the wagging tongue to shame."

"You want me to be good and hope no one believes him?" her friend said with damp sarcasm.

"Rowena once told me that a lady never lends dignity to the libelous by acting in a manner that reinforces their position. You cannot accuse a baron of slanderous acts with no proof and expect to escape without serious repercussions. As unfair as it is, people side with those whom they know, and you are largely *un*known save by the unfortunate choices you made during the last two years. Lord Marston is both respected and well-liked by many. There is nothing you can say against him without damaging yourself. Your only hope is to hold your tongue and let your good conduct and unrelenting temperance prove any negative rumors false."

Caroline's pale lips shook. "No one will believe I'm innocent if I don't protest."

"They will believe the one whose behavior shows the higher quality," Eleanor told her, softening. "A true gentleman never speaks ill of a lady. If he has broken this rule, he will incur Society's censure for it, and your exemplary conduct can only lift you in the eyes of those who doubt you. By using this approach, you risk nothing and stand to gain much."

"And what of Lord Wincanton?" Another tear slid down her friend's face. "Am I to allow poisonous gossip to reach him unimpeded?"

Conflicting emotions made Eleanor's already tense stomach squirm. Truly it was in Caroline's best interest to direct her hunt elsewhere for a husband. And, if she was willing to admit it, Eleanor would be enormously relieved, herself. But it would have to be a clean break. Caroline must understand that there was no chance of success or she would never give over. "You must cease your pursuit of him at once," she said in the same firm tone she'd heard Rowena use so many times when giving orders. "And not because of Lord Marston."

Caroline's brow puckered in confusion. "What do you mean? He cannot have any other cause to dislike me?"

"Dislike may be too harsh a word, but certainly you've given him ample cause for discomfort. Because you are my friend, he has been tolerant of your attempts to ensnare him—thus far. But his patience is not infinite." She braced herself as Caroline's eyes narrowed.

"You seem awfully certain of the gentleman's sentiment toward me, or rather the lack thereof. Tell me, is this advice based on factual knowledge or is it merely a supposition engendered by jealousy over his attentions?"

The accusation made Eleanor suddenly ill at ease. *Jealous?* Her first impulse was to deny it. She cared for and admired Sorin greatly, but to be jealous of his attentions implied another level of sentiment. *Am I jealous?* Part of her wanted to laugh at the suggestion; another part of her saw no humor in it whatsoever. But her feelings for Sorin—whatever they were—were irrelevant at the moment. What mattered right now was that Caroline comprehended the gravity of her situation. "Factual knowledge," she answered briskly.

Drawing herself up, Caroline raised her chin and looked down her nose at her. "I believe I have a right to know exactly how you acquired such *knowledge*."

Though Eleanor maintained her impassive stance, the coldness in her friend's voice made her shrink inside. She'd known better than to hope Caroline wouldn't ask for specifics. So be it. "Lord Wincanton recently invited Lady Ashford and me to accompany him to an event and, although I specifically mentioned that you are to stay with us in London, he very pointedly did not extend his invitation to include you."

An obstinate toss of red curls was her first answer. "Perhaps he wished to invite me himself and has simply not yet had an opportunity to do so."

Eleanor shook her head in denial of this postulation. "I've tried every means to gently dissuade you from your course, but it seems I've no choice but to tell you the truth. Lord Wincanton confided that he's concerned you may have mistaken his politeness for greater interest. His efforts to distance himself have been out of consideration for you because he does not wish to wound you with a more overt rejection. He expressed hope that your attentions will be diverted once we reach London, allowing him to avoid any further awkwardness."

Silence reigned for a very long, very uncomfortable moment.

"I see," replied Caroline faintly. A breathless little laugh escaped her as another tear slid down her face, which had grown dangerously pale. "Good Lord, what must he think of me? I've been the worst sort of flirt, and if Lord Marston *has* spoken to him of our past connection…" A careless shrug lifted her slumped shoulders for moment. "That's it, then. My chances are ruined. London no longer holds any promise for me."

"Of course it does!" Eleanor said. "There *are* other gentlemen, you know."

"Yes, but if *they* snub me—" Caroline jerked a thumb back toward the music room "—others will take their cue and do the same, especially once the old gossip starts again. I should return home this instant and save myself the humiliation."

"Sor—Lord Wincanton would never be so discourteous!" Eleanor flushed with embarrassment over the slip, but went on. "Besides, you are part of *my* circle, and I have many friends—friends who value my opinion far more than any gossip. One of them is sure to fall in love with you."

"Do you really believe that?"

"With all my heart," Eleanor replied, and she meant it. "I will do everything in my power to help you end the Season with a ring on your finger. But you *must* be careful. I beg you to heed my advice and conduct yourself at all times with the utmost decorum and dignity."

All remaining stubbornness faded from Caroline's eyes. "You're right, of course. This is my third year out, and I doubt my parents will deign to spend another shilling to promote me. I cannot afford to make any more mistakes." She sighed wistfully. "Countess would have been lovely, but I prefer to become a mere 'Mrs.' over spinsterhood."

Eleanor repressed a sigh of relief. Thank the Lord, Caroline was finally seeing sense! And it was good to see some of her tart humor coming back as well. "If it makes any difference at all, I believe your chances of making a happy match are much better without a title getting in the way. A woman who marries too far above her rank must deal with unhappy in-laws and their disdainful friends," she advised. "But a man need not have a title in order to possess wealth and status."

"Yes, well you needn't worry the more," said Caroline, her manner once more all business. "An undertaker could bend his knee to me this minute and I would accept him with gratitude—provided he has adequate means, of course," she added, ever pragmatic.

"And send your poor mama into a faint," Eleanor teased, glad to see her respond with a smile. "While I applaud your newfound enthusiasm, let us not be *too* hasty. I would not wish you to bind yourself to anyone unworthy."

Caroline's chin lifted a fraction and the fire returned to her eyes. "I may have adjusted my standards down somewhat, but they have not sunk to accepting anything less than an honorable man with a sufficient living."

"Good. But I still think you'll have better luck than to accept an undertaker's offer—especially when one considers that I know none."

Her words elicited another smile, this one mischievous. "A butcher's son, perhaps?"

"Heaven forefend. But truly, I think any gentleman would be lucky to have you for a wife." *Except Sorin.* Eleanor repressed a pang of guilty satisfaction over her successful intervention. This had nothing to do with jealousy. He would certainly be glad of the change, and she wouldn't have to watch Caroline destroy herself socially.

Caroline bowed her head and Eleanor heard a suspicious sniffle. "You are a good friend to say it. I'm sorry for the way I spoke to you, Ellie. Can you forgive me?"

Eleanor embraced her. "There is nothing to forgive." A clock chimed softly in the room. Bloody hell, it was nearly ten.

"We've been gone far too long," said Caroline, giving voice to her worry. "Lady Ashford will be furious. How will we ever explain ourselves?"

"We shall have to manufacture a plausible excuse for our

absence." Eleanor looked down with regret at her beautiful aqua gown. Reaching back, she grabbed a handful of silk, closed her eyes, and yanked.

Sorin watched with disquiet as Eleanor all but dragged her friend from the room.

"That's certainly put it in the fire," sighed Marston. "No doubt we've just missed a nasty scene. I remember Miss Caroline as having a particularly volatile disposition. I hope your Lady Eleanor is able to calm her down and bring her to her senses."

My Lady Eleanor. He hoped so, too. The look on the redhead's face had been nothing short of murderous. "I'm confident she will manage."

"As she's managed you?"

Heat crept up Sorin's neck. "I merely meant that she's a very competent and capable person."

"Naturally. One would only expect the daughter of a duke to be so."

A snort broke free before Sorin could stop it. "If you knew how ridiculous such an assumption is—I've had the opportunity to meet many dukes' daughters and found the majority of them vacuous, shallow, and uninspiring. I would trust very few with anything more important than arranging the dinner menu. Eleanor is…different. She would make a formidable duchess."

"Or countess, perhaps?" bantered Marston, clearly enjoying himself.

Sorin would have answered him smartly, but Rowena was coming over to join them with Charles in tow.

"I must apologize," she said with an awkward smile. "I can only assume Eleanor and her friend have encountered some sort of difficulty requiring their hasty departure. I'm sure neither of them meant to be rude."

"Of course not," he said, rising. "Unfortunately, we must also depart. Tonight's dinner and entertainments really have been a delight, but we must be going. Marston has agreed to accompany me to Holly Hall tonight and go on a hunting excursion with me tomorrow morning. One last parting shot, as you might say, before we take ourselves off to London."

Marston gave him a sharp look, but held his tongue.

"But you cannot go now," said Rowena, her tone one of worry. "Night has long since fallen, and it is far too dark to ride."

Smiling, Sorin cast a glance toward the long windows of the music room. "There is a good moon out tonight, nearly full, and I've ridden across these lands my entire life in both daylight and darkest night. There is not an inch between here and Holly Hall that I do not know intimately."

Charles frowned, though it looked more like a pout. "But we expected you to breakfast with us."

"I would, but we'd miss the early—" He stopped as Eleanor reappeared in the doorway, a much subdued looking Caroline just behind her.

"My apologies for our unceremonious departure," she said, her smile careful as she glided into the room. "One of the seams on the back of my gown tore when I sat and I was unaware of it until I rose from the pianoforte. It would have been unseemly for me to remain."

He was saved from having to say anything by Rowena. "I presume the matter has been corrected?" she asked coolly.

"Yes. Caroline summoned Fran and the damage has been repaired."

Rowena's gaze rested on her for a long moment before turning to Caroline, whose head was still bowed. "Thank you, Caroline. It was good of you to render assistance."

"It was my pleasure, Your Grace," said the girl.

It was an effort for Sorin to keep his mouth from dropping open. The change in the redhead's demeanor was astounding. But whatever had happened between the pair to elicit such a dramatic transformation, he knew he wouldn't learn of it tonight. "I'm afraid you've returned just as we were leaving."

Eleanor's gaze snapped up to meet his, and his heart warmed at the disappointment in her eyes. "I thought you were to overnight with us?"

Oh, no. He knew better than to give in to the desire to remain near her.

Rowena again stepped in and saved him from having to answer. "The gentlemen are obliged to be elsewhere at dawn," she explained. "We must not keep them further, as it is already late. I shall send for your horses to be brought around." She crooked a finger at the footman attending them. When he had gone, she turned back to the men. "We look forward to seeing you again Thursday. You and Lady Wincanton will join us here and we shall start out together, I presume?"

"Yes, along with Sir Yarborough and his mother," Sorin reminded them. He watched, irritation filling him as a flush crept into Eleanor's cheeks.

"Yes, yes. That is correct," said Charles with a peevish look at his wife. "Pity the lad could not join us tonight, but the arrangements had already been made and there was simply no time to add him to the party. Had I known you would be leaving so soon..."

It was a deliberate dig. Sorin knew he would have to explain later and hope his friend forgave him. "A pity, indeed. Perhaps next time." He turned and bowed to the ladies. "Lady

Ashford, Lady Eleanor, Miss Caroline."

"We bid you safe journey and good hunting tomorrow," said Rowena with a dignified nod as the others curtseyed.

"Thank you." He watched Eleanor from the corner of his eye while Marston said his farewells.

Eleanor's careful smiles and Caroline's unusually submissive manner practically shouted that some significant exchange had transpired between them. Whether it had ended in a clean victory or an uncomfortable stalemate was anybody's guess.

He and Marston found their horses waiting for them. Mounting, they rode in silence until they'd passed beyond the torch line. "I apologize if I've inconvenienced you," he said to Marston. "Given the circumstances, I could not imagine it would be good for either of us to remain."

"No, indeed not," said the other man, his tone grim. "And it is no inconvenience, provided you lend me something suitable to wear tomorrow morning. Truth be told, I'm grateful you pulled me from the trenches. Unfortunately, Ashford seemed quite put out over our defection."

"I'm sure he'll forgive us both once I explain the situation between you and Miss Caroline."

A sigh sounded in the night beside him. "I suppose it would be best for him to know the truth of it, though I'd hoped to spare her the embarrassment."

"I hope you won't think ill of me for saying it," Sorin said drily, "but any embarrassment the lady suffers is due entirely to her own inability to hold her temper in check."

"She has an impetuous nature, to be sure," conceded Marston. "But unlike you, I find her candor refreshing. So many women bury their true feelings behind an impenetrable mask. With Miss Caroline, one always knows where one stands...whether it's in the warm sunlight of her happy regard or the cold shadow beneath her heel," he said with a chuckle. "For the moment, I see only the bottom of her dainty slipper—but I'm looking up."

Sorin couldn't help but laugh. It seemed overloud against the soft backdrop of crickets and frog song. "Bollocks, man. You are the most optimistic fellow I've ever known."

"It's not optimism, my friend. It's desperation, pure and simple. I've sunk so low in her esteem that up is the only direction remaining open to me."

Sorin grimaced in the dark. He'd been in the same situation himself only recently. It was a sobering thought. "I'm sure she'll come around."

"Perhaps," murmured Marston. "I'd hoped to begin making amends tonight, but Fate seems to be set against me. She still paints me the villain of her fairy tale and will believe nothing else."

"Perhaps I can ask Eleanor to try to—"

"No," interrupted Marston. "I could never ask such a thing. It would only set her against her friend. Still, Lady Eleanor appears to be a good influence on her. They must've had quite a chat indeed. I've never seen Miss Caroline so…docile."

"I don't doubt it. Ellie can be quite persuasive."

"Persuasive? She pulled a bloody lion out of that room and brought a lamb back in. I'd like to know how she performed such a miracle. I don't suppose you'd be willing to ask her?"

He hated to crush the man's hopes. "Eleanor has never been one to prattle, and no amount of questioning will make her surrender that which she does not wish to reveal."

"A rare woman."

Indeed.

"I don't suppose we're really going hunting in the morning, are we?" asked Marston wistfully. "I'm afraid I failed to pack the proper attire for such an excursion."

"Why not?" Sorin answered. "I would not mind bagging a few more birds before leaving for Town. We'll find some clothes for you and you can have your pick of my rifles. As for the meat, it's been a hard winter here and I'm sure there are some families in the village that will appreciate a gift of fowl."

"When you put it like that, how can I refuse?" said Marston with a wry laugh.

"You cannot."

The men rode in companionable silence the rest of the way to Holly Hall at which point they parted for the night. Upon reaching his room, Sorin at once penned a note to Charles explaining the situation between Marston and Caroline and asking for his and Rowena's aid and discretion in managing the matter. Giving it to his valet, he ordered that it be delivered first thing in the morning.

As he lay awake, he thought, as always, of Eleanor. She had grown into an astounding woman in so many ways. Her ability to quash her friend's temper had been most impressive, yet he wondered how long the armistice she'd brokered would last. He also wondered if the women's friendship would survive once he began openly courting Eleanor—if indeed it ever came to that.

Chapter Nine

A pounding headache greeted Eleanor the following morning. She'd hardly slept for fretting about Caroline. And then there was Sorin. He'd left so abruptly, and his good-bye had been so formal and cool. She hadn't expected it.

"Lady Eleanor?"

She turned to answer the servant's inquiry. "Yes?"

"Her Grace has requested your presence in her sitting room."

No doubt to give me a good tongue-lashing for my conduct last night. "Thank you. Tell her I shall come as soon as I'm dressed." Sighing, she rose and rang for Fran. Going to the wardrobe, she grabbed the first serviceable gown she saw and prepared to don it. There was certainly no point in fussing over her appearance today.

When she arrived, Rowena wasted no time getting to the point of her summons. "I think taking Caroline with us to London would be a mistake. I plan to write to her parents today and tell them that we find ourselves unfortunately short of space."

Eleanor blinked in surprise and took a moment to steady herself. "You deserve an explanation for last night. In all honesty you need to know the truth in order to prevent any further incidents, but please wait until you hear what I have to say before you write to her family."

"I am already aware," interrupted Rowena, cutting her off. She rose, her long skirts hissing angrily as she paced the room. "She *knew* he had been invited," she said, her voice low and hard with suppressed fury. "Why did she not tell us? It would have saved everyone a great deal of discomfort!"

"She was too embarrassed," Eleanor said in her most soothing tone. "She truly thought she could be civil to him."

"Civil? She all but gave him the cut direct!"

"She was unprepared to learn that he was such close friends with Sor—with Lord Wincanton," Eleanor continued, desperate to calm her down. "When she saw them talking, she assumed the worst and thought Lord Marston was speaking ill of her to him. It upset her terribly."

Rowena sat on the edge of a settle and passed a hand over her pale, pinched face. A moment later, she withdrew a folded piece of paper from her pocket and held it out.

Taking it, Eleanor unfolded the missive, instantly recognizing Sorin's neat hand. Her heart sank as she quickly scanned the lines.

When she was done, Rowena took it back and began to refold it. "You realize this means I cannot invite Lord Marston to any of our at-home events in London. We cannot have that kind of tension in the atmosphere without it causing talk and endangering your chances."

"*My* chances? What of Caroline's?"

"She is not my primary concern."

"Neither am I," Eleanor retorted. "I don't intend to marry—and I wish you would stop trying to force it on me!

Besides, the matter is irrelevant, anyway."

"Irrelevant?" said Rowena, her voice rising. "The whole purpose of taking you to London is to—"

"That's not what I meant." She sighed. "I made a promise to Caroline and I won't break it." She then relayed the conversation she'd had with her friend the evening prior. "She vowed to behave herself, and I vowed I would help her find a suitable husband."

Rowena fixed her with a piercing gaze. "Do you honestly believe her to be sincere?"

"I do. She knows this is her last chance." Eleanor looked to her pleadingly. "I realize it will make things a bit difficult—"

"A bit?" Rowena's eyes were wide with incredulity.

"But there are ways around it," Eleanor hurried on, determined. "There is no rule demanding that we all must be in the same place at the same time. Under the circumstances, I don't believe Lord Marston will be offended by an occasional exclusion. When you do wish him to attend an event, Sorin can escort Caroline and me to another function somewhere else." *Please. Please. Please!*

Rowena took an agonizingly long time to answer. "Very well," she said at last. "I won't write to her parents *unless* things begin to degrade—and they had better not," she warned with a glare. "We will do our best to see her married quickly and without any scandal. God help us."

Elated, Eleanor opened her mouth to thank her.

But Rowena was not finished. "Understand that this in no way alters our plans for finding *you* a husband. Caroline's must not be the only wedding this autumn. As such, you will put forth the expected effort to that end once we reach London." Her face softened. "You cannot stay here forever, my dear," she said, reaching out to touch her cheek. "It would not be right. You need to build a life for yourself, have a family of your own. Your parents would want you to live fully and you cannot do so if you remain with us."

Eleanor's already heavy heart plummeted straight to her toes. So, he *had* been telling the truth. It wasn't that she'd doubted him—he'd never lied to her—but she'd rather hoped he'd been exaggerating things. "I understand," she murmured, numb.

The last vestiges of hardness melted from Rowena's face. "It's for your own good, my dear. I wish you would trust Charles and me. We just want you to be happy."

Eleanor wanted to scream that she was already happy, but the truth was that her sense of contentment had inexplicably begun to diminish. A strange sort of restlessness had overtaken her. Change was coming. It was inevitable.

She shook herself. Now was definitely not the time for melancholy rumination. Right now she had to appease the powers that be. "I know. Thank you for caring about me so much." She meant it. Her guardians' intentions were good, if misguided. "I cannot promise you that I will find an acceptable gentleman, but I'll try to be more open-minded."

It was enough. Satisfied, Rowena dismissed her.

The following days were filled with the business of preparing for their journey to London. Caroline remained unusually quiet throughout the controlled chaos, but Eleanor didn't worry overmuch. London would soon cure her of her brooding. Besides, she had enough to think about concerning her own dilemma. Each restless night brought her closer to Thursday and leaving Holbrook.

"It's been over a quarter of an hour since you last turned a page in that book," commented Rowena quietly as she ticked off items on the long list in her hand. It was the morning before their departure.

Eleanor looked up and blinked. "I guess I was woolgathering."

Rowena shot her a piercing glance. "You're not the only one to be acting queerly of late. Caroline has been far too quiet for my peace of mind. Is all well between you?"

"Quite. I was just thinking how much I shall miss this place," she said, looking around the room.

"You can always come and visit, my dear," said Rowena, frowning down at her list and crossing out a line. "In fact, I shall be quite upset if you don't make it a point to do so frequently, for I will greatly miss your company."

It took every bit of self-control for Eleanor to keep from showing her upset. She'd meant that she'd miss Holbrook while they were away in London, not forever! She hadn't yet given up all hope of remaining here. "Thank you," she replied past the sudden tightness in her throat. "Holbrook has been my home for so many years that I have great difficulty imagining myself anywhere else."

"I missed my home when I married Charles. But I soon grew to like it here, and I'm sure you'll come to love your new home as well." The corners of her mouth lifted in a gentle smile. "Especially once you and your husband begin filling it with children."

My husband? As if there was any man on earth I'd be willing to marry!

Unbidden, an image of Sorin flashed in Eleanor's mind. Shock suffused her, followed closely by utter confusion. *Why in heaven's name did I think of* him*?* Sorin was the stiffest, sternest, most proper gentleman in all of England—possibly the entire world. He'd scold and correct her at every turn, just as he'd always done, and though she *was* quite fond of him, she would eventually resent him for it. They'd make a terrible couple!

The ridiculousness of the whole idea almost made her laugh aloud. It was ludicrous! Even if she were to consider him for a husband, he would never agree to it. *In his mind, I'm still a child.*

But that thought harkened back to Rowena's last comment concerning children. Longing seized her heart in an iron grip. She couldn't deny that she wanted children. But freedom and children were mutually exclusive. If she wanted the latter, she would have to give up the former.

The thought of filling Holly Hall with Sorin's children, particularly of the act that precipitated such events, brought instant, scorching heat to her face and an uncomfortable tension throughout her whole body. She looked up to see Rowena staring at her. "Yes, I—I suppose I shall." She ducked her head over her book once more, ignoring Rowena's soft chuckle. But throughout the rest of the day, her thoughts kept wandering back to the idea. It was a source of both frustration and bewilderment that she could not put it out of her mind. That night as she lay abed, unable to find peace or slumber, she determined to settle the futile argument with herself once and for all. Sorin would *never* consider her for a wife—and despite her high regard for him, she'd *never* be happy with so overbearing a husband.

There! Satisfied, Eleanor closed her eyes and kept them shut, until at last sleep took her.

Thursday morning arrived, and with it complete turmoil. Maids and footmen rushed to and fro making final preparations for their employers' departure. Traveling trunks were trundled off to the carriages and the servants' wagons for loading. An early breakfast was bolted down. Finally, Sorin and his mother arrived followed closely by the Yarboroughs, and then it was time.

"Do you not think him completely handsome?" whispered Caroline as they walked to the carriage.

Eleanor followed her gaze to find that it rested on

Yarborough. She ought to be thankful that the comment had referred to someone other than Sorin, but all she could muster was a faint sense of unease. "I suppose," she answered with a shrug.

"His jacket is simply splendid," Caroline went on, her voice eager.

She looked again. Indeed it was—and far more suitable for a promenade down Rotten Row than for the start of a six-day journey on horseback. He looked every inch the dandy from the top of his jaunty felt hat down to his gleaming and obviously new Hessians. The ensemble had no doubt cost a fortune, but Eleanor knew the difference between a surface gloss and deep shine. No amount of expensive trappings would ever make a true gentleman of Donald Yarborough.

Her gaze lit then upon Sorin beside him. By contrast, the Earl of Wincanton wore the modest, practical clothes appropriate for a long journey. The morning sun kissed his hair and face with gentle golden light as he soothed his overeager horse and jested with Charles. He'd never been unpleasant to look at, but it struck her now that he was actually quite handsome.

"Eleanor?"

The insistent inquiry forced her to return her attention to Caroline. "Remember what we discussed," she said quietly. "Be polite during our journey, but do not encourage him overmuch. You don't wish to give the impression that he has your favor before we reach London, lest he boast of it to others upon our arrival and lead them to think you already spoken for."

"But what if— "

"You have only just met him," Eleanor cut in, giving her a stern look. "Neither of you knows anything about the other, much less whether or not you will suit. Let his actions speak for his character along the way without your prompting. If you still find him of interest after we arrive, I'll be glad to help further the connection." She lightened a little. "Be patient, and keep in mind that you may soon have many more appealing options to consider. You don't want to limit yourself before you've even seen what is available."

The pout didn't entirely disappear from Caroline's face, but she nonetheless nodded, albeit reluctantly. "Very well, I shall be careful not to let him think he has any advantage."

Satisfied, Eleanor led the way to the coach where Rowena waited for them with Lady Yarborough.

"*There* you are, my dear," the woman crowed as she approached. "I was beginning to think we might have to send a search party for you. London awaits—come, let us be off!"

A twinge of dislike ran through Eleanor as the lady gave her cheek a maternal pat before turning to board the coach. The woman was barely acquainted with her and ought not to be so familiar. She waited until Lady Yarborough's ample backside disappeared inside the vehicle's confines. Like her offspring, she was ridiculously overdressed for the occasion. With her feathered bonnet, heavily be-ringed hands, and the ceaseless prattle issuing from her mouth, Lady Yarborough reminded her of nothing so much as a stout magpie.

The ladies settled themselves while last-minute adjustments were made to the luggage to accommodate their traveling companions' trunks, and then they were off.

As Holbrook slipped past her window, Eleanor filled her eyes with its emerald lawns and sun-dappled woods. Already she felt a pang of homesickness. If she didn't return to Somerset, she would have to make a new home. Was there a way to marry *and* remain in Somerset? Yarborough was out of the question, of course. She'd sooner wed a pig! Again, her thoughts turned to Sorin.

Could I be happy as his wife? Another question arose, one that presented a whole new set of problems. *Could he be happy as my husband?*

Just as she held every man up to the standard he'd helped her set, so did he hold every woman up to his. A sense of hopelessness flooded her at the thought of Miss Jane Perfection Stafford. Over the years, he'd painted a vivid picture of the woman as meek and mild, patient and kind, never uttering a wrong word or acting in any way other than modest and proper.

How in heaven's name am I ever to measure up to that?

The answer was she couldn't. She wasn't meek, she was rarely mild, and while kindhearted, she often lacked patience. Speaking her mind was one of her biggest faults. How many times had she argued with Sorin? Between him and Rowena, she'd learned modesty and propriety, but the urge to rebel against starchiness was still strong. No matter how much she aspired to be like Jane, she always fell short of the mark.

And I always will. I cannot become something I'm not.

He'd said he had yet to find Jane's equal, but that didn't mean there wasn't one out there. She could see it now: he'd find a quiet little ingénue tucked away in a corner at some ball, her shy and retiring demeanor the perfect antidote to the brazen behavior he so deplored, and Saint Jane would be replaced by Saint Someone Else.

A sudden wave of nausea threatened. The swaying of the coach was causing her difficulty. *Strange, I've never suffered carriage sickness before…* Taking a deep breath, she tried looking through the window to settle her stomach. But the feeling only receded a little, leaving behind an uncomfortable tightness.

What really rankled was knowing he'd see some girl straight out of the schoolroom as more of an adult than her.

Age wasn't her problem. The problem was his perception of her. Hers was a war with two fronts; on one side hovered the inviolable specter of Jane, on the other stood Sorin's view of her as an eternal child.

What if she *did* manage to succeed in making him see her in a romantic way? What if they *did* marry? What would it be like? Would their friendship hold, or would they find life with each other intolerable? She didn't like to consider the latter. The thought of losing his friendship pained her more than she'd thought possible.

"I suppose you must be very excited to see London again, Lady Eleanor," chirped Lady Yarborough. "I have not been in years, myself. Not since Sir Yarborough died."

In a way, Eleanor was grateful to the woman for breaking her melancholy woolgathering. At least if she was busy being talked to death she wouldn't have time for pessimistic what-iffing about impossible things. "I'm quite happy in the countryside, but I'll admit to missing the variety of musical entertainments offered in Town."

"I am *so* looking forward to seeing several of my old friends," continued Lady Yarborough with a dramatic sigh. "We've written countless letters, of course, but it's not the same as seeing one another."

No, it was certainly not. "I'm sure you will be received with great joy," Eleanor answered politely.

The woman's face pinked at the compliment. "My son jested this very morning that he fears I might not wish to return at the end of the Season and that he'll have to send me home tied in a sack," she said with a giggle that sounded absurd coming from a woman her age.

Eleanor bit back a groan. "I'm certain we will all be glad to return home once the heat arrives. London is simply not to be borne in summer."

"*Mmm*, I suppose you're right," said Lady Yarborough. Another lengthy sigh burst from her. "And yet I shall miss the thrill of it all. There is nothing like London during the Season. Tell me, Lady Eleanor, have you already made a great many plans for while you are there?"

And thus began the anticipated fishing. A mischievous urge came over Eleanor to bait the hook with misinformation, but she squelched it. "Indeed. Several," she replied lightly.

Lady Yarborough deflated a little, plainly disappointed. Having been left with no openings to further the thread she'd attempted to begin, she turned to Rowena. "I also greatly anticipate seeing our new London residence for the first time. It is in a *very* fashionable part of town—Golden Square." She paused, clearly expecting a reaction to the announcement that she and her progeny had risen in the world.

Immediately, questions arose in Eleanor's mind as to how they could afford such an address. It was no secret that the late Sir Yarborough had been suffering financial difficulties. Everyone in the county knew he'd been depending on his son to secure the family fortunes by means of an advantageous marriage.

"How lovely for you," said Rowena, sounding only mildly awkward. "I'm sure you will enjoy it immensely."

Lady Yarborough's plump cheeks lifted in a smug smile. "I'm sure I shall. My Donald surprised me with the news of our relocation upon his arrival. At first, I was quite wroth with him for his tardiness, but I forgave him at once—his delay was owed to the need for the house to be refurbished, you see. According to him, the previous owners lacked taste entirely. Donald described the place as being utterly *ghastly*." She drew the word out, emphasizing it with a disdainful wave of her pudgy, glittering hand. "He said the house looked like a fusty Tudor relic, and that there was no alternative but to gut and redecorate—in the Greek style, naturally." She sniffed. "He tells me the gardens are in need of a complete redesign, but that will have to wait until next year so as not to interfere with several events we plan to host over the Season."

Eleanor ignored the blatant hint, privately mourning for the house in Golden Square. To think of it being gutted and "modernized" made her sick at heart. She sincerely hoped the previous owners never saw what had become of their former residence.

After a moment, Lady Yarborough shook her head and again sighed. "If only my husband had lived to see our son's triumph."

Eleanor braced herself. *Here it comes...*

"The fine education he insisted upon for our Donald has greatly benefitted him, you know. Within the space of just one year he's improved the estate in ways his father never imagined."

As determined as she was to refrain from encouraging the woman, Eleanor couldn't help herself. "How so, if you don't mind my inquiring?"

The gleam that entered Lady Yarborough's eyes confirmed it was just the sort of question for which she'd hoped. "Not at all, my dear," she said, reaching across to pat her hand as if it were the most natural and appropriate thing in the world.

Eleanor barely stopped herself from jerking away. Fixing a placid smile on her face, she prompted her to continue. "Do go on, Lady Yarborough."

The smug smile broadened. "Well you see, ten years ago my husband inherited land in Ireland, a great lot of land that was unfortunately populated by slothful tenants who rarely paid their rents and produced nothing save grief and more mouths to feed. I *tried* to convince him to do as some of his friends had and raise the rents, which would have enabled him to rid us of the squatters and thus free the property for more profitable uses, but he refused. My late husband always was far too softhearted, bless him."

The woman's tight lipped, scornful demeanor told Eleanor that the statement was anything but a fond eulogy.

In an instant, however, Lady Yarborough's scowl disappeared, replaced by a sickly sweet smile. "My Donald, however, saw at once the merit of such a plan and began to implement it immediately upon inheriting, thank heaven," she said with aplomb.

Eleanor's stomach turned. The woman's tone was so pompous—as if rack-renting and the forced eviction of the humblest of the working poor were acts worthy of pride! It was painfully clear now that the bully of her childhood had not changed one bit. He was still a brute. And now she knew where he'd learned to be so callous. The old Sir Yarborough might have been softhearted, but at least he'd *had* a heart.

Lady Yarborough nattered on, apparently unaware that there was anything in her boasts to inspire bile. "Fortunately, a much more pleasant alternative was found before he'd invested too much effort. While seeking an agent to oversee the management of our Irish interests, Donald learned that several of his friends' families had sold similar Irish millstones to private investors—investors willing to pay a good deal more than the pittance the crown had offered," she said with a hard nod that jiggled her chins. "He made arrangements to meet with one such man. The negotiations went *very* well." A toothy smile spread across her face as she reached up to finger the ostentatious necklace of gold and pearls nestled against her décolletage. "A most pleasing end to a terrible bother."

"And what of the tenants?" Eleanor asked, ignoring Rowena's warning glare.

An indifferent shrug lifted Lady Yarborough's round

shoulders. "No longer our concern, thank goodness. Donald told me the new owner has already begun a purge."

Eleanor struggled to keep from showing her anger and disgust…and failed miserably. "I cannot begin to imagine committing such a contemptible act against another human being." Across the way, she saw Rowena close her eyes in defeat. But it was too late now. "You speak not of vermin, madam, but of men who have very likely worked that land all their lives, men whose fathers probably worked it for several generations. Men with families—innocent children who will now be condemned to suffer the most inhumane privation, possibly even death. Are they not deserving of some compassion?"

The subject of her censure flushed an ugly brick red. Holding her spine stiff, Eleanor steeled herself. But though the woman was clearly displeased, the anticipated explosion didn't occur.

Instead, Lady Yarborough fixed her with a cold stare and smiled unpleasantly. "Your concern for your fellow man is quite admirable, my dear. Such altruistic idealism is fine for one so young and unburdened with responsibility. But we who *are* so burdened must be more practical. Those…" She paused for a beat and then began afresh, her tone growing even more patronizing. "Those *people* were not paying their rents. The land was supporting them while doing nothing for its rightful owners. You cannot expect us to have supported them without compensation indefinitely." In an obvious dismissal, she then directed her full attention to Rowena. "With the proceeds from the sale, we will improve and modernize our properties here in England. Golden Square is but the first step of many."

And the next will no doubt be to secure a rich, gullible wife for your hateful son. Eleanor fumed silently as the woman continued to boast about their plans. Plans that were, for all their surface polish, full of holes.

Over the years, the Yarborough estate in Somerset had slowly dwindled as outlying portions of it had been sold off to neighboring landowners in order to cover its owners' mounting debts. It was unlikely the little that remained would be sufficient to support the family without the Irish rents to provide a steady, if modest, income. Old Sir Yarborough had been right to hold on to his Irish inheritance. By selling it, his foolhardy son and greedy widow had effectually condemned themselves to a slow decline. The money from the sale was a temporary sop for an incurable financial hemorrhage and wouldn't support them forever. It would have been wiser to sell off the remainder of their English estate and relocate to Ireland. Looking at her, Eleanor knew Lady Yarborough would probably sooner die than give up the pleasures of London.

It struck her then that the house in Golden Square, the new baubles and finery, all of it was an expensive ruse. A carefully baited hook to lure some unsuspecting heiress into marriage so that they could use her wealth and connections to save themselves from ruin. The insult was that the woman thought her too stupid to see it.

She started as an elbow connected with her ribcage. Turning, she saw Caroline staring at her with a worried expression.

But before she could respond, Lady Yarborough again spoke. "Do any of you know anyone else in Golden Square?" she demanded, her nasal voice grating on Eleanor's nerves like the screech of an un-oiled carriage wheel.

"We do not," answered Rowena.

A smile tugged at Eleanor's mouth, and she ducked her head to hide it. Rowena's response had been decidedly chilly. At least she was not the only one to find their traveling companion vulgar and irritating!

"I believe Lady Wincanton may have a friend there," offered Caroline, speaking up for the first time. "I heard her tell Lord Wincanton this morning that they must visit her the week after their arrival. She specifically mentioned that she lived in Golden Square."

"Oh, indeed?" said Lady Yarborough, visibly delighted. "Thank you, Miss Caroline. You are a most helpful young lady," she added, flicking a cold glance at Eleanor to let her know *she* was *not*. "I shall have to inquire of Lady Wincanton and ask to be introduced."

Eleanor didn't know whether to cringe in horror or laugh. It was one thing for a friend to ask you to introduce them to someone else in your circle, but Lady Yarborough had never been among Lady Wincanton's set.

According to Rowena, upon marrying Sir Yarborough, the woman had spent just one summer in the country before claiming an adverse reaction to the air and insisting on remaining in London year-round for the sake of her delicate constitution. Looking at her now, Eleanor found it hard to imagine anyone less delicate. It was rumored that she'd returned to Somerset only because her lord husband had finally put his foot down after their son had been born, refusing to let the child be raised in Town.

Lady Yarborough had mourned her exile bitterly and publicly, effectively alienating everyone in the county that might have been willing to offer friendship. Now that her son was on the market, however, she was trying to be sociable—an endeavor which was fast proving disastrous. Lady Wincanton would undoubtedly deem any request for an introduction highly improper, to say nothing of the insult of being perceived as naught more than a rung on the social ladder. To Eleanor's knowledge, the only time the two women saw each other was at church.

Rowena must have been thinking along the same lines. "Oh, yes. I do remember something about her having a friend there now—but I don't think she would be anyone of interest to you," she said carefully. "If my memory serves, the lady in question is quite elderly."

But Lady Yarborough wouldn't be dissuaded. "Nonsense! I shall be most obliged to meet her and extend the hand of friendship. After all, we'll practically be neighbors." A calculating look entered her eyes, and she laughed a little. "I shall at the very least invite her to tea. Perhaps *you* might join us, Miss Caroline?"

Eleanor looked at once to Rowena, but her face remained impassive save for a slight tightening around the eyes. For Lady Yarborough to so obviously exclude them was a deliberate and shocking affront, especially when one considered that she was being allowed to share *their* transport to London. Now Eleanor knew just how angry the woman really was over her chastisement—enough to toss all good sense straight to hell.

By contrast, Caroline's face was full of worry—a good sign in Eleanor's opinion. Perhaps *now* she had a better understanding of what she'd be getting into if she encouraged the woman's spawn. "Caroline? I'm sure you'd find that lovely, would you not?" she prompted, giving her friend the tiniest of nods to let her know all was well and to accept the invitation. To decline would only set the ill-mannered cat against her, too, and Caroline could ill afford an enemy.

"I—I should be delighted," answered Caroline, looking anything but.

Lady Yarborough's haughty gaze rested squarely on Eleanor as she replied, "Excellent. I shall be sure to send an invitation as soon as we are settled. Now, how far did you say it was to our first stopping point, Lady Ashford?"

Too far, thought Eleanor, turning to look out of the window so as not to further provoke the contemptible woman. There were 116 miles between Holbrook and London. It was going to be a very long journey. She wondered how the gentlemen were faring.

They'd not yet traveled five miles before the pressure building at the back of his head made Sorin want to turn his horse around and gallop straight back to Holly Hall. Yarborough had not ceased bragging about his so-called "accomplishments" since they'd passed the main gate at Holbrook. The lad was more of a fool than he'd thought possible. Worse, he was a fool with a cruel streak as broad as the Thames.

The blackguard seemed to delight in the misery of those he viewed as less clever than himself—which, Sorin suspected, was everyone. His caustic witticisms spared none, not even those he named friends.

A rich, but rather dim cousin duped into marrying a pauper by means of borrowed gowns and paste jewelry was the source of amused warnings and much unsolicited advice on how to avoid being similarly deceived. Then there was the chum from university unfortunate enough to marry the toast of the Season only to find himself a cuckold a few months later, a story that elicited Yarborough's crude laughter and bawdy jests about how to be certain one's wife truly bore her lord's fruit and not the offspring of a lover. "Not that *I* shall ever have to worry about that," he'd added with a nasty leer. "I shall keep *my* field well planted and leave no room for another to till it."

Several times Sorin experienced an almost overpowering urge to draw his horse alongside and knock Yarborough senseless. Had Eleanor not been a member of their party, he would have done it. He could tell Charles was growing annoyed, as well, and wondered how the ladies were faring.

"Mother and I plan to host a ball this Season," said Yarborough for the third time. "The ballroom in our new house in Golden Square is simply splendid. I thought at first to have the frescos redone but in the end I decided I rather liked the existing ones, even if they are a bit out of fashion. I've furnished the place with the best London has to offer, though I expect my bride will want to redecorate according to her own taste." He glanced back at the coach and smirked. "I shall, of course, defer to m'lady's wishes."

Sorin ground his teeth. If this lack-wit thought Eleanor would succumb to his smooth words and dubious charms, he had a rude awakening ahead of him. "One hopes that your bride and your lady mother will be in accord regarding such matters," he said, striving for detachment.

Ahead of them, Charles began to chuckle. "He's right, you know," he cast back over his shoulder. "Many a marriage has been soured by contention between warring females. When I first married, I was more worried about how my wife and my mother would get on than anything else. I count myself blessed that they liked each other so well." Another chuckle. "Though I will admit it could be quite uncomfortable when all of the females in my house were united against me."

An impertinent grin split Yarborough's face. "My mother will be so happy to see me married that I doubt she'll object to anything my wife wishes. Her sole desire is to witness the birth of my heir—which will of course be my first priority once married."

Again, Sorin's jaw tightened as Yarborough once more glanced back at the coach bearing Eleanor. The thought of this wheckering muck-spout ever spawning was bad enough, but to imagine Eleanor as the vessel turned his stomach. "I'm going to fall back and check on my mother," he announced, reining in.

The look Charles shot him was a piercing one, and again he wondered if his old friend suspected something. It didn't matter. Another minute of listening to Yarborough and he would open his mouth and give himself away for certain. As he fell back, the coach containing Eleanor passed him by. Someone—Eleanor—was delivering what was unmistakably a scathing recrimination. Before he could catch any more than the briefest snatch of the conversation, however, the carriage passed out of earshot.

He smiled grimly. It appeared things were going as well for the ladies as they were for the gentlemen. Drawing alongside his own carriage, he tapped on the window. The curtain twitched aside, revealing his mother's annoyed countenance. A moment later, one of the smaller side windows opened.

"What is it? Have we encountered a problem?"

"All is well, Mother," he assured. "I simply wanted to be sure of your comfort."

A frosted brow lifted. "Comfort is not something one associates with travel." Her gaze flicked over his face and narrowed. "I sense there is another reason why you abandoned Ashford. Is the Yarborough fellow really so intolerable?"

There was no point in hiding it. "He shall count himself fortunate if I don't throttle him before our journey's end."

"How glad I am that I did not offer to share *my* conveyance." Amusement lit her eyes.

A laugh forced its way out before he could stop it. "I'd vow the ladies of Holbrook are wishing they'd kept to themselves, too."

"Oh?"

"I chanced to overhear a rather heated conversation as I passed their coach," he confessed, unable to help smiling. "Eleanor was delivering a rather impassioned denunciation. I believe I heard her use the term 'vermin.'"

"If things have begun to deteriorate at this early juncture, it is doubtful they will make it to London with any civility intact." Her lips pursed. "Perhaps I ought to have Eleanor join me. What think you?"

"I think such an invitation would be received with much gratitude," he said at once.

"So be it. Ask her—ah, *just* Eleanor, if you please—to join me when we stop. Until then, I shall rest." Without further comment, she withdrew and the window snapped shut.

Smiling, Sorin made his way back up front. As he passed the other carriage, he heard Rowena's voice, though it remained low enough that her words were indistinguishable. Hopefully, she'd be able to smooth things over. He restrained a sigh as he approached the head of the line. Yarborough was still blathering on.

Charles glanced at him as he drew up, scowling. "Great galloping galligaskins, will he never cease?" he muttered. "We have six *days* of this to endure."

"Cheer up," Sorin said with a grin. "Eventually, he'll run out of things to say about himself."

A soft snort erupted from Charles. "I'd be slow to lay any wagers on it. I fear our only hope lies in the sudden onset of a malady of the throat. One severe enough to keep him hoarse until London," he added, his scowl deepening.

Sorin didn't bother smothering his laughter even when Yarborough turned to peer at them curiously. He didn't offer any explanation for his outburst either. Let the oaf think what he would and continue acting like an ass. Sir Yarborough's conduct would only serve to drive Eleanor away—hopefully straight into his waiting arms. *If I can manage to make her see me as more than a friend, that is.* And then there was the matter of convincing Charles not to run him through.

He wouldn't be the only one to ask for Eleanor's hand, of that much he was certain. Yarborough was quite obviously seeking to impress her family. No doubt he would approach Charles with hat in hand soon after they reached London. But Sorin knew all the boasting in the world would not avail him. If the look on Charles's face was any indication, he was already developing a passionate dislike for their new traveling companion.

"Did I tell you that Lord Winthrop invited me to dine with him and his family next week?" Yarborough called back, eliciting a low groan from Charles. "He was an old friend of my father's. It is my hope that he'll support my ambition to take a seat in the Commons."

Now that *was* a surprise.

"Did he just say that he plans to become a Member of *Parliament*?" whispered Charles, clearly just as taken aback as he was.

"I believe he did."

"God help us all."

"I do hope you'll both support me as well," continued Yarborough loudly, flashing a winning grin at them over his shoulder.

"In a pig's eye," said Charles through his teeth as he smiled back and nodded.

Sorin kept his mouth shut and pondered this news in silence. Unless he'd by some unknown means increased his family's worth, Yarborough *couldn't* run for a seat. His father had sold off too much of their property in recent years for him to be eligible. Something wasn't right. The fellow was throwing around money like he had no end of it, and now he was boasting about his plans to enter into politics. Something had certainly changed his income and prospects, but what?

"I've been meaning to ask a favor of you," said Charles quietly.

Sorin looked to his friend, marking his serious manner. "You know you have only to name it."

"Yes, well, it may prove a bit awkward for you, this particular favor," said Charles, eyeing him. "I need someone to help me keep an eye on Ellie this Season."

Sorin did his best to maintain a placid demeanor. "Are you anticipating some sort of trouble?"

"A bit, yes. Not from Ellie, of course," amended Charles hastily. "Rather from her friend, Miss Caroline. Rowena confided in me that the girl has been...well, let us just say she's been restless of late. She also has an unfortunate tendency toward reckless behavior. Scandal has haunted her footsteps almost since she came out. If she trips the edge and becomes embroiled in anything serious, I want to ensure none of it touches Ellie."

"I can hardly prevent Miss Caroline from behaving inappropriately," Sorin began, keeping his voice low so as not to be overheard.

"No, but you *can* ensure that Ellie is with someone who will watch out for her and behave properly in her company while Rowena and I have our hands full. Your presence at her side will discourage any adventurers from thinking her unattended." His friend looked at him sidelong. "I would have asked you to help look after Miss Caroline, but I suspect she'd only try to entrap you. An idea that—unless I'm woefully lacking in intuition—likely holds no appeal for you."

"Indeed it does not," Sorin said drily. "I am most grateful for your mercy and will gladly act as Ellie's chaperone, if that is your desire." Though the windfall elated him, he felt rather like a fox that had just been asked to guard a henhouse.

"Wonderful!" said Charles, his smile returning. "Ah, but perhaps it might be best not to tell her what you're on about, if you know what I mean," he said with a wink. "I know you're fast friends and all that, but she might not take too kindly to your playing the watchdog."

Watchdog indeed. "I shall be discreet." He had to ask it. "Are you not concerned that my hovering might cause people to think us a pair?"

Charles's indignant snort would have wounded him had he not been anticipating it. "Not bloody likely," said his friend, chuckling. "All of London knows you're an old friend of the family's, a sort of older brother to Ellie. I've no worries over the rumor mill saying anything to the contrary. She's safe with you, and that is my chief concern." He paused and cleared his throat. "I don't suppose there's any chance you might be willing to help with a bit of matchmaking while you're 'hovering'?"

Sorin forced a negligent shrug. "If you think she'd be receptive to such guidance, I'll certainly do my best to steer her aright."

"Excellent! You'll be my eyes and ears on the front, then," said Charles, his eyes twinkling. "If you see any likely prospects and are able to make any progress with getting her to consider them, you'll let me know, eh?"

It really was quite difficult to smile when one truly wanted to scowl, but Sorin made the effort and brought one to his lips. "Naturally."

Deeper and deeper seemed the hole into which he'd dug himself. Still, there might be a way to turn this around to his benefit. The letters they'd exchanged were all well and good, but what they really needed was time spent together in meaningful conversation. Now that Eleanor was an adult, she needed to get to know him as an equal. As a man. If she could but see him in a different light, it might engender romantic sentiments toward him. He needed to open her eyes.

It must be done gradually, so as not to shock her. Changing her view of him from "brotherly friend" to "potential lover" would take time.

It would have to be done subtly, as well. Ideally, if all worked out as he hoped, she would be the one to tip her hand first. If he could make her fall in love with him, then, as his mother had suggested, Charles would gladly give his blessing.

It must be done with utmost care for her reputation. The last thing he wanted was for her to accept his offer of marriage only to avoid a scandal. He wanted her to choose him of her own accord.

Chaperoning Ellie would provide him the opportunity to be close to her without raising suspicion. Now he just needed a means by which to gently remove the veil from her sight and make her see him as a potential husband.

Chapter Ten

Stepping down, Eleanor breathed a sigh of relief as her legs, stiff from remaining so long in the same cramped position, slowly un-kinked. While the horses rested, she would take advantage of the welcome, albeit brief, respite from the close air in the box—and from the dreadful Lady Yarborough. An area of smooth grass ran along the wayside, away from the dust of the road. She made for it. "We've come farther on this leg of the journey than we did last year," she remarked as Sorin joined her.

"Well, the weather appears to be cooperating, which helps," he said, matching her stride as she marched along the hedgerow toward a shaded copse a little way beyond. "God willing, it will stay fair the whole of the journey."

"If my prayers have any influence in heaven, it will," she muttered, sending up another silent one.

"That bad?"

"Bad enough that I wish horses could fly."

"If wishes were fishes," he said, laughing. "I've heard it said that anticipation only lengthens the road." His hazel eyes crinkled at the corners, the tanned flesh contrasting sharply with his white smile, making it appear all the brighter. Somewhere along the way, he'd removed his jacket and cravat and had loosened his shirt about the throat, leaving it bare. He must have gone without a cravat for an extended period of time recently, for the skin there was just as sun-kissed as that above.

To her shock, Eleanor found herself wondering if it was the same golden hue all the way down to—

"Wherever it is you've gone, it must be far away from here," murmured Sorin.

Heat flooded her cheeks. "It's not anticipation that makes me long for speed. I—I'm simply weary of riding in the coach."

"A rather ill omen this early in the voyage, if I may say so," he said, his smile widening a fraction. "But in light of your confession, perhaps my news will be welcome."

"News? Do tell," she replied, glad to latch onto anything that might distract.

"My mother is regretting her lack of a traveling companion and has asked me to invite you to share a seat in our coach. If you are amenable to the idea, of course."

Amenable? She could have kissed him, she was so happy! An image of her flinging her arms about his neck and doing exactly that popped into her mind. Heat again flared in her face. *For shame, Eleanor—discipline your mind!* Whatever was the matter with her? Ever since the preposterous idea of marrying him had occurred to her, her thoughts had run wild. She struggled for composure. "I would be absolutely delighted to join her," she said, privately wondering if her face would hereafter ever lack a blush in his presence.

"Excellent. Then I shall inform Charles and Rowena of the change and fetch your things." His mouth twitched, and his eyes lit with amusement. "I'm sure Lady Yarborough will be glad of the additional space as well."

He knows! The dam burst. "Oh, if you'd *heard* some of the things that woman said to me about— "

His laughter cut in, a low rumble that made her insides quiver in the oddest manner. "If she's anything at all like her odious offspring, I can only empathize. Give me but a moment to relay my mother's wishes and I shall rejoin you."

The tension drained out of her as he turned and strode back to the coaches. Of course he would understand her. Despite his disapproving demeanor, she knew he'd *always* understood her, sometimes better than she understood herself. She watched him, marking that he took no time to linger but came back straightaway. "Has he been awful?" she asked as he approached, jerking her chin back toward Yarborough.

"Insufferable." He offered his arm, which she took, and his smile returned as they began to walk. "Charles is praying for a plague to strike him dumb the length of our journey. Personally, I'm praying for something a bit more permanent."

Smothering a laugh, she looked at him with sympathy. "If it is any consolation, I don't believe they will be accompanying us for the return."

"God willing," he muttered. "If you should at some point discover otherwise, I beg you to send me warning so that I may make other arrangements."

"I see. So you would leave me to suffer and endure while you make a merry road of your own?"

"Never," he vowed. "I would find some way to include you in my escape."

She all but squirmed beneath his gaze. It felt as if he were searching her soul, trying to fathom all of her secrets. The idea that he might somehow discern her recent, inappropriate thoughts concerning him made her palms sweat. She turned her attention to the path. Some blessed soul had planted a few trees just ahead and had erected a little bench in their shade.

Moving on before her, Sorin went and cleared it of leaves and debris.

How thoughtful and dear he was! Never had she met a more considerate man, not even her cousin. She doubted whether Yarborough would have done the same. Her back prickled unpleasantly, and she glanced behind her. Thankfully, no one had followed them. Everyone, including her bête noire, seemed otherwise occupied. Though they were in plain sight of anyone who cared to look, they were also quite alone.

With a glad heart she entered the cool shade. "Thank you," she murmured, sitting on the freshly swept bench.

Sorin stood before her, the dappled sunlight on his hair highlighting little glints of gold amid the darker brown waves. A breeze ruffled through it, lifting it from his brow. "Eleanor, I wish to ask you something," he said at last, his manner solemn. "I meant to do so before we left for London, but I've been unable to get a moment in private with you until now." He let out an awkward laugh. "I would not have the courage if I did not know for certain that you above all people will answer me with absolute sincerity."

"Of course I will," she promised, mystified.

"My mother has adjured me to take a wife, but the truth is that I find myself in the awkward position of having been out of circulation for what is undoubtedly a lengthy amount of time." His brow furrowed. "I simply don't know how to court a lady anymore—things have changed so much since I wooed Jane. At the least, I fear I shall appear antiquated and dull. At worst, I fear I'll become a laughingstock. I require guidance."

"Guidance?" An incredulous laugh escaped her. "Surely you cannot look to me for advice. I'm hardly qualified, given that I've decided never to marry." The words had a bitter tang of deceit now that she was indeed considering exactly that course of action.

His lips pressed together for a moment. "If I am to succeed in bringing home a bride, I require a modern female perspective on courtship, and you are the only one I trust."

He trusted her, and all she could think of was how to use his situation to her advantage. *Some friend I am!* She resolved not to do it, not to sacrifice their friendship to her childish desire to remain in Somerset. *He deserves better from me.* "What of your mother? I'm certain she would be happy to make some suitable arrangement for you."

"Modern, Ellie," he reminded her gently. "Please say you'll help me?"

His quiet plea pierced her. Unable to look at him, she closed her eyes. "Very well," she answered at last. *I'm such a fool. How could I have ever imagined he might want to marry someone like me?* "If that is your wish, then so be it. I will try."

"Thank you," he said, sounding relieved.

She opened her eyes and stared dully at the ground. "I think we should return," she said, forcing herself to look up and back to where the rest of their party was gathered.

Her stomach clenched and began to churn. Yarborough was staring straight at her, and even at this distance she could tell he was angry. In an instant, her upset transformed into cold fury. He had no claim on her whatsoever and no right to be jealous! Her thoughts raced. There had to be a way to dissuade the beastly man.

Sorin cleared his throat, and Eleanor realized there *was* a way—and it was standing right in front of her. If Sorin wanted to use her knowledge to help him obtain a bride, then she would use him to rid herself of a nuisance.

Dredging up a smile she hoped looked genuine, she again addressed him. "I'm honored by your trust. But if you wish my assistance in this most delicate matter, then we must contrive a means by which we may be allowed to spend time together in privacy so that I may instruct you."

"That should prove easy enough."

"Oh? Why is that?" she said with a frown, forgetting for a moment that she was supposed to look happy for the sake of their audience.

"Charles has already enlisted my agreement to escort you this Season."

Two minutes ago, she would have been pleased to no end to hear such news. Now, however…"Does he think me incapable of behaving appropriately on my own?"

"Not at all," he said smoothly. "He meant no insult, I assure you. In fact, it is a mark of his confidence in you that he does not feel impelled to safeguard you himself."

"I don't see why I need to be 'safeguarded' at all," she muttered, not caring anymore if she sounded like a recalcitrant child.

"Because he does not wish you to be left alone and vulnerable while he is otherwise occupied."

"Occupied? What in heaven's name would…" She stopped. "Caroline." She knew it for a certainty, even before he confirmed it with a nod. "And you are the only person Charles trusts with me while he and Rowena keep close watch on her."

"Yes."

Which led to another question, one she almost dared not ask. "And what will people say when you and I are seen much about Town together?"

"That your cousin has saddled you with an old hound to keep the young pups at bay," he drawled. "I'll be exceedingly flattered should anyone assume differently."

If she had her way, that was exactly what they would do, right up until the moment he proposed to someone else. In the meantime, Yarborough would give up on her and find a new target for his ambitions. *It's perfect!* She hugged the thought to herself and kept it locked away where it wouldn't show on her face. "Well, given the fact that he's been badgering me to marry, I would have thought him happy to allow me a bit more leash."

"Oh, don't mistake his intentions. Your cousin wants you married—but he also wishes to make certain you marry the right sort of man."

"And he trusts you to make that determination, does he?"

"Like him, I have your best interests at heart. He knows this."

Heat rose in her cheeks again. "Perhaps he's right, at that. And after all, you *do* know my standards." It was a rash thing to say, and she knew it. But it couldn't be unsaid. She softened. "If any gentleman is able to pass muster with you as his judge, I say let him come forth and seek to win me."

His hazel eyes hardened. "If any man is able to pass muster with me as his judge, he will be a remarkable fellow indeed, for it will be most difficult for me to deem any man worthy of you." He blinked and the strange, almost savage look was gone before she could question it.

Charles could not have given her a more protective guardian. With any luck, Sorin's watchful presence at her side in London would stave off any serious pursuit. A faint call made her look back to the coaches, where Charles was waving to signal their impending departure.

Sorin, taking note, offered her his arm.

She groped for words to make small talk as they walked back together, but all pleasantries seemed to have vanished from her vocabulary. Neither did he deign to speak. The air between them seemed heavy with unspoken thoughts, and her conscience pricked her.

Am I doing the right thing?

"Your essentials have been transferred to Lady Wincanton's carriage," said her cousin as they approached.

"Thank you, Charles." Lady Yarborough, who looked as if she'd just swallowed something bitter, glared at her as she passed. Had she lacked better manners, Eleanor would have stuck her tongue out and asked her how *she* liked being excluded. Instead, she settled for sailing by with her head high. Lord willing, Sorin's mother would find her company pleasant enough that she wouldn't be required to ride with Lady Yarborough again. The thought was reinforced as they passed her son, who was complaining stridently about the dust ruining the shine on his boots.

"Now, if only it would contrive to rain," murmured Sorin for her ears only as he walked beside her.

"You would *prolong* our suffering?" she replied just as quietly, though they'd already passed out of earshot.

The grin he shot her was devilish. "I would claim a seat aboard my own conveyance, naturally. Owing to its smaller compartment and my mother's need for leg room—her joints ache terribly if she does not stretch every now and again—Charles and Yarborough would have to ride in the other."

"I see. What an unfortunate arrangement for Charles and Rowena," she mused with a little devilishness of her own.

"Indeed. But as they were the ones to extend the invitation, I feel they ought to bear the majority of the consequences, don't you?"

So droll and full of mischief was his manner that she couldn't help laughing. "Though I quite agree, you are wicked to actually say it." She glanced back to see Lady Yarborough shaking a chubby finger first at a footman and then at a piece of luggage—presumably hers—tied atop the coach. The woman was honking orders to have it brought down at once.

Charles stood by, watch in hand, looking rather put out. She turned back to Sorin with a grimace. "Instead of praying for rain, I think we ought to pray for a miracle—in the form of another coach for hire."

Though he laughed at her sharp jest, Sorin shot a quick, silent prayer heavenward. *Please let it rain!* His mother would be with them in the coach of course, but it would still be another opportunity to be close to Eleanor.

A month, he vowed. One month, and he would make her see him as more than a fusty bachelor. More than just an old friend.

He had not missed the black look on Yarborough's face. It was brash of the young whelp to direct such open malice at him, but such were the vagaries of youth. There was no love in the man's heart for Eleanor, of that much he was certain. His designs on her were driven purely by the potential for gain. She knew it, too, he suspected.

As they approached his carriage, he surreptitiously waved the waiting servant off so that he could hand her up himself. Before he could do so, however, Eleanor turned to him as if about to say something, but then appeared to change her mind. His eye was drawn to where the white pearls of her teeth clamped down on her rosy bottom lip.

Hoping to ease the tension, he whispered, "I'll check in on you and Mother from time to time to make certain you don't get gobbled up."

"Thank you," she replied in a small voice, looking down. "I'll do my best to be good company for her."

"You are always good company, Ellie," he said as he opened the carriage door. A shy smile was his reward. He returned it, extending his hand and enjoying their brief touch as he helped her step up on the sideboard. It was a wrench having to leave her, but it couldn't be helped.

His mother poked her head around and fixed him with a questioning look. "You did send ahead to the inn, yes? They expect us?"

"Charles said his man returned two days ago," he replied with a subtle nod, answering her unspoken inquiry as well. "Arrangements have been made at all overnight stops."

"Excellent. I shall require hot water to be brought to my room immediately upon arrival, and I shall want dinner sent up. I will be too exhausted for words by the time we reach the place." She shifted a little and winced, ruining the effect of her imperious demands. "When we reach London, I shall ask you to have an upholsterer refurbish the cushions in this carriage," she added. "The padding is inferior and needs replacing."

"I beg your pardon, Mother. I'll do so and order extra care with the stuffing. For now, I'll have some pillows and blankets brought down." Ignoring his mother's spluttering, half-hearted objections, he summoned a servant. From the corner of his eye, he saw the tiniest smile of approval curl the corner of Eleanor's mouth.

"Ladies, I leave you in good hands," he said as the servants began to bring the requested items. Now to ready himself for the next leg of the day's journey. From the look on Yarborough's face, it was likely to be an arduous affair. Resigned, he made his way back up front.

"Lady Eleanor is well, I hope?" asked Yarborough.

"Quite." He took grim satisfaction in the grimace of displeasure that furrowed the other man's brow. Without another word, he mounted and moved to the fore to join Charles.

"How are things?" his friend asked quietly.

"Perfectly adequate, save for a complaint concerning the

relationship between posterior and cushion."

"I meant between you and Eleanor."

Sorin stared at him, unsure how to respond.

Charles chuckled. "Come now, I'm not blind. I know the pair of you had a disagreement of some sort. And so does Yarborough, for that matter. I assume it was quickly resolved?"

"Oh, that. Yes. Merely a small misunderstanding."

"You two seem to be experiencing a number of those lately. I certainly hope it won't impede your ability to keep an eye on her in London."

"It won't. In fact, that was the subject of our discussion. I had to tell her."

"What? I thought we were agreed not to—"

"She objected, of course," Sorin cut in with a shrug. "But once she understood why you made such a request of me, she was amenable to the idea." He pinned Charles with a look. "She is very much aware of her friend's propensity for scandal and agreed that preventive measures must be taken."

"Well, thank God for that!" said Charles, relief spreading across his face. Then his eyes narrowed suddenly. "I hope this is not some ruse on her part, pretending cooperation now only to lead us a merry chase later. She is most displeased over our plans for her this Season."

"She'll be perfectly well behaved, I assure you." He hoped. "And I will ensure that the gentlemen seeking her company are mindful of their manners as well." He glanced back to see Yarborough coming toward them, his face as sour as vinegar. He must have gotten quite an earful from his mother. "Speaking of which, here comes our new friend."

At once, Charles whistled and waved his hand to signal the lead rider to move out before the lad could catch up to them.

Sorin didn't bother to stifle his amusement this time, either.

Chapter Eleven

Eleanor forced herself not to squirm as the Dowager Countess of Wincanton inspected her. Her gaze was not unkind, but it *was* penetrating. Just outside, she heard Sorin issuing commands concerning pillows and such. Desperate to escape the intense scrutiny of her new traveling companion, she peeked out from between the curtains.

It afforded her a rare opportunity to observe Sorin's profile for a moment unseen. Or so she thought. Turning, he caught her eye and smiled. At once she dropped the curtain and looked down at her lap, unwilling to expose her burning face to the carriage's other occupant. The door opened again, causing her to flinch, but it was only a servant bringing in blankets.

Once everything was in place and the servants gone, the carriage lurched into motion, forcing both ladies to steady themselves until the rocking settled into a more predictable rhythm.

"Thank you for inviting me to join you," Eleanor said at last, breaking the deepening silence. Her face once more cool, she risked raising it.

"You are most welcome," replied Lady Wincanton with a brief smile. "I can well imagine how uncomfortable you must have been. Four together in one carriage seems to me unbearably crowded."

"Yes. It was quite close," she said, trying to sound nonchalant.

"Even more uncomfortable when confined with an individual for whom one has little liking," added Lady Wincanton, a knowing twinkle in her eye.

Eleanor felt her cheeks again grow warm. Just how much had Sorin overheard? And how much of it had he told his mother? "No doubt," she finally replied, her voice coming out sounding choked.

The woman's smile returned, and this time it was warm and genuine. "I think we can agree that a journey may be either lengthened or shortened by the quality of one's traveling companions."

"Indeed we can," Eleanor replied, half laughing at herself. Ironically, it seemed she'd jumped from the boiling pot directly into the fire.

"Then let us shorten our journey, shall we?" said the older woman with relish. "I have not bothered to keep up with the news of the county for an age. Nothing has seemed worthy of my interest—until now. Tell me of young Sir Yarborough," she demanded. "Sorin says you knew each other as children. What think you of the lad and his mother?"

Again, Eleanor wondered just how much the woman already knew. "I, ah…"

The Dowager Countess chuckled. "I've put you on the spot now, but you needn't worry, my dear. For your sake, I shall for the moment forego polite speech and tell you that my own impression is not a flattering one. The woman is garish and coarse, and her son is no better than a puffed-up fool of a peacock." She sat back and pursed her lips. "There. Now you may proceed without concern for my delicate sensibilities."

A laugh borne purely of surprise escaped Eleanor and she clapped her hands over her mouth, horrified.

But Lady Wincanton merely smiled. "I can see I've shocked you. I should have perhaps waited a bit longer before so freely offering my opinion, but I cannot help thinking you share it."

"I would be lying if I said I did not," Eleanor admitted, surrendering. "He was a horrid little boy who has grown into an equally horrid man. As for his mother…" She relayed the conversation that had caused such an uproar. "I know I should have held my tongue, but the wrongness of it was such that I simply could not remain silent, not even for the sake of peace."

Lady Wincanton nodded. "I agree. To have done so would have led her to believe you were in agreement with her."

"And it would have encouraged her to continue in her attempts to sway my cousin to favor her son's suit," Eleanor added drily.

"Ah, now we come to it," said Lady Wincanton, her eyes robin-bright. "I *thought* there was an ulterior motive behind their wanting to join our party. Their coach could easily have been repaired in time for the journey. So your old enemy has decided to woo you, has he?"

"He thinks only of my purse—and perhaps a bit of revenge for my embarrassing him when we were young." She didn't elaborate further. Sorin might understand her reasons for having knocked the brute on his arse, but his mother might not. "It is my hope that in light of our recent disagreement, Lady Yarborough will now reconsider me as a daughter-in-law and persuade him to look elsewhere for a bride."

"And if she does not?"

Eleanor pressed her lips together briefly. "Then I shall

have little choice but to make my feelings on the matter unmistakably clear." And she would do so in a manner guaranteed to put off any further pursuit.

As though she'd heard the rebellious thought, Lady Wincanton nodded, her expression grim but approving. "You have no fear of making enemies, do you?"

It wasn't really a question, but Eleanor answered it anyway. "No. I don't," she said recklessly. And if she did, she wasn't about to show it.

"Sorin told me I'd like you even better now that you are grown. He was right."

Eleanor barely refrained from gaping in astonishment. *He told her he thinks me grown?* She had no time to ponder the revelation.

"But then, my son has always been a good judge of character," continued the old woman, seemingly oblivious to her companion's increasing shock. "Jane was a very nice girl, too, though I vow she was much milder in temperament. A timid soul, she was—almost passive. You, however, are anything but a silent observer. Where Jane took great pains to avoid confrontation, you, I think, would rather lead the charge."

Oh, dear...

Eleanor's heart paused in its rhythm as Lady Wincanton lifted her chin high. "I have decided that I like you and that we shall be friends, you and I. As such, you need not worry should the Yarboroughs attempt to discredit you. If they should be so foolish, know that they will find themselves fighting a battle on more than one front." Her gleaming eyes narrowed even as Eleanor's widened. "I may be old, but I'm anything but toothless. London is still *my* bailiwick, and those two vulgar upstarts would be wise not to cross me."

It was a continuing struggle to hide her surprise. Lady Wincanton was nothing like she remembered. But then, she'd only been a slip of a girl the last time they'd spoken at length—if a mere ten minute conversation could be considered as such. "Th-thank you, madam," Eleanor finally stammered. "Your confidence is most appreciated."

"As I said, I have decided that I like you. Now, I think it is time for some refreshment. Let us see what awaits us inside this hamper."

As Sorin's mother rummaged through the contents of the basket, Eleanor breathed a quiet sigh of relief. She had passed some sort of test, apparently. It felt good knowing she wasn't alone in her disapproval of the Yarboroughs. By contrast, Rowena had been unhappy with her outspokenness and would no doubt have a few choice words for her tonight. She'd do her best to smooth things over, but that wouldn't extend to making an apology to Lady Yarborough. She'd sooner cut out her own tongue than kowtow to that woman!

The two of them chatted over lemonade and an assortment of carefully packed delicacies, passing the time in as pleasant a manner as could be had whilst being jostled about in the confines of a carriage. Surprisingly, Eleanor discovered they had much in common. The more they talked, the more she genuinely liked Lady Wincanton. Even so, she was careful not to reveal too much of herself, and she especially avoided talking about her relationship with Sorin.

After a while, they fell into a companionable silence, and Lady Wincanton's head began to nod.

Now she had time to contemplate all that had been said. *He thinks of me as grown…* A thrill of gleeful triumph ran through her. That thought led to another, less innocent one. *If he's willing to alter his view of me from child to adult, might he be willing to alter it further?* She'd meant only to use Sorin's situation to help her dissuade Yarborough, but she had to consider the opportunity presented.

He wanted her help to find a wife. How could she help him unless she knew what sort of woman he sought? If she herself could manage to fit that description… *I might not have to leave Somerset after all.* Again, she wondered at the wisdom of even contemplating a union with him. They were good friends, but marriage? *Could it work?*

Far sooner than expected, a bright ray of amber light peeked through the swaying curtains, its angle telling her that the time had indeed passed swiftly. The coach slowed, and Eleanor looked out to see the small, bustling village of Hindon. Eventually, they rolled to a stop in the twilit courtyard of the Ellington Arms coaching inn.

As she disembarked from the carriage, she caught Caroline's eye. She looked positively miserable. Lady Yarborough took her son's arm and without a word to her traveling party, began walking.

"Did I not tell you? A fine place!" boomed Yarborough, gesturing about with his other hand as though he were the proud proprietor himself.

Sorin, who was supporting his mother, glanced back at her with a sardonic look.

Eleanor stifled a laugh and followed on.

A portly, balding man hurried forth, bowing and scraping, to ask which of their party Lord Wincanton was.

"I am he," said Sorin.

The man bowed deeply. "I received your message, my lord, and have prepared a private dining room for your party."

Yarborough's bewildered expression began to turn downright nasty.

"Thank you," said Sorin with a kind nod. "My mother, however, will wish to dine in her— " He paused as his mother patted his arm and shook her head. "Never mind, it appears we shall all be dining together."

At the innkeeper's bidding, they proceeded into a small room clearly set aside for guests of prominence. Eleanor hurried around the opposite side to sit between her cousin and Rowena, narrowly avoiding the hasty chair Yarborough pulled out as she passed. She pretended she had not noticed, leaving Caroline to claim it.

Unfortunately, her position put her directly across from Lady Yarborough, who fixed her with a baleful glare. Eleanor ignored her in favor of the bowl of steaming soup that was promptly placed before her. There was little talk during the first course as everyone was hungry and tired. But as the second course appeared and the wine began to flow, so did conversation. Keeping her head down over her plate, Eleanor refrained from making eye contact with anyone at the table. Perhaps if she finished her meal quickly, she might be excused before any more disasters could occur.

No such luck.

Lady Yarborough cleared her throat loudly, drawing everyone's gaze. "Lady Wincanton, young Miss Caroline here has informed me that you have an acquaintance residing in Golden Square."

Eleanor caught Caroline's pained expression just as Lady Wincanton paused in her repast to fix her inquisitor with a steely eye.

"So I do," the Dowager replied flatly.

Lady Yarborough waited, but Lady Wincanton offered nothing further. A tiny bit of red crept above the neckline of her gown. "How delightful," she said rather awkwardly. "For *we* now also reside in Golden Square." Again she waited. In vain. The red crept higher. "I wonder if perhaps you might introduce me," she pressed on. "After all, we'll be neighbors." It was said with a sickly smile that slowly faded as the Dowager Countess of Wincanton again lifted her head to regard the woman with chilly disdain.

Looking at them, Eleanor thought Sorin's mother looked like a fierce lioness regarding a plump housecat.

"Miss Caroline is right," said Lady Wincanton at last. "The lady in question happens to be my sister-in-law. Happily, she is away caring for her daughter who is expecting the arrival of my grandniece or nephew any day now. I do not expect her to return to London this Season, so I'm afraid there is no one to whom you may be introduced at this time. As for your other neighbors, I know them not. But I'm sure they will come to know *you* in due course."

Eleanor hid her smile by taking a bite of roast chicken and watched the scarlet of mortification creep the rest of the way up Lady Yarborough's neck to flood her face. It would have been perfectly delightful had the woman not immediately turned her narrowed, spiteful gaze upon her. Eleanor hadn't mentioned anything to Lady Wincanton about her desire to be introduced to anyone, but damned if Lady Yarborough would ever believe it. There was nothing she could possibly do or say to mitigate the unbridled hatred shining from the woman's eyes.

"Ah! Rowena," continued Lady Wincanton as though oblivious to the rising tension in the room. "I want to ask you if Eleanor might come and join me Tuesday afternoons for tea with some of my friends and their daughters while she is in London. You are, of course, aware that I quite enjoy her company, and as I have no daughters of my own…"

Rowena glanced at her in open surprise before answering in a rather startled voice, "Oh, of—of course she may. I'm delighted that you've had such a pleasant time together."

"Excellent," said the older woman. "Then it is settled. Now, I do hope you will all forgive me, but I believe I shall go to my room now. I'm quite exhausted. Far too much so to even consider the temptation of dessert. Sorin, if you don't mind."

At once he rose and offered her his arm. Just as they made the turn, Lady Wincanton looked back at Eleanor and winked.

For the second time that day, Eleanor wanted to kiss a Wincanton. She'd just been placed under the aegis of one of London's most respected matrons.

Before anyone else could speak, Lady Yarborough, who was now a rather interesting shade of violet, rose also. Rage radiated from her like the spines on a hedgehog. "I'm quite fatigued as well," she bit out. "Donald, you will escort me to my room. Now."

Eleanor almost pitied him as he reluctantly left his half-eaten dinner to do her bidding. Almost. She watched as, without so much as a fare-thee-well, Lady Yarborough grabbed her son's arm and stalked out of the room.

Rowena turned to her with a baffled countenance. "What in heaven's name have you done to Lady Wincanton?"

"I—I've done nothing," she answered truthfully.

"Well, she certainly has taken a liking to you," said Charles.

"Unlike Lady Yarborough," said Rowena, her tone dour. "Eleanor, I must ask you to at least attempt to make amends with the woman. I *know* she's horrid," she added more quietly. "But we are forced to travel with her for the next several days, and I'm not entirely certain I shall be able to reestablish good relations without your help."

She felt her pulse quicken with outrage. "I will not retract a single word," she vowed.

"Eleanor, please!" hissed Rowena. "It's not that I disagree with you—I fully share your opinion on the matter of contention—but she complained about you for a solid hour after you left! I worry for your reputation should she reach London in such a state. Even *if* Lady Wincanton has decided to take you under her wing, Lady Yarborough could still inflict a lot of damage. And not just to you," she added, shooting a nervous glance toward Caroline.

Despite her growing fury, the sight of Caroline's desperate face moved her. "Very well. I dislike being held hostage in this manner, but for Caroline's sake I'll make the effort." The visible relief on Rowena's face at the concession grated on her nerves. "However, do not expect me to apologize to her for what I said—or to accept her son's suit. He is a brute and a liar, and I will have no part of him."

"Of course not," said Charles without hesitation. "I don't know what passed between you and his mother, though I expect to be fully informed forthwith," he added, looking pointedly at his wife, "but after spending a full day in his company, I can honestly say I have no desire to see the Yarboroughs become part of our family."

Unexpectedly, Rowena nodded agreement. "I am of like mind. Should he press for your hand, his suit will not be considered." She paused, seeming to wrestle with herself for a moment. "Eleanor, I would not ask you to humble yourself if I thought there was any other way. I did try, but Lady Yarborough will only accept your contrition."

"That will be most difficult, as I have none," Eleanor snapped. That she should bend knee, albeit metaphorically, to such a woman was both ridiculous and insulting. But she would do it for Caroline. "However, I'll do my best to at least appear remorseful."

"Thank you."

"Don't thank me yet," Eleanor warned. "She's furious with me and from the look she gave me just now that's not likely to change over a few words."

"Nevertheless, I do appreciate your willingness to try." Rowena looked at her with such concern that it made her heart turn. "Do be careful, dear. Neither of them is of significant rank, but their newfound wealth may broaden their sphere of influence. And duke's daughter or not, you are as vulnerable as any when it comes to gossip. There is only so much we can do to protect you."

"I understand," Eleanor replied. She stood just as servants entered bearing dessert. "If you will excuse me, my appetite is quite gone. I think I shall go to bed now."

Charles rose, too, waving off the attendants and their sweets. "And I, as well. You and Caroline are sharing the room next to ours. We will escort you upstairs."

Eleanor followed them in silence, wishing with all her might that they were back at home where she could retreat in privacy. Then she remembered that Holbrook wasn't really "home" anymore.

"I shall call for hot water to be brought up to you," said Rowena as they unlocked the door.

"Thank you," said both Eleanor and Caroline at the same time.

Charles poked his head in and glanced around the room. "Not that I expect any trouble, but you have only to knock on the wall or call out if we are needed," he said quietly. "Wincanton is just on the other side of you, as well."

So close… Eleanor's spine tingled, and she wondered at it. Was it her conscience pricking her again, or was it something else? She had no time to decide either way.

"Where are Sir Yarborough and his mother staying?" whispered Caroline, speaking for the first time in more than half an hour.

"Across the hall," answered Charles, jerking his chin in that general direction. "So watch how loudly you converse."

"Good night, Ellie, Caroline," said Rowena. "Lock the door behind us."

Immediately after doing so, Eleanor went to the narrow

bed against the far wall and sat, claiming it. On the other side of this wall, there might be another bed just like this one. And in it, Sorin might be resting even now, his head on a pillow, just inches away. The thought was both comforting and disturbing.

"I'm so sorry, Eleanor," said Caroline, coming to sit beside her.

"It was not your fault," Eleanor answered, wishing she would just be quiet and let it go. "It was mine. I ventured my opinion without thinking of the impact it might have on others. I should have had better self-discipline than to allow her to get under my skin."

"If it is any consolation, I agree with everything you said to her," said Caroline. "And—and I can definitely see now that Sir Yarborough is not someone I would ever want as a suitor. You were right about him." She made a face. "But even if he were not a complete ass, I certainly would not want *her* for my mother-in-law. I'll do my best to distance myself from him during the remainder of our journey."

Though glad to hear it, Eleanor knew it wouldn't be that simple. "You've accepted an invitation to tea, remember? You cannot renege without a valid excuse, of course, but I would advise that you break ties with them soon afterward, lest everyone assume you are being considered for a match."

Caroline frowned. "You were just invited to tea by Lady Wincanton. Does that not put you in the same position?"

Eleanor blinked in surprise and then forced out a little laugh. "Our situations are entirely different. I've known Lord and Lady Wincanton practically all my life, while you've only just met the Yarboroughs. Everyone knows Sorin is a sort of older brother to me—perhaps even an uncle, given the difference in our ages. No one will think anything of it."

Inwardly, she squirmed. 'Uncle' was a bit of a stretch, but it was too late now. She was determined to use such assumptions to her advantage, but she would have to be careful. Her best hope now lay in Lady Wincanton, who had referred to her in very motherly terms tonight. She would foster that rapport—in private and in public. Not only would it fend off the Yarboroughs, but it *might* help Sorin see her potential as a wife.

Again, she quailed at the thought of what might happen if she succeeded in changing his view of her. *Is that something I truly want?* She tried to sort out the muddle of thoughts and feelings provoked by the idea, concentrating on the positives. *He* is *handsome. And intelligent. And kind to a fault. He's a good man—one of the finest I know. And despite his sometimes starchy demeanor, he has a rare sense of humor. We've always gotten on quite well. Altogether, it would be an excellent—*

"I have little reason to believe either Lady Yarborough or her son has any genuine interest in me, anyway," said Caroline, her face settling into an expression of grim resignation. In truth, I really think they've only been nice to me in order to get to you." She sighed. "I did not anticipate needing to be concerned with such ruses until after we reached London."

"Caroline, there *will* be gentlemen interested in you for more than just your fortune and connections. You must believe that."

"Oh, I do," said Caroline, her chin rising. "But Sir Yarborough is not among them. He would not have looked at me twice were I not your friend."

"How can you be certain?" she asked kindly, though she knew it was the truth.

"Papa once told me *no* man sells his land unless he has no other alternative," explained Caroline, her tone matter-of-fact. "And he's done exactly that." Her eyes narrowed. "The Yarboroughs are awfully anxious to give the impression of wealth, but I'd be willing to wager that once the money he received for that land runs out he'll be a pauper—unless he marries well. I am certainly no heiress. It would not surprise me at all if Lady Yarborough withdraws her support of me the moment she realizes you're a lost cause." She tossed her curls. "It'll be a relief."

Eleanor looked at her with new respect. "I did not think you would see it—about the money, I mean."

"Neither did Lady Yarborough," replied Caroline archly. "I hope she won't brag about her son's exploits to any other prospective brides. Or maybe I do. It would serve them both right if her flapping jaws ruined his chances of bagging an heiress."

"Little chance of that," Eleanor sighed. "Unfortunately, there will be plenty of naive young debutantes just waiting to be taken advantage of by people like the Yarboroughs. Let us just be glad we are not among them."

Later that night, when the candles had been extinguished and Caroline was fast asleep, Eleanor lay awake, staring at the faint light shining from the gap beneath their door. She'd heard no evidence of anyone occupying the adjacent room since the inn had quieted. Even so, she swore she could feel Sorin's presence emanating from the other side of the wall.

Closing her eyes, she tried to put it out of her mind. But thoughts of him would not desist. Eventually, fatigue claimed her and she slipped into the realm of dreams.

Sorin lay still as death. Eleanor was so close. He could hear everything on the other side of the wall, from her gentle laughter as she talked with her friend to the splash of water as she bathed. The thought of her bathing sent a flash of heat through his body, tightening his loins. He thanked the Lord they'd left for London a week before most other families *and* that he'd had the forethought to make clear in his advance letters that he wanted a room of his own. After the day he'd spent listening to Yarborough, it would have been absolutely unbearable to have to share a room with him.

When all was quiet and he could hear nothing more, he turned onto his side and stared at the dim line of light under the door. His mother had certainly put Lady Yarborough in her place tonight. Even so, there would likely be trouble for Eleanor from that source later on. Mother's sponsorship would help stave off any attacks on her character, but she wouldn't always be there to act as a buffer.

I, on the other hand, will. It was a promise he intended to keep.

Rolling over again, he faced the darkness and closed his eyes, trying to find sleep. Despite being weary from the day's long ride, a great restlessness had taken him the instant he'd lain down. His thoughts refused to settle. He longed to be with Eleanor somewhere quiet where he could work on her unimpeded. London was just too full of distraction and turmoil.

If only I'd come home sooner…

Opening his eyes, Sorin was startled to find his valet standing over him with a lit candle. Groggily, he rose and went to the window. Opening the shutters, he saw faint streaks of predawn light on the eastern horizon, and cursed beneath his breath. It certainly didn't *feel* like he'd slept. Dressing with all speed, he went downstairs and joined the others at table. Two members of their party were conspicuously absent.

"Where is Lady Yarborough?" he asked Charles, taking the seat beside him.

"Like your mother, she's taking the morning meal in her room," his friend muttered around a forkful of ham. "*Un*like your mother, her choice to do so is doubtless a form of protest over last night's defeat," he added with a chuckle.

"She'll be down soon enough. Or she'll get left behind," Sorin replied, taking a sip of what the serving woman had alleged was tea. He cast a covert glance down the table. Yarborough had sat himself opposite Caroline at the other end of the table and was already filling the air with boastful chatter. Eleanor, who'd made a place for herself in the middle of the long trestle away from everyone, appeared quite content eating her breakfast alone and in peace.

She looked up from her plate and smiled at him warmly. He smiled back and lifted his cup in silent salute. The serving woman chose that moment to come back and load his plate, coming between them. By the time she moved out of the way, Eleanor had finished her repast and was rising. Rowena, who'd also finished, came over to her and together the ladies excused themselves.

Sorin bolted his food as quickly as possible and got up, leaving behind a rather startled Charles. He was just entering the common room when he noticed Lady Yarborough coming down the stairs. Not wishing to start the morning off with an unpleasant encounter, he hung back and waited, hoping she would go the other way. To his disappointment, however, she made a beeline to where Eleanor and Rowena now sat with their backs to the room, warming themselves by the fire.

Alongside his mother.

He scowled in surprise. What was she doing downstairs this early? She never emerged from her chamber until just before it was time to depart. Curiosity drove him to follow Lady Yarborough at a distance and quietly take a nearby wingback chair that faced away from them.

"Good morning Lady Ashford, Lady Wincanton," he heard Lady Yarborough say. There was a heavy pause, and then,

"Good morning, Lady Eleanor. I do hope everyone rested well."

"Quite," answered his mother. "One expects the bedding in such establishments to be disagreeable at best; however, I found mine surprisingly tolerable."

"I'm glad to hear it," replied Lady Yarborough. "I will relay your compliment to my son, who suggested this establishment. He expects the best, you know. As do I. I have no forbearance for things that are not of the very highest quality."

Silence.

"Lady Yarborough, might I have a word with you in private?" he heard Eleanor ask after a moment.

"My dear child," said Lady Yarborough in an oily manner that made his skin crawl with distaste, "whatever you have to say to me may surely be said before your family and friends."

After a moment's hesitation Eleanor again spoke, her voice sounding a bit strangled, "Yes, of course. Lady Yarborough, I wish to express my…regret over the unfortunate misunderstanding between us yesterday."

"Misunderstanding?" The flatly spoken word was laden with displeasure.

"Yes," answered Eleanor. "I've had time to think about what transpired. You were correct in that I have never been so unfortunate as to be faced with a decision like that which was forced upon your son. Though I would like to think I would have chosen differently, I cannot be absolutely certain I would have done so had I been in his place. As such, I ask that you forgive my having spoken in haste. I'm afraid I let my passion carry me beyond the bounds of polite manners."

Tucked away in his chair, Sorin covered his mouth to hide a broad grin. *Clever girl!* She hadn't at all apologized for what she'd said, but rather the manner of its delivery.

"Why, of *course* I forgive you," replied Lady Yarborough

in a saccharine tone. "I know you meant no disrespect. Your words were borne of a tender heart—a most commendable attribute in a young lady." A heavy sigh. "Would that my own circumstances had allowed me to remain so sheltered and idealistic. But alas, my naïveté was extinguished long before its time."

Sorin's mother cleared her throat loudly. "In my opinion, it is a mark of her exemplary upbringing that she has retained such charming ingenuousness, especially when one considers the degradation of society these days. Would you not agree, Lady Yarborough?"

Sorin muffled a laugh.

"Er, yes. Quite so," said Lady Yarborough after a moment.

"Then, as we all seem to be in happy agreement, may I assume the aforementioned 'misunderstanding' has been resolved?" continued his mother.

"Of course," said Lady Yarborough in a strained voice. "Yes, of course it has. It was really nothing to begin with."

"Excellent!" his mother interrupted, though the other woman was clearly not finished. "Then I shall go and find my son so that we may depart."

Grimacing, Sorin sank a little deeper into his seat and hoped to escape notice.

"Eavesdropping, are we? Shame on you."

The quiet voice at his ear made him jump, and Sorin bit back a curse. "Damn it all, Charles!" he hissed. "Don't sneak up on a body so!"

"Judging by the stiffness of Lady Yarborough's spine, it must have been well worth hearing," whispered his friend, who was smiling from ear to ear. "Come, their backs are turned. Stand, and we'll act as though you've just come in with me."

Too grateful to turn down the offer, Sorin did as he was told.

"You must tell me everything when we have a private moment," murmured Charles. "Not that I'm avid for gossip, but for once I'd like to know what my wife does before she tells me only the bits she deems important."

"It'll be my pleasure," Sorin answered, doing his best to appear nonchalant as his mother approached them.

"Lord Ashford," she said with a brisk nod of greeting. "How perfect your timing is. Might I borrow my son for a moment?"

"Of course, madam."

Sorin mouthed the word "traitor" at him as he turned, earning in response a wicked and completely unrepentant grin. Before his mother could speak, however, a nearby disturbance drew their attention.

"What do you mean I owe you a crown?" growled Yarborough angrily, his demeanor menacing as he addressed the owner of the establishment. "I thought we had an understanding."

Very politely, but also very firmly, the innkeeper clarified. "My lord, you and your lady mother had the use of two of my best rooms last night. The cost of meals was included in the price, which is half a crown apiece. The others in your party have already settled their accounts."

Yarborough's face and neck grew mottled. "I bring you business of the highest order—a duke *and* a bloody earl—and this is how you repay my kindness? I could have advised them to go by way of Chilmark rather than stopping here!"

"And your recommendation is greatly appreciated, my lord. But at no time did I ever agree to let my rooms free of charge." Arms folded, the innkeeper stood before him, waiting.

"Gentlemen, is there a problem?" Sorin asked, stepping in.

Yarborough, who looked ready to murder, blinked in surprise at his intrusion. "Not at all. Just taking care of a bit of private business. I'll be along in a moment."

"*After* rendering payment in full," said the innkeeper quickly, holding out his hand toward Yarborough. "Which I'll be having now, my lord, if you please."

An impatient sigh burst from Yarborough. "You are inconveniencing not only me, but the other members of my party with this boorish persistence!" he hissed to the innkeeper. "We'll discuss it when I return from London."

"Take your time, please," Sorin interjected loudly. "I'm in no hurry to remount. In fact, I'll wait with you while you settle your bill."

Jaw clenched, Yarborough snatched his purse from his belt and began to count out coins into the happy proprietor's hand. When he'd slapped the last one into the waiting palm, the innkeeper smiled broadly and bid him good day and safe journey. He did not, notably, encourage Yarborough to come back on his return trip, as he had Sorin earlier that morning.

Clearly, Yarborough had not expected to have to pay for lodgings. Either he was a stingy blackguard bent on getting something for nothing or he had money trouble. Neither was good, but if parting with a mere crown was painful…

The extravagant clothing, the new London address, cozying up to the Ashfords—suddenly, it all made sense. "When in doubt, brazen it out," the old saying went. He'd be willing to bet a thousand pounds that the Yarboroughs had spent every penny on this trip in an effort to fool and catch a rich heiress.

And that rich heiress was undoubtedly Eleanor.

Chapter Twelve

With great anticipation, Eleanor watched London's busy streets pass by her window. The leaden sky and drizzle bothered her not at all, though she wished the inclement weather had come a bit sooner so that Sorin might have ridden with her. It had begun just as they'd crossed into the outskirts of Town, and he'd elected to remain mounted rather than bring the damp into the carriage with him.

Despite having enjoyed the comforts of Lady Wincanton's carriage and companionship, both of which were far superior to the alternative, it had been a long and wearying road. Every night Caroline had bemoaned at length her having to endure Lady Yarborough's constant poking and prying into her personal business, and every night Eleanor had felt terrible for not being able to share her own good fortune. It wasn't her carriage to offer, and it would have been inappropriate to ask her hostess to further alter arrangements.

Still, she was here. The Season had never before held much charm or significance for her, but now it was everything. It was an opportunity. If Sorin, who was now officially on the market, could somehow be made to see her as the best possible match…

This time, the prospect of marrying Sorin inspired neither panic nor guilt, but rather excitement.

If I must wed, then why not *marry someone I already know? Someone I'm quite fond of and who lives close to Holbrook?* It made perfect sense, really. Holly Hall was but a stone's throw from home. And Charles would doubtless be more than pleased to have his dearest friend become part of the family.

The more she thought about it, the more convinced she became that it was the wisest course of action. *Who better to marry my friend than me?* True, he'd been stern and disapproving in the past, but things might be different now that he saw her as a woman grown and not a schoolgirl needing constant correction. In the course of one conversation, a whole new world of possibility had opened up. *Now to see if it is indeed possible…*

"I can see you're just as pleased as I to have arrived," said Lady Wincanton with a smile that transformed at once into a frown as one of their wheels hit a bump, jostling them. "Merciful God. My posterior will certainly be glad of a change in attitude."

"Mine, too," Eleanor agreed with a rueful laugh. She felt completely at ease with Sorin's mother now. Rather than being cool or aloof as she'd once thought her, Lady Wincanton was warm and kind. The lady had also proven to possess not only a sharp wit, but a far more playful sense of humor than she'd thought possible. Sorin was very much like her. "I confess I will be delighted to see the outside of this carriage," she admitted. "I long for a proper hot bath."

"That shall be my first order of business as well," agreed Lady Wincanton. "Along with a glass of mulled wine."

They fell into amiable silence as the coach wended its slow way through London's sodden streets to St. James Square, where they both made their London homes. Eleanor felt like cheering when they at last came to a full stop. She smiled at Lady Wincanton. "Thank you again, madam, for so generously sharing your carriage with me."

"The pleasure was all mine, my dear. I shall look forward to seeing you again on Tuesday."

The door opened then and Eleanor disembarked, glad for the large umbrella the footman held over her head. The other carriage had already stopped ahead of them. Issuing from within its confines were the shrill complaints of Lady Yarborough concerning the weather. She grinned as Caroline all but leaped from the conveyance in her hurry to get away. Even Rowena, who was normally so calm and patient, looked harried as she quickly followed suit.

Her view was blocked then as Sorin rode up between them, the water dripping from the brim of his hat as he looked down at her with a warm smile. "I shall make an appointment at Rundell & Bridge's and send a message to let you know when it has been set."

"I look forward to it," she replied, marking the avid gleam in the eye of the footman awaiting her leisure. *That* juicy bit would no doubt be halfway across London within the hour. *So much the better!*

With a polite tip of his sodden hat, Sorin hailed the driver of the carriage bearing his mother and moved to ride ahead of it.

Eleanor watched him for a moment. Now that she was really looking at him, she noticed what a truly fine figure he cut even in the rain.

Sorin. The only one who had understood her grief and had treated it with respect because he'd suffered a similar loss himself. The only person who'd let her cry and never told her not to be sad or to keep a stiff upper lip. Sorin, her friend and guide, ever sensible, always wise. The more she thought about it, the more the idea of a union appealed.

He's not so stern and uncompromising, really. I think I could *be happy as his wife.*

Only when he'd faded into the gray curtain of rain did she turn away. She shivered, marking the chill that had crept in to grip her fingers and toes. The warmth of a fire would be most welcome indeed.

Before she could set foot on the first step, however, someone else called out her name. Cringing, she stopped. *Damn.* Of course Yarborough would want to say a parting word. Likely several. Assuredly too many. Pasting a cool smile on her lips, she turned.

What a sorry sight he was with the water dripping off his new—and no doubt ruined—hat. He'd wanted to dismount and ride in the carriage when the rain had started, she remembered, but when Sorin and Charles had themselves declined the option, he'd changed his mind. Unlike the other men, who'd seemed almost to enjoy the rain, he looked utterly miserable.

"Sir Yarborough, I do hope you won't think me rude for my haste, but…" She gestured at the increasingly heavy downpour.

"Not at all, Eleanor," said he, his smile strained. "I don't wish to detain you long, only a moment to bid you a warm welcome home and to say that your delightful company has been the highlight of my journey. I hope to see you again very soon."

She only just managed to keep her mouth from dropping open. Not only was his familiarity of address impertinent, but he'd hardly spoken two words to her since her confrontation with his mother! Then she marked that his gaze rested not on *her*, but rather on the footman standing *beside* her. So, he planned to use the servants' grapevine as well, did he? Indignation heated her blood, driving off the cold.

"Why thank you, Sir Yarborough," she said, deliberately using formal address. Damned if she'd be quoted as having used his Christian name! "And know that you also have my thanks for your kindness to Caroline. I fear she would have been desolate when Lady Wincanton stole me back in Hindon were it not for your constant attentiveness and gallantry toward her. And do also please relay my heartfelt thanks to your dear mama for inviting her to tea. I'm sure it also lightened her spirits considerably."

His smile slipped a little. "Yes, of course."

At that moment, it began to rain in earnest. Blessing the weather, she dipped the tiniest curtsy, so as not to soak her hem. "You'd best go before you catch your death," she said loudly over the splatting of raindrops. "Caroline will scold me most fiercely for keeping you out in this. I'm sure we'll meet again in passing sometime soon! Good-bye, Sir Yarborough!"

Without giving him a chance to respond, she turned and hurried up the steps, forcing the footman to follow with the umbrella. She chuckled to herself as they left the despicable Donald Yarborough behind in the deluge. Up, up she went, not once glancing back. The footman sheltering her could take *that* conversation to the other side of London, too!

"Good Lord, Ellie!" exclaimed Rowena, who was waiting for her in the foyer. "Your boots are likely wet through. What in heaven's name were you doing lingering out there?"

"Saying good-bye to Sir Yarborough."

Rowena's brow shot up at her sour tone. "Go and get out of those wet things at once," she ordered softly. "And then you can tell me everything over a hot pot of tea."

It felt so good to be warm and dry that it was hard to imagine venturing out again into the chill air, but Sorin was determined not to delay. There were preparations to make that he hadn't been able to see to while in Somerset, and there were certain people he needed to speak with as well.

Happy was the chance that had made him look back at Eleanor. Had he not, he wouldn't have seen Yarborough still sniffing about. Considering the conflict between Eleanor and Lady Yarborough, he'd thought that perhaps the fellow had decided to leave off pursuit. Not so, apparently.

It wasn't that the blackguard represented any sort of romantic threat—Eleanor could hardly stand the fellow—but rather the trouble he might stir up that worried Sorin. Yarborough was up to something, and whatever it was it couldn't be good for Eleanor.

Rising, he called for his valet to bring his other boots and ready the light carriage. Rain or not, some things simply couldn't wait. He needed answers, and he needed them quickly. His mother came in just as he was preparing to leave.

"I take it you're going to see Stafford?"

"As a matter of fact I am," he said, frowning. "Lord, woman. Were you not my own mother, I'd swear you were a Gypsy fortune-teller. One day, I'll have to figure out how you do that."

A thin smile was her only acknowledgement of the compliment. "It was merely a logical assumption on my part. You're suspicious of Yarborough. Stafford possesses the means to confirm those suspicions or lay them to rest. You being the decisive person that you are, I would not have expected you to wait a moment longer than necessary to seek out his services."

"I could just be going out for an evening's entertainment, you know."

"On your first night in London after a six-day journey and in this biblical downpour?" she scoffed. "And with *that* look on your face? You look like you're either going to attend a funeral or planning to cause one."

"Stafford should hire you," Sorin grumbled good-naturedly. "I think I'll just tell him to come 'round with some of his cold cases and let you have a peek. You'd probably solve the lot of them over tea."

"What nonsense," she replied, but her expression was smug. "I myself began to seriously wonder about Yarborough when you told me of his reluctance to pay his bill that first night. And then there was that whole 'Irish land sale' business Eleanor told me about. He brags and makes a show of prosperity, but begrudges an innkeeper a measly crown. Something is not right."

It was uncanny how similar they were in nature. "I know it. But John will ferret out the truth," he assured her, pulling on his gloves.

"And what will you tell her?"

"Eleanor?" he asked. "Hardly necessary to let her in on it, I should think. I might tell Charles, though. Just so he can keep an eye on her when I'm not around."

Her mouth thinned. "Yes, well tell him to be sure that Rowena goes with Eleanor's little redheaded friend whenever she visits them so as to prevent her becoming a source of information. I would not put it past that pair to attempt extortion." Moving to the chair he'd vacated, she sat with an indelicate grunt and stretched her feet out before the fire.

The trip had taken a heavy toll on her joints, Sorin knew. He was thankful they'd arrived before this cold snap had fully settled in. He'd stop by the apothecary along the way and bring back something to ease her discomfort. "Rowena will want to throttle me if she finds out I'm interfering, you know."

"If it prevents a disaster, I'm sure she won't mind. If you're going, you had better do so now before it grows too late in the day," she said, waving him off and closing her eyes. "Wait," she said suddenly, opening them again.

"Yes?"

"On your way out, have Jacobson bring up some of that cognac I know he's hidden away, will you? Quietly."

He fought back a grin. "Of course, Mother." The liquor was probably far better than any apothecary's tonic. As a rule, ladies weren't supposed to drink hard liquor, but when her joints pained her his mother was apt to bend the rules a bit. At least she would sleep peacefully and pain-free tonight. With a short bow, he departed.

"Take me to Bow Street, George," he told the driver, a man who'd been in his family's employ since early boyhood. A man he could trust to keep quiet. Boarding the carriage, he sat back and rapped twice on the roof, signaling his readiness to depart. He could have sent for John to come and see him tomorrow, but he didn't want the household servants getting wind of such a visit. There were no secrets in London—or at least they were damnably hard to keep. Better that everyone think him off to Covent Garden for a bit of fun.

The streets weren't very congested. A good portion of London's population preferred to remain indoors when it rained like this, but even so it took him a bit longer to get to Bow Street than he'd have liked. It didn't matter. John's door was always open, whether at the office or at home.

An hour later, the two of them were talking over a pint at the Dove and Duck. John had agreed to put eyes on Yarborough, and they'd moved on to more pleasant matters.

"So you're on the market this year," said John, lifting his

glass. “Good. About time you put on the shackles. My sister would want you to be happy.”

Sorin knew the time for mourning Jane was long past, but the mention of her name still elicited a pang of sadness. Her death had extinguished the light in his world for so long—but not anymore. His spirits rose at the thought of Eleanor. “I’ve not been completely unhappy. I’ve travelled the world and come home a far richer man than when I left, and I have a great many friends.”

“It’s not the same as having a family.” John’s knowing eyes watched him over the rim of his glass as he took another swallow. “Believe me, I know. I waited far too long to do it, myself. Should have done it ten years ago rather than waiting until this old pate started showing through,” he said with a laugh as he reached up to pat his thinning hair. “Still, my Winnie never seems to mind, bless her. She says I’m still of some use.”

“Well, I’m determined to marry before I’m too old to be of use to anyone,” Sorin said, taking a long drink.

“I’m glad,” said John, his solemnity returning. “You know, I thought I’d have a harder time adjusting to married life after all I’ve seen. But the truth is that it’s good to be able to come home and leave all of it behind. When I’m with Winifred and the children, the darkness just can’t take hold of me.”

His candor took Sorin completely by surprise. He’d been friends with Jane’s brother since the day they’d met, and in all that time John had never once mentioned experiencing any discomfort related to his work. Sorin had never understood how the man managed to sleep after witnessing firsthand the nightly tragedies that played out on London’s streets. How could any man have any peace after being exposed to such constant danger, corruption, and death? “Do you not worry for their safety? Does that concern not divide you at all?”

He'd wanted to ask it for years.

John nodded slowly, considering. "At first I thought marrying *would* weaken me, make me more vulnerable. I fully expected to have to resign. But the truth is that with Winnie I'm stronger. Knowing I've got her and the children waiting for me at home gives me something to look forward to. Something to think about that's not so awful as what I have to sometimes deal with. As far as their safety is concerned, I'm well-equipped to ensure nothing happens to them. Benefit of being the Director," he said, baring his teeth in a knowing grin. "They're better looked after than the bloody king."

His words again awakened in Sorin the fierce need to protect Eleanor. For a moment, he considered asking his old friend to set a Runner to watch over her, but that would probably be going a step too far at this juncture. First, he needed to know if there was even a legitimate threat. "Marriage has changed you. In a good way, of course," he added quickly.

"I think you'll find marriage will change you, too. In a good way, of course," John shot back with a wink. "Provided you find the right woman, that is." He sat back, looking smug. "Which, unless I'm mistaken—and I'm usually not—you've already done. A man doesn't have a fellow watched for no reason. Who is she?"

Bloody hell. He should have known better than to think he'd be able to get away with it. "Lady Eleanor Cramley, daughter of the late Duke of Ashford and cousin to the current duke."

John's brows knit. "The girl you mentioned in your letters?"

"The same," he admitted, feeling his neck growing hot.

A slow smile spread across his friend's face. "I was wondering when you'd realize it. Don't look so shocked," he said softly. "Your letters have been full of her for ages. I kept expecting to hear that you'd proposed to her, but you never did, and I could not understand why when you're so obviously well suited."

"She was—*is*—a good deal younger than me, John," Sorin explained uncomfortably. "I was away at Eton when she was born, but I've known her since she was in pinafores. I practically helped Charles and Rowena raise her. I'm sure you can see the complications, both with her and with her family."

The other man brushed the excuses aside with a wave. "None of that will matter if you truly love each other. She's grown now, after all." He peered at Sorin, his eyes glinting in the firelight. "She doesn't know how you feel, does she?"

"No." At least he didn't believe so. "And before you say anything, I cannot just *tell* her without risking a great deal of upheaval. I must be sure of her feelings first."

John looked thoughtful for a long moment. "You know, I think this Eleanor of yours was the saving of you. After Jane's death, you needed something to concentrate on other than your grief, someone to look after. Your Eleanor filled the hole Jane left behind."

Sorin's heart clenched. "I suppose she did, in a way. You know, after a few years I tried looking for someone else, someone like your sister. But Jane was one of a kind." He laughed to himself. "As is Eleanor. To find myself attracted to her was confounding, to say the least. She and Jane are so different in temperament that I never would have thought…"

John's smile was gentle and a little sad. "Maybe that's no bad thing. I would not dwell too hard upon it. Just accept the fact that she's what you need now, and don't let her slip away."

He didn't intend to. "I'm planning to remain close to her throughout the Season. I'll know which direction to take soon enough." He hoped.

"There is only one direction that will lead to happiness for you. Don't be foolish enough to take any other. Tell her."

"I will, when the time is right." If indeed that time ever came.

"Love makes fools of us all." John shook his head and took another swallow.

He could only laugh in rueful agreement as the barkeep refilled their glasses.

"You won't ask me, proud ass that you are," said John, taking out his pipe and knocking out the dottle. "But I'll do it anyway because it'll give you peace. I'll have a man posted to watch her house. If your fellow so much as twitches his nose at her, we'll know about it. And if he's into anything that a gentleman ought not to be into, I'll have it."

"John, I don't know how to thank you," Sorin replied, both grateful and relieved.

The other man paused in the process of refilling his pipe and winked at him. "You'll be thanking me aplenty when the bill hits your purse."

"I meant personally. You're a good man, John. And a damned good friend."

"That's the only kind to have," said his friend with aplomb. He laughed. "I'd never have thought love would bring you to my door again. But I'm glad it did. Here's to love and to the saving of us poor fools who fall into it."

As they again lifted their glasses, Sorin thought to himself that John was right, more right than he knew. From the moment he'd met her, Eleanor had been, and continued to be, the saving of him.

Chapter Thirteen

Eleanor luxuriated in layers of muslin so fine they were nearly transparent, the outermost sprigged with delicately embroidered violets. If one couldn't wear silk, then this was surely the next best thing. An exquisite gold chain bearing a single pearl set in a circle of amethysts graced her throat, and tiny matching earrings dangled from her lobes. Her hair was braided in a high coronet with a few artful curls left loose here and there. It was a shame to cover such a masterpiece, but she couldn't run around London with a bare head. Carefully, so as not to disturb the arrangement too much, she put on her bonnet and arranged the bow charmingly off-center beneath her left jaw.

Tucking a small posy of freshly picked violets into the pale green sash tied beneath her breasts, she spun before the mirror, watching the diaphanous material bell out ever so slightly. When the weather warmed a bit, she'd dispense with most of the underlying petticoats. The walking dress would have a much slimmer silhouette with only a single opaque underskirt, and it would also be far more daring. Too bad this was an afternoon outing rather than an evening affair, for then she'd be able to leave off the fichu that covered her to the collarbone.

Still, the gown was quite flattering and therefore absolutely acceptable for her outing with Sorin. *And Rowena*, she reminded herself, trying not to resent the fact. It was only proper, after all. No matter how close Sorin was to her family, he was still unmarried.

But not for long…

Her stomach trembled at the thought of what she was about to attempt. Nerves. Never had she thought to suffer from them. But she seemed to be *all* nerves when it came to anything having to do with Sorin these days.

Relax. She made herself take a deep breath. *He has stated his intent to select a wife. Why* not *me? We already know each other, after all.*

But her unrelenting conscience refused to leave it alone. What if true love was waiting for him out there? What if through her machinations she prevented his finding it? She would rob him of the greatest happiness anyone could hope for on this earth.

Then again, there were entire books of prose expounding on the cruel nature of romantic love. Many considered it a curse. *Better to marry a friend who will never subject him to such ill treatment.*

Satisfied, she patted down a stray hair and smoothed it into place. But as she stared back at her reflection in the mirror, the pessimistic little voice again intruded: *But what if I win his heart and hand only to make him* un*happy in the end, despite all efforts?*

The knock on her door made her jump.

"The Spencer, Fran! Quickly," she urged her maid, pointing. "And the shawl. The shawl—over there!" The weather had improved significantly, but it was still nippy in the shade. Fran rushed to fetch the short jacket and hold it out for her. Eleanor's fingers shook too badly to negotiate the frogs. Finally, she gave up and let her maid do them up for her. Throwing the thick cashmere over her arm and grabbing her gloves and reticule, Eleanor darted from the room. Hearing voices below as she neared the stairs, she slowed to a more dignified pace.

Sorin stood at the bottom, his smile gratifyingly appreciative as she descended. "How lovely you look today, Ellie."

Warmth suffused her from the inside out, and her lips began to tingle. The sensation spread, until her whole body felt alive and awake as never before. *How peculiar?* Was this heightened self-awareness due to the fact that she now regarded him as the potential companion of her life? Had she considered another, would it have been the same?

"Lady Ashford has already gone out to the carriage," he continued. "Shall we?"

Taking his arm, she walked out with her head high and her spirits light. Happiness swelled within her. Nothing could possibly ruin this day! Had there been a torrential downpour awaiting her outside, still she would have been elated. "I'm so pleased that you asked me to help you," she told him quietly as they approached the carriage. "Truly, it was an unexpected honor. I only hope my selection is to your mother's taste."

"I would not worry overmuch," he replied, giving her hand a pat. "Having spent five days with her in close quarters, you'll likely know what pleases her better than I. After all, ladies will often reveal to others of their own sex things they won't discuss with menfolk. Whatever you select will be perfect, I'm sure. In any case, I trust your judgment."

The compliment and his lingering gaze sent a pleasant

shiver of delight up her spine. He entered the carriage before her and then extended a hand to help her up before taking a seat opposite Rowena, who was already present.

"How pretty you look," said Rowena with a smile as she sat down beside her. "Did I not tell you this new style would be fetching?" She turned to Sorin. "She hardly allowed me to have her fitted for it. I'm afraid our Eleanor is slow to approve of change."

The butterflies in Eleanor's stomach began to flutter anew. "I won't disagree with you, but I *will* own that once I find something that pleases me, I keep it close to my heart and greatly dislike parting with it." Plucking up her courage, she looked directly at Sorin. "Having said so, I'll also admit that change can be good—when it is the right sort of change."

His eyes widened a fraction just before he quickly looked away out of the window, and panic tightened her midsection. Had she gone too far? *Oh, sweet Lord!* "Rather than making me sound so set in my ways," she hurried on, "let us instead say that I am not overly fond of changes that come with undue haste." *Damn, but that came out wrong!* "Prudence never did a lady any harm," she added lamely.

"How…interesting," said Rowena, her brows rising. "I think you are finally growing up, Eleanor."

Eleanor cringed. Rowena hadn't meant to sound so patronizing, she was sure. She flinched a little as the older woman laid a gentle hand on her arm.

"You've matured into a fine young woman," said Rowena. "Your mother would be quite proud of you, as am I."

A sudden sting of tears threatened to ruin Eleanor's composure. "Thank you," she whispered.

"Indeed she would," added Sorin softly, looking at her with an expression of tender approval.

But was it the approval of a mentor who'd once scolded

her to act like a lady or the approval of a man who thought her worthy of bearing his name and children? The world around her faded as she stared into his eyes, becoming lost in the slow, rhythmic thunder of her own heartbeat.

The air in the carriage fairly crackled.

"I think I shall buy a new timepiece for Charles while we are at Rundell & Bridge's," said Rowena, breaking the spell. "I noticed his has become a bit worn."

The world returned with a crash and Eleanor looked away, mortified. Good heavens, what must he think of her, staring at him like any bold miss on the street? "I think my cousin would like that very much," she said quickly, focusing on Rowena. "But nothing too fancy, I should think. He always complains that his father's watch is too ornate."

"True enough. Most men do seem to prefer things that are direct and uncomplicated," answered Rowena.

Knots began to form in Eleanor's gut. *Oh, no. No, no, no…* Had Rowena seen her staring at Sorin? Was her comment intended as advice on how to behave with him? She searched Rowena's face for clues, but found none. *I'm probably panicking over nothing.* Still… "I might also have a look while we are there," she said brightly, hoping to steer the discussion into safer waters. "I've nothing to wear with the new ball gown that was delivered this morning."

"The rose one?" asked Rowena. "I think that a fine idea." She turned her attention to Sorin. "Rundell & Bridges is rather out of the way, and it may be some time before we have occasion to visit again. Perhaps you'll do me the favor of helping Eleanor make her selection while I peruse the watches? After all, as a gentleman, you'll be able to offer her a different perspective regarding what is considered attractive on a lady."

Eleanor's mouth went completely dry. Her gaze snapped

back to Sorin as, with bated breath, she awaited his response. Rowena surely hadn't meant anything by her request, but…

"I'm delighted to be of assistance, of course," he replied with a cordial nod. The smile he turned on her was utterly benign. Relief flooded her, making her almost giddy. *He suspects nothing. Breathe.*

The rest of the journey was passed in light—and thankfully innocuous—conversation.

When they at last arrived at the esteemed jeweler's, Eleanor couldn't help feeling a little intimidated. The foyer was sumptuous, the atmosphere as hushed and reverent as a cathedral. A liveried manservant minced forth to take their names and to bid them make themselves comfortable while he made the proprietor aware of their arrival. Another servant, this one only slightly less haughty, came to take their jackets and cloaks.

As she perched on one of the plush chairs, Eleanor thought to herself that only the king's palace had more marble and gilt. She'd only just begun to wonder how long they would be made to wait when the first man returned.

"Master Rundell will be pleased see you now," he murmured, bowing as he held the door open for them.

The room within had been painted white, and the furniture it contained was white, too. Unlike other jewelry shops she'd visited, this one had no jewelry on display. No glass boxes containing marble busts wearing necklaces. No cases of jewel-encrusted rings and earrings. No rows of glittering bracelets. There was not a single jewel to be seen.

There were, however, a great many mirrors. They graced every wall at close intervals, interspersed with wall-mounted candelabra. Candelabra were also scattered about on pedestals throughout the room, casting luxuriant, bright light. There was not a dark corner to be found in the room save beneath the furniture.

"Welcome, honored guests," said the portly gentleman who waited within. He gestured to the cushioned benches. "I am Master Rundell, and I am at your service. Please, sit."

Eleanor took the seat Sorin offered her and folded nervous hands in her lap.

"You are here to view rings, my lady?" asked Rundell, coming to her first.

Before she could open her mouth to stammer out a polite denial, Sorin spoke. "We came to commission a piece for my mother, but both Lady Ashford and Lady Eleanor have expressed an interest in viewing some of your ready pieces. Lady Ashford is looking for a watch for her husband, and Lady Eleanor requires jewels to match a particular ball gown."

The proprietor's round face wrinkled in a broad, happy smile. "It will be my delight to show you our finest pieces, of course." Going to a pedestal by a curtained doorway, he took from it a small bell and rang it twice.

At once, two men entered the room, both dressed in unrelieved black, a sharp contrast to the rest of the room.

Master Rundell spent a moment delivering quick, quiet instructions before turning back to face them. "Hans will attend Lady Ashford," he said. The one called Hans went immediately to Rowena and bowed low before her. "Geoff will assist me. Now, do you already have something in mind or shall I bring out a few items for inspiration?"

They spent the next half an hour looking at various pieces of jewelry—*spectacular* pieces of jewelry. Even Eleanor, for whom such baubles held little import, was impressed. There was not a flaw to be found in any piece, neither in the stones nor in their settings. Every item shown her was a breathtakingly beautiful example of perfection and skill. At last, they agreed upon an emerald brooch that would have the

Wincanton crest worked into the setting with diamond accents.

"And now what may we show you, Lady Eleanor?" asked the jeweler, again smiling.

Sorin watched Eleanor most intently and soon came to the conclusion that choosing a gift for her wouldn't be as easy as he'd hoped. She hardly glanced at the rings, asking instead to see other wares.

"The gown I wish to match is pale rose," she told the proprietor.

"Ahh," said he, his eyes lighting. "Rubies with pearl accents, perhaps?"

"No pearls," she said at once. "And while rubies would be lovely, I fear they would not be deemed appropriate," she said a bit wistfully.

"Why not?" Sorin asked, confounded. "Rubies are the favorite of our queen, and Her Majesty would never wear anything improper."

A faint blush stained her cheeks. "My mother once told me that only married ladies ought to wear rubies because red is considered the color of passion."

Now *that* was a bit of useful information. "I see." He turned to the jeweler. "What else can you suggest?"

The little man's ever-present smile widened another increment. "If rubies and pearls are not an option, then I'm afraid the only other thing that would go well with pale rose would be diamonds."

"Why not a gold filigree piece?" said Eleanor with a nervous glance at Rowena, who was busy poring over another tray of watches.

Sorin could stand it no longer. He leaned down to murmur at her ear, "You are a duke's daughter, Ellie. While I agree that you should avoid vulgar ostentation, you must not be afraid to show your rank and quality. If you wear unadorned gold people may make incorrect assumptions about your circumstances."

It was complete and utter drivel, but it would serve his purpose. He stood and addressed the jeweler with a look that would keep the price range within reason. "Bring the diamonds. We seek something simple but elegant—tasteful."

The jeweler snapped his fingers, at once summoning his hovering assistant to his side. "Bring out the Rani collection." With a smart bow, the one called Geoff vanished behind the heavy velvet drape, returning a few moments later with a large, flat box of highly polished wood. Another servant preceded him with two short tables, both of which he placed before Eleanor. A candelabra was borrowed from a stand and placed upon one table, the box upon the other.

"These are some of our finest diamonds from India," said Master Rundell, opening the box with a flourish.

Sorin was pleased to hear a soft gasp from Eleanor. "Well? What think you?" he asked her after a moment. They were dazzling, but the design was a bit too busy for his liking. Still, if she liked it…

"They are breathtaking," she answered, sounding as if her breath had indeed been stolen a little. "But I think I should like something a little more open."

Again, the little man snapped his fingers. "The Estrellis collection," he said to his assistant without looking away.

The lid closed and the box was withdrawn. Another quickly replaced it. This time when the lid was raised, Eleanor gave a warm hum of approval.

"Would you like to try them, my lady?"

She nodded, and the man carefully lifted a glittering necklace from its velvet bed. Sorin cleared his throat softly.

The proprietor looked up at once. "My Lord Wincanton, perhaps you might assist the lady while I unfix the earrings?" he said, offering up the necklace, which Sorin took with a small nod of thanks.

The assistant held a polished glass before Eleanor as Sorin moved behind her to fasten the necklace about her throat. A hard tremor shook her as his fingertips grazed the nape of her neck, and in the mirror he saw her close her eyes and swallow. Was her reaction one of desire or repugnance? Gently, he placed a hand on her shoulder. She didn't flinch beneath it. "You can look now," he said at her ear.

Her eyes opened, their usual spring green darkening to forest shade as she met his gaze in the reflection.

Desire lanced through his vitals. Now it was his turn to tremble. Stepping back quickly, he nodded approval. "I think the necklace quite tasteful and appropriate."

Her hand rose to touch the gleaming jewels at her throat. "It *is* lovely, but…"

"Oh, Eleanor, it's absolutely stunning!" exclaimed Rowena from the other side of the room. "Do try on the rest," she said, rising and coming over to join them.

Eleanor was handed the earrings which she affixed to her lobes, and then the bracelet. But when the proprietor proffered the matching ring, she politely declined. "It is beautiful, truly, but…"

Sorin looked to her in surprise, observing the way her pearly teeth tormented her full bottom lip for a moment. "Is there something you dislike about it?"

"No, not at all. It's only that, well… Mama always said a lady's fingers ought to remain unadorned until she receives her wedding ring. I prefer to carry on her tradition and wait."

His pulse began to pound as the words sank in. Hope sprang anew. *Has she changed her mind about marriage?*

Rundell's face fell, but he put the ring back in its place. "Of course, my lady. What think you of the rest?"

"I think we'll take it," answered Rowena for her, much to the jeweler's transparent delight. "That is, if you like it, my dear."

Eleanor's face shone. "How could I not like it?" Her smile faltered. "But Rowena, it's far more than I should like to—"

"Let it be a gift from your cousin and me," interrupted Rowena, patting her hand. She addressed Master Rundell. "Have these, the watch, and my other selections sent to my London residence."

"Yes, Your Grace."

They waited while Eleanor removed the jewelry. Sorin saw her gaze linger for a moment on the ring, a magnificent white diamond of at least two karats surrounded by smaller stones, as it was separated from the rest and taken away to the back.

"I think you ought to wear them to the Blessington ball next week," said Rowena as their carriage rolled away, leaving the exclusive shop behind.

"But I thought to save the rose gown for the Cleveland ball," replied Eleanor.

Rowena shook her head. "That's almost a month away. You mustn't wait. First impressions are often the longest to linger. Young ladies should always come out as strong as possible at the very start of the Season. It helps weed out those who know themselves unqualified to seek your hand. You want to clear the field of clutter, enabling you to focus your attention on only those gentlemen equal to or higher than your own rank."

"General Rowena," teased Eleanor with only the slightest

edge in her voice. "Always drawing battle plans."

"So I am, and I won't apologize for it. I fully intend to see you married this Season."

Sorin's heart again leaped when Eleanor declined to rebut her assertion. Another good sign. Perhaps her headstrong resolve to remain unwed had at last given way to good sense. Out of consideration for the ladies as well as his own growling stomach, he offered to treat them to a late afternoon tea at Devereux Court.

They arrived just in time. When Eleanor went to visit the powder room, Sorin took the opportunity to broach the delicate matter at hand. "Lady Ashford, I'd like to discuss the upcoming—"

"How long have you been in love with her?"

The bluntness of her inquiry caught him off guard. *Fool!* He'd been too obvious in his conduct today. "I have, as you know, always been very fond of Eleanor," he stammered, unsure of her mood and intent. Her face was closed and unreadable.

"What I observed in the way you looked at her this afternoon goes beyond 'fondness'," she said quietly.

Panic set in. He could only attempt to explain himself and hope. "As a child, Eleanor charmed me to the point of spoiling her as I might have done a younger sister. When she grew older, however, the nature of my affection changed—not through any fault of hers, but wholly through my own."

Her brow furrowed.

"I was not as careful with her as I should have been," he rushed on. "In my weakness, my own selfish and irresponsible need to be adored, I indulged her. I let her remain too familiar with me for too long and failed to enforce the rules of propriety with her until it was too late." He ran shaking hands over his hot face. *God, help me.*

"Go on," she prompted.

"Everything began to change when I came home the year of her sixteenth birthday," he told her. "Out of innocent affection, she offered her usual effusive greeting and embraced me. To my eternal shame, I..." He swallowed and took a deep breath. Her face was as pale as parchment, but he wouldn't coat the truth. "I reacted as no gentleman ought."

All remaining color leached from her cheeks and lips.

Panic turned into utter terror. "In my haste to correct myself, I admonished her most assiduously for her demonstrative behavior and in the process wounded her deeply. The breach was mended, but only just, and it has never been the same between us since." He peered into her eyes, imploring her to understand, to forgive. "I have tried every possible way to dissuade myself of..." He faltered again. "All efforts to expunge such feelings have failed." He steeled himself, expecting a look of revulsion to cross her features, but none came.

"And that was the real reason you left and stayed away for so long," said Rowena, her voice not ungentle, though her countenance remained dangerously pale.

He nodded. "I'd hoped that she would marry and be gone before I came back. But year after year she did not, and I could not stay away forever. When I returned home this time, I knew I could no longer run. I'll either have to watch her fall in love and marry another or find a way to persuade her to marry me. I have little hope of the latter."

"But why? Why do you assume she won't return the sentiment?"

"Because she confessed to me only weeks ago that she looks to me as a model for the kind of man she wishes to marry," he said flatly. "But it is plain she does not see *me* in that role."

"Perceptions change."

"Perhaps, but not overnight. I spent *years* lecturing and correcting her at every turn. I pointed out every infinitesimal fault, from the way she walked and spoke to how she held a teacup. More recently, I called into question her very judgment." A strangled laugh forced its way out. "I've been a mentor and a chaperone to her, an older brother almost. Sibling affection is rather a significant hurdle to overcome when one is contemplating a marriage, would you not agree?"

"Not so significant as you might think," she replied with an arch smile. "I saw the way she looked at you at the jeweler's. I find it not unreasonable to believe that time has changed the nature of her affection for you, as well. We must find out."

Hope again flared within him. "Therein lies the chief problem," he told her. "I don't know how to approach her to fathom out the depth or nature of her feelings for me without risking exposure of my own—which, if her view of me remains unaltered, would forever ruin our friendship. I won't risk injuring her. Surely you must comprehend my prudence?"

Rowena slowly shook her head. "You know each other so well, and yet you've been blind to each other for so long. It is clear to me at least that she loves you, dear friend. Deeply, and not, I think, in a sisterly fashion."

His face heated once more. "If I am to marry her, there can be no doubt," he insisted. "I want her to marry me to satisfy her own heart's desire and for no other reason. If she wishes me to serve in the capacity of a husband, I will most happily oblige. But if not, then I would rather remain silent and preserve both her ignorance and, therefore, her happiness."

Rowena again shook her head. "If you think this is something that can be hidden from her in perpetuity, you are much mistaken. How will you go about gaining such surety without revealing yourself?"

"For now, my intent is to remain near her and allow her to once again become comfortable in our friendship." He closed his eyes for a moment and sent up a brief prayer. "I've made so many mistakes with her. Mistakes I must now overcome. The barriers I strove to put between us must now be dismantled, and I fear it won't be easy. My past rejection of her innocent affection has left her wary. And then there is the matter of Charles. I fear he will take great umbrage when I reveal my true intent, which I cannot do until I ascertain her feelings."

"Allow me to help you with that," offered Rowena. "I cannot imagine he would ever disapprove of your marrying Eleanor. If anything, he should welcome the idea. We could certainly choose no better match for her. Let me talk to him."

"No," he said at once. "I and I alone must speak with him about this. He would see it as a betrayal of his trust if he discovered it by any other means."

"You discredit the strength of his love for you," she said sternly. "Charles views you as a brother."

"Well do I know it. And because of his faith in me, he has placed Eleanor in my care this Season." He took a steadying breath. "Rowena, please…"

Pursing her lips, she sat back with a sigh. "Very well. But unless you are more discreet than you were this afternoon, he will see the truth for himself, as I did. A blind man would have seen your love for her."

Indeed, he must exercise more care. A great deal more. The struggle to keep his true feelings from showing was getting harder every day. "Agreed."

"And then there is Eleanor herself to consider," she went on. "She is not so practiced at concealing her heart. If she falls in love with you, Charles will see it. There, I think, lies the solution to your dilemma. And there is where I *can* help you," she said, holding up a hand to forestall the objections piling up behind his teeth. "I'll create opportunities for you to spend time with her, and I'll keep Charles's attention focused elsewhere. Our having agreed to host Caroline for the Season should be enough to occupy his mind," she said darkly. "But I advise you not to take too long in finding out what you need to know."

"Thank you," he said simply. "Your trust means more to me than I can say."

Her expression again turned arch. "Oh, I fully expect to be rewarded for my trust in the form of a ring on Eleanor's finger. Yours."

"If it is within the realm of possibility, I shall," he promised. At that moment, Eleanor reappeared and began making her way toward them. There was little time. "To begin, I would like to escort her to the Blessington ball. If arrangements have not already been made, that is," he added quickly, letting her know with a jerk of his chin that they wouldn't be alone for much longer.

"We would be delighted if you would join us," she replied with a bright smile.

"Join us for what?" asked Eleanor as Sorin stood to greet her.

"Lord Wincanton has agreed to accompany us to the Blessington ball," said Rowena.

Eleanor's eyes lit. "How wonderful! Will your mother join us as well?"

"I'm afraid she's already accepted an invitation for another event that evening." So had he, actually, thanks to her having answered affirmatively on his behalf. He would have to send his regrets, but as long as Mother attended they wouldn't feel slighted. She wouldn't mind making his excuses. After all, he was on the market now and must focus his attentions on bringing home a bride—Eleanor.

Chapter Fourteen

The sun shone bright and hot, making it the perfect day for a picnic. Eleanor was careful to keep her parasol positioned to prevent any light getting through. The Blessington ball was in just two days.

Never had she prepared so assiduously for an event in all her life, not even her debut. Lemon water had been daubed on her nightly to ensure her face and shoulders remained free of freckles. Milk baths had been taken. And she'd been careful to keep her bonnet on and her shoulders covered when in the sun. Every inch of skin from her fingertips to her hairline had been plied with lotions and creams in order to make it as soft as butter. She wasn't about to spoil it all now.

Anything that smacked of childishness, whether in appearance or behavior, had to be avoided at all costs—and a freckled face screamed immaturity. Grown ladies did not expose their faces to the sun.

I'm an adult now, and I must look and act like one. It was vital that Sorin see her as his equal, his match, in every respect.

He'd gone to fetch her some lemonade, leaving her to

wander along the banks of the pond and admire the swans as they made long vees on the water's surface. He would be back at any moment, but for now she was free to let her mind wander. Edging beneath the shade of an obliging willow, she leaned back against its trunk, closing her parasol.

In just two days, she would don the rose gown, her new diamonds, and her most seductive smile. He would come and offer her his arm. They would appear together and be announced together. And then they would dance. Closing her eyes, she imagined herself in his arms, floating across the ballroom floor. He would look at her, and he would say—

"Lady Eleanor, how delighted I am to see you again."

A little yelp of surprise burst from her as she jumped and turned to face the unwelcome intruder, her skin crawling with distaste. Fighting the urge to scowl at him, she affected a polite smile. "Good afternoon, Sir Yarborough."

Coming closer, he made an elegant leg before her. "Surely you and I have known each other long enough for you to call me by my Christian name?"

"Oh, but I mustn't," she said, stepping away from the tree to give herself plenty of maneuvering room in case she needed to retreat in haste. "It would be highly improper of me, Sir Yarborough."

His smile widened, and he took a step closer. "Since when have *you* ever worried about propriety?" he asked, reaching up to rub his jaw, a deliberate reminder.

Damn.

He laughed. "You needn't scowl. I came not to stir up old grievances, but rather to let you know that I've missed your company. I can only assume that, like so many, you've found London's distractions pleasant and absorbing."

It was an unsubtle hint that she'd been ignoring the almost daily invitations he'd been sending. "Indeed," she said brightly, snapping her parasol up and open, though there was no need. "I've been so very busy. In fact, this *was* the first time I'd been afforded a moment's peace." One unsubtle hint deserved another.

A crease marred the space between his brows, and he took another step closer. "Perhaps you should take some rest from this whirlwind of activity. I should dislike it very much if you were to fall ill from overexertion."

She'd show him "overexertion" if he came any nearer! Her fingers gripped the ivory-headed handle of her parasol. "I can assure you, *Sir* Yarborough, that the state of my health is more than satisfactory." Behind her back, she balled her other hand into a fist and braced herself. "One might even go so far as to say it is robust."

"Indeed, quite so," said another voice. It was Sorin. He parted the trailing willow branches and entered the shade bearing two cups. "She has practically run me to Bedlam these last few days. Ellie, your lemonade."

She accepted the cup he proffered and took a grateful sip to hide a grin of pure glee. The look on Yarborough's face was one of frustrated indecision. She understood his conundrum well enough. On the one hand, being considered a friend of the Earl of Wincanton would do him no harm socially. On the other, the illustrious Earl appeared to be blocking his efforts to woo the object of his desire—thanks be to heaven. One day, perhaps, she would find the opportunity to thank her rescuer properly. Or perhaps *im*properly…

"Lord Wincanton, a pleasure to see you again as well," said Yarborough finally, though the words sounded empty. "I met Miss Caroline near the bowling lawn a short while ago. She told me she was looking for you."

Sorin's eyes flashed with amusement. "Yes, I know. I spoke with her just a moment ago." He turned to face Eleanor fully, giving Yarborough his back and blocking the fellow's view. "She was most troubled concerning a letter she received from her aunt regarding a young cousin."

Eagerly, she took up the thread. "Yes. Apparently, she was proposed to by a young man to whom the family strongly objects. They wish her to refuse him, but she is being most intractable." She moved closer and lowered her voice just enough to make it plain that she was excluding certain parties from the conversation, but not enough to prevent that conversation being overheard. "She claims it is a love match, but her family feels the young man has mercenary motives."

"Perhaps they ought to reconsider their position," interjected Yarborough, coming around to again stand before them. "After all, the young lady may never receive another offer of marriage."

Eleanor felt her hackles rise. "I can think of far more tragic circumstances than spinsterhood, Sir Yarborough—one of them being that of a young woman trapped in an imprudent marriage to a man who claims to love her while his true and only interest is in pilfering her purse."

Now it was Yarborough's turn to bristle, but any rejoinder he might have given was cut off by Sorin before it could be voiced. "I can only agree," said he. "Better for her to remain unwed than marry a fool, or worse, a deceiver."

Eleanor observed that his eyes were fixed on Yarborough as he said it. *Oh, my.*

All color, save two high splotches of red on his cheeks, drained from the younger man's face as he visibly struggled for composure. Finally, he cast his gaze down and bowed shortly. "I'm afraid I've intruded upon a conversation that was intended to be private. Please excuse me." Turning on his heel, he stalked away, leaving the two of them alone.

"Oh, bravo, my friend," she murmured to Sorin, setting

her cup down on a nearby stump. "I could not have done that better myself."

"I must apologize," he said at once, coming over to set his still-full cup beside hers. "I should have been more forbearing. He is, after all, still very young."

"He is a year older than I," she objected, looking down so that he wouldn't see her disappointment.

"Perhaps, but you are far wiser."

Something in his voice drew her gaze back up again. Beneath the budding willow branches, his hazel eyes were so very green, so intense in their regard of her. "Am I?" Her voice shook just a little.

He drifted closer. "Of course you are. You have a maturity about you to which that whelp can hardly ever hope to aspire, as well as many other fine qualities."

Light and warmth blossomed within her. She allowed the current that had been steadily tugging her toward him draw her a step nearer. "Such a compliment from you is high indeed and worth more to me than any he could ever give. Yours are genuine, while his are no more than empty words contrived to lead me astray."

They were less than an arm's length away from each other now. All she had to do was reach out and she could touch him, place her hand upon his chest. Her heart hammered wildly as his gaze dropped to her mouth.

With a suddenness that left her swaying on the spot, he drew back and turned to walk to the edge of the pond. Stooping, he picked up a small twig that had fallen from the willow and twirled it for a moment between his fingers before casting it lightly into the water. The swans turned curiously, no doubt hoping to receive an offering of bread. "I'm glad to hear you say it," he said without looking at her. "It shows you've learned the art of discernment. Another mark of wisdom."

Mortification flooded through her, leaving behind a bitter taste. *Damn, damn, and damn!* For a moment, just a brief happy moment, she'd thought he might kiss her. But no, not Sorin. Wisdom indeed! She was an unmitigated fool. Stooping, she too picked up an object, a fist-sized stone. Since his back was turned, she indulged her ire and flung it with all her might into the pond. It sank with a loud *thwunk* and a satisfyingly large splash. The poor swans fled the disturbance in a flurry of wings, honking protest.

Not wanting to endure censure over having abused the wildlife, she began walking. She'd only gone a few steps, however, when a warm hand grasped her elbow—a hand that was just as quickly snatched back as though it couldn't bear to touch her. She stopped, squeezing her eyes shut to prevent tears from starting.

"If I have given you offense, then please accept my apology," said Sorin softly. "Truly, I did not mean to sound so condescending."

She turned and looked up at him in anger and frustration. But his face was full of such remorse that she couldn't stay wroth. The wind, as he would have said, had been taken out of her sails. "No. The fault is mine. You spoke of my 'wisdom' a moment ago, but I fear I must disagree with you and therefore make myself even more unpleasant." His frown told her she'd only managed to confuse him further. She sighed. "Increasingly of late, I find myself prone to grossly misunderstanding the intentions of those around me, even those whom I have long known. Forgive my conduct just now. I reacted in a manner most unbecoming."

"It seems we both suffer the same malady," he replied heavily. "I, too, have been guilty of misinterpreting the words and actions of even my closest friends in recent days. Come," he said, offering his arm. "Let us forget our shared inclination toward misperception and enjoy this fine day and each other's company."

"Agreed." Indeed. She vowed from that moment on to never again read more into his words than what was on the surface. Taking his arm, she let him lead her out from beneath the willow branches and into the sunshine. She was sorely tempted to leave her parasol closed and just enjoy the warm sun on her skin. What was the point of preserving herself from freckles if he never looked at her with anything more than benign detachment? Vanity, however, won out in the end.

"Shall we see if the others would like to play a game of bowls?" he asked politely as she paused to open her parasol.

"Why not?" she answered in the same, too-light tone, reining in an urge to smack him with the contraption. It wasn't his fault he wasn't attracted to her.

Bollocks, but that was close! Sorin breathed a slow, silent sigh of relief. What in the seven hells was the matter with him, staring at her like that? Now she was all nervous and fidgety. Truly, he had not meant to sound like such a condescending ass, but as with just about every conversation he'd had with her of late, he'd said the wrong thing. "Will you be joining Mother for tea this week?" he asked in an attempt to keep her talking as they traversed the wide lawn between the pond and the house.

"I shall," she answered, her gaze fixed on a point somewhere amid the colorful blankets and parasols dotting the green expanse.

"I'm glad. She's looking forward to your weekly visits as she has not anticipated anything in years."

"As am I," she answered at once. "She also promised to

introduce me to several friends with unattached sons and grandsons. Apparently, she's in agreement with my cousin on the matter of my unwed state. She said it was high time I overcame my reticence."

An icy fingertip brushed his spine. *Did she, now?* It took every scrap of control to keep his tone nonchalant. "I can only imagine that you will benefit greatly from her connections. She knows everyone of importance and has much influence."

"I really ought to be more grateful for her sponsorship," she mused, sounding contrite. "Charles will certainly be pleased, as will Rowena."

"And you?" he finally asked. "Your opinions regarding matrimony are certainly known to me, but I don't suppose you've shared them with Mother?"

She shot him a wry, sidelong look. "I would have declined her offer of assistance, but I feared she would persist in spite of my objections and I did not wish her to feel slighted. Nor did I wish her to tell my cousin that I'm being uncooperative. Privately, I will tell you that I dread the idea of her playing matchmaker. Of all my acquaintances—excepting you and Rowena, of course—she is the most likely to influence his decisions. If she indicates her approval of a particular gentleman, Charles will surely insist that I seriously consider him."

Just what the bloody hell is Mother playing at? He must dissuade her from any further benevolent interference as quickly as possible before her "master plan" misfired. It rankled, but he knew he had no right to be so possessive of Eleanor. She was nothing of his to prevent her from meeting other men, and he was nothing to her but a friend. And that was how he must behave now or else risk exposure.

"Well, as my mother is not a person to be persuaded once she's made up her mind, I'm afraid you'll have to endure her meddling." He clamped down hard on his reluctance and forced himself to continue in a cheerful tone. "She but seeks to assist you in much the same manner as you've agreed to assist me," he reminded her, watching her closely. "You may of course choose to decline any offers that come your way, but I cannot so easily avoid the marital noose. I'm expected to bring home a bride, and shall therefore need all the help you can give me in order to make the right choice."

"Well," she said, again averting her gaze. "I can certainly be your eyes and ears and help to determine the true character of your considerations, just as you will doubtless do for me. I want you to know that I'm very grateful to have you as an ally in this matter. I only hope I prove equally worthy of your trust and confidence."

Was it possible to feel any worse than this? Here they were, arm in arm, walking in the bright sunshine—discussing marrying people other than each other. His spirits had not been this low since he'd first fled England's shores. He led her over to the shady plot where her family had staked a claim.

"Eleanor! Do come and sit beside me," said Caroline, patting the blanket beside her. "Penwaithe has gone to fetch me some lemonade," she announced without preamble, a smug little smile forming on her mouth.

Sorin's head began to pound. Lemonade. What he needed was a stiff brandy. A large one. Eleanor obligingly sat where she was directed, and he waited to see if she would offer him the place beside her as she usually did. She quite markedly did not. So he sat next to Rowena.

"You've made progress in gaining his attention, then," said Eleanor to her friend. "I congratulate you. I understand he's difficult to approach and that he does not often deign to converse with people with whom he is unfamiliar."

"Well, he has deigned to do so with me," replied Caroline, sticking her nose in the air. The effect was completely ruined by the unabashed grin under it. "He happened into the library while I was there, and—"

"You were in the library?" interrupted Eleanor, her brows rising.

"Yes, and you needn't make it sound as though I mistook it for the ladies' respite room," snapped Caroline. "I went to look for some poems recommended by another friend, but got distracted by a book concerning Greek myths. I was looking at it when Lord Penwaithe entered. He immediately took notice and then proceeded to converse with me on the subject. He's a great admirer of all things Greek."

"How wonderful for you to have found something in common upon which to begin building a rapport," said Eleanor. "Many married couples have nothing at all in common, a circumstance which I feel causes much disharmony. If I am ever to marry, he must be someone with whom I can feel completely at ease discussing any subject."

He could take no more. Standing, Sorin bowed. "Ladies, if you will excuse me."

"You are leaving so soon?" said Eleanor, frowning. "I thought you wished to play at bowls?"

He wondered if her disappointment was personal or just an expression of general politesse. "I did, yes—but I'm afraid I forgot a promise I made earlier." His mind raced, looking for a likely excuse. "I was to meet with Lord Brampton," he lied. "I'm woefully late already and must take my leave at once. I wish you all a most pleasant afternoon." He bowed again and turned before anyone else could object.

Coward! His back prickled as he strode away across the field. How he was to survive this Season was unknown. One thing was certain; Ellie would *never* find anyone more compatible than himself. If by some miracle she did, he would be hard pressed not to kill the bastard.

Chapter Fifteen

Solemn green eyes stared back at Eleanor from the reflection. She looked every inch a lady tonight. While the soft rose of the gown was certainly acceptable for an unwed woman, its cut was quite modern and daring. Grateful now for her prudence concerning the parasol at the picnic, she searched the wide span of flesh exposed between shoulders barely covered by tiny, puffed sleeves. Not a freckle in sight.

Everything was just as it ought to be. The diamond necklace Sorin had helped her select glittered above a décolletage flattered by the design of the dress. Matching earrings swayed from her lobes, and her hair rose in an elegant braided twist with curls piled high atop, giving her the appearance of greater height. It was by far the most elegant and attractive she'd ever looked.

And it was all for naught, as the one man who interested her was completely blind to her.

I might as well be wearing a smelly old sack for all he'll look at me. A fit of ill temper made her slam the jewelry box lid closed with a loud *clack!*

This whole week had been a right disaster, starting with the picnic where everything had gone wrong with Sorin. Since then, Yarborough had continued to be a bother. He'd sent two more invitations, both of which she'd very politely refused. Then it had come to her attention yesterday that a friend of Rowena's had heard Lady Yarborough sniping about her "overweening pride" to a group of contemporaries. Add to these things the fact that Caroline, despite her promise to behave herself, was near to the point of open warfare with Marston and that Rowena had begun to feel ill, and one had the perfect recipe for insomnia.

Poor Rowena. She was trying to put on a brave face and keep her condition a secret, but Eleanor knew it wouldn't be long before Charles found her out. His nerves were already on edge from having to deal with Caroline and patience was in short supply. The instant he learned his wife was again with child, there would be absolute chaos in this house.

To top it all off, tea with Sorin's mother yesterday had been exceedingly awkward and uncomfortable. The enjoyable event she'd come to anticipate had turned into a stiff, stale discussion devoid of any amusement at all after *he* had elected to join them. One simply couldn't talk of certain things in the presence of a man, including Rowena's being *enceinte*. He would have been honor-bound to inform Charles.

Eventually, Lady Wincanton had taken the matter in hand and asked her son outright why he'd suddenly decided to intrude. He'd flushed to the roots of his hair and excused himself at once, apologizing profusely for his unwanted presence.

Though she'd felt bad for him, Eleanor couldn't help also wondering why he'd done it. It wasn't as if there were any other males present from which she must be protected.

Sighing, she reflected that it didn't really matter. Her

weekly tea appointment with Lady Wincanton would only last until Sorin married. The moment he brought home a bride, there would be no more time for 'little Ellie' in their lives. In all honesty, she'd count it a blessing, for it would save her from having to endure further torment.

Tears welled in her eyes. The one thing she hadn't expected in all of this was how much it hurt to have all of her assumptions regarding Sorin's perception of her confirmed. Not only was she no closer to her goal of staying in Somerset, but the thought of remaining there and seeing him married to someone else made her positively ill.

"Heaven preserve me from my own idiocy!" she muttered, tossing aside her brush and swiping at her eyes.

A soft voice called from the doorway. "Ellie? Whatever is the matter?"

Turning, Eleanor tried to put on a brave smile for Rowena's sake, but it was no use. Such was her misery that it could not be hidden. "If you must know, I'm not looking forward to tonight."

"Why not? Are you unwell?"

She considered saying yes, but Rowena's alarmed expression stopped her. Given her delicate condition, Eleanor could not in good conscience deliberately cause her distress. "Oh, no. Nothing like that. I—I fear I've made a terrible mistake." At Rowena's askance look, she elucidated. "I promised to help...someone...make a match this Season, and now I'm not certain I can go through with it."

"Has Caroline been causing trouble again?" asked Rowena, her voice turning sharp.

"Not at all." Eleanor looked at her and made a decision. "It's Sorin. He asked me to help him select a bride." Rowena's brows rose in evident surprise. "I told him I would. And now... well, now I'm forced to keep my promise, despite...despite..."

To Eleanor's mortification, the tears she'd thought under control escaped to run down her face. Grabbing a handkerchief, she rushed to blot them before they could spot her gown. "Oh, Rowena! He trusts me to help him, and I simply *cannot.*" Gentle arms closed about her shoulders, and she sagged against them. "Whomever I choose will be all wrong for him, I'm certain of it. I don't want to be responsible for his happiness."

"You know, the man has some say as to whom he offers his hand," answered Rowena, her tone wry. "But tell me, why do you assume you'll err? Do you not know him better than anyone else, save perhaps his mother?"

"There are times I think I do, but then he says or does something that proves me wrong. He can be so frustrating at times!" Feeling utterly wretched, she dashed away more tears.

"Then he is no different from any other man," said Rowena, laughing a little. "Charles drives me absolutely mad on a daily basis, yet I love him to distraction. He knows it, too." She paused, and then, "I believe Lord Wincanton knows how deeply you care for him, Ellie, else he would not have singled *you* out to ask for help. He trusts you, because he knows you would never want him to be anything less than perfectly happy."

Yes, and it was making *her* perfectly miserable! "I know, and that makes it even more difficult. I don't think anyone can possibly be good enough for him." *Though I would have tried my best…* She buried her face in her hands. "What am I to do?"

Rowena sat silent for a long moment. "Let us approach this from a standpoint of logic. What particular qualities does he seek in a wife?"

She thought back. "He never actually listed them," she blurted, blowing her nose with vigor and not caring that it made a loud, honking noise like that of an angry goose. Sorin would certainly not have approved. *And there's one answer.* "He's always been most adamant that a lady's manners and sense of propriety must be beyond reproach."

"A good place to begin," said Rowena with a thoughtful nod. "You ought to be quite the expert at judging such things, given that he himself often instructed you in comportment."

So I should, she told herself bitterly. Manners and propriety! What good had they done her? Her thoughts turned to that paragon of virtue, Saint Jane. "And…I suppose she must be biddable, compliant, and meek of temperament."

This earned her a doubtful frown. "Are you certain? Look at the women closest to him. Neither you nor his mother are any of those things, if you'll pardon my saying it. You are both strong-minded, and I doubt he has ever described either of you as being 'meek'."

It made her smile, as doubtless intended. "Lady Wincanton *is* quite a force of nature. But a man might not want to marry a woman so like his mother." *Like me.*

Pursing her lips, Rowena nodded slowly. "Perhaps, yet it seems to me he prefers the company of strong women."

"Not so when it comes to his bride," she replied sadly. "His first choice, Jane, was—according to him—'perfection', and he always described her as the most temperate of women."

"The choices made in one's youth are not always the right ones," answered Rowena. She folded her hands in her lap. "I met her, you know. Jane. She was lovely and sweet, but I remember very clearly thinking she was all wrong for him. Timid to a fault, she was. Constantly needing reassurance. I recall hearing him once tell her not to be so fearful of everything."

"He's never said such a thing to me," Eleanor responded with a grimace. "If anything, he's always adjured me to have more caution and curb my impulsivity."

"And yet I've always heard him praise your courage," mused Rowena. "He cares for you a great deal, you know." Again, she paused as if debating what to say next. "Enough that at one point, I actually thought of proposing a match."

Hearing this only made Eleanor feel worse. *But he does not care for me the way a man cares for a woman he wishes to marry.* Oh, how she wished he did! And not just so she could stay in Somerset. She longed for him to *see* her as a woman. But it was not meant to be. "It would never have worked," she said aloud, her chest constricting. "He looks on me as a sister."

Rowena's eyes took on an expression of deepest compassion. "And…how do you view him?"

The question brought Eleanor up short. In her mind's eye she pictured Sorin, his mouth quirked in a gentle smile, the sun on his hair, the light in his hazel eyes as he laughed. *He is everything I want and cannot have.* The shock of realization prickled across her flesh like a thousand stings. She didn't just want someone *like* Sorin—she wanted *him*. All of him. His heart, his mind, his tall, lean body—with a ferocity that shook her to the very seat of her soul.

Her mouth formed very different words, however. "He is ever my dearest friend." She dredged up a watery smile. "Worry not. I *will* help him, as I promised. I'm sure there must be someone worthy of his good name."

A knock saved her from having to answer any more uncomfortable questions. Fran informed her that Lord Ashford was awaiting them downstairs.

Eleanor avoided Rowena's eyes, took up her accoutrements, and trudged out and down the stairs, her feet leaden. Her cousin greeted them with a grunt, a frown creasing his brow. He was alone.

"Is Lord Wincanton not here?" she asked him, almost

afraid to hear his answer.

"I'm afraid Wincanton won't be joining us tonight. He's just sent a note saying he's been detained. He'll meet us at the ball if he can manage to get away."

It was with the greatest effort that she kept her face passive. "I hope it's not anything too serious." She looked around again. "Where is Caroline?"

"Here," said her friend from the top of the stairs. "I went to find you a moment ago to ask your opinion, but you'd already gone." She descended and turned, showing the beautifully draped back of her new gown. The pale azure silk complemented her vibrant coloring perfectly.

"You are an absolute vision," Eleanor told her, smiling. "You'll be the toast of the Season, Caroline. I just know it."

"I think you both look lovely," said Rowena, joining her husband. "Come, it is time we were on our way."

Eleanor was relieved to see she looked as if their conversation of a moment ago had never happened. Her spirits rose an increment. With Sorin otherwise occupied tonight, she would at least have a chance to regroup.

I cannot stay in Somerset if he weds another. Perhaps I can find a dedicated spinster to serve as my companion. I'll buy a nice cottage for us to live in—in another county… It would mean being far removed from her loved ones and her childhood home—everything familiar would be lost, but it was the only viable option.

Almost as soon as the carriage began to move, Rowena propped herself against a cushion in the corner and closed her eyes tightly. Eleanor hoped she would last the night. Charles, thankfully, seemed totally absorbed by the view from his window.

"I'm hoping Penwaithe will notice me this evening," whispered Caroline as they wended their way through London.

"I wore my hair this way just to catch his eye."

"I wondered why it was up like that," Eleanor whispered back, eyeing the arrangement. Rather than the profusion of fiery curls that were Caroline's hallmark, she wore her hair in a high coronet, every strand tamed into submission by pearl pins. "You look very regal."

"That was my intent," said her friend, eyes sparkling with excitement. Taking up her fan, she opened it and held it up between them and Charles. "He made such a fuss over a statue of Athena we saw in the gardens during the picnic." She leaned closer, her voice lowering so that it was barely audible over the noise of wheels against cobblestones. "I said in jest that she must not have had red hair, and he replied that indeed he could not imagine a goddess like Athena with such hair as mine, so tonight I shall prove him wrong." She giggled softly. "He said the only goddess likely to have hair like mine would be Aphrodite rising from the sea. A promising comment, would you not agree?"

Certainly—if one were seeking an illicit affair! Calming herself, Eleanor leaned even closer so there would be no chance of Charles overhearing her. "Caroline, I know you won't like what I'm going to say—I can see you frowning already—but as your friend I must speak honestly. Such a comment was nothing short of an indecent proposal. Any man who would compare you to a deity known for debauched behavior is obviously lacking in respect for you."

As anticipated, Caroline's lips thinned, her delight exchanged for hot wrath. "You would make every comment from a man mean something lewd!" she hissed. "He made a *jest*, Eleanor! Nothing more. I wore my hair this way tonight merely to let him know that I was paying attention and to further the rapport between us. The man has a sense of humor, and now he will see that I do as well—unlike some people!"

Snapping her fan shut, she leaned back against the squabs and folded her arms.

Now it was Eleanor's turn to open her fan and use it as a screen. "I stand firm in my opinion," she insisted quietly, ignoring the barb. "By playing to his 'jest' as you call it, you might very well send him the wrong message. You don't want him to think you're willing to engage in improper behavior!"

But Caroline's expression remained recalcitrant. "You presume that I'm too ignorant to know when a man has lascivious intentions," she whispered back. "I can assure you I'm not. As it is with you, this is not my first Season." Her anger faded into hurt. "Why can you never simply trust me?"

Guilt slithered into Eleanor's heart. "You are one of my closest friends. If I'm overly protective, it is simply because I cannot stop worrying that someone will hurt you, the thought of which causes me great pain. Just…be careful with him. Please?" She glanced at Rowena, who was still slumped in the corner with her eyes shut. Bending, she murmured directly into Caroline's ear. "I don't know if you've noticed, but Rowena has not been well of late."

"I have indeed," replied Caroline in just as quiet a voice. "Is she…?"

Eleanor nodded. "And she needs no additional burdens to worry her," she added pointedly.

The light of battle died in Caroline's eyes. "I will give her none."

Glancing across the carriage at her cousin, Eleanor realized he was peering at them with curious eyes. Snapping her fan shut, she offered him a quick and, she hoped, reassuring smile.

No excitement stirred in her breast when their carriage arrived at its destination. This was the first real ball of the Season, and she ought to have at least a tiny thrill of joy at the prospect of dancing. But without Sorin to dance with, there was no charm in it. No matter who she partnered with, she knew she'd only imagine and wish that it was him.

I love him. Over and over, the three words repeated in her mind. *Is this what being in love is like?* Every tragic poem she'd ever read on the subject of romance came flooding back. She'd hoped to spare Sorin such cruelty, and now she was caught in its nets herself.

She waited half an hour, but still he failed to appear. Finally, and only because Rowena was giving her "the look," she allowed Marston to partner her in a quadrille after which she was fair game for the other gentlemen who'd been hanging about. Her dance card was filling with alarming speed. Taking a moment in the powder room, she wrote false names in the few remaining empty spaces left later that evening just in case Sorin showed up.

Why am I even bothering? Yet she continued to write.

Back into the fray. After nearly an hour without pause she scurried, head down, off the ballroom floor to sit out the next dance somewhere quiet.

Just as she approached the safety of the stairs, she heard a familiar voice and looked up. Dread filled her at the sight of Yarborough with his head tilted back in laughter. She altered course before he could spot her, but then spied his mother heading toward her from the opposite direction. It was stand and be pinned down or hide. She took the better part of valor and ducked behind a potted tree, praying she'd not been noticed by either of them. After a moment, she risked a peek.

"I was hoping to find you before the next dance."

She nearly screamed in fright, only just catching herself in time to release her breath in a more dignified manner. Turning, she faced Sorin with as pleasant an expression as she could muster, given her mortification over having been found crouched behind an ornament. "Lord Wincanton. I'm so glad to see you were able to join the festivities."

"My apologies, I did not mean to startle you." His brows knit. "Whom are you trying to avoid?"

"The Yarboroughs, of course. I've been fortunate thus far, but you just witnessed a very near miss." A tiny curl of warmth unfurled in her belly as the tension eased from his face. She knew beyond a doubt that he'd been worried her answer might be him. *Do I dare hold to such thin hope?*

"Allow me to assist you." He offered his arm, which she took. "I'm sorry I could not be here sooner."

Did he really mean that? Or was he merely being gentlemanly again? "As am I." How else could one reply? Silence stretched between them, intensifying her nervousness.

She longed to reach out and touch him, to know the feel of his strong arms around her, the texture of his skin, the taste of his kisses. It was the sort of yearning that made imprudent ladies fly into men's arms and surrender all respectability. *Say something!* "I've been waiting for you—to tell you about Miss Margaret Rutherford," she amended quickly, grasping at straws.

He frowned. "Miss Margaret…who?"

I made a promise, and this is as good a way to keep him talking as any. Steeling herself, she elaborated. "Miss Margaret Rutherford is the daughter of Mister Rutherford, a coal magnate, and Lady Abigail Rutherford, formerly Lady Fentonwick. She remarried after the death of her first husband, the Earl of Fentonwick, and her son's subsequent assumption of the title." She waited, but he said nothing, so she continued. "I realize, of course, that Miss Rutherford is only a Miss, but her mother was once a countess and has raised the children born to her second marriage thusly. Margaret is a modest young woman of impeccable reputation whom I vow would be a credit to any gentleman."

He stared at her and did not answer.

She rushed on, determined to see this through. "If Miss Rutherford is not to your liking, then might I suggest Lady Rothchild's daughter, Lady Eugenia? She would bring you both wealth and beauty, and her reputation is equally without blemish. If you would like, I would be happy to make the introductions."

Sorin's stomach roiled as though he'd just swallowed a large mouthful of something particularly vile. She was playing matchmaker. For him. That it was exactly what he'd asked her to do mattered not at all. She was staring, waiting. He needed to say something. Something other than the flood of invective currently held back only by his tightly clenched teeth. "I...confess I did not expect you to find suitable candidates so quickly."

"I was fortunate enough to meet both ladies on the day of the picnic," she explained. "They are acquaintances of Lady Blithesby, a friend of Rowena's. Her ladyship had only the highest words of praise for them both."

"I see." He took a breath to steady himself. "Well then, I suppose I ought to meet these paragons." His heart sank as a proud smile lifted the corners of her mouth.

"Incidentally, Miss Rutherford brings more wealth than Lady Eugenia," she continued in a hushed voice. "I overheard her mother say she'll bring sixty-three thousand to a marriage. Although a duke's daughter, Lady Eugenia will bring only twenty-five." She patted his arm absently. "Of course I know money means nothing to you, but you should still be aware.

Given her vast wealth, you'll probably find it more difficult to gain Miss Rutherford's favor, if only because she's already gathered so many admirers. Even so, should she be your choice, I have every confidence in your ability to win her."

Wonderful. "I think you have a good deal more faith in me than perhaps you ought," he said, trying to sound amused as opposed to miserable.

"Nonsense," was her brisk reply. "Being an earl, you're quite the catch yourself. You'll have no trouble at all finding a bride. Now, I'm given to understand that Miss Rutherford enjoys outdoor sport more than most ladies—riding, archery, hunting, and such. She's well-educated, of course, but not the bookish sort. Lady Eugenia, I'm told, is more content with reading or needlework. She also enjoys music and is highly appreciative of chocolate in all forms, an excellent bit of information for any gentleman coming to call."

Unable to bear hearing any more talk of Miss Rutherford and Lady Eugenia, he stopped and turned to her. "Would you honor me with the next dance?"

She blinked in surprise and after a brief hesitation, nodded. He propelled her to the dance floor past several gentlemen who looked on with appreciative and eager eyes. When Sorin at last stopped in line to face her across the aisle for the *danse écossaise*, he suddenly understood why she'd attracted so much attention.

What stood before him was a completely dazzling woman, a perfect rose in full, glorious bloom. He'd been so unsettled by their conversation and so intent upon observing her face for even the smallest clue as to her true state of mind concerning him that he'd been all but blind to anything else.

He was certainly not so now. Dumbstruck, he could only stare at the slender curves revealed by the fall of her skirts as she moved. Creamy skin glowed in the candlelight, its velvet richness offset by the fiery glimmer of diamonds. Diamonds he'd helped select. His fingers itched with the memory of how soft the flesh of her nape had been as he'd helped her first try them on.

Desire threatened to drown him as he bowed in response to her curtsy, and then the dance commenced. Weaving through the line, they promenaded. Then began the series of turns that brought them together time and again. Her warm fingertips briefly brushed his palm, each touch fanning the embers within him until they blazed white-hot.

Their eyes locked, and everything else was cast into insignificance. All thoughts save those of want evaporated as wild imaginings rose in his mind. Visions of pulling her into his arms and kissing her right there on the ballroom floor, of sweeping her up and carrying her off to some secluded place and making slow, passionate love to her flashed through his head.

Then the dance was over. She again dipped before him, her breathing rapid and her color high, no doubt from exertion. It couldn't be anything more, not with her trying to marry him off to Miss Weatherford or Lady whatever-her-name-was. Before he could say anything, another man stepped up between them and claimed the next dance. The next instant, she was gone without a backward glance.

A sense of loss engulfed him as he watched her trip the reel with her partner. Light as eiderdown, she was, and her smile shone like a thousand suns. But that smile was not for him. Jealousy raged in his blood until the heat of it was almost unbearable. In that moment, he knew there was no escape from the desire that bound him to her. It was an invisible, inexorable force, like gravity. How could she not feel it, too?

She passed by, and their glances caught and held for a moment. Heat rose in his face as her brows drew together in a look of consternation just before she was whirled away. *Bollocks.* He needed to regain his composure before he made an idiot of himself in front of the whole bloody assembly. He turned—and found himself face-to-face with Yarborough.

"You think I don't know what you're playing at?" the man accused him bitterly.

"I beg your pardon?"

The younger man's eyes burned with malice. "You pretend to be a friend to me and to her. But I see the truth of it. You want her for yourself."

Sorin froze. "Of whom are we speaking, exactly?"

"Eleanor, of course!" said Yarborough, spitting her given name like a curse. "You needn't act the fool with me. I've seen you, the way you look at her, the way you hover over her and drive off her other prospects. Well, I can tell you that she wants none of you."

Blood pounded at Sorin's temples, yet he held himself in check. "You presume too much," he said with far more calm than he felt. "If I'm protective of Eleanor, it is because I *know* what kind of men hunt her." He stared pointedly at the other man.

Yarborough puffed up like a rotten carcass. "Protective!" He sneered. "Is that what you call it?"

"I've known her since before you showed your ugly face in Wincanton," Sorin growled, stepping close enough to prevent anyone overhearing. "I have no shame in admitting she is dear to me. And as long as I draw breath, I will protect her from greedy little bastards like you. If you have any wisdom at all, you'll leave off and seek your fortune elsewhere."

"If you cannot have her, no one can—is that it?" said Yarborough, sarcasm dripping from each and every word. "I should think the lady has a right to choose her own husband."

Ice filled Sorin's veins, eradicating the heat of before in

an instant. "Indeed she does—but she won't choose you. That I can promise."

Yarborough looked at him with open contempt. "You are neither her father nor her brother to speak for her. You are nothing to her. I *will* woo Eleanor, and I will win her—whether you approve or not."

The time for gentle manners was long past. *Time to take off the gloves.* "You've already tried and failed," Sorin told him bluntly. "The lady has ignored your invitations, eschewed your company, and given you no encouragement whatsoever. Why do you continue to lay siege to a woman who is so plainly uninterested in you?"

"She would not be so difficult if *you* did not influence her!" snapped the other man, his face reddening.

His words were a balm to Sorin's soul. He crossed his arms and regarded the pompous little whelp with amusement. "First you say I am 'nothing' to the lady, and then in the next breath you cite my influence as a stumbling block. Which am I?" He chuckled, further enraging his would-be rival. "Don't let temper overrule good sense, my lad. If you think I cannot put an end to your unwanted pursuit, you are wrong. One way or another, you will leave her be." He lowered his voice. "Don't make me call you out."

Yarborough paled, yet still he had the stones to scoff at the threat. "Don't be ridiculous. People don't duel anymore. It's against the law. Yet another sign that you're a relic, an old man dreaming of something he can never have."

Sorin skewered him with a hard stare and spoke quietly. "I wonder, were we to face each other on the field of honor, how quickly your bravado would crumble?"

"Are you challenging me?" said the other man, his voice trembling.

Sorin let a slow smile take over his mouth. How he would

like to do just that! But it would cause a terrible scandal, and Eleanor would bear the consequences of it. "Consider this the warning shot across your bow," he said lightly. Stepping an inch closer, he breathed, "You've already committed offenses against one whom I love. If you continue on your present course, know that I will indeed challenge you. Know also that should it come to that end, I won't hesitate to kill you."

All color fled Yarborough's face.

"This is the only warning you will receive," Sorin continued. "Think carefully before committing yourself to any act you might come to regret." Not waiting for a response, he gave Yarborough his back and strode away.

Perhaps it had been unwise to show his cards, but he had no regrets. He'd be happy to lay down his life for Eleanor's sake, but doubted Yarborough felt likewise. If the man's greed was such that it drove him to act rashly, however, then so be it. Sorin, being a perfect shot and equally as deadly with a blade, didn't fear a confrontation.

Ascending to the gallery, he leaned against the balustrade to observe the ballroom from a better vantage point. He wanted to have an eye on Ellie, not because he was worried that Yarborough might tell her about their little tête-à-tête—only a total fool would tell a woman he wanted for himself that another man was willing to die for her—but because Yarborough wasn't the only man out to bag an heiress.

Unfortunately, she was nowhere to be seen. Where the devil had she got to? He peered out at the swirling mass, searching for her rose gown.

A hand touched his sleeve, causing him to start. Turning, he came face-to-face with the very one he sought.

"Come with me, quickly," she urged, drawing him away.

The look on her face told him there was trouble. "What has happened?"

"It is Caroline," she answered, her features pinched with concern. "She has just had an argument with…" Her eyes surveyed the closeness of the crowd, and she lowered her voice. "A certain gentleman of our acquaintance. Come. This way."

She led him through the crush and then ducked down a relatively quiet hall. Stopping in front of a closed door near the far end, she knocked twice, paused, and knocked again. The door opened a crack, and a red-rimmed eye the color of cornflower peered through the aperture briefly before the door swung wide to admit them.

"I've brought Lord Wincanton," murmured Eleanor as she entered. "He will take us home."

"Thank you," said the girl thickly, her face blotchy and streaked with tears.

"What of Charles and Rowena?" Sorin asked. "Why are they not here?"

A guilty look crossed Eleanor's features. "I went to them first and told them Caroline was unwell and that you'd already agreed to escort us home. I know it was wrong of me," she rushed as his frown deepened, "but I did not wish to upset Rowena."

He stared at her reddening cheeks, incredulous. "You lied to them?"

"Sorin, please. You misunderstand my intent." She came to him and laid a gentle hand on his arm. "Rowena is with child again—but you must not tell Charles! She wants to wait awhile before informing him. I did not tell them about this because I did not want to increase her worry. She's been so ill of late and the added stress…"

"I understand," he said at once, joy for his friends' good fortune warring with a sudden pang of envy. "Wait here," he commanded, going to the door.

Finding a servant in the hallway, he paid the man half a crown to discreetly see to arranging transport. Briefly, he pondered the wisdom of seeking out Marston for a quick word, but quashed the notion. There was enough on his plate at the moment, and that would likely add another entire meal. He'd learn what happened soon enough anyway.

The servant returned and informed him that his carriage would be brought around to the back of the manor to avoid the congestion. Dropping another coin into his palm, Sorin told him to wait. Returning to the ladies, he brought them out and had the servant lead them through the halls, by request avoiding the ballroom.

The last thing he needed was for Yarborough to see him bundling Eleanor and her friend off into his carriage.

Only after they'd successfully boarded the conveyance did he finally relax. The atmosphere in the carriage was, at best, oppressive. Caroline stared, empty-eyed, at the floor, while Eleanor fussed over her and offered what comfort she could. He met her eyes several times, unable to help himself. But each time, she merely shook her head a little in warning and mouthed "later."

The storm broke half a mile later when Caroline suddenly burst into hysterical sobs. "Oh, Eleanor!" she wailed. "I don't *want* to love him, but I cannot help it! I've tried and tried, but no matter how I tell myself that I hate him, my heart gives me such pain when I see him!" Turning, she laid her head on Eleanor's shoulder and wept such as only one with an utterly broken heart can.

"I know. I know, dear," murmured Eleanor, stroking her friend's hair.

He could do naught but feel both helpless and awkward when she met his gaze over her friend's shoulder.

"The things I s—said to him," the redhead continued,

horror evident in her shaky whisper. "Such terrible things! And all he did was tell me that he still cared for me. But I was just so *angry* with him still!" Her ire quickly faded again into hopelessness. "I was hateful toward him when I ought to have been forgiving. We have both made egregious errors, but had I been a better person and able to overcome my temper we might be mending things even now instead of…this. And my heart might have what it truly wants."

He watched as Eleanor held her tight, heedless of the water threat posed to her gown. "Love, it seems, never offers us an easy path," she offered her friend softly.

Sorin stared at them, his own heart leaden. Would it not be better to just tell her the truth, have done, and see what happened? Part of him wanted to do so desperately, to be free of the terrible burden of secrecy. But fear still barred that path with sharp brambles. If she rejected him after such a confession, he would never recover from it. Their friendship would be over, and she would never again look upon him with trust or affection.

"I want to leave," wept Caroline.

"We are leaving," said Eleanor.

"No, I mean leave London. I can never face him again—I want to go home and I never want to speak of him again!"

For Sorin, her words were the validation of his greatest fear concerning Eleanor. He'd keep his mouth shut. At least for now. He started as Caroline unexpectedly addressed him.

"Lord Wincanton, you have graciously provided both your carriage and escort after bearing witness to my shame, and you've offered neither censure nor derision. I'm humbled by your generosity." She dragged her watery gaze up to meet his. "My behavior toward you has been inexcusable, and I know that it has brought you great discomfort. I humbly ask your forgiveness and hope that in time we may become true friends."

The misery in her eyes tugged at his heart. "I already consider us friends, Miss Caroline. And I will do everything I can to help you if you'll permit me. I'm very good friends with Lord Marston."

A faint smile shook the corners of her mouth for a split second. "Thank you for your kindness, but I'm afraid there is nothing that can be done now. I've just set fire to the last stick of bridge between us, you see. He will never forgive me for the things I said to him tonight."

"I'm sure it's not as bad as that," soothed Eleanor.

"Allow me to at least try, Miss Caroline," he insisted, something inside him desperate to see *someone* achieve the happiness that seemed destined to elude him. The look Eleanor cast him was one of hopeful adoration. That she should have such trust and confidence in him was almost unbearable when he couldn't even admit to her the truth of his own heart.

Caroline shook her head sadly, more tears streaming from her eyes. "I doubt whether anyone can mend what I have broken. For either of us."

Chapter Sixteen

"Yet another invitation from Yarborough." Eleanor cast the page into the grate, her irritation mounting as its edges flared orange and began to shrivel amongst the coals. It was better to focus on her anger toward Yarborough than on how awful she felt every time she was reminded of Sorin. "Why can he not simply leave me alone? I've been polite, but no more than what good manners demand. I've certainly given him no encouragement to hound me so."

"Well, he seems oblivious to your dislike," said Caroline, looking up from her embroidery. "You'll have to make your position clear."

"If I made it any plainer, I'd be walking out with a sign hung 'round my neck." With Caroline, at least, she could vent her frustration openly. "The man is a menace! People are actually beginning to show him sympathy. Him! Thanks to his deceitful devil-woman of a mother, all of London 'knows' we were childhood friends and simply cannot understand why I slight him so. According to increasingly popular opinion, which *every*one feels quite free to share with me at *every* opportunity, I ought to be delighted at the prospect of a suitor with whom I am so familiar. I'll be a pariah by the end of the Season." She plonked herself down on a chair and scowled.

"And yet thus far your only response to such comments has been, 'We are not well suited.' Eleanor, you cannot continue trying to deal with this passively. Being polite about it and then changing the subject won't work anymore. People want to know why you choose to ignore him."

"Of course they do," Eleanor snapped. "As if they have a right to ask such intimate questions of me." Yes, she'd heard the murmurs and whispers concerning her of late. And the more she heard, the more annoyed she became. The more annoyed she became, the less tolerant she grew to curious inquiry. "The next time someone asks me inappropriate questions regarding the matter, I'll answer them with my back," she vowed.

"And alienate those who might be counted among your allies, should it come to an open dispute like the one in which I currently find myself," warned her friend.

"I don't care what other people think!" Eleanor huffed. Which wasn't entirely true, but those whose opinions counted already understood her plight. "It might be wrongheaded of me, but it seems far better to remain silent than to constantly dole out excuses in a vain attempt to placate those who should have more respect for another's privacy."

But Caroline shook her head. "They will never stop speculating. You really only have two options from which to choose. You must tell your inquisitors the truth—which we both know would lead straight to scandal—or confront him in private and give him the chance to walk away with his pride intact."

Eleanor's temples had begun to throb. She didn't want to confront him, but she didn't seem to have much choice. "I'll think on it," she promised. Putting down the post she'd been crumpling, she eyed her friend. "Speaking of confrontations, you've been very quiet of late. Still determined to avoid him?"

"I'm determined not to make a fool of myself," replied Caroline coolly. "I've wounded him. If I try to recant now, he will only reject me. Again." Her shoulders slumped. "I have no desire to be publicly humiliated. Neither do I wish to cause him further pain."

"Why not let Lord Wincanton speak with him and ascertain his mood? He might have had a change of—"

"No! He must not interfere. Marston would be ashamed to learn that others are aware of what occurred between us. Let the matter remain private, I beg you."

Though she had deep misgivings, Eleanor nodded. Excusing herself, she went downstairs. As she neared the family sitting room, she heard Rowena speaking and paused a moment to listen.

"I cannot help but suspect that this sudden illness was a sham," she heard Rowena say. "I'm certain something happened between them but what, exactly, I know not. Thus far there have been no rumors but even if nothing surfaces, I still—"

"Let it be," interrupted Charles. "Whatever happened, it appears to have been kept private or we would have heard something by now. We ought to be grateful the girl seems to have finally learned her lesson without causing permanent damage to her reputation."

There was a moment of silence, and then Rowena again spoke. "Charles…there is something else I wish to speak with you about."

Eleanor waited, barely breathing.

"What is it, my sweet?"

The concern in his voice as well as his use of the pet name made Eleanor smile.

"I'm with child again," came Rowena's soft reply.

A soft exclamation erupted from Charles. "You are certain?" he asked in a quavering voice.

"I am. I saw Doctor Harper yesterday and confirmed it. Provided all goes well, our next child should be born in late autumn." Her words were followed by the sound of someone rising in haste, no doubt to embrace the bearer of such good news.

Reluctant to intrude on such a private moment, Eleanor retreated. Later that night, she found her thoughts returning to that moment. All day long, there had been a quiet feeling of joy throughout the house. The servants knew, and word was no doubt spreading across London even now. While she was pleased for Charles and Rowena, she couldn't help feeling lonely.

I'll never experience that sort of happiness...

She was not the only one suffering. Though Caroline had also offered them both heartfelt congratulations, Eleanor had caught a look of profound sadness in her eyes as she'd turned away. She said nothing, however, for fear of making her friend feel even worse.

As she lay abed listening to the rain against the window panes, Eleanor's thoughts turned to Sorin. Things had improved since the night they'd brought Caroline home, and she lived in terror of saying the wrong thing, of ruining the growing warmth between them. Despite her earlier resolve to become a spinster, she'd again begun to hope to change his view of her. Rowena had dismissed Jane's example, but Eleanor wasn't so sure Sorin desired something different.

I have to try. If Jane pleased him by being demure and proper, so can I.

But in her secret, innermost thoughts, she longed to please him in other ways—ways no proper lady would even imagine, much less act upon. Things she wouldn't have any knowledge of if it weren't for Caroline sharing certain scandalous conversations she'd overheard between her married sisters. Things that made her feel hot and uncomfortable to think about now. If Sorin knew she was having such thoughts about him he would be shocked. Maybe even appalled.

He would certainly think her far too wicked to consider for a wife.

Lightning flickered, causing shadows to leap and dance throughout the room. An earth-shaking rumble of thunder followed an instant later, and the rain began to lash the windows in earnest. A painful sob heaved its way up from her chest, and tears streamed from her eyes as if mirroring the torrent outside. All the frustration and fear she'd been holding in for so long, she now released. No one would hear. No one would know.

"Eleanor?"

Eleanor leaped from the bed with a squeak of fright, her heart pounding. "Sweet Lord above!" she gasped, trying surreptitiously to wipe her eyes. "Caroline, what in heaven's name are you doing up and about at this hour?" Despite the rug, the floor was frigid. She eased herself back onto the bed and tucked her feet beneath the covers.

"I'm sorry," said her friend, coming into the room fully. "I did not mean to frighten you. I came because I could not sleep."

"Marston?"

"Yes. But that is nothing new." She joined Eleanor on the bed. "You, however, have been crying. Are you still upset about Yarborough?"

Though her conscience pricked her, she couldn't tell Caroline the truth. Better for her to believe she already knew the answer. "He and his horrid mother have all but ruined

London for me this year. My only consolation is that he will soon have no choice but to pursue someone else. After all, he must marry by the end of the Season, and he's already wasted so much time chasing after me—or rather, my inheritance." She sat up, gladly turning her mind from her misery. "In fact, I think I'll put it to him in just those words."

"Then you will speak with him?"

She nodded. "At the Cleveland ball. I just have to figure out a way to do it without causing a scene."

Caroline's gaze bored into her, and for a moment Eleanor feared her misdirection had been too obvious. "I agree," her friend said at last. "I think it wise to deal with him quickly and in as direct a manner as possible."

The tension in Eleanor's stomach began to ease.

"But are you sure there's not something…*else* bothering you?"

"Nothing," Eleanor answered firmly, avoiding her eyes. "I've been so worried that this business with Yarborough would get out of hand and cause Rowena and Charles unnecessary concern. You're right, of course. I cannot remain passive anymore and must take action. I'll speak with Charles and let him know my plans. He will support me."

"Good." Caroline rose. "Well, as you've problems enough of your own, I won't bother you with my well-trodden woes."

"Nonsense, I'm always happy to listen to whatever you have to say." Reaching out, Eleanor caught her hand. "Please, stay and talk."

"No, really, I'm quite all right now," said Caroline, giving her fingers a quick, reassuring squeeze before letting go. "I really just needed to hear a friendly voice, I think, and your good company has eased my heart enough that I feel able to sleep now. Good night, Eleanor."

"Good night," she replied, feeling helpless as she watched

the door close. With Caroline gone, Eleanor's thoughts returned to her true problem. Pointing out eligible prospects to Sorin had resulted in a most puzzling and enlightening experience. His flustered reaction had been such that she was sure now he hadn't actually meant for her to take up the role of matchmaker. But if he didn't really want her help finding a bride, what *was* his reason for asking her to assist him?

There was only one thing to do if she wanted to find out, and that was continue until either she figured out the truth or he told her to stop. By Jove, he'd asked her to help him find a suitable wife, and that was what she was going to do—to all appearances, at least.

Sorin watched from the corner of his eye as Eleanor walked beside him exploring the new tulip beds he'd had installed in the garden. Her behavior was growing stranger and stranger. Instead of easing into comfortable familiarity as he'd been trying so hard to get her to do, she'd gone the opposite direction, becoming more and more formal. She had also been driving him to Bedlam trying to suggest possible matches for him.

Already, he had endured no less than nine introductions. He'd begun to feel like a fattened goose on Christmas Eve—every time he bowed before one of her "finds" he could almost hear the sound of an axe being sharpened. Though all the ladies in question had been lovely and were no doubt delightful under other circumstances, he'd not found a single one even remotely interesting. Of course, he'd known this would happen. Until Eleanor married and was once and for all unavailable, he would be unable to truly consider anyone else.

"Next year, I think I should like to replant these roses along the back wall, over there," he said just to break the silence. "Several of them have stopped blooming."

"Is your gardener fertilizing them properly?"

He marked that she maintained her distance, never coming closer than arm's length. They used to walk with their arms linked. "I've asked him, and he swears he's done everything correctly. He seems to think they suffer from a disease, but has been unable to determine which. There is no indication of mildew or spotting. He's checking the roots tomorrow to be sure it's not soil-related."

"You should write to the king's chief gardener and ask his opinion," she suggested, keeping her hands folded primly behind her. The sun on her hair made it shine like burnished gold. "After all, as a peer, you have the privilege."

"I had not thought of that, but you're quite right. I shall do so later today." He turned to her. "How goes it with Miss Caroline?"

A crease marred the perfection of her brow. "Not well, I fear. She's far too quiet. Charles and Rowena are delighted by her apparent reformation, of course, but I dislike it. She is not herself."

"Neither are you of late."

She glanced up at him, startled. "I? How so?"

It was a risk, but he had to know if there was a problem. "You've not been as open with me as you once were. It has been many a day since you spoke to me of anything beyond that which may be covered in drawing room small talk."

Her cheeks flushed, and she looked down. "I meant nothing by it, I assure you. I've been…distracted."

"By?"

"Yarborough, if you must know," she replied, her voice taking on an edge. "He seems determined to remain a nuisance, and I've been trying to decide how best to deal with him."

Calm. He must remain calm. "How has he been troubling you?"

"He writes daily, just a line or two, but it is enough to set the servants talking. And the invitations from his mother to come and call remain unceasing. People are calling me a heartless ice maiden while admiring his dedication and her forbearance."

Sorin struggled to rein in a sudden flare of fury. Yarborough had not heeded his warning in the least! "You should have Ashford speak with him."

She shook her head. "I was planning to do so, but my cousin has enough to worry about with Rowena. The doctor says all is well with both her and the babe, but nausea has rendered her unable to leave the house for nearly a week now." Her mouth thinned. "I must deal with Yarborough myself. At the first opportunity, I'm going to speak with him, refuse his suit, and then point out that it is in his best interest to look elsewhere before it grows too late in the Season. He cannot, after all, concentrate on wooing another when he is openly set on conquering me."

Sorin felt the blood leave his face. It seemed he and Yarborough had something in common, after all.

"It is my hope that he will see reason and desist," she went on, oblivious. "I would ask Charles to intervene in the event Yarborough takes it badly, but…"

"I would be honored to assist you in his stead," he finished for her in as neutral a tone as he could manage. A thrill raced through him at the prospect of being her champion. Unfortunately, he would have to wait until *after* she tried to dissuade the blackguard herself. He almost hoped the bastard would provide him with such an opportunity. "Let me know when you plan to speak with him so that I may make myself available."

"Easily done," she said with a grim smile. "People might arrive at the wrong conclusion if I allow him to call on me at home, so I've decided to address him at the Cleveland ball—discreetly of course. My purpose is not to humiliate him, but simply to make him understand that I am uninterested in his suit."

He nodded. It was just a week away. "That seems a wise course. He's less likely to react poorly in a public setting."

"Just so," she confirmed, her expression softening. "I knew you would see the logic of it at once."

An hour later, Sorin strode into John Stafford's office.

"I was just going to send you a message," said John, looking up with a smile. "I found the information you wanted."

"Let us hope it is enough to frighten the bastard off and keep me from having to shoot him."

John's brows rose. "Things have not been going well, I take it."

"Not particularly." He didn't feel like elaborating. "What have you discovered?"

"Well, the Yarboroughs' financial dealings, while they appear to be disappointingly legal, indicate that they are quite thinly stretched. Your fellow is up to his eyeballs in debt."

Sorin frowned. "But what of the Irish property?"

"Oh, it was sold," said John, smirking. "But not for anywhere near the amount they would have everyone believe. The estate was small, only about a third the size of yours. The proceeds from that along with the sale of their old London residence were enough to pay for the house in Golden Square as well as a few relatively minor purchases—a new carriage and four, some jewelry. As for the improvements to the property in Golden Square, they were contracted to the lowest bidder who would require only half the money up front. The new furnishings were all bought on credit as was the majority of their new finery. I would venture to say that Yarborough's very teeth are in danger if he does not marry exceedingly well."

"They are frauds, then," Sorin muttered. "They haven't a penny to their name, yet they're living like kings—on credit."

John nodded. "A practice all too commonly employed, I'm afraid. I also discovered that their house in Somerset has been rented to a family from Derbyshire. A solicitor friend of mine at Bailey & Gerald informed me the contract has been drawn up, signed, and that a deposit has been made—and doubtless already spent."

"They never intended to return to Somerset," Sorin said, experiencing a twinge of guilty relief at the knowledge that he wouldn't have to put up with the pair on the return trip. "They plan to remain in London and live off his bride's inheritance."

"A right assumption, if you ask me," agreed John. "He's going to look for the biggest purse he can find and marry it quick as you like—before his creditors can come after him and have him locked up in Marshalsea. It's no wonder the fellow is so reluctant to give her up."

All of London knew Eleanor's inheritance was substantial, but few knew the exact amount. Charles and Rowena had done everything in their power to keep that information a secret. The family's solicitor was one person who knew. Sorin was another. Though they'd passed her off as no wealthier than any of half a dozen other heiresses currently on the market, he knew she was 'worth' a little more than two hundred thousand pounds. The question was, did Yarborough know it, and if so, how?

"And you say he's done nothing illegal?" he asked John.

"Naught that could land him in prison—yet," added John with a wink. "Best be having an eye on that lady of yours, though. He's not afraid of dirtying his hands to get what he wants. The man that oversaw the work on his house said he feared for his life after he demanded the rest of what was due. Said Yarborough threatened harm to his wife and daughter if he said aught to anyone about anything. The only reason the fellow talked to me was so that if something *did* happen, we would know where to look first—an idea I'm proud to say I helped plant." He sucked his teeth and shook his head. "Any man who would threaten another man's family, well, I would not put it past him to try anything. Especially if he's desperate."

"Thank you, John," Sorin replied, his thoughts spinning as he declined a visit to the pub and departed. It was clear now that the whispers about Town concerning the pair, no doubt largely generated by Yarborough's mother, were part of a greater plan.

The pieces began to fit together. They were laying a siege and had planned their battle strategy down to the smallest detail. Yarborough's familiar and suggestive manner with her, the constant barrage of letters, the way he was always lurking about watching her, and the intimidation of her rivals. As with the previous two Seasons, there should have been swarms of men beating down Ashford's door to court Eleanor, but there had been only a few this year and they'd not lingered very long.

Taking a step back, he could see it all clearly. Everything Yarborough had done from the moment he'd arrived in Wincanton was carefully constructed to discredit Eleanor's public rejection of him, to make people believe there was a secret relationship between them that did not, in fact, exist. No doubt he planned to come forth with news of a secret engagement or something of that nature. Eleanor would deny it, of course, but the damage would be irreversible.

All the elements were against her. They were from the same county. They'd known each other from childhood. She'd refused all her other suitors. Though she would deny any relationship, her character would fall under suspicion. There would be enormous pressure to marry him in order to avoid a scandal. It was clever. Quite clever. And it showed the Yarboroughs capable of playing a long game indeed—if he could confirm his suspicion.

Upon returning home, he received an invitation from Charles for an evening at White's along with Marston. Blessing his good fortune, he replied acceptance at once. It was the perfect opportunity to have a look at The Book. A most useful tool for enlightenment concerning current gossip, it should provide confirmation, if any existed. He played a few hands of cards before quietly going to consult the infamous Tome of the Ton. An unpleasant prickle spread across his flesh as he turned back through the more recent pages to find an alarming number of wagers concerning Lady E. and Sir Y.

Charles must be informed immediately and action taken before it was too late.

As he was preparing to leave, however, Marston pulled him aside. "You're not going to like this. I just overheard a man say that Yarborough boasted to him—in strictest confidence, of course," he added with a snort, "that on the way to London he and Eleanor had become 'very close,' but that she'd given him the cold shoulder upon arrival because her redheaded friend had advised her to try for a bigger catch. The man claims Yarborough is heartbroken but determined not to give up."

Beneath his breath, Sorin uttered a stream of blasphemy that would no doubt earn him several days in purgatory. "I knew something like this was brewing, but I did not expect it quite this soon."

"If you are to act, it needs to be swiftly, before something untoward happens," said Marston.

"He won't harm her. I'll kill him first, and he knows it."

"I'll second you, if it comes to it."

Sorin looked at Marston for a long moment, considering. "I appreciate that, old friend. It may very well come to that, but I intend to try another way first."

"You should speak to Charles at once," urged Marston. "Explain the situation and ask him for her hand. He will support you. It is the simplest way to eliminate the threat. Safely married, she can no longer be a target."

"Charles is not the one who concerns me most. The lady herself has to accept my offer."

Marston's smile was a gentle reproach. "I still think you're wrong about her. I think she loves you. Adores you, actually."

"Perhaps, but she does not love me the way a wife should love a husband," he answered with a grimace.

"Love can change, and marriage comes with certain expectations that will help you in that." A knowing look lit Marston's eyes. "She'll want children. Marry her first and work on the rest later when you have the luxury of time."

Blood rushed to Sorin's face.

The other man chuckled at his discomfiture. "Rest assured the pleasures of the marriage bed will forever alter her view of you, my friend. And when she sees you as the father of her firstborn, they will alter yet more." He sobered. "Regardless, I'm certain she would much rather marry you than that miscreant."

"I'm not so certain she's going to want to marry anyone, but I will do whatever is necessary to protect her." Even if it meant deceiving her, though he would prefer another alternative.

The entries in the betting book were clear. Something was expected to happen soon. The Cleveland ball was but a week away. The night Eleanor planned to speak with Yarborough. As far as he was aware, she planned to attend no other events of significance between now and then. Every instinct told him the blackguard would make his move that night. He would be there, ready.

Chapter Seventeen

The Cleveland Ball

Eleanor drifted amid the crush, looking for Sorin. Again, she'd dressed to please him and wore the soft salmon pink he'd once claimed to be a favorite color on her. In spite of all her dashed hopes, she still wanted to be beautiful for him. After all, a miracle might occur to change his unromantic perception of her.

"May I have the honor of partnering you in the first dance, Lady Eleanor?"

Turning, she faced Lord Marston with a smile. She'd hoped to dance with Sorin first, but he was nowhere to be seen. "You may," she told him, dipping a curtsy and taking his arm.

"Is Miss Caroline here tonight?"

The abruptness of his inquiry caught her by surprise. "I—yes, she is," she answered with no small amount of trepidation.

"My apologies," he said at once, looking embarrassed. "I've no manners tonight, apparently."

"It's quite all right," she murmured, keenly aware of his

pain, which was so similar to her own. "She deeply regrets what passed between you," she ventured carefully.

"As do I. I love her still, you know."

"Your affection is not unreciprocated," she said, ready to brave Caroline's wrath.

His eyes lit. "She told you this?"

"She did." She laid her other hand on his arm, stopping their progress. "She is desolate over what happened. I worry for her. For you both. Won't you go to her?"

He shook his head sadly. "Even if what you say is true, I fear she would lose her temper with me again, and that would do neither of us any good at all. Come, let us join the other dancers."

Together they walked to the ballroom floor to join the forming lines. To her shock, she spied Sorin four couples down opposite none other than the raven-haired Lady Eugenia, one of the women to whom she'd introduced him a few weeks prior. The little heifer was looking at him with bold, appreciative eyes. Even more alarming, he seemed quite pleased with her company.

Pain lanced through her at the sight of his lopsided smile. It doubled when he broke into laughter. Sorin was not the sort to laugh easily, especially in public. If he was comfortable enough with Lady Eugenia to do so, it was a sure sign that he favored her greatly. Feeling ill, she tore her gaze away from the happy couple to regard Marston, who was peering at her with an expression of deep concern.

"Lady Eleanor, are you feeling well?"

She forced a smile. "I'm perfectly fine." Fortunately, at that moment the music began, sparing her the need for further explanation. Though she tried and tried not to look at Sorin, she couldn't help herself. When the cotillion brought her and Marston 'round on promenade between the lines, she kept her gaze straight ahead, refusing to look at Sorin.

Over and over, she and her partner wove about the other dancers in the complex steps. Over and over, she passed by Sorin and Eugenia. Over and over, her thoughts ran wild with suppositions.

Did Eugenia's hands tingle after each touch the way hers did? Did Sorin's? Was that why he seemed so oblivious to everything else? Did he have a preference for women with dark hair? Lush figures? Sultry laughs? Such thoughts raced through her mind, each one chipping away at her soul.

She tripped and barely caught herself, embarrassed to have been paying so little attention to what she was doing. Thankfully, Marston seemed not to have noticed. *Please let this dance end soon!* She needed to get out of here and find a place where she could breathe and settle her frayed nerves. Dipping her curtsy at the end of the dance, she fled.

And very nearly slammed right into Yarborough.

"Lady Eleanor," he exclaimed with a delighted smile. "How very fortunate. I was hoping to see you here tonight. I've been meaning to talk to you."

His words were lost on her, for at that moment Sorin passed by, Lady Eugenia on his arm. The jealousy that had been steadily gnawing at Eleanor intensified, ripping at her heart like a vicious, ravening beast.

Turning to Yarborough, she smiled brightly. "I've been meaning to speak with you, as well. Could we find somewhere a bit more private? Over there, perhaps?" she suggested, nodding toward the terrace doors. Their path would take her right past Sorin.

"Of course," said Yarborough, offering his arm.

But Sorin was facing away when she passed. Frustration ate at her.

"May I offer you a glass of champagne?" said her escort,

gesturing for a passing servant to stop with his tray.

"No, thank you." Her confidence slipped as Yarborough's smile faded. "But I would greatly appreciate some punch."

"It will be my pleasure," he said, his smile instantly returning.

Watching as he strode away to do her bidding, Eleanor debated whether to disappear. No. To run away now would ill serve her in too many ways. Besides, she really *did* need to speak with him. Spotting a nearby vacant chair, she sat and scanned the crowd for Sorin. There he was. All she could see of him was his back.

And Eugenia was still hanging on his arm.

An idea formed in her mind. A sly, underhanded idea. It was so wrong, but desperation drove her to take desperate measures. Her discussion with Yarborough could wait just a little while longer—just until after they danced. Given the rumors running about Town, it would cause too great a stir for Sorin to ignore.

"Your punch, Lady Eleanor."

She looked up to see Yarborough standing before her, glass in his hand. "Thank you," she said, taking it. Thirsty, she swallowed several gulps before realizing how bitter it was. *Ugh!* Someone had forgotten to sweeten it. Struggling not to make a face, she set the half-empty glass aside and stood.

But Yarborough wasn't ready to dance just yet. "You know, I must admit that I did not expect you to be here when I returned."

He'd never know how close he was to the truth. "I would never be so discourteous."

"And yet you do not answer any of my letters or accept any of my invitations."

Her cheeks warmed at the gentle recrimination. "That is part of the reason I wished to speak with you tonight." Hell, she was going to *have* to do this now rather than wait. "I think that perhaps you've been laboring under the misimpression that I seek more than your friendship. If I have in any way given you cause to believe it to be so, then I must apologize, for it was entirely unintended."

A twitch of his jaw muscle was the only betrayal of his displeasure. "Lady Eleanor, I would not dream of asking more of you than you're willing to—"

"Excellent," she said, smiling in spite of a sudden rush of dizziness. She sank back down onto her seat, all thoughts of a hasty retreat gone. Her upset over Sorin must have been greater than she'd imagined, for she'd never before experienced the faintness so many ladies claimed accompanied emotional upheaval. "I worried that you might be in disagreement with me on the matter," she continued. "I've been hearing the most alarming rumors concerning us. Rumors we both know to be untrue."

He stared at her for a long moment, his face inscrutable. "Yes, of course. Please don't take this the wrong way, Ellie, but you look a bit pale."

Ellie!? She decided to let it pass. It wasn't worth causing a scene. "It's a bit stuffy in here."

"Indeed it is. Perhaps a breath of fresh air is in order?" He nodded to the doors immediately to her left.

How very convenient. Looking at him, she grew even more suspicious of his polite manner. Surely a great bully like him would react more unpleasantly to her rejection than this? But perhaps she'd been wrong about him. He was, after all, much older now.

Her head felt strange, as if it were full of wool. She attempted to stand and found her legs weak. A silk-sleeved arm hovered before her. She took it and allowed him to help her rise, feeling much steadier for the support.

Thoughts of Sorin swirled. Longing, confusion, and most of all hurt.

Yarborough opened the door and led her out onto the terrace. Even in her muzzy state, Eleanor had enough sense to stop before attempting the stairs leading down to the garden. Not only were stairs a non-negotiable obstacle at the moment, but a tour of the gardens by night was off limits to any young lady of good reputation—or at least as long as she was with anyone other than Sorin.

Sorin… She would happily go anywhere with him.

"You look lovely tonight, Eleanor," said Yarborough, interrupting the pleasant thought.

She frowned. Hadn't they just agreed there was to be nothing between them but friendship? At best? At worst, she disliked him. Intensely. He ought to be grateful she'd rejected him so politely.

"Thank you," she said, turning away. But the quick movement unbalanced her, forcing her to grab the balustrade for support or topple over. *What in heaven's name is the matter with me?*

"You know, I think you may have judged me wrongly," said Yarborough, repositioning himself to again face her.

Once more, she tried to turn away but for some reason was unable to do so. Confused at her sudden immobility, she looked down to see that he had his hand on her arm. She hadn't even felt him touch her. "Sir Yarborough, please. I don't feel at all well," she said, her tongue seeming thick and unwieldy. It was an effort to speak clearly. "I don't think this an appropriate time for such a discussion. If I've misjudged you, then allow me to review my opinion when I am in possession of all my faculties."

A slow smile stretched his lips as he moved closer, pinning her between himself and the balustrade. "Ah, but it is the perfect time for us to discuss our future, my dear, dear *Ellie*."

She could only watch as he came closer. Her head spun, the ground felt terribly far away, and she now began to fear she would faint. "Sir Y—" She had to stop and take a breath, having suddenly lost all the air in her lungs. "Please…remove yourself at…at once," she gasped.

He didn't budge.

With great effort, she lifted leaden arms and pushed at him with all her might. But all strength seemed to have deserted her. Though it seemed her body could only move at a snail's pace, her mind raced. Something was terribly wrong. She licked her now dry lips and recoiled at the bitter taste.

The punch. He put something in it. Alarm should have jolted her to action, but she found herself incapable of more than another feeble attempt to dislodge herself from his embrace. "No…I won't let you…" It came out as a whisper.

"My darling, in your current state you will let me do anything I please," he said, his smile sanguine. "You've had too much champagne, you see. And thanks to your lack of inhibition, your passion for me can no longer be contained or kept secret."

Hatred slowly blossomed in her belly, burning there like a coal straight from the fiery pit. The force of her anger gave her a spurt of strength, which she used to lift and draw back her arm.

The bastard laughed and grasped her wrist, holding it away. "Now, now. Don't start our marriage off this way. After all, once we are wed I'll have every right to retaliate in kind. By the bye, you may be thankful I've chosen to forgive your previous transgression against me in that regard. I blame Ashford for not teaching you your place. That said, know that I will not be so lenient again."

Dully, she registered shock at the implication of his words. Bully indeed.

"In truth, I have no desire to hurt you," he said, his gaze drifting down to her décolletage, infuriating her further. "You've grown into a beautiful woman." A fingertip followed the path his eyes had taken, and her stomach knotted in revulsion. "I can make it pleasant for you, if you cooperate. If not…well, I leave it to you to decide the temperature of our marriage bed. Warm or cold, I'll still enjoy my time between its sheets—and your legs." His eyes were full of gleeful malice.

Panic, pure and simple, set in. If something didn't happen this very instant to stop this, she would be in serious trouble. She was *already* in serious trouble. But whatever he'd put in her punch made movement difficult. It was making thinking difficult, too.

Laughter filtered in from somewhere below and behind her. It took a moment for her to place it. The garden. People were coming up the stairs from the garden. If she faked a faint, someone might come to help. They were coming closer. Closer. They were almost here…

"Perfect timing," murmured Yarborough.

Disgust filled her as he leaned in and his mouth ground against hers. She would have screamed in outrage, but the instant she opened her mouth it was filled with his tongue. Nausea struck, and bile rose in her throat. All attempts to dislodge him were in vain.

He's so strong! There was only one thing to do. Determined to end the revolting contact, she bit down hard on his tongue. The salt tang of blood filled her mouth, and with a hiss of pain he withdrew. All strength left her. As she slumped to the ground, she heard Yarborough cursing and another familiar voice shouting. Strong hands grasped her about the waist and lifted her.

No! She began to struggle against her assailant.

"Lady Eleanor!"

Opening her eyes, she saw Marston bending over her.

"She was feeling faint," she heard Yarborough say. She felt him beside her, but his voice sounded so far away. "I brought her out for some air, and she—"

"Stow it, Yarborough!" hissed Marston. "You'll be lucky if he doesn't bloody well run you through for this. Lady Eleanor…Eleanor!"

Run him through? He must mean Charles. "No," she mumbled. "Don't tell Charles. He cannot know…the children, the babe…"

"Hush, now," Marston said at her ear. "Can you manage to stand and walk a little bit? You don't have to go very far, just a short way."

He sounded so desperate that she determined to try, and though it was difficult, she managed to take a few steps. Now that she knew she was safe, she felt so warm and cozy. Sleep beckoned. Someone was shaking her.

"Eleanor!" snapped Marston. "You must stay awake for me, do you understand? You cannot go to sleep, not yet."

A palm tapped against her cheek, and she opened her eyes, confused. She was back in the ballroom. Sweet music drifted on the air, and everything was edged in a soft nimbus of golden light.

Marston hauled her up against his side and led her away. She protested, wanting to go back and look at the lights, but he was too strong. "Fetch Lord Wincanton at once," she heard him say. "Tell him it is a matter of extreme urgency and bring him back with you."

The light receded farther as they again began to move. Time slowed as she struggled to keep her feet beneath her. Just when she thought she couldn't move another step, the world tilted on its side. Giving in to gravity, she laid down. Something cool brushed across her forehead and cheeks. She didn't much care for it. It interfered with the warmth wrapped around her. Blurred sounds reached her as though from a long way away. A distant door closed, and there were more voices.

Someone was terribly angry. For some reason it didn't frighten her. In fact, it made her very, very happy. More movement. She was floating. It was just like one of those queer flying dreams she'd had as a child. She imagined herself lifting high above the treetops, flying up, up toward the moon.

So happy…

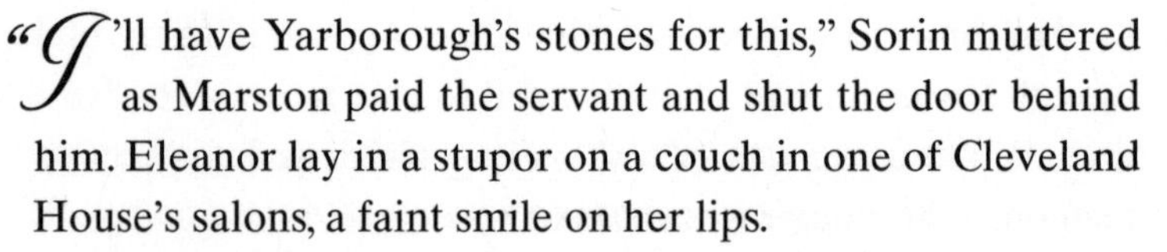

"I'll have Yarborough's stones for this," Sorin muttered as Marston paid the servant and shut the door behind him. Eleanor lay in a stupor on a couch in one of Cleveland House's salons, a faint smile on her lips.

"Worry about that later," said his friend. Leaning over Eleanor, Marston lifted one of her eyelids, eliciting a weak protest. He cursed softly. "Her pupils are like pinpricks. The bastard dosed her with something, likely an opiate. We have to find Charles and—"

"No," Sorin interrupted quickly. "If we tell Charles now, he'll call Yarborough out."

"Under the circumstances, I'm afraid I don't really see how it can be avoided," said Marston, shaking his head slowly. "There were witnesses."

"Lady Ashford is with child, and the pregnancy is causing her a great deal of discomfort," Sorin explained awkwardly. "The stress would endanger both her and the child. I'll tell him everything later in private where we can decide how to handle the matter without her being the wiser. But first we must get Ellie out of here as quickly and quietly as possible."

"Agreed," said the other man after a moment. Again he bent to peel back one of Eleanor's lids. "Considering that he was after her inheritance, I doubt Yarborough gave her enough of anything to put her in danger but—"

"I'll send for a physician as soon as we get to Ashford's house," Sorin assured him. *And then I'm going to hunt down Yarborough, run him through from bow to stern with a dull sword, and rub salt in his wounds.*

"How may I be of assistance?"

The question brought Sorin back to the present. "Wait until after I get her out and then go find Charles. Tell him she fell ill and that I escorted her home. Assure him it's nothing urgent, and above all mention nothing of Yarborough. I want no suspicions raised over her departure. I'll stay with her until they arrive home."

With Marston going ahead to ensure the path was clear, Sorin carried Eleanor through the servants' corridors to better avoid encountering anyone they knew. He hardly breathed until they put her in his carriage. Propping Eleanor up in the opposite corner, he watched to make sure she didn't fall as they began to move.

Everything went smoothly until they made the first turn out onto the street. Dislodged by the motion, Eleanor slumped and swayed dangerously. Leaping up, he went and sat beside her to prevent her tumbling onto the floor. A pothole then necessitated flinging an arm across her chest to hold her steady.

Turning with a deep sigh, Eleanor snuggled into him.

Panic, along with a tearing streak of desire, sucked all the breath from Sorin's lungs. His mouth went dry as she mumbled something unintelligible, her lips parting less than a hand span from his. Very carefully, he tried to reposition her facing away so as to facilitate an escape to the safety of the other seat.

But the lady was having none of that. Now that she'd been roused to wakefulness, she seemed intent on seeking out human contact. He froze as she scooted closer—and laid back across his lap. Paralyzed, he waited, hoping she would subside back into a somnolent state.

Instead, she arched up, nuzzling against his chest and neck.

Closing his eyes, he rubbed his cheek against the golden softness of her hair and inhaled deeply of her lavender scent. He was unlikely to ever have another chance to hold her. This would end in a moment, and she would never be this close to him again. He let her rest against him, content with her unknowing gift—until she reached up, pulled his head down, and covered his mouth with her own.

A shock of want lanced down from the point of contact all the way through his vitals to the seat of his desire, hardening him with dizzying, near-painful haste. The carriage jolted, and some devil-cursed instinct made his arms tighten around her, drawing her closer. His will unraveled as with a groan Eleanor opened her mouth farther and ran the tip of her tongue along the crease of his lips.

All restraint went straight to hell.

Pulling her hard against him, he gave free reign to his desire and kissed her with all the passion he'd withheld for so long, taking what she gave and returning it in full measure. His hands roamed, discovering her shape, skimming at will across her back and down her flanks, moving to cup perfect breasts barely covered by the low neckline of her gown.

She arched her back, and the gentle swells enticed him, their hardening peaks just visible beneath material pulled taut over them. At the brush of his thumb across one, the woman in his arms breathed a low moan against his lips. His heart hammered like a battering ram against his chest as her breath became fast and uneven.

Eleanor... Eleanor...

His hand wandered lower, finding the hem of her dress and running beneath it to caress a slim, stockinged calf, knee, and then thigh. He toyed with the garter for a moment before continuing up, driven by the need to touch her, to feel her silken flesh against his palm. She squirmed as he neared the juncture of her thighs, but she didn't pull away, not even when his fingers brushed the soft curls that concealed her womanhood.

Cupping the plump, hot mound, he drew his thumb up along the delicate crease and heard her breath catch on a soft cry as he found the swollen jewel nestled within. Thrilling to the sound, he stroked the slick, sensitive bud until she writhed against him. Reaching down, she covered his hand with her own, urging him on.

She was ready. Slipping lower, he dipped a little farther and gently pressed, following the rhythm of her breathing until he felt her body stiffen in his arms and her passage clench. Covering her mouth with his own, he muffled her outcry even as he worked to prolong her climax.

When she at last relaxed against him, he withdrew his hand and looked down—into her open eyes. Eyes glazed with pure, unadulterated lust.

Everything—including, it seemed, his heart—simply stopped. Time didn't resume its steady march until her eyes drifted shut a moment later. With a long, contented sigh, Eleanor sank back into the arms of oblivion, a woman's smile curling lips swollen from his kisses.

Reality came thundering down on Sorin like a landslide as he pulled back and settled her against the squabs. Part of him felt no regret—the animal part that was even now aroused almost beyond the point of self-control. The other part, the decent part of him, recoiled over his deplorable conduct. He'd damned near lost control of himself. Another moment or two and he would have taken her right here in the carriage.

Only a scoundrel would take advantage of a lady in her condition. *I'm no better than Yarborough.*

Turning, Eleanor flung an arm over her head and muttered incoherently, snuggling deeper into the cushioned seat. In all of her mumblings, he'd heard no mention of love—for him or anyone else. *Does she even know I'm here?* She'd looked right *at* him a moment ago, but had she truly seen him? Were her actions spurred on by a hidden desire for him or was it merely animal need, incited by the drug, that had driven her to behave like a wanton?

The drug. If it truly was an opiate Yarborough had given her, it couldn't have been the sole impetus. She would certainly have been incapacitated, but not impassioned. Had he given her something else? Alarmed, he checked her pulse. It was slow, but steady, as was her breathing. She was in a deep sleep.

He sat back, feeling hollow inside, drained.

Will she remember? Some—not all, but some—did recall events that occurred while they soared on the wings of opium. His heart seized at the thought. Would she hate him? It was too much to hope that she would remember the pleasure and crave his touch again. He wouldn't allow his heart to cling to such a fantasy. Better to hope instead that she would have *no* memory of the incident at all.

He would have no way of knowing until she awakened fully.

While he ruminated over his troubles, Eleanor slept peacefully the rest of the way to St. James's Square.

When they arrived at Ashford's house, he sent the driver to get help. Though he longed to hold her in his arms again, he couldn't risk another unconscious attempt on her part to seduce him. Ashford's staff would be scandalized enough already. Two footmen came out to assist him, as well as her maid.

Sorin waited outside Eleanor's room while the housekeeper and servants got her settled and sent for a physician. Then, despite vociferous protest from the housekeeper, he pulled up a chair and waited by her bedside, unwilling to leave her.

Charles and Rowena arrived half an hour later. Leaving his beloved to the womenfolk, Sorin drew Charles aside and asked to speak with him privately. "She is not ill," he told his friend as soon as the door closed. "She was drugged."

"Drugged?" Charles sat abruptly, paling. "Are you certain? Marston said she'd grown sick and— "

"It was Yarborough."

"Tell me everything," demanded his friend.

"Marston was helping me keep an eye on Eleanor and saw them go out onto the terrace. When he followed a few minutes later, he discovered Yarborough attempting to compromise her." Sorin watched his friend's pallor disappear, replaced by an unhealthy brick-red flush. "She collapsed just as he reached them. When he discerned her condition, he accused Yarborough of treachery. The bastard denied any wrongdoing, of course, and fled. Marston managed to help her to a salon and then sent for me. We both suspect Yarborough gave her some sort of opiate. A physician has already been sent for."

"Did anyone see them?"

Sorin remembered what Marston had said and forced himself to repeat it. "Marston said a couple coming back from the garden witnessed the incident. How much they saw is in question, and they may or may not talk of it, depending on whether or not theirs was an illicit tryst."

"Dear God," muttered Charles, passing a trembling hand over his face. "If they *do* talk, it'll be her ruination, drug or no drug. Why in the seven hells would Yarborough take such a terrible risk? He might have killed her!"

"Is not her inheritance enough of a reason? Had he actually managed to compromise her, you'd have had no—"

"I would have had no choice but to call him out," interrupted Charles flatly.

"That, or convince her to marry him and avoid such unpleasantness," Sorin said, hating every word.

"Force her to marry a man who would take her against her will?" Charles snorted. "I'd sooner send her off to America! Eleanor is more a sister to me than a cousin. I would never ask her to do such a thing."

Sorin squirmed inside, feeling the acid burn of shame and guilt. No. He hadn't taken Ellie against her will, but he'd come very damned close. And no matter how he tried to rationalize what he'd done, there was no acceptable justification. He'd fallen prey to lust, plain and simple. Charles would never forgive him if he found out. Everything depended on Eleanor now, on whether she remembered the ride home and, if so, how she felt about what had happened.

He debated for a moment the wisdom of it, but then decided it was best that Charles knew of his visit to Bow Street and the findings of his investigation. At least he could do that much to help further ensure her safety.

"The greedy bastard!" swore Charles, eyes bulging as he listened. "I'll have him hung! I'll tie the bloody knot myself. I'll—I'll—"

"You'll keep quiet," cut in Rowena.

They both turned to see her standing in the doorway. Neither man had heard her come in.

"I've been listening for some time now," she said calmly. "The physician arrived almost immediately after you two left. He said she appears to have taken too much laudanum, but that she should be well enough by morning. Sorin, I cannot thank you enough for your help. There is no possible way to express my gratitude to you and Lord Marston for taking care of this matter so discreetly."

Entering the room, she came and laid a hand on her husband's arm. "Charles, if you call him out, it will not only result in you having to risk your life, but it will cause a terrible scandal that will ruin Eleanor. And before you object, understand that it *will* ruin her, no matter the outcome. In this case, the reality of her innocence does not matter in the face of what people will think. If all remains quiet, we should leave it and be thankful."

Charles's face fell. "I suppose you must be right—but it sits not well with me at all!" He smacked a fist into his palm. "The blackguard deserves a good thrashing at the very least!"

"We will deal with this quietly," she insisted, shaking her head. "Tomorrow morning, you will speak with Yarborough *in private* and warn him that any further offense will result in serious consequences for his entire family. I'll leave it to you gentlemen to determine what that will entail in the event he is foolish enough not to comply."

Sorin looked at Charles. "I think it's time I visited Bow Street again." He would see Stafford first thing in the morning. And this time, he wouldn't come back empty-handed.

Chapter Eighteen

Eleanor's eyes felt like someone had poured sand under the lids and her head ached with a dull throb that matched the beating of her heart. Certain other parts throbbed, too, she noted—but in a more frustratingly pleasant sort of way. She turned over, unwilling to let go of the delicious dream.

"Good. You're awake."

Too lethargic to jump in surprise, Eleanor merely groaned in protest and rolled over to peer at Rowena. "I feel terrible," she croaked. Her mouth was ash dry. "May I have some water?" She closed her eyes and lay back again, partly to ease her pounding head and partly to try and recapture a little more of that dream before it dissolved completely—in it, Sorin had been kissing her, touching her. The cool rim of a cup against her lips shattered the final remnants of that lovely vision.

Damn.

"Not too much at first," cautioned Rowena, pulling it away before she could gulp down any more. "You've had a bad turn."

Confusion set in as she looked around. “It’s morning,” she said, blinking. She’d been at the Cleveland ball… “How did I get here?”

Rowena turned away, but not before Eleanor saw a black look cross her features. “What do you remember of last night?”

Eleanor tried to concentrate and found it hard to do for the lingering fog in her mind. “I danced with Lord Marston, and then I saw…” She stopped. She’d been about to say she saw Sorin flirting with that dark-haired witch, Eugenia. Pain tore at her heart. *Get over it and move on…* She took a steadying breath. “I went to the terrace with Sir Yarborough to speak with him privately. I was going to explain to him the futility of his continued pursuit.”

Rowena’s gaze sharpened. “And?”

“He seemed to receive my refusal quite w— ” She frowned as a muddled memory surfaced. An ugly one. “No, wait. He was…” She struggled to bring it back, but all she could recall were flashes of his snarling face and her own vague feelings of anger and disgust. And fear. “He was wroth with me. And I was angry with him. I— ”

“He drugged you,” interrupted Rowena, her voice hard. “According to the physician that attended you last night, he used laudanum. Quite a lot of it.”

Eleanor flinched as, all at once, every nerve in her body sprang wide awake. She fought down a sudden urge to vomit. “The punch! He offered me champagne at first, but I refused. I sent him to fetch me some punch instead. It tasted bitter—I thought they’d forgotten to sweeten it.” Horrified, she covered her mouth with her hands. “What…did anything h—happen?” she asked weakly, afraid to hear.

“Nothing more than a kiss, thank God,” answered Rowena, coming to sit beside her on the bed. “Lord Marston said he found you with Yarborough, just as you collapsed. Yarborough told him you'd fainted, but our friend quickly realized it was a lie and got you safely away. Sorin brought you here in his carriage and called for a physician while Lord Marston came to tell us you'd taken ill."

"Did anyone see me?" Was all of London abuzz this morning with the juicy tale of her disgrace?

Her guardian's pause made her squirm with apprehension.

Rowena met her eyes. "According to Lord Marston, there was a couple coming up from the garden about the same time you fainted. We don't know who they are or how much they saw. Only two of the Clevelands' servants know you left the ball early and they were told you'd taken ill."

Eleanor sagged against the pillows, tears stinging her sore eyes. Rage washed everything in red, rage the likes of which she'd never known could exist within her. "If I *ever* see Donald Yarborough again, I'll kill him."

Reaching out, Rowena clasped her hand. "We both know that cannot happen, but if you wish, you may have Charles bring charges against him on your behalf. As your guardian and as a peer of the realm, he has that right. If you testify along with Lord Marston and the physician who examined you last night, there is little doubt that Yarborough will be thrown in prison. However, such a course would likely result in a monumental scandal, one you might not survive with your reputation intact, no matter your innocence."

Breathing slowly, Eleanor steadied her racing heart. "If I do, he'll only refute my accusations and drag my name through the sewer," she said flatly. "And yours, as well. Even if he loses, even if he is thrown in prison to rot forever, he will still win." Yarborough's ugly words resurfaced through the fog. "He resents my having laid him low when we were children and would relish the thought of returning the favor."

"I concur. But we will support you, whatever your decision.

If you choose not to involve the magistrate, however, Charles is prepared to speak with him privately."

"I will not allow Charles to call him out," Eleanor said at once, terrified at the prospect.

"No, nor will I," agreed Rowena with a vehement shake of her head. "But there are other methods of persuasion that may be brought to bear, if the threat of being dragged before the magistrate is not enough to deter him."

Her head hurt. And her heart, as well. *It should never have come to this.* "As long as he can promise me that it won't result in a duel, I would have Charles address him privately."

Rowena nodded and stood, straightening her skirts. "I'll tell him."

Eleanor closed her eyes. What a disaster. She'd wanted nothing more than to end this in a civilized manner, one that would—*should*—have allowed Yarborough to walk away with his pride and honor intact. If he'd had any to begin with, that is. If he didn't cooperate…

"Shall I tell the kitchen to send up some breakfast?" asked Rowena.

The very mention of food brought on a wave of nausea. "Thank you, but no. Perhaps some tea, but nothing more—for now," Eleanor amended with a smile, not wishing to upset her any more than she was already.

"I'll have Charles inform Lord Marston and Sorin of your decision." She shook her head. "Poor Sorin was beside himself last night. I know he'll be especially relieved to learn you are well. You know for a moment, I thought that perhaps…"

Eleanor's breath caught at the sight of the sad little smile hovering about Rowena's mouth. "What? You thought what?" She twisted the coverlet in her hands.

"In all the many years I've known him, I've never seen him so furious," said Rowena. "Charles had to physically prevent him leaving here last night once he was certain you were out of danger. Such was his anger over your ill treatment that we both feared he would seek out Yarborough and challenge him." Her gaze pierced Eleanor. "You are very dear to him, you know."

Tender pain blossomed in her heart. *But not dear enough.* She looked down and began smoothing out the wrinkles she'd put in the coverlet. "As he is to me." It came out sounding rather strangled.

Several heartbeats passed in silence before Rowena spoke again. "I'll see about having tea sent up for you."

"Thank you." Unwilling to raise her watering eyes, she waited until Rowena departed, leaving her alone with her thoughts. The knowledge that Sorin had been so angry on her behalf both pleased and frightened her. Guilt crept in alongside the fear. If she hadn't been trying to make him jealous, this would never have happened. This was her fault for being fool enough to think herself safe with Yarborough under *any* circumstance. For pity's sake, he'd drugged her in plain sight of everyone! Had he succeeded in his dreadful scheme, she would no doubt have awakened to the news of her upcoming nuptials.

If Marston hadn't found her in time. If Sorin hadn't secreted her away. If, if, if…

She had to see him. At once. If only to thank him and know in her heart that he wasn't wroth with her. And she must write a letter expressing her gratitude to Lord Marston, as well. Scrambling out of bed, she rang for Fran. "Tell Lady Ashford I've changed my mind and will come down for breakfast. Tell her, and then come right back and help me dress. Hurry."

Eleanor turned to her wardrobe, snatched out her new lavender walking gown, and threw it across the rumpled bed. As she pulled her nightdress off over her head, her thoughts returned to her scandalous dream. The curious floating sensations, the feelings of warmth and safety—and above all the memory of passionate kisses and touches shared with the man she loved.

Memory...

Memory?

Her hands froze in the act of pulling on a stocking. *No. Not memory. Vision. Wild imagining. Dream. It was a dream. Only a dream.* One by one, she tallied all the many reasons why he would never behave in such a manner, the final being that even if he did by some miracle secretly desire her, he was far too honorable a man to take advantage of her in her weakened state.

An irony-laden laugh forced its way up from the depths to choke her. No, the images in her mind were no more than a result of longing and lust mingled with whatever Yarborough had slipped into her glass. A mere dream.

But what a dream! Even now, her body still tingled.

Standing before the mirror in her stockings and shift, she let her hands trace the shape of her hips, moving up until they cupped her breasts. Her nipples, just visible beneath the near-transparent batiste, were dark, rosy shadows. She closed her eyes and stroked one, imitating the actions Sorin had taken in her erotic dream. Lightning pleasure shot straight down to her belly as the sensitive nub contracted, causing her to gasp.

It was the same feeling as in the dream, only far less intense. The juncture of her thighs pulsed with sudden heat, making her legs feel weak. Reaching beneath the hem of her shift with a trembling hand, she was shocked to find her secret flesh slick and burning as with a fever. An unbearable tension seemed to build within her at her own touch. What would happen if she were to stroke there as he had?

The doorknob rattled. With a tiny squeak of guilty fright,

Eleanor leaped away from the mirror, snatched up her wrapper, and enfolded herself in it just as Fran entered.

"Lady Ashford says she'll have Cook make you something fresh when you come down, my lady." The maid came over to the bed to fetch the gown that had been carelessly tossed atop it. "She's been so worried. Said nobody ought to ever eat meat that's not served hot when away from home."

Eleanor breathed a silent sigh of relief. "I can only agree and say that I will certainly never do so again."

"Poor thing," said Fran, looking at her with pity. "Oh, and she also said to tell you Lord Wincanton will be calling later today. Such a nice gentleman he is."

"Yes, he is," Eleanor said absently as Fran helped her don the gown. Would she be able to look him in the eye? Another fear clawed its way to the surface. What if it hadn't *all* been a dream? It had certainly seemed very real. What if in her intoxicated state she had behaved inappropriately toward him? Her heart quailed.

"Eleanor?"

Turning, she saw Caroline peeking in from the doorway with eyes full of worry. "I'm perfectly fine," she said at once, reaching out to embrace her friend as she entered.

"When I heard what happened, I—" Caroline drew back to search her face. "They told me you left the ball ill," she breathed, one eye on Fran, who was just leaving. She waited until the door closed before continuing. "Lady Ashford asked Lady Heston if she would mind taking me home after the ball, so I knew nothing until after I arrived." Her eyes narrowed in fury. "The beast ought to be hung!"

"I cannot say that I disagree with you," Eleanor replied, grimacing. "But no matter how much I would love to see him brought to justice, we must avoid a scandal. I'm surprised Rowena told you what really happened."

Caroline's face flushed. "In truth, she did not. When I came in, I heard Lord Marston speaking to Lord Ashford and remained hidden so they would not see me. I know I ought not to have listened, but I could not help myself. I was completely horrified and so very angry for you! I had to wait until they moved on before I could go up to your room." She stopped and took a deep breath. "Lord Wincanton was here with you when I came in."

"He was?" Hope flared in Eleanor's heart as her friend nodded.

"Yes, and his distress frightened me terribly. I thought that perhaps…" She paused, and Eleanor saw tears form in her eyes. "I thought you'd *died*. But as soon as he saw me, he assured me you were not in danger and that you would recover fully. And then he told me that I must have nothing more to do with the Yarboroughs—and why." Her blue eyes burned with hatred through their bright veil of tears. "You may be confident that I shall never again speak to either of them!"

"Caroline, you must never tell anyone what really happened," Eleanor urged. "Promise me!"

"I already promised the same to Lord Wincanton, but I'm happy to make the same vow to you."

Relieved, Eleanor again embraced her friend. "Thank you."

"I pray that *pig* Yarborough gets what he deserves," muttered the redhead, hugging her back fiercely. "I hope he's forced to marry Lottie Winthrop!" she burst out. "She'd be a perfect match for him, the horrid little cow."

In spite of being almost overwhelmed by doubt and fear, Eleanor began to giggle. Miss Winthrop was truly not a very nice person, but even so, she wouldn't wish anyone, even Lottie, to be stuck with the likes of Donald Yarborough for a husband.

With patience worn thin as parchment, Sorin waited, one eye on the mantel clock. Rowena had sent a note this morning to tell him Ellie was fine, but he needed to see for himself. He also needed to speak with Charles. How that conversation went would depend upon how much she remembered and her feelings about it.

Stafford had not disappointed him this time. Just thinking about what he'd learned made Sorin's jaw tighten. It might not be his place to challenge Yarborough openly—but that didn't mean he couldn't find another way to get to the bastard. And he had.

Angry over having been cheated out of his fee, one of Yarborough's solicitors had provided evidence concerning an illegal investment Yarborough had made with the aid of a rival solicitor. Under a false name, Yarborough had taken some of the proceeds from the sale of his Irish property and invested in a "coffee farm" that was, in fact, a slave operation. Things had gone sour, however, and his investment had not provided adequate returns. He was in imminent danger of bankruptcy.

This same informant also claimed Yarborough had made some interesting inquiries of a junior clerk employed by Ashford's solicitor—inquiries specifically regarding the amount of Eleanor's inheritance. Yarborough had not been given exact information, but he'd learned enough to know that marrying her would enable him to pay all of his debts and live quite well on annual dividends from the remainder.

Even if Eleanor decided not to prosecute, and he didn't think she would, Yarborough was still on the wrong side of the crown. And Sorin was going to make certain the blackguard saw the full measure of consequences for his crimes.

Alerted by the sound of approaching footsteps, he turned to see Eleanor. Her smile was subdued, but she was clearly pleased to see him. Like a cool rain, relief washed over him. Either she didn't remember anything of his actions last night—or she returned his affection for her in kind. If the former, he would allow her to remain in blissful ignorance of his imposition. If the latter, he was prepared to drop knee this instant. The ring practically burned a hole in his pocket. "Ellie, I cannot tell you how happy I am to see you well."

"Thanks in part to you, as I understand it," she replied. "I owe you an enormous debt of gratitude. Had it not been for you and Lord Marston—"

"Think nothing of it." *Please…*

Her brow furrowed. "Such a selfless act cannot be considered insignificant." She looked to the floor, but not before he saw a blush begin to stain her cheeks. "Had I been more prudent, my rescue would not have been necessary. And had you been less discreet, I would be facing an entirely different situation than the one I do now."

A selfless act. Again, he was struck low by shame. And—if he was honest with himself—sore disappointment. It was at once evident that their passionate interlude was, for her, lost to oblivion. No hidden amour for him dwelt in her breast. *It's for the best,* he told himself, overriding the protest of his heart, which felt like someone was trying to tear it from its mooring.

It took him a moment to gather his wits enough to speak. "I'm honored to have been able to render assistance. As is Marston, I'm sure. Which reminds me…" Reaching into his pocket, he pulled out a sealed envelope. The ring, he left concealed. "He came by this morning and asked me to deliver this to Miss Caroline. I believe it may be a final effort to reconcile differences."

With ginger fingers she took it. A twinge of unease ran

through him at how careful she was to avoid touching him. He brushed it off. It was only natural that she would now be reluctant to make physical contact with any man.

"I cannot break the confidence with which I've been entrusted," she said, her voice breaking a little as she looked up at him. "But I can tell you that this letter will be most welcome. Thank you for bringing it."

Before he could respond, Charles walked in and the moment was lost amid friendly greetings and more undeserved thanks.

"Gentlemen," interrupted Eleanor. "If you will excuse me, there is something I must see to at once."

"Yes, of course," said Charles, dismissing her with an impatient wave. "We have business to discuss, anyway."

Her eyes hardened. "Business concerning Yarborough?"

"Yes," said Charles after a moment's pause. "Rowena told me you'd agreed to have me speak with him privately rather than haul him up before the magistrate. Is that truly what you want?"

"I wish to avoid a scandal," she said with calm that was belied by her worried eyes.

Sorin's temper flared. "If there is a scandal, *you* won't be the cause of it. The fault will be entirely his."

"Regardless of who is at fault, a scandal would impact more than just me," she answered back. "There are others to consider." Turning to her cousin, she dipped a curtsy. "I shall leave you to your discussion."

"What news?" asked Charles as soon as the door closed behind her.

Prevaricating would serve no purpose. "Yarborough is due to be arrested tomorrow morning."

"What? But I just agreed not to—"

"For reasons having nothing to do with Eleanor," Sorin

interjected. He then told him what he'd learned that morning. "He'll be sent to a penal colony—if he's lucky enough to escape the noose," he said, taking grim satisfaction in the pronouncement.

"George's gouty toe," swore Charles softly. He frowned. "Wait. Why tomorrow and not immediately?"

"Stafford agreed to wait until morning because I asked him for time so I might warn you. It is my hope that Yarborough will simply blame his creditors, but if he learns of my friendship with Stafford, he'll rightly assume that I was involved. Given recent events, he might also suspect you."

Charles regarded him with sharp eyes. "And if Yarborough thinks we have anything to do with his arrest…"

"He might attempt revenge of some kind," Sorin finished for him. "The most obvious means of getting at either of us would be to threaten Eleanor. It would be an easy matter to spread lies from the confines of his cell and tarnish her good name."

"Perhaps, but I shan't worry much over it," said Charles, shrugging. "Who would believe the words of a traitor?" He squared his shoulders. "Well, if the blackguard is to be arrested tomorrow, then I fail to see the point in speaking to him today. I'll go and tell El—"

"You cannot," Sorin interrupted. "You must go and confront him."

"Why? As of now, the events of last night are known only to a very few. Why not simply let the matter rest?"

"Because we don't know who else saw them. Marston said there were witnesses. He knew none of them, but that does not mean Ellie went unrecognized. And because we don't know who he may have talked to about last night, and because he'll expect you to come pounding on his door in a state of righteous anger. If it does not happen, he'll wonder why," Sorin stressed. "Then, when they come for him tomorrow…"

Crestfallen, his friend nodded understanding. "Very well. I shall leave at once. Better to have done with the nasty business quickly. What should I tell Rowena and Eleanor?"

"Nothing," Sorin replied. "The less they know the better. When you see Yarborough, you must give no hint that you know what is to happen. If he is forewarned, he will flee."

"Either way, the man is finished," Charles told him with a humorless chuckle. "In truth, I care not what happens to the bastard as long as he troubles us no more."

"I can find nothing to disagree with in that statement."

But that night as he sat before the fire at his favorite club nursing his aching heart and his third brandy with Marston, Sorin began to care. He began to care very much indeed.

A group of rowdy young men intent on making merry came in and seated themselves a few tables away behind them. Their noisy discussion informed all in the room that they were recently come from taking their pleasure in Covent Garden. Ribald jests were traded, as well as some good-natured ribbing about a particularly buxom barmaid.

"Come, let us leave and go somewhere less crowded," said Marston, draining his glass.

Before he could stand, however, Sorin heard Yarborough's obnoxious voice rise above the others, boasting about how he'd lifted the barmaid's skirts. Sorin's blood heated, and he resettled himself. "I won't be driven from my place by such as him, lest everyone think me craven," he told Marston, who was looking at him askance.

"What does it matter what anyone thinks?" hissed his friend. "By this time tomorrow he'll be bragging to the rats in his cell!"

Sorin eyed him for a moment. Pride and sheer stubbornness urged him to remain. But reason won out. "You're right, of course. Come. Let us go someplace less polluted." But just as he again prepared to stand, raucous laughter broke out behind him.

"I heard a somewhat different tale," said one of the men in Yarborough's party. "I heard that her-high-and-mightiness left early after taking ill."

There was a derisive snort, Yarborough's. "If she was ill, then I'm the king's long-lost twin. The *lady* in question was the epitome of robust health, I tell you. Thankfully, her little swooning act seems to have fooled everyone. Truth be told, I'm just glad her cousin failed to call me out over the incident when he came to see me—or worse, force me to marry her."

Sorin gripped the arms of his chair until the wood creaked softly in protest. All the pain of this morning's disappointment came flooding back, along with all his wrath over how Ellie had been treated by the bastard. That this swaggering imbecile should speak so of her, when any man would be more than blessed to call her his wife…

"Force?" said another of Yarborough's companions. "I should dance down the bloody aisle to be so lucky! The wench brings a fortune with her, and she's not bad looking either. I'd certainly not mind playing a bit of bread and butter with her."

Another round of laughter followed, as well as a few more ripe comments from the men. Again, Yarborough's voice rose above the others. "Yes, yes. Her fortune might tempt another, less discerning man, but I tell you there is not money enough in the world to make me want to marry that succubus. Her… *appetites* are such that I'd never know if the babe in her belly was my get or a footman's."

There was a moment of shocked silence followed by a spattering of nervous laughter. The man had just gone beyond the pale and everyone present knew it.

Heat flashed across Sorin's skin, and his heart began to pound.

"Don't," mouthed Marston, shaking his head.

But it was too late for that. Rising from his seat, he went to confront Eleanor's detractor. "What interesting tales you tell, Sir Yarborough. Do continue."

Blanching, Yarborough nevertheless stood to face him. "What business is it of yours what I say about some nameless whore?"

A hush fell in the room, and Sorin felt all eyes on him. *Steady, now*. "I should think it both an honor and a duty to warn one's friends concerning such a female as you have just described," he said lightly, gesturing to the other man's companions. "Come. You *are* among friends, are you not? Speak her name so that we may be warned against this man-trap." He waited while beads of sweat formed on Yarborough's brow. "No? How very curious. Don't you think it curious?" he asked Marston, who'd come to stand at his side.

"Indeed," agreed Marston with a toothy grin. "One wonders at the meaning of his sudden silence when but a moment ago he was a veritable magpie."

Yarborough's eyes darted between them. "You have no proof that I was speaking of…*her*," he finished low through clenched teeth.

The blood roaring in his ears, Sorin smiled. "I don't *need* proof." Without offering any other warning, he followed his statement with a satisfying fist to the other man's jaw.

It was a brawl worthy of any dockside tavern. The pair that had come in with Yarborough leaped to their feet in his defense, and within seconds everyone in the room was trading indiscriminate blows. The club's frantic proprietor came running in to break up the fight and received a punch to the nose for his trouble. Thus were the odds evened, for the man at once charged back into the fray like a maddened bull. Though the reinforcement was welcome, Sorin and Marston needed no help. Having spent a goodly amount of time as sailors, both knew how to take a man down quickly and did so now with great gusto.

When at last Yarborough lay moaning on the floor in bloody surrender, Sorin looked down on him in contempt. "Get up."

Yarborough stared up at him with fear-filled eyes. "If you mean to challenge me—"

"Oh, I do." Consequences be damned. He'd already broken the rules of gentlemanly conduct by striking the blackguard. "I warned you this would happen. At your own peril you chose to ignore that warning. Now name your weapon and choose your second."

"I hate to disappoint you," gasped the other man, swiping at the blood trickling from his nose, "but allow me to remind you that the king has declared a prohibition against dueling."

"Only within the boundaries of London itself," replied Sorin, feeling the red tide of rage rise up in him once more. "I believe we both possess horses, do we not?"

But Yarborough only shook his head and spat out a bloody tooth. "I will neither defy my king nor risk my life for the sake of satisfying your antiquated code of honor."

Those watching muttered in frank disapproval. No true gentleman would publicly disparage a female so, or fail to answer such a challenge.

Fury set fire to Sorin's veins. "Coward. You risked your worthless life the moment you opened your lying mouth to wrongly malign the woman I love."

"Love?" Yarborough let out an irreverent snort. "If you think she could ever love you, then you really *are* an old fool."

"Perhaps I am, at that," Sorin replied, gratified to see the younger man flinch as he took a step closer and bent low to peer into his battered face. "But this *fool* will gladly lay down his life to defend her good name. If you will not answer my challenge, then you admit your statements concerning the lady are false in their entirety."

His pale face flushing, Yarborough glanced around at the men circling them.

Sorin could see there was not a sympathetic face among the lot. Even the braggart's friends, those who'd defended him with their fists only moments ago, stared down at the fallen man with hard eyes. *If a man has not his honor, he has nothing...*

Swallowing, Yarborough bowed his head in defeat. "Very well. Before these witnesses, I offer you my humble apology and retract my offensive words concerning the lady." He looked up and met Sorin's gaze. "You have taken my dignity, sir, and can ask no further reparation. Do you accept?"

Utter disdain filled Sorin, and he did nothing to prevent it showing on his face. "You leave me little choice." He weighted his next words with deadly cold. "But know this: if I ever hear you speak falsely of her again—in fact, if I ever hear you've spoken of her at all, prohibition or not, I will find you and put a hole in your craven hide."

Turning to the proprietor, whose previously nondescript face now bore a great deal of character in the form of a spectacularly broken nose and an assortment of cuts and bruises, he took out his purse. "My apologies," he said, dropping enough money into the man's outstretched hand to cover the cost of reparations thrice over.

"Nod ad all, by lord," said the man, smiling in spite of what had to be a painfully split lip. He bowed, making it clear to all that Sorin, at least, would be welcomed back.

"You know you've just committed yourself to a course from which there is no turning back," said Marston as they walked out. "It'll be all over London by morning. The good and the bad. You must go and see Ashford at once."

"Agreed. But I cannot take myself to his house at this hour, especially looking as I must." His right cuff was torn, and his cravat and jacket were spattered with blood—Yarborough's, he hoped—and he could feel the beginnings of an ache in his jaw where someone's fist had connected with it. "I'll go first thing in the morning."

Marston eyed him. "Perhaps you're right. When you do see him, best be prepared to tell the truth."

The truth. Though part of Sorin dreaded the prospect, another rejoiced. Whatever the outcome, there would be no more secrets, no more lies. He would learn once and for all the nature of Eleanor's feelings for him. Then he would have to live with them—one way or another.

Now that he'd declared his love for her publicly and drawn blood in defense of her good name, they must marry. There was no other way to avoid what would doubtless be the scandal of the Season. Eleanor would marry him, but the nature of their marriage would be determined by her will alone.

If by some miracle she found it within herself to eventually return his full affection, he would give heartfelt thanks to God every day for the rest of his life. Even now he prayed it would be so.

If, however, the only thing she would accept was the protection of his name, then so be it. Through no fault of hers, it had come to this. He wouldn't impose upon her more than she desired. He wouldn't even subject her to his presence, if such was her wish. To ensure her happiness, he would deny her nothing within his power to give, even if it was his absence.

If she found his love repugnant, he'd simply have to learn to live without his heart, for it would remain with her no matter how far away he went. Such would be the penance for his selfish act, for having robbed her of the life she would have had with someone more deserving.

Chapter Nineteen

Pacing the familiar length of the salon, Sorin was more nervous than he had ever been in his life. He'd tiptoed out at dawn to walk the short distance to Charles's house, something he hadn't done since before his days at university. But he had needed to get out before Mother awakened—before she could hear of his disgraceful conduct last night and panic over the unfolding disaster. He would explain everything to her later, after it was done.

"My apologies for keeping you waiting. I came as soon as I could get away," said Charles, coming in. "What brings you here so early? Has Yarborough been arrested?"

He'd forgotten all about that, actually. "It should be happening as we speak, but my visit is not about that." His gut tightened at the perplexed look on his friend's face. "I can see the gossip has not yet reached you. I'm glad. I wanted to tell you myself."

"Tell me what?" Charles shook his head. "What gossip? Bloody hell!" he exclaimed as he came closer. "What happened to your face?"

Sorin put a hand to his sore, purpling jaw. "It's nothing. Charles, I've done something that I fear will have significant consequences for all of us." He took a deep breath. "Last night while Marston and I were at the club, Yarborough came in and began speaking ill of Eleanor to his fellows. I'm afraid I quite lost my temper."

Charles frowned. "I don't…" Comprehension dawned across his features. "You hit him."

Though he tried to dredge up a modicum of remorse for his actions, Sorin couldn't fool himself and wouldn't attempt to fool his best friend. "I laid him out on the floor in front of nearly a dozen witnesses," he said unabashedly. "I challenged him, but the coward refused to face me. He offered a full apology for the insult. I accepted. It's done."

Quick as lightning, his friend's bewilderment turned to anger. "The man is going to *prison* this morning!" he spluttered. "Could you not have held your peace for one bloody night? No one would have believed him! But *now*—you should have walked away and let him be!"

The very idea made Sorin's blood hot all over again. "To do so would have been to let his lies go unchallenged and let everyone think I cared nothing for her honor!"

"Her honor was not yours to defend!" snapped Charles, his face reddening. "But now everyone will assume otherwise!"

"Believe me, I *know* what a bloody mess this makes of things, Charles!" He lowered his voice. "Which is why I've come to ask for her hand. At least as my wife, Eleanor will be safe from the storm that is about to break."

"A storm of *your* making!" accused his friend, jabbing an angry finger at him. "None of this would be happening had you simply kept to the plan. *Your* plan!"

"I'm keenly aware that the fault is mine, and I will do everything I can to minimize the damage," Sorin vowed. "A marriage will help. We are, after all, already well-associated in Society's eyes."

"*If* she'll agree to it," said Charles, clearly doubtful.

"She must. And for more reason than just her reputation." He stood before his closest friend and steeled himself. It was time. "I'd hoped to woo her slowly over the course of the Season, but now everything has gone wrong and there is simply no more time."

"Woo her? What the devil do you mean, 'woo her'?" Charles's wroth expression transformed to one of profound shock. "Are y—are you in *love* with Eleanor?"

Sorin forced himself to meet his eyes. "I've tried to deny my feelings for her, but my efforts have proven ineffectual. I did everything in my power to stop it, Charles. I even left England. At the time, travel was a welcome escape from the torment of watching her succumb, as I thought she surely must, to some other man's charm. But year after year I waited for the news that never came, until I finally had no choice but to return."

"Upon my word," whispered Charles with wide eyes. "I think I need a brandy." Rising, he went to the decanter and poured out a glass. He downed it, and then poured himself another. Lifting the decanter, he offered his guest a glass.

"Thank you, but no," Sorin responded, feeling slightly queasy. "I had enough last night to have lost my taste for it today."

Charles came and sat back down. "Why the devil did you not say something before now?"

"I did not wish to put a strain on our friendship, especially after you entrusted me to act as her chaperone." A trust which he'd broken in the most flagrant manner possible.

A frown again creased Charles's brow. "Though I admit to being displeased by the deception, I understand why you felt it necessary. But surely you must know I would not have objected to your suit. Eleanor could ask for no better match, in my opinion."

"That is exactly what I told him," said Rowena, entering the room.

"You knew of this?" said Charles with unconcealed hurt.

She entered and closed the door behind her. "I began to suspect it during our journey to London, but I learned the truth of it only a short time ago."

"And yet you shared neither your suspicion nor its confirmation with me," her husband said grimly.

"Don't blame her," Sorin told him. "I made her promise not to tell anyone, including you. I felt it only right that I should be the one to inform you of my intent. As to why I waited to do so, I could not risk Eleanor learning of my true sentiments prematurely."

"As she would have done had you begun dropping 'helpful' hints," cut in Rowena, patting her husband's arm. "I offered to speak with her on his behalf, as well, but he made me swear not to say anything that might influence her."

"Why?" asked Charles, baffled. "We would have been glad to intercede on your behalf. I've no doubt it would have been an easy matter to convince her to accept you—she adores you already."

"As a friend only," Sorin clarified bitterly. "I wanted to wait until I'd had the opportunity to make her see me as more."

"Yes, well, as you've said, time has run out," his best friend pointed out.

"Charles." Rowena stared at him, one brow arched in silent command.

Closing his eyes, her husband passed a hand over his face. "Of course. Yes. I give you leave to ask for Eleanor's hand."

"Thank you," Sorin replied, every bone and sinew atremble

with relief. He sat in the nearest chair and tried to gather his wits. "I've so dreaded telling you the truth. In all honesty, I was unsure how you'd react."

The look Charles directed at him was one of compassion. "Daft fool. You ought to have known better. I've considered you family almost from the day we met."

Sorin found speech impossible at the moment, so he nodded. Taking a deep breath, he marshaled his self-control. "Now I must decide how to tell Eleanor." If telling Charles had been hard, telling her would be bloody awful.

"A word of advice, if I may," said Rowena, her eyes boring into his. "Under the circumstances, she has little choice but to accept you. But if you declare yourself now, at least she'll know your proposal is more than just a matter of honor. Tell her the truth."

Rowena was right. Come what may, it was time. He nodded.

"I'll go and get her," she said, rising.

Feeling like a leaf caught on the surface of a rushing river, Sorin watched her leave. His fate was out of his hands now. All he could do was hope.

Charles looked at him for a long moment. "You know, I'd venture to say your worries are needless."

"What? Why?"

His friend's face was wry. "Because at one point I thought I might have to speak to Eleanor about you. She pestered you so when she was younger, always hanging at your elbow, full of endless prattle. Everything was 'Sorin said this' or 'Sorin did that.' She practically worshipped you. I thought it would diminish as she grew older and made other friends, and it did, to some extent. But not nearly enough. I worried that you would be bothered by it, but you never seemed to mind."

"No. I never minded," Sorin replied, smiling fondly. "Our

friendship has always been a natural and easy one. If I was overly tolerant, it was because I knew how much she needed someone to just listen." He looked at Charles. "You must believe that I never intended anything more than friendship. When I realized my feelings had begun to change, I fled on the fastest ship I could find."

"She was devastated when you left," said Charles, shaking his head. "Such that I was concerned she'd developed the sort of *tendre* dramatic young ladies sometimes do for an older gentleman in their acquaintance. But after we returned from London her melancholy seemed to ease. I introduced her to every young man we knew, hoping one of them would catch her eye. But none did, and I could not understand it." He fixed Sorin with a piercing gaze. "Now I begin to wonder if I was right after all and she already had her heart set on someone else."

The temperature in the room climbed a notch, and Sorin debated confiding in him that Eleanor had been comparing those other men to him. He elected against it. She'd included Charles as part of her comparison criteria, after all, and she certainly hadn't given him any reason to believe that he was viewed any differently than her cousin. With one exception. And that event was not something he cared to divulge to Charles. Ever. "If so, then she concealed it from me." He shifted nervously. "Charles, I will not impose myself on her against her wishes."

His friend flushed to the roots of his hair. "You cannot make such a promise. Not when you both love her and require an heir."

"I won't sacrifice her happiness for my own," Sorin insisted, vowing it to himself at the same time. "I've controlled myself thus far. I can do so forever, as long as she is happy."

His friend chuckled. "If there is one thing I've learned

from marriage, it is that a wife is never content unless she owns her husband body and soul. And a husband in love with his wife is never satisfied with less than his love returned fully."

"He did *what?*" Eleanor sat abruptly as flashes of heat and cold warred with each other across the battlefield of her flesh.

"*Shh*!" hissed Caroline, hurrying to close the door. She lowered her voice yet further, so that it was barely above a whisper. "I overheard one of the footmen say he'd heard it from his sister who works as a maid for Lady Wincanton that Lord Wincanton came to blows with Yarborough last night at his club. And now he's here—before breakfast!—asking to speak with your cousin."

It couldn't be true. "Are you absolutely certain the footman was not speaking of someone else?" Her heart seemed to pause as one fiery brow lifted in answer. She bit her lip. "Yarborough must have said something truly vile."

"I know not what prompted Lord Wincanton's violent reaction, but whatever the circumstances leading up to the event; I think we can be assured of what will follow," said Caroline with a mischievous smirk. "Any moment now, you'll be summoned so that he may ask for your hand."

Eleanor suppressed a sudden urge to run downstairs to find out if it was true. Guilt and excitement mingled, making her head throb as her heart began to gallop. She folded her shaking hands in her lap to prevent giving away just how anxious she was. "That would be most inconvenient," she said, struggling to project outward detachment.

"Inconvenient?"

"Yes. Inconvenient. For I should be forced to refuse him."

Caroline's eyes widened. "Why? You love him, do you not?"

Stunned, Eleanor could formulate no reply to the blunt—and very accurate—assertion.

"I began to suspect the truth some time ago," said Caroline, her blue eyes full of compassion. "But I was not certain until the night I discovered you crying. As one who has suffered a broken heart, I know another when I see it. By the bye, mine is mended."

Eleanor looked askance at her. "The letter?"

Caroline nodded, her cheeks flaring with color. "It was an apology—a very good one. I'm no longer wroth with him. In fact, I'm quite ready to apologize for my part in our long misunderstanding and accept his offer of marriage. He plans to visit later this week to formally ask for my hand."

"Oh, Caroline, I'm so pleased for you," Eleanor said, setting aside her own troubles for a moment to hug her friend. It had been a long time coming, and she was truly glad to see it finally happen.

"Thank you—Ellie, I hope you won't make the same mistake I did and assume the worst," said Caroline, pulling back to look her in the eyes. "A broken heart is not something you'll want to live with in perpetuity. I barely survived mine."

Embarrassment loosened Eleanor's tongue. "You may have come to an understanding with Lord Marston, but that does not make you an expert in all matters of love," she retorted. "My heart is not broken!"

"Perhaps not yet entirely, but it is certainly beginning to crack," her friend shot back. "And there is little point in denying the cause." A wry smile curled her lips. "You've allowed very few gentlemen close enough to elicit such strong emotions."

Eleanor's determination crumbled, bringing both a sense of relief as well as great pain. The secret she'd held so close to her heart was finally a secret no more, but it made no difference. "If he asks for my hand, it will be because he feels it is the honorable thing to do. It won't be because he wants me," she said, mortified to find herself crying. Taking out a kerchief, she blotted her eyes. "I'm naught but a child to him—a sort of y-younger sister," she said through her tears.

Caroline just stared at her with wide eyes. "Not to be vulgar," she said slowly, "but he *will* eventually require an heir. So even if you are correct about his indifference, which I cannot help but doubt, I'm sure you'll manage to convince him to do his duty. In fact, I might even venture to say he'll be—"

A knock interrupted her, and the door opened to reveal Rowena. "Please excuse me, ladies, but I'm afraid this cannot wait. Eleanor, I need to speak with you privately. Now."

Caroline rose and, casting Eleanor a final encouraging look that did nothing to lift her spirits, left the room.

Rowena came and sat down beside her. "I'd hoped to be the one to tell you, but I can see that Caroline has once again managed to beat me to the mark."

Before she could stop herself, Eleanor burst into sobs. Rowena's arms closed about her shoulders, and she surrendered, letting loose the flood she'd been holding back. When the worst of the tempest had passed, she pulled away, her eyes sore and her heart heavy.

"I thought you would be happy," said Rowena, clearly taken aback.

Happy? How could she be happy knowing that Sorin would resent her for the rest of his life? A fresh wave of tears gushed forth.

"My dear child," murmured Rowena. "I cannot tell you how sorry I am that it had to happen in this manner. I know this is hardly the way any woman wants to find out she is to marry, but the scandal will die down soon. And more importantly, you'll be wed to a good man who truly cares for you."

"I would rather remain unwed and suffer the scandal than be forced into a passionless union," Eleanor blurted with a loud hiccup.

Rowena's brow furrowed. "Passionless?"

"Yes, passionless. If he asks for my hand, I shall refuse him."

"Eleanor! You cannot—"

"I can," she insisted. "I have my inheritance. I'll go somewhere far away and live quietly so as not to bring further shame on you and Charles, but I will *not* force my friend to marry someone he does not desire!"

Rising, Eleanor fled the room over Rowena's fading protestations, unwilling to hear another word. She needed to compose herself and marshal her strength before seeing Sorin. Refusing him would be the most difficult challenge she'd ever face, but face it she must, and with as much dignity as she could muster.

Caroline's room was mercifully vacant when she entered it. Going to the wash basin, she poured some water into the bowl and splashed her face. The mirror on the wall revealed her frightful state as she blotted herself dry and tried to pat her hair smooth. There was nothing to be done about her red, puffy eyes, but circumstances being what they were, she supposed tears wouldn't be unexpected.

Still, it would upset Sorin to see her cry.

She stared at her reflection. "I will control myself," she whispered to herself. "It's only for a little while longer. For his sake. Just long enough to free him. Then I can fall apart at my leisure knowing I've done the right thing. I won't let him sacrifice himself on the altar of my honor."

But if I do, he'll be mine, the wicked part of her replied.

Sorin did care for her, after all—enough to make him defend her good name at the risk of matrimonial imprisonment. Many marriages were founded on far less, and she *would* do her best to make him happy. But would it be enough to justify such a selfish act? What if after marrying her he met another Jane? He'd regret his decision and resent her for having trapped him. That he would break his vows was not a concern. The Sorin she knew would never do such a thing. But he might want to, and then he wouldn't be the Sorin she knew anymore. Could she do that to him?

But he would be mine…

Caroline's words echoed in her mind. He *did* have a duty to fulfill. He might not want to consummate the marriage at first, but time would be on her side. And there were ways to persuade even the most reluctant man. Perhaps—provided he met no one else—he might in time come to desire her.

Both paths beckoned. One altruistic, the other, anything but. Both were paved with liberal amounts of dishonesty. Until she chose which to take, she would exist in an unbearable state of limbo.

Leaving Caroline's room, she made her way to the stairs. Each step felt like a little death, an incremental descent into Hades as she made her slow way down. Pausing outside the door of the salon, she gathered her courage.

This is it.

She opened the door to find both Charles and Sorin waiting for her. Her cousin's face was inscrutable, but Sorin's… he looked haggard, as though he'd not slept in days, and there was a nasty bruise along his jaw. Her heart ached at the sight. This was all her fault. If she'd just been clear with Yarborough in the beginning, he would never have pursued her and Sorin would never have felt obligated to defend her.

Both men stood as she entered. She dipped a dutiful curtsy and waited, her heart in her throat, as Sorin bowed.

"Eleanor, Lord Wincanton has requested to speak with you privately," said Charles, his manner frighteningly formal. "I'll be waiting in the library."

Her heart raced as the door shut with a muted *click* behind him. All the careful words she'd been rehearsing jumbled together on the tip of her tongue and remained there, unable to escape, as Sorin came to stand before her.

"I'm sure Rowena has made you aware of what transpired last night," he said quietly.

Though her informant had in fact been Caroline, Eleanor nodded.

"Firstly, know that it was only because of my high regard and long affection for you that I acted in such a manner," he continued, his deep voice rougher than she'd ever heard it, save in her dreams. "Yarborough's words angered me such that I was drawn beyond the point of considering the consequences you would have to bear for my reaction to them. Please forgive me."

"There is nothing to forgive," she said, finding her voice. Silently, she cursed the tears that began to cloud her vision. "By coming to my defense, you did what any true friend would have done."

He shook his head. "No. Were I a true friend, I would have answered his lies with words rather than brute violence, thereby accomplishing the revelation of truth without condemning you. Instead, I let my heart and my temper overrule all good sense." He looked down. "I struck him because it was what *I* wanted. It was purely selfish of me, and now there is only one way to prevent your ruination."

The blood began to whoosh in her ears. "I beg you not to say another word!" she burst out. "If you care for me at all, you will leave this instant and let the matter play out as it will without interfering—I will *not* allow you to be punished for defending me!"

"Punished?" He let out a cracked laugh. "If anyone is to suffer for my impetuous behavior, it is you, not I."

It was both dream and nightmare as he reached into his pocket, pulled out a small gilt box, and dropped to one knee before her. "Eleanor," he said softly. "I love you—I have for quite some time now. Will you do me the great honor of becoming my wife?"

Tears ran unchecked down her face, and a great sob lodged in her throat. She clapped a hand over her mouth to prevent its escape. The temptation was so great! All she had to do was say 'yes' and she'd have everything she wanted.

Except for his heart. He might have said the words, but she knew they could not be true. *Already I have corrupted him, caused him to lie on my behalf.*

After a moment, she took a deep breath and forced the dreaded words she'd rehearsed past trembling lips. "It is with regret that I must refuse your very kind offer." She closed her watering eyes and made herself speak the rest before he could object. "You care for me—I know this—but it's not enough. I cannot allow you to marry me out of some misplaced sense of honor or obligation. Not when you might still marry someone who can truly make you happy as I know I cannot." *Someone like your Jane.* She swallowed another sob. "I won't rob you of that joy."

"Eleanor, look at me."

The command was not to be refused, especially when she felt the warm touch of his fingers beneath her chin. She opened her eyes and looked down into his luminous hazel ones, expecting to see relief. Instead, there was a look of such hurt in them that it stole her breath.

"I've been dishonest with you for so long," he said after what seemed an eternity. "Like a coward, I hid my true feelings from you, afraid of how you might react. But no more."

For an instant, wild hope flared in her breast. But it was quickly snuffed out. "You would say anything to persuade me, to protect me. But I'm not a child to be protected anymore, and I will not be persuaded in this. I release you from any obligation to me, real or imagined." She turned to leave but his hand shot out to clasp her wrist, holding her in place.

"It's not an obligation!" he insisted, pulling her back. Taking her hand, he pressed the little box into her palm. "Open it," he demanded gruffly.

The box's hard edges pressed into her flesh as she stood there, her throat too tight to speak. Opening it was the last thing she wanted to do. To see the symbol of what might have been could, and probably would, break her will to refuse him.

"Eleanor, please," he urged gently. "Just look at it—and then I promise I'll ask nothing more of you unless you wish it." He released her, leaving behind an invisible, tingling imprint on her skin.

With trembling fingers, she did as he bade and opened the lid. Inside on a nest of freshly picked scarlet rose petals lay a sparkling diamond ring. She frowned. It looked strangely familiar, but it couldn't be. Instead of diamonds, there were tiny blood-red rubies encircling the central stone. "This cannot be the…"

"It is," he cut in. "Read the inscription."

Picking it from amongst the fragrant petals, she brought it close and peered at the tiny words carved inside the golden circle. "The truest love begins in friendship," she read aloud, her voice breaking on the last word.

"Were you to put it on, I believe you would find it a perfect fit," he said, bringing his hands up to cup hers. "The proprietor assured me he could gauge a woman's ring size with a single glance."

Though she'd not tried it on at the time, Eleanor knew that in addition to the added rubies, this ring had been several sizes too large and there had been no inscription. Realization slowly dawned. "But—that was nearly two months ago," she whispered in astonishment, her gaze rising to meet his as he stood.

"I went back the next day and commissioned the work, replacing the outer stones and having it resized and engraved in the hope that you would one day wear it as my wife. You, Eleanor. No one else."

Her knees began to shake so that she felt they might give way beneath her.

"It's time you knew the truth," he murmured, his warm fingers stroking hers. "That day I scolded you so assiduously for being too familiar—I did it because I was terrified. My reaction to your embrace was…" He paused, his Adam's apple bobbing, his cheeks awash with sudden color. "You must understand that I had no warning and no control. In that instant, the affection I'd borne for you since we first met began to transform into something I knew you did not—and thought that you probably never would—reciprocate. I could not bear the thought of losing your friendship and trust because of my shameful desire."

She knew her mouth was hanging open and didn't care. It all made sense now. The way he'd subsequently avoided her—or whenever he *had* been with her, the way he'd behaved with such sternness, always correcting, always criticizing. He'd done it all to distance himself and keep her unaware of his true feelings for her. "That's why you left!"

A wry smile tugged at one corner of his mouth. "Yes. That, and the fact that I could not endure the torment of watching you fall in love with and marry someone else, as I thought must surely happen. But running away did no good at all. You followed me with your letters and kept the wound fresh, so to speak. Your heart was in them, and though distance prevented me from exposing myself, it did nothing to stop my love for you growing ever deeper. When I finally returned home and you were yet unwed, I thought I would go mad. It is only because of my mother and good friends that I began to consider trying to find a way to make you see me differently."

The irony of his admission nearly made her laugh aloud. They'd both been scheming and plotting to change each other's perception, all the while never guessing their work had already been done.

Taking her hand and easing the ring from between her fingers, he again knelt. "I offer you not only my name, Eleanor, but my heart and my absolute devotion. It is my greatest hope that one day you will return my affection, and I'll gladly spend the rest of my life in pursuit of that end. Please say that you will marry me."

If a heart could burst from happiness, then hers was surely in danger of doing so now. "I will," she finally choked out. "But you should know that you are not the only one to have kept a secret. I've been just as guilty as you in that regard." Laughter broke through her tears at his puzzled expression. "We've been so at odds, neither of us knowing the other's heart for fear of revealing our own! But never again."

Reaching out, she caressed his face. "I was so accustomed to loving you that I failed to even notice how that love had changed. I think now that I began to realize you were the only man I could ever marry the day you questioned my 'high standards.'" She moved closer and whispered, "You are not just the example of what I should want in a husband—you *are* the husband I've always wanted."

A fire kindled in his hazel eyes. With utmost tenderness, he took her hand, kissed it, and then slid the ring onto her third finger. "Then I am yours." Standing, he took her in his arms.

"I have dreamed of this moment," she said happily, stroking the back of his neck as he brought her close.

Stiffening suddenly, he drew back.

"What is it? What is wrong?" she asked, fear creeping back into her heart.

"Eleanor, I have another confession to make, one I cannot withhold from you though it will likely forever darken your view of me." His face and neck reddened. "The night Yarborough drugged you, when I took you home…I'm afraid I took liberties no gentleman sh— "

"It was *not* a dream!" she blurted, certain now that what she'd thought was wishful thinking had in fact been quite real. "You kissed me!" She hadn't meant it to sound accusatory, but such was her shock that he had behaved in so bold a manner that it couldn't be helped.

One corner of his mouth twitched. "Actually, you kissed me first."

Now it was her turn to blush. Apparently, her concerns about having acted inappropriately with him had been quite valid. "I—you—I did?"

"You really don't remember?"

She didn't remember how it all started, but she did know there had been a good deal more than just kissing. He'd touched her in ways no gentleman should ever touch a lady outside the marriage bed. Her cheeks stung, and she knew her entire face must be awash with color.

So much for the proprieties—and after all his lecturing! Despite her outrage, a delicious shiver rippled across her skin as she recalled that night, her wantonness, and his desire.

His desire.

The shiver became a lightning blaze as the realization hit her that love wasn't *all* that motivated him to want to marry her. *He desires me!* Enough that he'd set aside all self-discipline and behaved as no true gentleman would. And she'd liked it. She'd liked it a *lot*. So much, in fact, that she wanted him to do it again at the earliest opportunity.

After we are married, of course, she corrected herself. … *Or at least not until after our engagement has been properly announced.*

"You were delirious," he explained, clearly mistaking her silence for umbrage. "While I was trying to keep you from falling over in the carriage, you kissed me. Quite ardently." His flush deepened. "I'm ashamed to say that I took advantage of your impassioned state. I thought I might never have another chance, you see," he rushed on. "Had you recalled the incident the following day, I would have asked for your hand at once, but you seemed to have lost all memory of it—and all desire for me. I thought the drug responsible for your actions, and I did not wish to impose on you, if I was not truly wanted."

Oh, she'd wanted him. And in her compromised condition, she'd had no qualms about letting him know it. *And he wants me!* The wicked part of her rejoiced. Stretching up, Eleanor put her lips close by his ear. "My dear Lord Wincanton, when we are married you may impose upon me as often as you please, and I can promise you will suffer no complaint from me."

The bold words set her cheeks aflame all over again, and for a moment she worried that she might have stepped beyond the bounds of propriety—even for a fiancée who'd already been compromised by her intended.

Saint Jane would certainly never have acted so brazenly… but then I doubt he ever behaved with her the way he did with me. Her concerns vanished an instant later as her husband-to-be leaned down and took her mouth in a sweet, molten kiss that sent rivers of heat snaking down into her belly.

No, she wasn't Jane. She wasn't meek or mild, and patience wasn't her strongest suit. She often spoke her mind, and while she'd learned modesty and propriety, there were times when they could and ought to be set aside. Now was just such a time.

Reveling in the solidity of Sorin's impassioned embrace, Eleanor leaned into him and allowed herself to be swept away.

Propriety be damned!

Epilogue

Eleanor beamed down at young Edward Tristan Latham, the future Earl of Wincanton, as he rolled about on the blanket beside her and played with his chubby, adorable feet. Looking up, she saw her husband watching her with a tender look in his eyes and the same lopsided smile as his son. Two years ago on this very day they'd spoken their vows. It seemed like only yesterday.

"He is growing so quickly," she murmured. "Too quickly, I fear. We'll see him in shorts all too soon."

"He'll be in good company," said Sorin, nodding toward the wood.

Turning around to peer over her shoulder, she saw a group of familiar people approaching. Caroline, Lord Marston, and their son were coming up the well-worn path that led from Holly Hall to Holbrook, where they'd gone this morning to pay a visit to Charles and Rowena. Marston hung behind, shepherding little Winston along. The boy was almost two now and a very independent lad who insisted on walking everywhere by himself.

"Come join us!" Eleanor called out, waving as Sorin levered himself up.

Caroline smiled brightly and took a spot on the blanket beside little Edward. She tickled his feet, eliciting a squeal of delight. "I have news," she announced with a gleam in her eye. "Lady Yarborough has married again."

"Married?" Eleanor could hardly contain her astonishment. After her son had been convicted for his crimes and sent off to Sydney, Lady Yarborough had gone into mourning as though he'd died. The woman had disavowed all knowledge of his illegal activities, of course. According to Lord Marston, she'd displayed such anguish during his sentencing that the magistrate had shown her pity, allowing her to retain the family house in Wincanton as well as the jointure provided by her late husband. Naturally, she'd chosen to continue leasing the house out while she remained in London as the permanent guest of a friend. She'd been living off the income provided by the rent. Since then, she'd all but disappeared from Society. "I cannot believe it. To whom?"

"An American by the name of John Copperfield," replied Caroline. "He was a friend of the Fenbridges—the people she was staying with. He came to London to visit them and not a month later asked her to marry him. It was very nearly a scandal. They were wed three days ago, according to Lady Rothchild who was one of only a few people in attendance. They set sail for America next week." Picking a grape from the picnic basket, she popped it into her mouth.

"She's abandoning London?" Eleanor whispered, still stunned.

Caroline nodded. "Lady Rothchild said she'd never seen her so happy. I don't wonder that she'd want to leave. Apparently, disowning her son did nothing to redeem her in the eyes of most of her so-called friends. Losing their association greatly diminished her pleasure in Town."

"I suppose you'll have new neighbors soon," Sorin told Marston, who had at last arrived with his son. "The heir will no doubt come to claim what remains of his estate."

Marston's eyes were full of laughter. "He already has. Sir Reginald Farnes, a distant Scottish cousin to the Yarboroughs, has already moved in. The fortunate man had never even met his English relations before coming to finalize the matter of his inheritance."

"A very nice gentleman he is, too," added Caroline, selecting another grape. "We are quite pleased with him. Now that he has inherited, he need only find a suitable wife."

Eleanor looked at her with open suspicion. "Don't tell me you've already got matchmaking designs on the poor man?"

"Me?" said her friend, her bright blue eyes widening. "I would never—even if there *is* a perfectly suitable young lady available."

"Who?" Eleanor demanded. "Every female of age in the vicinity is already married, and the next 'batch' of debutantes won't be coming out for at least another year."

"Which leaves Miss Anne Wheaton in the perfect position to snap him up," replied Caroline.

Knowing she'd been beaten, Eleanor bit. "And who, exactly, is Miss Anne Wheaton?"

"A recent addition from Devonshire," answered Caroline, her tone matter-of-fact. "She and her widowed mother have taken up residence at Woodbury Cottage. Miss Anne is both pretty and modest, a delightful young lady of the highest quality. Sir Farnes is sure to notice her without any help at all."

Eleanor wasn't fooled by her prim manner for a second. "But were we to take her on, it would no doubt ensure her success," she said drily, earning a hopeful smile. "Very well. We shall see what can be done."

Beside her, Sorin chuckled. "You intend to see every soul in the county married, don't you?" he said for her ears alone.

"Nonsense," she replied sotto voce, occupying herself with adjusting little Edward's position on the blanket. He'd wriggled almost to the edge. "But what would it hurt to try?" She looked into his smiling hazel eyes. "Is it so awful to want everyone to be as happy as I am?"

His warm hand covered hers, stilling it. "Not at all, my darling. If your happiness is such that you wish to share it with others, then I've done my duty well and shall be glad of it." Breaking all the rules of propriety, he dropped a quick kiss on her lips.

Eleanor blushed as their audience smiled and pointedly looked elsewhere. "There was a time when you would have frowned upon such bold conduct," she quietly teased. "I remember a certain lecture pertaining to inappropriate displays of—"

Another kiss silenced her.

"What a monumental fool I must have been," murmured her husband with a shameless grin. "You must remind me frequently of the many reasons why I should never again be so absurd."

"You may rest assured that I shall," she replied, her smile promising him just such a "reminder" later.

Acknowledgments

My family, for encouraging my obsession with words and supporting me through long hours spent stringing them together and moving them around. (And for tolerating lots of sandwiches for dinner.)

Barbara Rosenberg of The Rosenberg Group, not just for sealing the deal, but also for her sharp eyes and priceless feedback.

Erin Molta, Senior Editor at Entangled Publishing, and Stacy Abrams, Executive Editorial Director at Entangled Publishing, for helping me bring Sorin and Eleanor to life.

My ARWA sisters and brothers, for their unfailing support and encouragement. I wouldn't be here without you.

Romance Writers of America's online Chapter, The Beau Monde, for helping me understand and navigate the many rules of the Regency era.

Don't miss these other thrilling reads from Entangled

Less than a Lady
by Eva Devon

To win a lord, you can't be a lady…

Darcy Blake, Earl of Chase, is a solider, rogue, and a loyal King's man. Commanded to spy on the luscious actress Amelia Fox, Darcy must pretend to be her student for a court theatrical. He is certain he can school her in the art of seduction while discovering if she is a traitor. But to his shock, he finds Mrs. Fox teaching him an entirely different kind of lesson.

As London's most popular actress, Amelia is famous at court, and she doesn't have a husband to tell her what do. Unfortunately, the king has ordered her to train the rakehell, Lord Chase to act for the court. Before long, the Earl is driving her wild with desire and awakening her heart to love. As an actress, society dictates she can never be more than Lord Chase's mistress, and Amelia has vowed never to be less than a lady.

When Darcy learns the witty actress is indeed linked to a traitor, he'll have to decide if love or loyalty will rule the day.

One Step Behind
by Brianna Labuskes

Lucas Stone, the Earl of Winchester, has a reputation for arrogance and a soft-spot for his sister, which is how he ends up in the predicament of hiding behind a curtain at midnight with the dreadfully dull Miss Imogen Lancaster. But he soon discovers appearances can be deceiving when the country mouse turns into a spitfire in front of his eyes. Now they must work together, which would be fine, if they could decide if they'd rather fall in love or kill one each other.